GWYNETH JONES

WHITE QUEEN

CASSELL PLC

VISTA

First published in Great Britain 1991
by Victor Gollancz

This Vista edition published 1998
Vista is an imprint of the Cassell Group
Wellington House, 125 Strand, London WC2R 0BB

A catalogue record for this book is
available from the British Library.

ISBN 0 575 60378 X

Printed and bound in Great Britain by
Cox & Wyman Ltd, Reading, Berks

98 99   10 9 8 7 6 5 4 3 2 1

ACKNOWLEDGMENTS

Thank you: Storm Constantine for the use of her pronouns. Sam Daniels for the petrovirus. Dr A.J. Power for the blue sun. Richard Ridley-Jones for a patriotic sentiment. Ruth Sinclair-Jones for vetting KT 2583. Peter Gwilliam for support, advice, criticism; and, not least, for the paradise slices.

Aleutian Comms Tech courtesy of D&P: Thank you very much.

Thank you also (a short bibliography): Chuck Jones for *What's Opera, Doc?*; Wole Soyinka, Chinua Achebe and others, for all their West African novels; Louise Gerard for *The Golden Centipede*, the book that distantly started it all; and the chickenpox virus. Thank you Susako Endo, Murasaki Shikibu; and Sakyo Komatsu for the brilliant *Japan Sinks*. Ian Stewart for *Does God Play Dice?*; Gaston Bachelard for *The Poetics of Space*; Powys Mathers, the translator, and Chauras the original composer of the Sanskrit poem known in English as *Black Marigolds*.

Gerardville, West Africa; June, 2038

1: BirdDog

i

Johnny could never sleep in Africa. Sometimes he would force himself to be sensible about it: get up and wander the streets. Then he would find plenty of other people around, dancing to muted Natural in half-empty marquees, walking dreamily in the bluey gloom, sitting chatting on the fissured pavements. He would step over bodies of the fallen, sometimes catching the sigh of their peaceful breath. Their casual poses reminded him of Bella, who at eighteen months old couldn't understand that you had to go to the place assigned for rest before you could lie down. There were no improper places in her world. She was never away from home.

At last this particular night ended. The pattern of his mosquito net printed itself on the clammy dawn. He put Robert in his pocket, left his room to the native roaches and went out into the old city, to his customary breakfast bar. It was the rainy season – not that there was much difference here, even nowadays, between rainy and slightly less rainy. The lumpy clay fragments of the pagan palace glistened behind their crumbling UNESCO barricades. Across the road the Islamic Palace, which still housed some of the country's administration, presented a high, blank wall to the world. The new city, over the river, was a misty vision of white towers and greenery.

Johnny crossed the railway line (defunct) and bought a faxed American paper from his usual copyshop. As always a foolish soreness prevented him from buying his own paper in this crude form. In the ex-goods yard a market came and went according to the local calendar (except when a lucky trading day fell on a Friday). Alongside its site stood a row of eating booths.

He liked Mama's because the clientele was sufficiently mixed that he didn't stand out more than he must. It was a ramshackle construction of canvas and scaffolding, with a dirt floor. But the presence of Mama, a big woman with an air of sleepy authority and a taste for rich and complex headties, gave the place a touch of class.

Out in the open a party of revellers in tired evening clothes were finishing their night with coffee and brandies. He sat down inside with his paper, nodding shyly at his fellow breakfasters. Under the counter three children in painful school uniform sat gobbling breakfast, eyes glued to an ancient cartoon show. The presence of the tv depressed Johnny, but he gazed at the kids hungrily: children and home!

Dominic, who was eight and liked soccer but preferred cricket, brought cornmeal porridge and chopped banana; and a tumbler of 'sour coffee' in a battered metal holder.

'Oye! Mr American. Eat well.'

Heads turned as the foreigner's identity was announced. The city was small, gossip endemic. Johnny tried to control his piteous cringing. One of the all-night revellers looked up and turned out to be David Mungea, Johnny's best friend in the city. He came strolling over, lanky and graceful.

'Your good news continues!'

He was pointing to the paper, which was full of garbled accounts of the revolution that was going on in the USA. Asabaland had had a Marxist regime for a few years, and for some weird reason they were sentimental about it. Notwithstanding a cheerfully brutal open economy, and one of the worst energy audits on the continent, they were all socialists here.

Johnny shrugged.

David, Minister of Transport and indefatigable party-animal, was actually past sixty; old enough to remember what exile meant.

'Oh, only a fool would not be cynical. But you'll be cleared, Johnny. You'll see your family again.'

'Shit, I don't know. Fucking revolutions: they never do any good.' His hope was painful today, he didn't want it touched.

David tactfully changed the subject, nodding at the other foreigner across the table. 'This is what makes me love my city, Johnny. Here we are, Americans, Africans, lecturers, truck drivers, sitting down to breakfast together. This is the way life should be – diversity and harmony!'

It was the girl.

She had been following Johnny about for a long time, almost since the day he arrived. He still knew nothing about her. Johnny had two reasons for being in Africa. In the first place, he might as well be here as anywhere. The other reason was too absurd to mention: but just for fun, it could be that he was on to something, a story; and *something* might involve this girl.

She seemed to agree with David. She then seemed to return to a warm conversation with the woman beside her – university teacher, by the formal clothes. Johnny wondered how he hadn't noticed her when he sat down. He stared, trying to see, for once, *what actually happened*. She did not speak. No words came out of her mouth. He was damned sure of it.

'I think she likes you,' said David. 'Lucky man. We were just saying, over there, that's a very attractive young lady.' He considered. 'Not my type, of course. I prefer to wrestle only with someone who could break my arm if she felt so inclined . . . But the personality – mmm. You know her?'

'Nobody does,' said Johnny.

'Aha! I knew you were interested. That's a good sign.' He lifted Johnny's hand and gripped it. 'Be happy, my friend. Believe that good things do happen. Remember, I'm praying for you.'

Johnny left soon after the girl, tipping the *Tribune* into a cycle bin as he walked out. Dominic took the American's bowl and tumbler in his gloved hands and carried them to a skinny young man who was hunkered down in the back doing the special washing up. He returned with a bucket of hot water and bleach, and sluiced Johnny's place.

Johnny wondered if the minister's prayers would do him any good. David claimed that he tried to be a decent Christian, but that gorgeous heavyweight jazz singer with him at Mama's was not his wife. And the country was littered with young roads blighted at birth by some Mungea connection's greater need for a couple of new Jaguar XL tilt-rotors.

He followed the girl to a small supermarket and watched her buy a pack of salted roast broad beans and a big carton of sanitary towels. He asked about her at the check-out. The local English was heavily contaminated with French, besides Arabic and other unnameable African influences. He managed to get by.

The young woman beamed. '*Ah, l'Américaine! La jolie-laide*! So much a nice girl.' But she knew nothing.

The mystery girl was tall and slight, with a touch of coltish awkwardness as if she hadn't finished growing. She had dark hair, and a dusky olive complexion that didn't absolutely rule out many nationalities. He was personally gut-sure that she was not from America, north or south. In crude terms, the mystery had only two elements. There was the way this other foreigner followed Johnny around but was not staying anywhere and could not be cornered. And there was the bad harelip which left her almost no nose and a split upper lip. The deformity explained her reluctance to speak out loud: but was apparently invisible to everyone but Johnny. The pretty American!

She wasn't in sight outside.

He walked on to the yard gate of a plastics smeltery, quiet now until the industrial power-hours began. No more hotels or shops this way. She was gone. It didn't matter. His interest was only a half-conscious, half-deluded fantasy, latest move in the lonely game he was using to while away his exile.

Good things do happen, thought Johnny. He felt a rush of gratitude to whoever had brought up this young woman: giving her such sunny confidence, such an affirmed self-image that her deformity meant nothing to her or to anyone who met her.

Because of the great river that formed its northern boundary, landlocked Asabaland had never been isolated. Without gold or oil, this area had been a significant continental trading mart since before the pyramids were raised. The modern country was a palimpsest of sub-Saharan history. Since the end of 'pagan times', early thirteenth century by Christian reckoning, it had been Islamic, then Portuguese, then 'pagan' again: then, for a formative period, French, then briefly German; and finally British. After the British it had suffered a bloody right-wing dictatorship, followed by mad Marxists and economic collapse. In the mid-to late-twentieth century it lost fifty per cent of its forest cover, and had a population explosion. Between 1985 and 2010 it lost another thirty per cent forest, and population was hacked back by unprecedented disease and famine; but losses never approached a return to the pre-industrial numbers. At present Asaba had a small war and a desertification problem in the north. But basically it was busy creating wealth by supposedly benign means.

The capital, Gerardville, was called 'Fo', a Fulani term of disputed etymology, by everyone and in every location except on the road signs to the airport. It lay in the foothills of the highland, removed from invasion routes. No one here seemed to worry much about the desert, or the tribal dispute that still lingered on where the Treaty of Versailles had meddled with an ancient frontier. Asaba's ambition – David said – was to be a *leafy suburb* of the global village. Fo saw itself as already there. It was a strange image for Johnny, far removed from the Africa that people wanted to buy at home. He kept wondering – nerves twitching for the amputated limb of that skill he would never use again – exactly how he'd angle this version to get it through the tube.

Johnny crossed into the new city over the small local river by the Gromyko bridge that carried Granderoute Macmillan, the road south. He continued on foot through Fo's morning clangor of trams, oxcarts, pushbikes, gashog taxis and humming leclecs. He was reticent about using public transport. He was morally certain he could do his neighbours no harm. But that would not make the experience of being spotted and thrown off any more pleasant.

You had to walk to the American embassy anyway if you didn't arrive by chopper. The folks hadn't encouraged casual visitors, even before things at home reached crisis point. You couldn't get a pushbike up the drive now. Grass-grown and choked with rampant African weeds, the approach to the eagle-crowned gateway was a green tunnel leading to some enchanted land, the kingdom of sleeping beauty.

The complex was a shock after Fo: the big white dishes mooning out from the roofs, the meagre human accommodation dominated by that crown. Even now that most world business was done by undersea cable, the US government stuck faithfully by the old icons. Johnny felt the reversed balance, and swallowed the bad message it had for him personally. This was still a homecoming.

'I'm sorry I had to have the gate let you in. We've paid off the local staff, you know. Austerity measures.'

The American ambassador was a courteous mid-westerner called Joseph (Josh) Kent. Johnny didn't know what cross-wired instructions Kent was getting from the presidential retreat and from the new occupiers of the White House, but the man managed to stay remarkably calm.

Johnny remained standing. He must touch nothing in this room. The soles of his shoes were a problem the ambassador stretched a point to ignore. The apology about the gate was part of the routine: though it was true that Josh Kent was now alone here.

'Josh, I want to talk to you.'

'About what, Johnny? Fire away, I've plenty of time.'

About what! Disingenuous bastard. Johnny controlled his fury. 'I read in the paper about Barr and Matthias and Ledern. Josh, is there any hope?'

Kent looked reproachful. 'Johnny, the leaders of this interregnum situation have to break up the overtly racial appearance of their coup. Of course they're going to rehabilitate white liberal "criminals" of the dissent programme, as far as they can. But your case can't be affected. You know that.'

'I was framed,' said Johnny.

He wondered how Kent managed not to laugh in his face. It's amazing how naive an acute, sophisticated journalist can become when the situation is personal. The toppled regime could be accused of anything but this: it *could not* be admitted that any agency had ever had the power to subvert the National Institute of Health. The Big Machinery, Our God-Given Systems, must be above suspicion. He felt the truth of it, written in his own stupidest, deepest convictions. He looked at the desk where his file lay open on the integral screen. John Francis Guglioli, twenty-six, twelve years younger than the century. He had always hated the name Francis — Frank, an old guy with a paunch and grey bristles, fond of baseball, sitting in front of a tv wall in his undershirt . . . It was good of Kent to leave the page open like that, but it was a painful reminder that Johnny Guglioli had once been an insider, someone allowed behind the screens and into the critical files.

He had the dizzying feeling that he wasn't in this room. He was looking at Kent through a screen. If he reached out, if they gripped hands (which Kent would not, for all his courtesy), it would still be unreal. There was no contact, none possible.

Joseph Kent studied his visitor — a slightly gangling young man with straight hair brushed back into a neat braid. Shabby but decent clothing, an open, childishly rounded face that showed no sign yet of ill health. He was sincerely sorry for the boy.

'You were a foreign correspondent, Johnny. Travelling, lonely, sometimes starved of information, maybe experimenting in stupid ways. Be honest. You cannot know *for certain* that you're clean. But suppose you are.' He paused. 'I'm not a socialist. I reckon it's a compliment to these people that I'm not afraid to say so. If they win fair elections, soon, I'll accept them the way I would any elected administration. That's my best offer.'

Good for Josh. This room was livespace, of course, like any public office. Not much chance that anyone was grabbing, but it's always worth turning your good profile.

'But you are one of them, Johnny. It looks like your side gets to win this time. If it helps, think of yourself as a human sacrifice.'

Johnny nodded dully.

Kent pushed a couple of envelopes across the screen. One contained Johnny's regular pocket money, in Asa pound notes. The other was from home. Since Johnny didn't have a phone number now, the only communications he received came by freight.

'Mail for you. There's a picture of your little girl. She's very sweet.'

'Thanks.'

The ambassador pondered. Johnny, feeling undismissed, could not control a throb of hope.

'One thing puzzles me, Johnny. What exactly are you doing in Africa, in Gerardville? You've been here, what, three months?'

'No reason. It's as good as anywhere.'

'Nothing political, I hope?'

Johnny laughed. 'Not in the least.'

'Good. Goodbye, Johnny. Thanks for dropping in.'

When Johnny and Izabel decided to get married, Johnny took her out into the open (real wilderness, no theme park), and told her that he was a trade union activist. They were both nineteen. He'd been the pampered property of a media corporation for years, talent-scouted out of high school into intensive training. He was an eejay, an engineer-journalist: Johnny Guglioli with his backpack of fantastic equipment, one of the few who brought the World Outside home to the USA. He loved his work, but he wanted artistic control.

He believed, naively, that in fighting for the right to report honestly he was doing all anyone in the bleeding crowd could ask of him.

Izzy had always been scared. But she surely hadn't turned him in. Probably he would never know who had done that. The puzzle wasn't high on his agenda. He didn't blame her for the divorce. He didn't even miss her, not in any way that made sense. He missed their child, Bella, horribly. And without hope, because the baby who had been the light of his life didn't exist any more. It was two years now. *Two years.*

It would have been better for Johnny if the Revolution hadn't happened. At least then he'd still be a political exile, able to dream of the day when all injustice would be undone.

He threw his letters away unread. He nearly chucked the picture too, but some stubborn instinct of self-preservation prevented him. He walked about under the Gromyko bridge, social centre for the dregs of Fo society. It was raining hard now, the new city and the old had both vanished.

He studied the down-and-outs, and took grim warning.

Rationally he knew that he would never see his baby again. But he also knew that he had done nothing wrong. Something deeper than his pain told him to hang on. The innocent are not punished for ever. Everything would be restored to him, somehow. Until that day he must use whatever means necessary to survive intact: to remain Johnny Guglioli.

ii

Outside some workshops a fight had broken out. The two principals and their supporters screamed at each other and scuffled under the streaming rain. Meanwhile a caterpillar truck loaded with goods was stuck in a pothole. It struggled, signalling doggedly for human assistance. The trader finally pointed this out, his round, gaudily wrapped body shaking with indignation. The gawky driver broke off the quarrel to swing himself into the cab and cut out the alarm. Both of them callously returned to the fray.

No one was taking any notice of the explorers. They weren't behaving any differently from the local bystanders, who were standing around, nervous and excited, waiting to see if blood would be shed. But they were convinced that 'stranger' was written all over them. The explorers' captain was just about holding them together when the truckers suddenly decided to use the struggling machine as an excuse to back down. They converged on it, shoving and cursing. The driver gunned the engine, eliciting dreadful noises. Everyone felt awful: but the captain, that person whose aspect is always tenderness for the helpless, couldn't bear it any longer.

'Stop it! Stop it! Stop it!'

His sudden articulate yell panicked the others. As their leader ran back they scurried, confessing their fear and giving up any attempt at passing for normal. They hid behind some sheds on a dirt access road that led down to the big highway. In a short while the captain joined them, spattered with mud from head to foot. Luckily, no one seemed to have noticed the odd behaviour of a small group of noncombatants.

The others were shamed by the reminder of how quickly the small decencies of life had been muddied out of sight by adversity. That person whose obligation to principled action is unaffected by circumstance hadn't meant to embarrass anyone. He was embarrassed himself now; but unrepentant.

<Oh Agnès!> sighed his guardian. <Try to think of the rest of us. We can't all be as pure in spirit as you!>

Agnès was the local version of the captain's name.

<Well, anyway. I made them stop.>

It wasn't the captain's fault. The long-term effects of the crash were coming to the surface, not only in proliferating practical problems but also in low morale. People were afraid to be left alone. Whenever the person they depended on went foraging a search party would soon follow him, and become a liability. It was a silly situation. But someone had to go and do the shopping, and who else could it be?

He put his arm around his guardian as they piled into the car and brandished one of his parcels.

<Look! Clean underwear!>

<Oh Agnès!> Benoit hugged him.

What a charming presence it was, though nothing in Agnès's pleasantly irregular features deserved to be called beauty. The people here had a poetic term for the effect. It was a neat observation, the one arousal being near the other. Agnès was so often angry. Was it the way the world's pain drew sparks that made people want to be near him? Or was it just the sexy symptoms – the bright eyes, flushed skin, pouting nasal?

<No wonder we love you.> 'You're so sexy-looking when you're angry!'

The joke fell rather flat, and not only with those who didn't understand the spoken words. Most of Agnès's crew found it hard to make out that Benoit was conflating personality with physical appearance to be funny. They laughed, one after another: an absurd descant. The infection took hold, they laughed together; and felt better. Their captain felt worse.

Agnès had been eager to starve and wade through swamps. He hadn't anticipated the grim test of a shipwreck in the company of artisans and merchants. Momentarily exasperated beyond kindness he grumbled something to this effect – and spent the ride back to camp feeling the sting of his own comment far more sharply than said artisans and merchants themselves.

The expedition hadn't exactly become a disaster. There had been casualties, and the three parties found themselves widely separated. But the whole venture had been such a leap into the unknown: it was nonsense to complain that things weren't going to plan. At the landing, knowing that the other two parties had their own problems, Agnès had put a brave face on things. He had ordered the lander salvaged and led them off to explore, carrying the injured with them and caring for them as best they could.

Most of their trade goods were lost, but it's amazing what people will give for an object whose only attraction is that they've never seen anything like it before. The cars had been hired, with unlimited mileage, in exchange for some baby toys.

There had been consternation when, after carrying them for two days, the creatures collapsed in evident need of food. The captain's guardian had persuaded everyone to see the funny side. But the cost of the liquid food had curtailed their exploration. For a while now they had been camped in a pretty wooded park outside the city of Fo.

The more assertive members of the crew had represented to Agnès that there were surely plenty of hotels in the city. They were almost penniless, true, but there was nothing wrong with the credit of the other two parties. He had only to approach any significant local character; an arrangement must be possible. Agnès refused to consider the idea. He had not come all this way to sit in an hotel. They might have known. Their leader went mountaineering for fun at home.

Agnès was interested in loot and fame, in his own way. But he would never have left home merely for material profit, for show; or even for the fun of risking his neck. He was a poet. He was determined to go on as he had planned: to explore quietly and privately, to make as little impact as possible. He was not going to be co-opted into a state visit, nor a trade delegation. He had no particular desire to meet the local people. People are the same anywhere. He had come to stare, simply to stare . . . to store his mind with new sensibilities, new perceptions.

The camp's position was a compromise. It was buried deep in the park so Agnès could get on with his famous staring, but at least the very presence of trees, grass, shrubs, assured that human habitation couldn't be far away.

They spent the rest of that day calmly. Fairly large weapons occasionally stirred in the undergrowth. None of them seemed armed for serious damage, but a weapon without provenance was an eerie thing. They didn't attempt any form of retaliation. They had decided that it was better to ignore signs of hostility unless absolutely forced into self-defence.

The master at arms, a person with a strong sense of justice, still brooded on the perfidy of the car hire firm.

'Unlimited mileage!' he snarled, no less sore however often the liquid feed transaction was repeated.

Agnès visited the sick and then went off by himself, taking care to remain in sight. He sat between the roots of a huge tree. The wooden fans made a house around him. He laid his own hand next to the hand of a fallen leaf. Even to the stubby fifth leaflet the shape was an echo, an echo of home; an echo of self. To give and to receive the Self makes open palms. He shook hands with the fallen leaf, wondering what tiny faraway contact the local people felt. Perhaps none: they were not obliged to perceive him at all. He tasted the populated air, but none of its tiny messengers carried news for Agnès. The loneliness was dizzying. He took out his sketchpad and began to compose. *There*, the shape and texture of loneliness . . . and in loneliness a bodiless unity: the unity inescapable of the WorldSelf.

I came to find the new, but there is nothing new. There is only the WorldSelf, perceiving itself. Any shelter out of which I look is that of my own body. Any leaf is my hand. I cannot escape; I can never leave home.

He was nagged by that angry exclamation. The person whose obligation was to security and vigilance (and who was also the beloved partner of Agnès's guardian), did not take to formal words easily. That repeated outburst about the car-feed signalled growing concern about the future. Their lander was still providing shelter, but there was no one left who could repair it or even halt its decay. There were other daily needs, like food and clean underwear, equally beyond the skill of anyone left alive. Those who could bear to use local supplies did so: but soon there'd be no choice.

From the skin of Agnès's bare hands and wrists, from his face and throat, tiny particles sifted away; floating on the almost nonexistent breeze bringing the chemical touch of *Agnès* to the others in the clearing. The captain had a fleeting notion of how frighteningly few these wanderers were in the vast, alien crowd. He quashed it hurriedly: and luckily no one had noticed his half-remark. The idea had no hold on him; it winked out of existence. In commonsense, as in poetry, this world seemed so like home.

Agnès fell into another round of his dispute with distant Guillaume, leader of one of the other two parties. No one could quarrel with Eustache, who never worried about anything but practicalities, but between the other two there was constant friction. One reason why Agnès was camped in the park here was that he couldn't bear to be beholden to that shameless materialist for his mess bills. He knew he was going to have to give in soon. The thought didn't sweeten his temper; and of course Guillaume was crowing. Fortunately (as his guardian would often observe) they considered each other's worst insults to be compliments: which made for a kind of peace.

There were other thoughts . . . so much more pleasant. Agnès slipped away into stillness, luxury and delight.

<WorldSelf and I: *here begins a new life*. Here, in this strange city . . .>

Now that person whose aspect is bold action was shocked. In such a dangerous, even a desperate fix, how could the poet sink into one of those hedonistic fugues! The pure artist, who was supposed to be such a goodie-goodie, so concerned for his people's wellbeing . . . Agnès only chuckled.

<*You exaggerate* . . .> He drifted further.

At nightfall they changed their clothes and danced, all but the sick, and the expedition's baby. Agnès and his guardian handed each other through the figures, stooping as they passed him to include the baby, who sat clapping hands on the sidelines. The sound of feet scuffing on a floor of mud and leaves, the feel of branches snagging hair, had everyone giggling as usual. But the rite was taken seriously, nevertheless. What can't be conveyed by normal means of communication must be put into words. What is too deep for words is expressed in dance. The other crews, far away, were dancing too. Briefly, the three parties were peacefully united.

The baby, whose guardian was also Benoit, fell asleep after tearfully exhorted promises that nobody would sell anything else that he loved while he was unconscious. The adults sat and chatted. They would have watched tape, but that was another loss: there was no storybox mender among them. Agnès's chaplain was grieved and anxious. The captain teasingly begged him not to wallow in superstition. No one would collapse and die if separated from their narrative for a while. Although the locals seemed to believe otherwise . . .

'They live surrounded by ghosts,' he explained. 'The other world, the land of the dead, is on show everywhere. I don't know if they *have* any more rational knowledge of God.'

Some of his audience, unused to abstract description, didn't quite understand. They laughed, to be on the safe side, and were comforted. It was worth something to be in the company of a great poet, even if it was a little above one's head.

Agnès sat with his knees reversed in a relaxed posture, one hand cupped over his nasal against the chilly evening air. He argued with Guillaume about that episode in the workshop yard.

<I don't care,> he snapped. <I won't *stand* for people being mean to machines. And I think it's much more offensive to play

tricks of your kind. They'll find you out; and they'll get mad. We all
want to go home rich, of course. But lying and cheating isn't the
way ->

But with Agnès, Guillaume replied, pity was like a disease.
Which attitude would Agnès himself prefer from visiting strangers?
Agnès admitted, with a grin, that he would far prefer to be cheated.

Agnès's guardian, the person who can always find something to
smile about, came over to comb wanderers from the captain's hair.
The beloved leader, dear child, turned with a blind, nestling
movement to curl and bury his face in the other's lap. How sadly
sweet it was to feel him there: little grub, lost forever.

'What is your formal name here? I keep forgetting.'

'*Benoit*. At least, that's the nearest I can get.'

'If I win nothing else out of this life,' said Agnès, his voice muffled
by his guardian's clothes, 'at least from now on you and I will
always belong to each other.'

Endless speeches! This was one of the trials and fascinations of
being so close to Agnès. Benoit hugged, and they discussed in more
commonplace fashion the difficulties ahead. The accommodation
with Guillaume was inevitable. Naturally the value of this crew's
share in the adventure must take a fall.

<Never mind,> pointed out Benoit. <We knew what was likely
when we signed up with you!>

Rueful, smothered giggles from the poet. Agnès's lax grip on
material success was notorious, proverbial.

<No one is ever successful at anything for long. The difference,
my dear, is that you don't gloss things over. For some reason you
seem to value failure. And yet, mysteriously, people still long for a
chance to serve you. Yes, even Guillaume.>

Agnès uncurled, pulling faces.

<We'll hold out for a while longer.>

Guillaume, the wilful one, had always wanted to announce
himself and everyone else to the locals. Agnès had fought and won
on this point before they left home. Inevitably the tables would be
turned if he had to fling himself on the other's mercy. But the self-
styled 'Benoit' noted a last remark, informally expressed and
quickly retracted. Only someone who knew Agnès intimately
would have caught it. There: a message that had to be a misunderstanding.

<Indeed? For some new reason?>

Agnès shrugged. <If I told you you wouldn't believe me.>

In that night, another of the injured died. Agnès's physician had died in the crash. Anyone who had been seriously hurt was as it were still trapped in the wreckage: nothing could be done for them. It was no surprise. Anyone who had volunteered for this expedition must, by definition, have a tendency to court early and maybe violent death. But another deathbed brought their plight home to them once again. Agnès assisted his chaplain at the making of the person's last record, and then retired with his sketchpad and a lamp to the fan-rooted tree. He did not return to his poem. But he stayed out there for hours, copying carefully from memory certain odd patterns of lines and dots and curves.

He was even more determined to hold on to his independence: and not only for his own sake. He had to do his best for those who depended on him, in this life and the lives to come. Guillaume had put his efforts into making a big impression. Agnès knew there were things about this new world that the wilful one had not noticed, or had entirely misunderstood. Agnès would not come to their meeting, when it was eventually forced on him, completely empty-handed.

iii

L'Iceberg was one of those monster hotels left abandoned all over the globe by the collapse of long-haul tourism. Its yellowed tower rose up from the French-planned city centre, forlorn marker of the high point of a far-retreated tide. In fact the air of decay was an illusion. L'Iceberg (officially the St Maurice) survived very well. Johnny would not dare to enter its front doors, but there was a garden bar at the back called the Planter's which was less intimidating. It was the watering hole for every foreigner in town.

The Planter's was on Johnny's regular circuit in the search for the mystery girl. He'd never caught her in here yet, but there had to be a first time. Besides, his pocket money was burning a hole in his pocket. Greasy notes were not generally current in L'Iceberg, but the bar staff were friendly. Johnny bought a beer and carried it himself to a red plush island.

The glass wall to the garden was dark, the bar a gloomy cool cavern washed in the hiss of rain. On his screen talking heads around the Pacific Rim discussed with ill-concealed delight the demise of the New York stock exchange. By the bar a party of white South Africans arranged tours with their holiday guide. Two Fo bourgeois, a man and a woman, talked urgently and sadly in a tiny alcove. A group of businessmen passed by going out to eat, clapping each other across the back and showing big teeth. It was the dead time of the afternoon. Johnny nursed his beer, wondering how long before he got the bum's rush.

A white woman came down the stairs from the hotel wearing a small-waisted, dark dress with an effect somewhere between petals and armour. Between the segments of the skirt a cool green chemical glow came and went. Johnny registered the dress as Big World fashion. He was thinking that for a whore she looked too expensive for Fo, when he realised with horror that he *recognised* this person.

She saw him. She came over to his island with a false and meaningless smile on her face.

'It's Johnny Guglioli, isn't it? D'you remember, we net –'

The talking heads now surrounded a centrepiece illustration of Times Square. Thousands of bodies swirled to and fro under a signwriting of charged slogans. These rhetoric-parties had become a feature of New York life, apparently, like a dance craze. The truth was Johnny didn't give a shit for the Revolution. Hisps and Blacks duking it out with the Wasps and the Jews and nothing in it for Johnny. He was still dead meat. A plague upon both your houses.

The falsely smiling woman was called Braemar Wilson. She was British. European foreign correspondents, engineer-journalists like Johnny, worked for the national governments or the media giants. Wilson was either not good enough to be anyone's employee, or didn't have the right background. She was no eejay, just a glorified presenter. She did cod-intellectual 'development' on news stories and topical concerns, sold her stuff to packagers, scheduled tv, the Brit tabloids. Johnny had networked with her on a couple of gigs, but never met her in the flesh. Never wanted to. She made her living by telling the people what they wanted to hear. Close the dome. Chute the poor. It's not your responsibility. The Big Machines, or else Mother Nature – the Youro version – will decide who sinks, who swims.

It was the height of ill luck for anyone from the past to turn up here. Maybe he was glad it was an unsympathetic stranger.

'I heard about what happened. How awful for you, I'm so sorry. May I sit down?' She sat beside him. 'What a swell party they're having,' she remarked, with an edge of provocative scorn. 'Next July we collide with Mars, but who cares about trifles? You're well out of the whole fracas, in my opinion.'

Johnny glanced around and was immediately, painfully riveted by half-naked breasts rising from a calyx of dark petals. She had more of the chemical light on her mouth. It was wet ruby there, a brazen signal to all comers.

'I'd be home if I could. I love my country.'

'But I think you haven't much reason to do so, Johnny.'

He stared coldly. Everybody knew his business. 'I'm the victim of a freak medical error. The machines get it right for nearly all of the people nearly all of the time. I'm a democrat. I've nothing to bitch about.'

'Medical? I heard it was a political problem.' She took a matt black case from her purse, removed a tobacco cigarette and lit it. A coil of blue-silver poison rose as she turned her attention to Times Square. 'You know, I think it started with the identity crisis. American is what you are. One recognises the flavour. Capitalisto rococo, the children of Eldorado: same orgiastic violence, same oral-fixated dreamlife, same crazy gulf between rich and poor. If your lot had been able to make sense of that, instead of trying to pretend that the Third World was something that happened to other people – '

There was nothing unmannerly in Ms Wilson's approach. Her aggression was merely fashion. It was perfectly correct for her to address a slight acquaintance through what was going on on the screen they shared. Johnny had no right to take her remarks person-ally. But his bruised psyche got the better of him.

'Ma'am, you're wasting your time. If I need something with a face to hold my baggie, I generally call upon the ghost of my ex-wife. I find her rates are most competitive.'

Ms Wilson laughed. She leaned forward into his space with electrifying audacity: and was out again before he could gasp at the shock. She hadn't touched him. She had laid on the table a small rectangle of pale green pasteboard with a darker stripe, meticulously turned down at one corner.

Braemar Wilson

New Things Inc

More . . .

He did not touch it.

'I'm not selling,' she said. 'I'm buying. You and I have an interest in common.'

'Are you the real Braemar Wilson?' said Johnny. 'Gosh, I am impressed. You know, you look much younger on the screen.'

He got up and left.

Seimwa L'Etat, the proprietor of *The State of The Nation*, had been a very rich old lady before Johnny was born. By the time he met her (never in the flesh) she was fabulously old, fabulously rich and arguably quite insane. She acknowledged no family ties, allowed no one to refer to her or address her except by that *nom de guerre*. It was her pride that her small empire of news and entertainment holdings was scarcely contaminated by a human workforce except for the chosen few, her 'artists'. Johnny and Seimwa's relationship had been personal from the start. He humoured the old monster, enjoyed her, loved the life she gave him.

One day he discovered that she, or someone, was aware of his union activities. He braced himself for the earthquake: none came. The next time Johnny went on a trip it was up to the space station. In prospect this was an obscure piece of excitement. No one went to space any more. It was several years since the station had been abandoned. The crewed trip was a one-off: assess and retrieve. In practice, they discovered that eyes-on didn't differ materially from pictures relayed by the station's compromised communications; they retrieved nothing; and nobody watched them on tv. But at Johnny's medical debriefing, he was declared infected with Class Q petrovirus.

The petrovirus was one of a series that had been developed at the turn of the century by the military, designed to dissolve into organic polymers. The Class Q combined this ability with a propensity to attack the protein based 'living' material at the heart of the most advanced modern data processing. No one knew much about QV, except that it had appeared from nowhere and ruined the Mars Mission, soured the relationship between the USA and the USSR; and probably had been the final death knell of Man's attempts upon the High Frontier. No one had ever claimed responsibility for that debacle. The theory that QV was an artificial product, designed by terrorists, was perhaps no more than a reassuring myth.

The infection had been confined to space. Until Johnny's debriefing, there had been no positive evidence that the QV had reached earth at all. Research on the disaster suggested that QV had been spread around the machines through sweaty, bare fingertips on a keypad. But if it could penetrate plastic housing, maybe the virus could get through skinshield too. Johnny wasn't just a journalist, he was an engineer. He took things apart, he actually *handled* the magical 'blue clay' through nothing more than a skin of silky plastic. He would never be able to do that again. By US standards of disease control he was a risk even in normal life.

The QV killed humans, too. Death would come, at the best estimate, within two or three years, after a brief plunge into premature dementia. The infected space programme personnel had vanished into quarantine, and presumably died there. Johnny would have to live and die there too. Not many laws were still respected throughout the United States in the third decade of the twenty-first century, but that was one. Seimwa's doctor – a human being, for privacy and style – had given him the hint that it might be a few hours before his foreign correspondent's passport could be cancelled. Johnny just had time to get home and kiss goodbye. He'd taken flight, understanding that this mitigation came from Seimwa, as did his punishment. The doctor wouldn't have suggested such a thing on his own initiative.

He could have disappeared, gone native. But Johnny meant to survive. Therefore he kept himself registered, did the things notifiable disease people were supposed to do in countries that did not quarantine and continued to protest his innocence. He had a pension from the *State*, which was managed for him through the embassy in whatever country he was in. He still had contacts in long-haul travel who would give him rides. Though the trips were hedged around with gruesome indignities they provided some distraction. They permitted him to keep up his fantasy game, his imaginary treasure hunt. But life was awful, simply awful.

Johnny came home from L'Iceberg and lay on his cot staring up at Byron the Bulb, reviewing his horrible plight.

And the moral of the story is, he thought, don't tease the dinosaurs, children. Doesn't matter how decrepit those pea-brained bonepiles may seem. Their teeth go on getting bigger.

Johnny's hotel was called The Welcome Sight, a cheap doss but tolerant and friendly. The room was cleanish (he swept it himself) and furnished with an iron cot, a three-legged wardrobe and an antique beatbox. The Welcome Sight's economy version of en-suite entertainment. Room service was covered by the resident sticking his head out of the door and yelling; there was a public phone and message pad at the desk.

In his bathroom, a tiny closet, he was able to practise an ancient alchemy of coated-paper and light that produced reasonable still photos. On the beatbox he was able to record his notes, on metallic tape. By the bed lay a rigid leather suitcase, bloomed with age, that contained Johnny's library. In another life he had been a spendthrift book-collector. A chosen few from the surviving collection came everywhere with him: but everywhere. They were like diamonds, he told himself, sewed into a money belt. But to sell one of these would be truly desperate. It would put him well on the way to party time under the Gromyko.

A ten-centimetre skewbald cockroach crawled over his stomach, the rain rattled on murky plastic corrugations overhead. The back of the bathroom door was his photo gallery. It was a poor showing: mere glimpses of the mystery. Her eyes, a half-profile, her loose-limbed figure blurred and anonymous walking down the street. If that girl was what he thought she was, she might be Johnny's ticket home.

He stared impassively. He should be excited. If another pro was interested his fantasy could even be real. In fact he didn't know which depressed him most. Wilson's presence in Fo, or her body.

'Robert – '

The cockroach halted, directing its head towards the sound in a way that looked curiously purposeful. Johnny sat up, gathered a small plastic box from under his pillow and shooed his pet inside. A

scuffed label on the lid said dimly ESaZRT . . . The batch number
that followed, Robert's ID, had faded away.

'Problems. That ageing sex kitten isn't here for a de-tox.'

It was probably too late, but he stopped looking for the girl and
kept away from L'Iceberg. A few evenings later Braemar Wilson
turned up at Mama's, again dressed like an expensive tart. She
must be in her forties, he supposed. Which was nothing these
days, though Johnny's grandparents would have called her
middle-aged. However, that was hardly the point. Johnny
detested the kind of female executive Wilson epitomised. The
equation of whorishness and power, the way she oozed sex was
an affront: to Izzy, to any woman trying to live with dignity in a
man's world. He pretended total indifference. She ended up heading off with David Mungea and his friends, and Johnny had to
endure David's congratulations next morning.

'So, you've found yourself an African woman this time.'

Johnny was bemused. 'She's British.'

David laughed delightedly. 'We've all been British, it is an
occupational hazard around here. Your friend was born in
Kenya: Afrasian mother, she belongs to us. You lucky fellow. She
spent the whole night asking questions about you.'

Johnny didn't care. He took sour pleasure in imagining what
Ms Wilson would look like now if she'd stayed in Africa. In fact
she would look dead. Not many middle-aged East African whores
about these days.

It had to happen.

He crept, ratlike, into the Planter's, devoured by curiosity
after days of lurking in his room. 'Oye!' cried the barman. '*La
jolie-laide*, she was here, Johnny. She left you a message!'

He drank his beer standing, with nervous speed: remembered
too late that he couldn't afford another and tried to hang on to
the dregs. The barman whipped the glass away with slickly
gloved hands and thrust it into the superheat cabinet.

Johnny carried the scrap of printout to an island. The screen
was running a new Korean animation feature about '04. He
stared at his treasure in dismay. He piled prawn crackers from
the cocktail tray into a fantasy condo, and read the message
again.

'I must see you. I'll come to the Devereux fort at midnight, tonight and every night until you're there. Please be there.'

No address, no signature. Idiomatic English. She came to the bar and wrote it as if she'd been stood up by her boyfriend. *Hey, you, you know who you are? Where were you?*

He didn't know what to do.

The barman appeared and laid another beer.

'Who ordered this?'

The waiter grinned broadly. 'Your other girl, Johnny. You can stay a while, if she paying.'

But don't breathe on anything with a processor in it, said the man's pitying eyes.

Ms Wilson came down the steps from the hotel in a mulberry-coloured sheath of clinging and fluid bodywrap. He seriously wondered why she'd hauled these outfits to darkest Africa, if not for the sole purpose of making his life a misery. She must have suborned the bar staff, unless she had fixed her room system to trawl the hotel's entrances for something that looked like Johnny Guglioli. Which wasn't unlikely. It was the sort of thing people used to do all the time, in the lost world. She came slowly, giving him the chance to walk away. But he stayed.

The dress was the same shade as her hair. Something in its cut brought out the non-Caucasian in her features and in her skin, which was the colour of heavy cream.

'You speak French, don't you?' said Johnny, after a pregnant pause. 'What does the term *jolie-laide* mean?'

'In English? Attractively ugly, I suppose. Attractive, though one can't explain it as conventional good looks.' She smiled wickedly. 'Why d'you want to know?'

'It doesn't matter.'

Braemar sat down. 'Have you decided to stop freezing me out? I hope so. You need me, Johnny.'

'Oh?'

She sighed in exasperation. 'I don't want to hurt your pride, but how can I avoid it? You might have a hot story, my boy. Anything's possible. But you have no way to take it home.'

'Tell me about this story,' suggested Johnny.

She moved: into his space and out again. She was curled back on the red plush, the scrap of printout between her fingers.

'Oh, Johnny.' She grinned. 'It's been a long time, hasn't it? Since you last practised your profession, I mean. Surely one's supposed to eat these things after one has memorised them?'

Johnny was furious with himself, but only for a moment. He had a sudden and powerful intuition that Wilson wasn't such a threat as he'd feared.

He stood up.

'Okay, you win. Go along on your own. I can't stop you.' Braemar lit a cigarette and used it to point at Johnny's feet. His shoes were soaking from the walk over here. 'She wants you, Johnny. I think she might notice the difference. But the Devereux fort is thirty k out of Fo. Are you going to paddle all the way?'

'I have money.'

'Fine, you have money. No doubt you can even work out ways of spending it, here in darkest Africa. But are you going alone? Do you think that's wise?'

She looked past him through the screen into a sequence of astonishing technical bravura, the red chrysanthemums: terrible litany of fire. Asamayama, Asosan, Sakurajima, Mikhara, Fujiyama.

'I know how you feel. You're reduced to playing around with a loony sideshow when you should be at home covering the main event. It's demeaning. But a newspaper isn't print on paper, comic strip on a screen, a multipage charged up over the phone, or the program belonging to the proprietors. It is an assessment of newly critical events, sacred to words alone: a survival of human communication in a world that's reverting as fast as it can to chimpanzee bottom-jerking and grooming noises. You're an engineer-journalist, a reporter. They can stick you in the gulag but they can't stop you from doing what you do.'

Her eyes, dark and clear, told him *more* . . . Press my pad and I'll go on like this indefinitely. He'd been right first time. She was selling herself, her geisha presence and a discreet ego-massage in exchange for a piece of Johnny's fantasy game. He felt a surge of elation as he realised he was going to give way to temptation. It was something for nothing. He'd be mad to refuse.

She collected him from outside The Welcome Sight in a huge, horrible white convertible. The hotel's logo, a hologram of the tower, leapt up from the hood like a rhino horn as soon as she cut the engine. Johnny's whole street – nameless, like all the streets in the old city – came out in the dark to admire.

'What the fuck is that? It's disgusting.'

'I suspect the original germ plasm was nineteen fifty-eight Cadillac. What's wrong with a few fins, anyway? I thought you were supposed to be an American.'

He got in. She shut the door. Immediately, once more, she was in his space or he in hers: a profound shock. Johnny looked out of the window, grinning sourly. It was like being fourteen again. But he was a professional at this by now. He could deal with inappropriate sexual arousal. The car was semi-automatic. Fo was supposedly beaconed, but only a lunatic would auto on these roads. He could be thankful that she'd be pinned safely behind the wheel.

Macmillan was empty. Bandits and guerrillas lurked in the suburban darkness, by repute at any rate, but they left the mutated Cadillac alone. It rumbled like a tank over the potholes.

'What's it feel like, Johnny?'

'Huh?'

'To do it with a machine,' explained Braemar.

'I don't know.'

They reached the Devereux fort with an hour to spare. Once buried deep in forest, it was now surrounded by ribbon development and only a few hundred metres from the granderoute. There had been a half-hearted attempt to set it up as a tourist attraction. Braemar dropped him at the dilapidated gateway and went on to put the car out of sight. Johnny prowled the car park and helipad, feeling very exposed. He didn't need his flashlight. An invisible half moon silvered the clouds, and the random lights of nearby houses winked in the lower darkness.

The fort stood up against the dim sky, a pile of child's blocks. It had been Portuguese originally, before a consortium of local and stateless European entrepreneurs took it over. Inside the roofless keep you could see genuine relics of those days. The shelves where the goods were stored, stacked up like damp kindling; the rusty holes in the stone where chains had been pegged. Those South Africans would probably come here with their guide, point their cams, pose on top of the mouldering cannon. There were even free souvenirs to take away, if you cared to scratch the dirt. Some of them weren't very old. The Devereux had had a bad reputation in the bloody right-wing years.

Johnny had trained himself to avoid such times: silence inside, alertness without occupation. He had no purpose here. His only plan was to get home, somehow. To hold Bella in his arms again. The connection between that goal and a game of make-believe did not exist. It was an imaginary thread that vanished when you touched it. He felt utterly desolate.

Someone walked up behind him. It was Braemar, with a needle of light. She bent and pulled a spray of colourless flowers from a small mound which might have been an unmarked grave. '"*Flower of a heart whose trouble, must have been worse than mine* . . ." What a terrible place.'

'If it isn't haunted, it ought to be.'

'It is haunted. The word means the way we feel here. What we call "real" hauntings were invented, in their time, for the sort of clowns who now have to plug into a horror-feelie in order to get scared of death and pain.'

'I love the way you talk.'

'Thank you. It earns me a modest living.'

They retired to a heap of broken stonework and sat down. She touched the 360 perched like a large insect beside her face, read the shell closure light and sound at her wrist. They were in livespace.

Johnny shuddered. 'Why midnight, for heaven's sake?'

'Maybe your friend doesn't know what darkness means.'

'Ms Wilson – ?'

'Braemar. A *nom de guerre*, Johnny, same as your Seimwa. Do you know, by the way, why she adopted one? Is she a feminist?'

'I hardly think so. She does tend to split the world the way they do, into human and subhuman. But not along the gender line.'

No hit, Ms Wilson. I don't mind in the least bad-mouthing my ex-boss on the record.

He felt her smile.

'Braemar, what d'you really think will happen tonight?'

'You're going to meet your friend. And if it's possible, we're going to follow her home. Are you game for that?'

Even her absurd Brit jungle kit was sexified – cinched waist and breeches like second skin. He would save her up and use her for imagery. It wasn't true about Izzy. Fo was full of gorgeous women with whose ephemerides he'd shared intense, sticky fisted experiences: slick clefts he'd penetrated, mulberry nipples sucked and bitten. There was a special savour to this one. She talked to him and looked at him and smelled of the lost world. In fact, he didn't know what he'd been complaining about.

'I'm game.'

'What about you? What do you expect?'

Johnny hunkered over the ache in his groin and picked at moonlit pebbles.

'For a long time it's been part of my calculations that the visitors would turn up one day. Some people buy lottery tickets, some believe in God. I've been waiting for the aliens. I've imagined them as humanoid and more or less intelligible, not because I consider that likely but because . . . otherwise it's not such a fun game. I've made a study of the field and found nothing but nonsense. That didn't bother me. In fact it had the effect of making me feel, oh, something like – statistically, the real one has to be coming along soon. Maybe that doesn't make sense, but I'm still rational. If you hooked me to a lie detector it'd certainly tell you that even here tonight I don't believe . . . This hobby long predates my run in with the NIH. But then lately, which doesn't predate my problem but doesn't seem to me to be connected: recently I've begun to prefer one popular scenario above the others.'

'The one where they touch down quietly, and mingle for a while before – '

'Yeah. That one.'

'And this preference would be because, over the past year – '

'Not that long,' said Johnny.

'Why did you come to Fo?'

'Well, I started getting these weird dreams.' Johnny laughed. 'No, seriously, no dreams. There was a ufo report from down in the Asa warzone several months ago. I presume you know about that. It was probably a robot fighter blowing itself to quarks, the way the poor critters are trained to do nowadays so they won't rat on the bastards who build them. However, the obscure ones are the ones I prefer, and besides I can't get to Arizona any more. So I came here.'

'And found you had a funny-looking friend. More?'

He looked at her quizzically. 'I think you've heard this story before, Braemar.'

'Brae. My friends call me Brae. Is there more?'

'Only that I have a plan. You see . . . '

He had a heap of stones by now, and was trying patiently to build a little tower.

'I did not fuck with any machine. I would not knock it because I've never tried it, but computer-assisted sex has never come my way. It's true I've been to space. I saw the quarantine zone. But no one who was up there with me, including the monitoring systems, can think of or demonstrate how I could have got near. And I was not propositioned by so much as an electric can opener. I swear. I have never been in contact with contaminated nanotechnology.'

'Have you had a European test?'

The tower was six pebbles high. It wavered. Johnny corrected the second level with precise fingertips.

'I've had a whole lot of NIH-excluded tests. Inconclusive: verdict, I should refer to the system with the greatest expertise, which is unhelpfully circular advice.'

'Catch 22.'

'What?'

'It's from an old drama-movie. A shorthand term for your situation.'

He was annoyed. He considered himself cultured, but if she was going to start spiking the dialogue with crumblie fictional allusion . . .

'I don't rate them. Why watch actors working up a storm of pretend emotions when you can plug into subscriber soap? If you like that kind of exhibitionism . . . But the point is I know I'm clean. I have to persuade my boss to get the case reopened. Even in the middle of this revolution, I believe Seimwa can still do it. I plan to offer her the aliens, see if we can trade.'

Seimwa would like that, he thought. She delighted in barefaced insolence.

'What about the way you feel? Have you had any symptoms?'

Her timing was vicious.

'I feel terrible. Wouldn't you? In a year or so I'll start going senile and then they can bury me and feel justified. Braemar, I didn't ask you to join me on this trip. I don't expect you to drink out of the same cup. But take your risk and keep quiet about it, okay?'

'One more question.'

'One. And harmless, or I'm going to get mad.'

'Why the construction work?'

'Oh.'

He flicked the tower with his thumbnail, scattering it. 'A nervous twitch. Mama wanted me to be a regular engineer.'

Johnny entered the fort alone. The floor was earth, the air dank. He was in a tomb. He touched off his flashlight and the silver ribbed sky appeared in a circle overhead. There were two ways in, the one he'd used and a black hole with broken steps that led to the underground storage space. He stood where he could watch them both.

He was naked without a cam, without even a wire. But it would be crazy to break the rules of US quarantine in the very act of trying to win back his good name. He was actually frightened, too. He'd forgotten how this felt: the real/unreal danger of an eejay's life. The artificial stunts, the occasional genuine firefight. He had known both. It was dangerously difficult, once embarked, to remember which was which. This must be fake, however, or Braemar Wilson surely wouldn't be here.

Spiking the dialogue, what a kid's trick. Sneering at his country too. It was nothing internal that had brought the USA down. It was the '04 and its complex reverberations. And the rise of the European mega-state, gross industrial malpractice and economic warfare. Not that Braemar would care. She probably had a whole family of illiterate Romanians with rotten teeth cleaning her toilets. *Plug into a horror-feelie.* How he despised that kind of retro-slang.

Even if he did use it himself, all the time.

If it hadn't been for her he'd have found some reason to ignore the note. The game was to seek, not to find: to stretch out the interest over slow pedantic days, like an old convict building something pointless out of matchsticks. Was Braemar so naive that she thought this could be real? The 'alien' was a birth-defected rich kid in hiding recovering from disastrous gene-therapy. Rich enough so the locals knew better than to answer questions . . .

He heard a scrabbling sound, thrust the light at it and saw a dark shape wriggling in one of the crumbled slit windows. She dropped to the ground. Dim light welled between her fingers from a short, red, glowing dumbbell. She came towards him, then stood and gazed for a long time. The strangeness of her face began to melt. The split lip and concave nose became as invisible as the features, the beauty even, of a face loved and familiar. Maybe, he thought, she was trying to see him as human too.

'Hi. I'm John Francis Guglioli, late of New York City. Who are you?'

'I am you – '

She didn't have a cleft palate, then. She didn't make sense but her speech was normal, only slightly nasal. She was very young. Translate the measure any way you liked she was fifteen at the most, this alien. The way she looked at him, shy and daring and doubtful, made her seem irresistibly like a high school Juliet. She thought it would be romantic to meet in the broken tower at midnight: now she wasn't so sure.

'What do you want from me? Why did you ask me to meet you here? Who is it you're afraid of?'

<Afraid? Oh – !> The upper lip curled wide.

She pushed her torch into a loop on her sleeve to free her hands. She reached out to him. <I think I am your child. You are my daddy.> Her whole body was shaking. Her sweet eyes filled with tears. <Don't you know me? Please! You must know me!>

Johnny yelled, suddenly terrified. She wasn't speaking English! *The words were in his mind.* He dropped his flashlight, grovelled to retrieve it. Crouching, he brandished it at her.

'What are you talking about? My daughter's in New York.'

She seemed to get a shock, then came back fighting. She did not speak his language, not any language. He understood every word.

<No! You may believe that, but you're wrong. I know you, I can't be mistaken. I knew you the moment I saw you. Oh, Daddy!>

Johnny was suffering some kind of psychic invasion. 'No!' he shouted. 'You're crazy! It's not true! Get out of my mind!'

She heard something from outside. Her head jerked to the sound Johnny hadn't caught.

<Oh no,> she cried, *not using words.* <They've followed me!>

She dropped to her hands and . . . feet. Like a bear. She was wearing a loose khaki coloured jumpsuit, cuffed close at the wrists and ankles, with lots of loops. It was what she always wore, it made her look like a theatre nurse or a waste disposal worker: formal, but ready to get dirty. Her legs inside the trousers moved around, the joints turning upside down. It was obvious that the girl was doing this, it wasn't just happening; but hardly consciously. She was a wolf, a baboon with a semi-human face. She was above him, seeming much bigger than her real size, the way a big dog does when it gets too close. She howled something and leapt up the wall.

Johnny couldn't jump like that. He rushed out of the fort.

His flashlight, lost under the glow of the sky, caught a loping shadow. He heard a sharp intake of breath close by. It wasn't Braemar. The alien girl's enemies were around him. They either didn't see him or they didn't care. They ran and piled – several figures – into a big dark car. It rolled away, Johnny ran after it. Outside the gates the convertible was waiting. He leapt in.

Braemar had something else wrapped around her head besides the 360: a nightsight visor. She'd switched to the car's powerpack, which wasn't going to carry this juggernaut very far over rough roads, but never mind. For the moment they could follow the quarry lightless and practically silent.

'What happened, Johnny? Is she real?'

He had recovered some semblance of cool. 'I don't know. She panicked before we got anything going.'

'They were at the convertible. I went back for . . . to fetch something, and they were crawling over it like traffic wardens. Gave me a proper turn. They ran off when they heard me.'

About a mile beyond the last suburban lights the burr of a gashog engine left the Macmillan. Braemar turned after it on to a suicide track that had never been paved. The big car jounced and bounced along ruts deep as streambeds. Johnny could see nothing of Braemar's view.

'We're going to roll over,' she grumbled. 'I wonder what would happen if I tried to put the wheels away at this speed.'

'That's what I saw,' said Johnny. 'She put her wheels away.'

He couldn't hear the other engine any more.

'Lost them,' muttered Brae. 'Pulled off the road. Damn.'

But they hadn't pulled off the road, they'd pulled across it. Braemar gasped and thumped the brakes. The convertible's lights leapt out automatically, a safety routine. Dark figures appeared transfixed: one of them four-footed, big as a wolfhound at the shoulder. Braemar grabbed something and jumped out. It was a rifle. Johnny gaped in disbelief.

'Get out of the car, Johnny! Dear God, *get out*! It's tampered!'

But he couldn't move. One of the aliens walked down the lights. It was a ? a man ? The man-form held out its hands, making a soothing, sort of Christlike gesture. Johnny felt the car respond. The machine moaned, chugged. Its wheels retracted, it tried to put down its track. It closed its big white eyes and nestled down to sleep.

The aliens piled into their own car and drove away.

Johnny had begun to feel very sick. Saliva burst into his mouth, bile rose in his throat. He fell out of the convertible, staggered through wet grass that clung to his knees and fell against something, the bole of a tree. He felt unbelievably sick. A warm stream of piss poured down his thigh. Equal and terrible forces tried to drag him from the tree and mash him into its bark. So sick he couldn't move or breathe, must be dying . . .

He woke up in somebody's front parlour. He was lying on a mattress on a concrete floor under a brown and grey goatshair blanket and wearing some stranger's pyjamas. The concrete was extremely clean, the mattress thin as cardboard. At the foot of his bed a chunky monoscreen stood blank-faced on a plastic crate, on top of it a Christmas centrepiece of holly and Christmas roses. There was dim, dawnish light coming through unglazed windows, and through the muddy resmelted roofing.

He closed his eyes, recalling the second unscripted wilderness experience of his life. He and Braemar Wilson must have fallen in about fifteen rivers, climbed in and out of hundreds of thorny ditches before they found their way to this suburban street. Reports of Mother Nature's demise have been exaggerated.

He didn't care to think about what had gone before. He felt a complete fool. At least he didn't seem to have woken up in a spaceship. That would have been unbearably banal.

When he opened his eyes again Braemar was there, going through his personal effects surrounded by a mess of children. The monoscreen was blaring away and two African grown-ups in country clothes were reverently watching, sitting on the floor. Braemar had managed to open Robert's mobile home. Robert flopped out. She yelled, the children shrieked with laughter.

'Hey! That roach is under my protection, Ms Wilson!' If she was

embarrassed she brazened it out pretty well. 'Put the box down.'
Johnny leaned out of bed and rapped on the concrete with his
knuckle. 'Everything's okay, Robert. You go home.'

The big roach tasted the air in Johnny's direction, then crept
obediently back into its den.

'Smarter than your average orthopteron.'

She came over. The way she looked at him was a little too
knowing for comfort. 'My friend, the cockroach. Oh, Johnny. Why
don't you let them do their own dirty work?'

'He's a souvenir,' explained Johnny. 'We were in hospital
together once. One day the world will be ready for cute roaches.
Then I press the self-replicate button and restore my ruined
fortunes. What d'you think?'

'Too many legs.'

'What happened to my clothes?'

'They're being washed.'

'I pissed myself, didn't I? How disgusting. Thank you for looking
after me. I was totally helpless.'

'It's called culture shock.' Her face was still painted, but barely.
Beautiful women have to do it. Maybe paint was better than the
never-ending surgery or the new kind of cosmetic treatment that
could go so horribly wrong.

'Have you ever had anyone close to you die, Johnny? I have. It's
strange. It's, a kind of, Africa. There are parts of ourselves that we
can keep at bay, the way we fend off the parasites and bugs that
own this continent. But if it breaks through, or if we go outside,
Africa is what it always was: inimical paradise that made us but
God knows how . . . When you run into a big unevolved emotional
nexus, such as death of a spouse, such as meeting an alien, you fall
back into Eden. Doesn't matter how sophisticated your conscious
responses: things get strange.'

'You didn't collapse.'

'I wasn't in the car when it came alive. And I didn't meet that
friend of yours, she didn't talk to me.'

Johnny sat bolt upright, appalled.

'*Bella!*'

'Oh shit. Johnny, it's all right. I called your wife. Your little girl is
home and safe.'

'I told you?'

'Yes, you told me. You came out of whatever happened in the fort thinking the aliens had kidnapped your daughter. It's fugue, Johnny. Come on, you know all about it. Remember the scenarios. You've been drip-fed those scenes since you could sit up unaided.' She pulled her phone from her bag. 'Look, I'll try to get through again. You could listen.'

He could not speak to his daughter. Izzy wouldn't allow it. She said she had to protect the child. The thought that Braemar Wilson knew this stung him so that it took him a moment to read the full implication of her offer.

'You have my ex-wife's phone number.'

'Yes.'

He didn't keep phone numbers in his pockets. He held the ones that still had meaning in his head. What else did she know? How deep did she get? No point in asking. A US quarantine subject becomes a ward of the state, as far as data protection is concerned. Johnny had absconded, so he didn't even have that meagre protection. There was nothing he could do, no legal or practical recourse. Anyone who chose could delve into his private places.

'Nah, don't bother. It's the middle of the night. Too late for fairy stories.'

Braemar nodded, and put the phone away. It was a fine, economical communication, that nod. It accepted his unspoken contempt at her prying, almost with . . . humility. She went on looking at him, giving him this humility as though it were a present. Her eyes were brown: the iris not striated with grey or green as in most brown eyes, but opaque, glowing chestnut. In fascination he kept on returning her stare until it was like the preamble to a cat fight. One of them had to back away or else they had to fall on each other, clawing and grappling like maniacs.

She stood up.

'I'm old enough to be your mother.'

Their hostess had gone away and come back. She put a tray of coffee and porridge down beside Johnny and bent over him in concern.

'*On doit fai 'mene la para –* '

'She thinks you ought to see a doctor.' Braemar became professional. 'We don't want that. Too suggestive of the colonic irrigation in the spaceship, you know the one. Not right for us at all. The chopper'll be here soon. I'll ask her to fetch your clothes.'

'Come and have dinner with me,' she said, when they landed at L'Iceberg. 'Have dinner with me, and we'll talk.'

He returned to The Welcome Sight and spent the hours dozing, trying to work out what he really believed.

He and Braemar Wilson had scripted the stance he'd take in the intro carefully. It was meant to put him on a level with the audience, no sneering voyeur; and yet retain some intellectual credibility. It also dealt with the likelihood that Johnny Guglioli would spin any kind of yarn to get attention for his plight, and made that part of the story. But what was the truth? Something had brought him to Africa. Something had held his peripheral attention for years. He could not be counted among the believers. But a true disbeliever would reckon his files, his 'open-minded interest', so much crackbrained waste of paper and memory. One had to face that. Now he was inside one of those stupid real-life true stories. It had happened to him, and it still wasn't evidence. It seemed to him that his only evidence was that gut-wrenching, bone-deep terror, far more vivid than the inconclusive and easily faked events.

But Braemar apparently believed in something, something that made her willing to carry a deadly weapon. Whether she'd smuggled it or got hold of it in Fo, no journalist would take up a firearm lightly. It was ethically impossible: more to the point, she'd be as career-dead as Johnny if anyone caught her with it.

Was she faking? Was he being used by some unknown agency? He felt very angry when he thought about the gun.

They ate in the Planter's Bar, as if it had already become their sentimental rendezvous. She wore the glow-worm dress, he had hoped she would. Since it was her bill he chose fresh asparagus, carrot soufflé, *coeur de paume gratin aux truffes*, a silly confection of spun chocolate, cocoa liqueur, *marrons glacés* and ice cream; and a fancy bottle of wine. She accepted his raid on the menu with quiet amusement, then put him down (childishly, he thought) with an African and frugal order of foofoo and the local 'green stew'.

His meal was more food than he'd seen in one place for years. Unfortunately his stomach rebelled: he could not eat. He tried the wine. It smelled slightly of dogshit and tasted like caramelised printing ink. Bob Marley was on their screen, Johnny's choice. He sat staring at the grievous and beautiful prince of sound, Braemar's gorgeous body and the alien's swivelling joints entangled horribly in his mind.

'I wish he hadn't died of cancer. That's so defeatist.'

'You Americans. Can't a person simply fall ill, without being a moral degenerate?'

'Some diseases are willed. That's fact, Braemar.'

'And some are thrust upon us, eh, Johnny?' She'd finished the wine, but showed no sign of it. She shook out a couple of small lozenges from the base of her cigarette case and put them under her tongue.

Johnny was intrigued. Medics these days favoured pills taken by mouth. AIDS, polio, TB, malaria: everyone who travelled had to swallow their protection regularly. But strange drugs also had their place in the classic scenarios. He faced a possible ex-human, already in the thrall of the baboon-telepath invaders . . .

The waiter had left them with coffee and Armagnac. Johnny refused both. She touched off the screen, breaking contact with the hotel's systems.

'Alone at last. Shall we talk about aliens?' She smiled at him. 'Mind if I smoke?'

'Yes. So do all these other people.' There were two tables of other diners, far away in the recesses of the red cave. 'Why don't you take up a nice clean modern habit, liking chewing betel?'

Braemar sighed.

He reached across the table and picked up her purse. 'Fair exchange is no robbery, okay?' He shook out the contents on the cleared tablecloth. 'Take your phone. Don't tell me you never use it to record private conversations. Let me see you disable it. We're not going to say anything important. Call it a small courtesy.'

She pulled out the powerpack.

He flipped open her cigarette case, removed two of the lozenges, wrapped them in a scrap of paper napkin and put them away. She used a European passport, not a British one. He read the first page. He'd have liked to thumb the stripe but he would not: not even for revenge.

'I see we belong to the same one-eighth of the world's population. That should come in handy. A good colleague on this circuit has to be a blood brother. Or sister. Isn't that right?' He leered bitterly. Johnny's blood was good for nothing. 'Do you have an ex-husband, Brae? Can I have his number?'

She shook her head. 'If I had it, yes. I don't.'

'Why "Braemar", anyway? It sounds disgustingly Brit suburban: the name of a semi-detached villa on Acacia Avenue.'

'That's exactly right. It's the name of the place where I was living when I made my first tv sale. I thought it was appropriate for an obsolete housewife.'

'You don't look much like an obsolete housewife to me.'

'I was a lot older then. But the name still fits. I am the place. You are the thing. I am the place that you come into.' She dropped her eyes, glowing like a blow torch. 'Generically speaking, of course.'

Oh, it was a fun game, flirtation. He wondered if he could stand all the fun he was going to get if this partnership materialised. He wondered if she was just a clever tease, purely faking the heat that seemed to come back at him. He swept stuff back into her purse.

'I'm not into gender reification,' he told her. 'I thought we were supposed to be talking about aliens. As we both know, you can lie through your teeth and there is nothing I can do to defend myself. You can turn me inside out and I can't touch you. But tell me some sort of story. For the sake of appearances.'

She smiled patiently. 'Okay. This is what I have. There were three landings. There's an area in North America and another in Thailand. At both places there *may* be aliens interacting with the local people, but there's a – a wall. We can't get near. The humans who know about the aliens won't talk. I mean literally not a word, not to anyone. It seems the aliens don't wish their presence to be known, and have ways . . . I have friends in this search. We are almost if not entirely convinced that it's real this time. The Asa ufo was part of the same cluster but it was reported confusingly and we got on to it late. I came to Fo. When I found you here of course I looked you up. Anyone who is interested in aliens is interesting to me; I knew at once you must be on the same trail. I asked a few questions. I learned you had a contact of some kind. I made my offer. That's all.'

'You truly believe that those characters last night were, are, aliens from outer space?'

'Could be. And one of them is interested in you. And you're still talking. It's my intention to keep you talking.'

He recalled, horribly, the utterly disorienting *sound* of that voice in his mind. He believed nothing, except that there was a lot Braemar wasn't telling . . . and yet his simpler instincts cried that she must be mad if she wanted to share the experience he'd had last night.

'I see. I kiss and tell. You sell my story to the world.'

'Don't be disingenuous. You have the contact, I have the access to systems. I'm not trying to rip you off. All I want is to be close to them. From the first. To be one of the few.' She grinned. 'I'm a space-invaders groupie, and I think you can get me into the dressing room.'

Johnny was meant to be the observer, that was his role. He did not like this reversal. But if he was to be bought then he wanted Braemar Wilson's body, which he could not have. At this juncture, frankly, no other trade was remotely interesting. He'd rather have her, right now, than his old life back intact.

A laughing, talking mob of Africans came streaming by.

'Johnny! Braemar! My friends!'

David Mungea, high as a kite, swooped down on them and carried them away.

Johnny had been on the town with David often, though not since Braemar joined the gang. He had managed to enjoy himself in a distanced way. He appreciated the music, became passively stoned in smoke-filled clubrooms and got into tiring intellectual conversations with drunks. Tonight was different. He had to relax, he couldn't help it. He let himself enjoy the painful pleasure of being near Braemar without prissy reservations. He felt safe in the crowd: to tease her and get teased, meet the lick of her eyes. They sat around rickety tables in a concrete-floored shebeen. David put his arm around Brae and whispered loudly.

'Braemar, do you find this boy attractive?'

'Yes.'

'You sound sad about it, don't be sad. Everything is always coming right. All will be well.'

'Tell us that when you're sober,' said Johnny.

'But I am never sober,' laughed the minister. 'That's my great secret.'

In a canvas-walled dance hall with the rain rattling down outside he watched from the side while she danced, and let his imagination run riot. The floor was sheets of plastic, the musician at the desk sampled its crackle and slither, beat them and the rain into rhythm. Natural! everybody sang. This is Natural music. This is Natural music. Musiiique Naatuuurellle . . .

About two a.m. she'd had enough. He walked with her back to L'Iceberg. There was still a muted row from the Planter's Bar, but the front of the hotel was dark and quiet.

'Johnny,' she said. 'I realise that this coralin stuff is tricky. As I understand it, while the blue clay is more robust than any kind of etched crystal hardware, it's also marginally vulnerable in new ways. But data processing has always been vulnerable – to thunderstorms, hackers, fluff and dust and bugs physical and informational; to people pouring cups of coffee over their keys. There's caution and there's insane paranoia. You must know it's actually quite difficult to pass on a retrovirus. The processor in my global-phone is coralin, true. But even if you were not framed, you're unlikely to bring the invisible walls of the world crashing by handling its powerpack.'

Sex with a machine. The source of that nasty joke was that the QV was partly descended from the group that caused the last century's most famous plague. AIDS was unremarkable now, submerged in a slew of mystery-mutant-plague scares. But the joke had some point. Intimate contact, exchange of body fluids: Johnny had no right to risk any of that.

He stared ahead, aching, hating the sly liquid glance he caught as she smiled and talked. She couldn't mean it.

'Maybe you no longer have a career as an eejay. But look at me, Johnny. I'm no engineer. I still get my stuff on the screen, more or less. And no one expects my hands to be clean. The precautions are taken for me.' Again that soft, meaning glance. He hated her deeply. 'What's the point in this self-flagellation? Do you think that the Big Machines will look down and see how patiently you've suffered, and take pity?'

This was pretty well what Johnny did think: that if he kept the rules to the letter and beyond, somehow it would stand in his favour. It sounded ridiculous spelled out in cold blood, so he didn't answer. He didn't want to talk. He felt like a walking lump of tumescence: the horny adolescent boy, one of Mother Nature's more hideous practical jokes.

She used her roomcard to open the gates. A body lay curled peacefully by the watchman's hut. She touched the leaves of the shrubs that peered over a low wall. Dim lights sprang up like night-opening flowers. Braemar sat down by one of them.

'This city is on the brink and doesn't know it,' she said. 'Fo, New York, Seoul, Bruxelles . . . You and I are probably the only two people in Africa who can hear the seconds ticking away. It's a strange state to be in. It makes everything very intense, here in the last days. What d'you want to do now, Johnny?'

She looked up at him, so still that he knew she would not move if he touched her. He could do whatever he liked. He could peel back that petalled armour from her breasts, she would only stir to lift her throat so they rose more freely to his mouth. He could push up the glow-worm skirts, unfasten his pants and take her right here. She wanted him to do that. He had never been more certain of anything in his entire life.

This is how one becomes a rapist.

Johnny drew a breath of bitter outrage. 'What do I want to do now? As I believe you know very well, I want to fuck you until we're both unconscious. Since I can't do that, I think I'll crawl back home. Maybe stopping in some doorway on the way to jerk off. I haven't had a sexual partner for two solid years. If we are going to work together you'll have to understand what this means. I have a hormonal problem. It's something any young male of chaste habits has to live with. I cope, *but don't push your luck.* I'm bigger than you. Excuse my frankness. This is the twenty-first century and we're both grown-ups.'

He collapsed on the end of the wall, staring at his feet.

'Oh, I forgot. I tried to seduce a guy at a party in Amsterdam, a few months after I dodged quarantine. But I did not manage to persuade him to go all the way. Or even very far.'

'I didn't know you were bisexual.'

She had the nerve to find his plight funny.

'Not in any of those files you've been tampering with, eh? I'm not. I was utterly gonzo.'

His outburst had relieved the pressure momentarily. God bless words, he thought. Where would we be without them? He ought to leave now, find that doorway. But this thing had gone beyond mindless arousal. Brae's body had acquired meaning beyond itself. He put his fists to his eyes: images of those country people in their pitifully decent poverty, thoughts of what the coming of the visitors might mean to them, to billions. His memories were not to be trusted – the car that whined and lay down like a dog, his daughter kidnapped. Yet there had been a meeting. He was convinced, for now at any rate. The world would be changed for ever. But he would still be shut out. He wanted to be wrapped and hidden. Please. Let me come home.

'Johnny, come here.'

He was desperate enough to obey.

She took his hand, and closed it over a small, slick package. It was a gesture he had only seen in risqué foreign films. Decent kids in New York didn't need to be protected against casual pregnancy or disease. You got married, you stayed married: end of options. The touch of her hand, the sophisticated way she closed his fingers: the effect was incredibly erotic. His tongue was too thick for his mouth.

'That won't keep out the QV. Okay, you're not risking your job. What about your life?'

'I thought I'd made myself clear. I'll try again. You turn me on. I'm forty-seven years old. At my age one doesn't hesitate when lightning strikes. You tell me you haven't got QV: that's enough. One takes the reasonable precautions, one takes one's own risks. *C'est tout simple, l'amour.*'

'Or am I too old? Is that it?'

She laid his fist on her bare shoulder. He was in her space, and falling, dazed with gratitude.

A strange thing happened then. Braemar was not tumbled in the bushes, as she had fully expected to be. As soon as they were in each other's arms, the two figures stayed quite still: for so long it was as if they'd mysteriously found, these sparring strangers, that nothing more needed to be done or said. Johnny sighed. Braemar stood and took his hand; they walked sedately into the hotel.

She found a book in his bumbag: an ancient paperback, nearly a hundred years old, the pages protected by plastic film. He had

a weakness for old books, that was in the files. '"An abode without birds,"' she read, '"is like meat without seasoning. Such was
not my abode, for I found myself suddenly neighbour to the birds;
not by having imprisoned one, but having caged myself near
them."'

She remembered the baby-faced prince of that bizarre, brief
Camelot, twenty-first century New York, with his motorised
skateboard and a rather sickening line in clean-kid arrogance. He
always carried a silvery tool, stiffly prominent in a belt loop or
his jeans pocket. To her unregenerate eye it looked like some
kind of ancient druggie impedimenta. It was the shank of a coralin drill, the badge of the latest elite brotherhood, fusion of art
and science; engineers of the word. And now . . . She wondered if
Johnny was aware of the way he wore the ubiquitous crotch-
bulge bumbag of a young adult male slung on his shoulder. Of
course he knew. He wasn't stupid.

It was immeasurably touching that the young exiled American
should carry Walden in his pocket. The hunter who had been
condemned to become part of his quarry: birddog, caged among
the singing birds. And trying to like it. Good boy.

Saddest of all was his conviction that what had happened to
him had been done deliberately. She thought how strangely the
whole world spiralled back towards the mindset of old Africa. No
weather any more, only the effects of human villainy. No death
except by witchcraft.

Some people said the QV incident was invented from start to
finish. There never was such a virus. There was only an excuse to
close down a space programme that had become a meaningless
expense and political suicide, an excuse that only cost a few
space-jock disappeareds. Was that the truth? Maybe the truth
was worse, maybe the whole business was a random error thrown
up by Johnny's precious Big Machinery. Or maybe, why not, the
virus was real, the NIH was right, and she and Johnny were both
doomed. One could not know the truth, one could only choose
one's risk.

Through the glass doors to her balcony the sky was a mass of
baroque violet, magenta and heavy orange, folded and crumpled
down to the black and unlikely margin of Asaba's volcanic spine.
The chances that the curtains would part and the god appear in

person were poor, at this season, but it was still a wonderful show. Around the '04 you used to get sunrises like this in the tepid post-industrial UK, but that was over. You had to come far south nowadays to find a good, rich, poisoned sky.

She had lived through fire and flood and earthquake, and seen the world go on just the same. The plate armour of the soft earth shrugged: seas churned, the twisted islands fell burning into the abyss. The blue sky turned livid, wild lightnings wrecked the man-made networks that threaded the atmosphere. Cold and famine took the world that had been preparing for hot flushes and rising seas . . . Everyone got ready to die. But in a few years it was as if nothing had happened. The human race, somewhat rearranged, carried on getting and spending, making politics, having fun. Starving and suffering if anything a little less, just now, than when Braemar was young.

Though you wouldn't persuade Johnny to believe that.

She wondered how soon before the drug wore off (not the one she'd taken); and he started to think again. He would remember the rifle. Stupid panic, to have let him see it. She would have to do some nifty handwaving to get around that. But she would have help. Poor child, he'd been so much on his dignity at first – and rightly so – but here he was with his hand in the honey jar all the same. It was so easy, she ought to be ashamed. She was ashamed. She could only tell herself (fearing it was nonsense) that one day it might be possible to explain.

Leaning on the page she turned to look at Johnny, his bare arms startlingly white, vulnerable and pitiful as a child's despite the deep curves of muscle. Under the influence of Oneiricene, the drug that infects the waking world with the loose poetry of dreams, she saw a white hound lying there: clean-limbed, earnest-eyed, eager and absurdly faithful. The muscle-shadows of his power a dapple of urgent words. A lamed hound is a murdered hound. One more betrayal couldn't hurt him. She had not wronged him. Johnny was beyond harm.

On the bedside cabinet lay a crumpled 3D snapshot of a little girl (better put that away again) and a sprig of creeper in a tooth glass of water, the blue flowers already faded.

What a dog's life he'd been living. Johnny Guglioli, friend of roaches, with his leper's bell and his chastity. The power of

American New Age morality astounded her. To think, she murmured, I used to wonder how the devil people could hope to sell Coca-Cola with no sugar in it and no caffeine . . .

'I believe in pleasure,' said Braemar.

i

At ten fifty-eight a.m. (STZ10) on 15 July 2038, Colonel Hebron Everard, commander of USAF base St Francis, Cape Copper Ridge, Alaska, was in his public office with his PR. They were about to take access hour. The colonel, an ethnic Slav at the end of a routine career, had regarded this command as a peaceful prelude to retirement. He was not very wide awake, politically. The Revolution had plunged him into acute, almost pre-cancerous depression. There had been no enemy across the cold straits for a generation. But barely ten miles away there was a new town of some one and a half million people, a sprawling de facto arcology of modern plastic burrows, decrepit clapboard and half-empty power-starved towers. If revolutionary violence broke out in St Francis, Everard's duty was clear and horrible.

Major Louis Parker, the commander's PRO and (in the modern structure) his second in command, was a stocky Afro-American with a wife and two children on the base (Everard was a childless widower). He had a reputation among the men for cautious and intelligent kindness. As they waited for the floodgates to open, he listened patiently to Everard. St Francis town – the blue-lit burrows paved in spongy carpet tile that smelt always of stale beer and vomit, the miserable population, the mindless murders. There was nothing for the people to do, besides drink and watch fabulous animations in the movie theatres. Or else stay at home and spy on each other through the soap nets. They lived on handouts. They didn't go outside. No one stopped them. But there was nowhere to go, no fuel to spend.

The base had been at action stations, overground duties suspended, since the state of emergency was declared. The bunker's main screen window showed an idyllic scene: burrows and silos overgrown with nodding flowers, like the peaceful ruins of some long-dead civilisation. One all-weather strip and the perimeter fence spoiled the illusion.

'It's the death of capitalism,' said Everard. 'Okay, communism had to go first. But there's too many people, that's the beginning and end of it. No system can survive. We're going to see the Dark Ages return, Lou, right here in the USA.'

The Revolution, which had at first seemed such an ebullient success, had suffered a few mood swings in the last weeks. But the arcologists were unlikely to stampede, and almost certainly there would be no order to harm them if they did. Very shortly Parker expected to hear that the President had finally surrendered and the phoney civil war was over. But Everard was beyond reason in these moods.

An aircraft appeared, coming in to land. It touched down silently, a black and white chequered spaceplane without any visible ID. Both men stared at it, then, slowly, as if drawn up on strings, rose to their feet. Six people left the plane. Nothing else stirred.

'Oh, my God.'

'Systems failure,' stated Parker. 'Excuse me sir – '

The plane had not registered, did not register, on horizonless radar. It did not exist, it had never been in the sky. But there it stood.

There was no eyes-on human surveillance outside, nearer than the main gates. There was nothing on the board to show that any man on duty inside had noticed this invasion. Parker did not raise the alarm. Six figures crossed the window. A full frontal view of them, starred by frisking lines, showed at bunker access.

'Who are you?' said Parker. 'What do you want?'

The man was wearing a light brown coverall, again without any ID. He was unarmed, unaugmented, carried no communication devices.

'Access,' he explained, in nasal and oddly uninflected English. 'This is access time. Isn't that right?'

The visitors all wore light brown coveralls, but each of them had added some form of decoration. One wore plastic clamshell fragments knotted in her hair, another had a 'sealskin' tunic strung with fringing and beads; and so on. They were uniformly slender

limbed but bulky in the trunk. Their hair was dark and lank, their
skins medium light. They had no noses. They came into the
colonel's office smiling grotesquely, showing their open hands, the
fingers pointing downwards.

One of the six was a child of about ten years old. He perched
himself at the communications console to the right of the commander's desk. He ran his hands over the keypads: a strange gesture, as if
he was stroking a pet animal. Then he went in slickly, never
pausing for a second.

Louis Parker watched, fascinated, still unsure what kind of
incident he was facing. Public access – livespace – was such a sacred
concept that he would tolerate almost anything in this hour, in this
contained space. A bunch of naked feminists could come in and
spray graffiti over the walls, over himself and the colonel too: in
fact, they'd done it. And at this incredibly delicate juncture . . . He
told himself the kid could do no harm, no chance of him starting
World War Three. The Big Machines could look after themselves.
They had to, these days. No one else in charge!

The others stood around. They didn't speak, but their faces kept
twitching. It was eerie: they seemed evidently insane. But there
were no pre-violent indicators. The child accessed a gift catalogue,
the commander's morning paper and the LANDSAT gazetteer.
When he'd finished with LANDSAT he stood, swallowing a split-
lipped grin as if he thought it might give offence. He shrugged his
narrow shoulders.

'Thank you very much,' he said, in the flat adenoidal English.

Parker smiled warmly. 'Glad to oblige, kid. What were you
looking for, by the way?'

<Your seat of government, of course.>

The six noseless visitors joined hands and began to dance.

Louis Parker stared. Belief came over him in a rush, irrational but
complete. The dance over, they calmly turned to leave.

'Wait!' yelled Parker. 'Wait a moment. Can one of you kindly tell
me in plain English just what is going on?'

The one in the sealskin tunic was, by all non-verbals, their
leader. He raised his eyebrows. <Why d'you think we did the
dance?>

They walked out.

On one of the small screens a disconcerting image flickered.

Colonel Everard and the chief alien arranged armchair to armchair against a blue curtained backdrop. A ruddy aging blond, with the eyes of a worn-out peasant farmer, faced an olive, noseless savage . . . Some Public Domain trawler company was pasting up a news item. It whisked away.

Colonel Everard was shaking. He was sick as a dog, as if the room had been pumped full of nerve gas.

Got to get them back, Parker told himself, subvocal. *The girl, the one like a pretty girl with the clamshells in her hair. She's their weak link, sexual favours bimbo. We could turn her . . .*

It was the way he had been taught to assess terrorists.

'Oh, Lou,' gasped Everard, sweat standing on his pasty face. 'Oh, Lou . . . The aliens have landed!'

There was a knock on the door, a startlingly immediate and physical sound. Parker hesitated a split second: slapped the pad. The visitor with the clamshells marched in and stood, fists balled at her sides, within a foot of him.

<You're quite right! He isn't my daddy. Yes, I married him for gain. He knows that as well as you do. But how dare you assume that means I could be persuaded to take your part in a quarrel?>

A small red object, a little bug, crept out from under her hair. She put up one hand and absently tucked it into her mouth. The distraction seemed to calm her.

<You're a woman, aren't you? You should understand. Sex doesn't mean a thing. Loyalty is *important*.>

She marched out. She had not spoken a word. Parker saw that from Everard's face, and understood what had happened to him.

'What?' he yelled. He recoiled from the closed door. '*What!*'

Outside, through the screen, the chequered spaceplane quietly took to the air.

Parker recovered, feeling dizzy and stressed but in control again. The systems failure, the odd aircraft, would be explained somehow. He even knew about these noseless people. It was a Francistown cult, an algal bloom of the hopeless ocean. People had their noses cut off, ate no solid food and thereby became spiritually pure or whatever. Maybe it was a feminist thing, nose equals penis. Which made you wonder about the noseless men.

Colonel Everard was looking dog-eyes at his PR; a scared hound to his master. Parker laughed shortly. 'No such luck, Heb. No demigods are going to come and haul us out of the shit. It's a hoax. Listen to me. We're going to rub the camrecord for the last hour, including what I'm saying now. Nothing happened, okay? We don't want the media all over us. Let's get through with the Revolution, shall we, before we move on to alien invasion.'

The alien girl left another note for Johnny at the Planter's Bar. This time, the meeting went smoothly. Since Johnny wouldn't touch any of her coralin-based equipment, Braemar bought a 'dead' camcorder and stock, locally produced but still ridiculously expensive. The hotel terminal in her room had a port for her adaptor. It processed the taped images, constructing statistical approximations of the information unavailable to a flat lens.

She sat on her bed, remote in one hand, taking Johnny and his alien apart frame by frame: obverse profiles, upward angles, back views. Braemar had once saved her own life by exploiting a housewife's tv science of pop-anthropology, explaining to her fellow housewives the far-reaching implications of a bride's behaviour at an English middle-class wedding. She turned that science on the alien. She was trying to find answers, in gesture and glance and dress, for the questions which might be so vitally important.

What kind of people are these? What do they respect, what do they value? What do they fear?

Braemar gave up looking for the zip fastener very soon. The alien kept her overalls on, and her brown cloth baseball boots with the ankle ties. She did not, if one could express it so, *mug* 'alien life form' in any way; she didn't ham it up. But she was entirely convincing.

Johnny took the alien's hand. The creature allowed him. There were three rather short fingers, a thumb, the stub of a fourth finger. With the 'thumb' locked in a fist, pads on the outer surfaces formed a thick horny paw. The nails were trimmed claws. The skin of hands and face looked faintly scaly, with visible pores: goosebumped like chicken skin, but with no trace of down. He felt her forearm through the cloth, laid his own beside it.

'This is the pentadactyl limb!'

The alien observed his awe with mild amusement. Braemar saw her wondering, *Why shouldn't an arm be like another arm?* When Johnny ingenuously offered to trade nakedness, the alien was at first overcome with mirth: then suddenly deeply wary.

What was that anxiety? Not sexual, not simply sexual anyway.

They called her Agnès. It was the only name she offered aloud, and Johnny reported no other. Confusingly, she sometimes seemed to use it to 'name' Johnny as well as herself. It would do for the moment. So would 'her' gender. The alien seemed feminine to Johnny. Braemar accepted his attribution, but it took a very few frames to convince her this certainly was no woman. 'She' had not been aware that the name 'she' borrowed was a girl's name. The reaction to Johnny's probing – are you female? – was odd. 'She' did not appear to misunderstand, or even to find the question alien. She was embarrassed for Johnny. There was no sense of taboo broken, just a minor social gaffe. Johnny was continually embarrassing her. She didn't want to believe how easily he was impressed.

Johnny wanted to know: 'Why have you come here?'

<To be somewhere new. To taste the strange.>

Agnès saw that Johnny was dissatisfied. She shrugged in disappointment.

<You mean, practically speaking? Guillaume is the one you should talk to. He always has some smart, practical answer when you want to know why he does what. He wants to meet your leaders. I don't. I'm fighting with him about it.>

Braemar read body language: emotion and unconscious habit. No voice spoke in her mind. The alien's facial gesture was swift and delicate, but Braemar could not identify any organised system of sign. On the tape, Johnny spoke aloud and the alien girl rarely spoke at all. When the conversation became intellectual Braemar had to rely on Johnny's notes. As far as she could judge, the gaps in the dialogue were filled with reasonable likelihood by the 'telepathic communication' Johnny reported. But how much did that mean? Maybe nothing.

<Our planet is so like this one,> said Agnès. <Look up!> (On the screen, she pointed to the watery but potent rainy season sun.) <Your sun, it's like ours, except ours is blue. The way you live, the people out in the cities, the farms and the factories inside. The way you respect the dead, that's the same.>

('Inside' and 'outside' sic; Johnny's notes.)

<But Johnny don't you ever wonder what else there is to unite us to the Self, besides the dead? Those recorded images, is that all you know of religion? Do you never think of the Self alone, the

WorldSelf, that is the same everywhere, of which separate human life is only a small part?>

Not a word of this for Braemar, only a touching impression of unshakable youthful earnestness.

'What is this "Self"?' asked Johnny.

The alien spoke, plain English: one stiff intense phrase. 'The Self is God.'

She briefly covered her face: Braemar read, obviously, reverence.

Oh, it was for all the world like a serge-wrapped sweating missionary communing with a wondering savage.

Johnny's wonder, the alien's amused calm.

Is the laughter laughter? Is evasion evasion? Is reverence reverence? Is sexual attraction attraction?

Johnny was uneasy about the telepathy business (and who could blame him?). He approached the subject cautiously.

'Agnès, can you explain to me how we understand each other. How do you make me understand you? Have you learned my language or am I – uh – doing my own translation somehow?'

Now that worried her. Again, not seriously but socially. The missionary becomes a tourist, a tourist briefly afraid that this attractive bit of local talent is wanting in his wits.

Agnès was puzzled (reported Johnny). Puzzled tone. <This *is* my language. Surely Common Tongue is the same everywhere? None of us has had any problem communicating.>

On Braemar's screen the alien suddenly dismissed her doubts and became radiant. (A break in transmission, said Johnny's notes.)

<Oh! But you love words! You love them as much as I do. Give me time. I will learn to make you such terrific speeches!>

Agnès made no noises, no throat-clearings. None of that mechanical, casual humming and hawing the deaf have to suppress in social intercourse with the hearing. *They are naturally silent*, Braemar noted; and thought of animal comparisons.

There was a vertigo that could strike Braemar: a kind of horror, when looking at Agnès suddenly made her feel herself on the brink of some ultimate dissolution. She was attempting to find meaning, where no *meaning* of hers could exist . . . At moments she could taste Johnny's initial terror, bile in the mouth.

When the fugue came she would leave the interview tapes and think of glory: how the outcast eejay and the obsolete housewife were going to astonish the world with their noseless tourist.

They even had an alien artefact. Agnès refused to take Johnny back to the ship with the same firmness as she refused to remove her clothes; but she'd given him a present. It was a piece of rag-paper, grainy and rough, torn from the kind of child's jotter that you could buy in any street corner supermarket in Fo. An abstract pattern of colour covered it. The colouring medium might be ordinary wax crayon, but in the alien sweeps and dashes Braemar discerned (was this imaginary?) talent and skill. The alien is an artist.

The eye attached to the word-filled mind finds it extremely difficult to come to any image 'empty': simply to see. The farther a human artist strays from representation, the more literary a picture becomes, not less. Agnès did not struggle with the paradox. She called this a poem.

The coralin 'maker disc', which held the original record of Braemar's whole working life (and plenty of room for another few working lifetimes), was actually a cassette of incredibly fine tape laid with filaments of the blue clay. She transferred the reprocessed Agnès interviews to this disc as she studied them, and added Johnny's audio notes: a rough mix. The whole could be refined into 360 smoothness later, but not over-produced. They'd be careful to preserve the scrubby edges of romance.

Braemar studied Johnny as well. She had some tape of the night at the Devereux fort, and more of him in his room at The Welcome Sight – human interest, the background. Here was Johnny with his pocket Dante, running his finger from the Italian to the English, the picture of wronged innocence nobly improving himself. The Dante study was a myth. He'd only bought it for the miniature Doré engravings. Shame on you, Mr Guglioli. They'd laughed over putting that sequence together. He wouldn't laugh if he saw her poring over each frame, giving him the same treatment as she gave the alien. But she needed to know Johnny, too, and so did other people. We've caught one of the Chosen Ones. How does he jump? What makes him different? What makes him so attractive?

As soon as the stuff began to flow, Braemar started sending copies of everything home to her confederates. Had their moment really come? She felt sick at the thought. Let it be a hoax, she prayed. A subtly simple hoax that has fooled me and will embarrass me to death. Or let it be a *weird occurrence*. Let 'Agnès' vanish, (promising to write), and Johnny and I spend the rest of our lives struggling in vain to prove she really happened. Let this be anything but what it seems. She had been prepared for anything when she came to Africa. Except (she now discovered) for success.

Johnny was surprised that his parner didn't clamour to meet their alien. She allowed him to think that she was simply scared. Why get complicated? It was the truth. She refused to believe in magic. There must be some other explanation for what Johnny called 'telepathy'. But it would be stupid for Braemar to take the chance.

ii

It was 31 July. Instead of the customary hot, dull summer drought, London was having a welcome early monsoon. The air was fresh and cool as Ellen took the waterbus, half empty at this hour, down from Brentford; the dawn sky was blue and piled with brilliant thunderheads over the eastern horizon. Treatment pans along the river bloomed in purple and gold, putting the miserable little plane tree saplings up on the barrage to shame. There was hardly any smell. These latest cultures seemed to have improved that problem. Ellen mused on the EC ruling about urban shit, and its witty reversal of the old adage. Nowadays, civilisation is measured by the distance people *don't* put between themselves and their excrement.

Leaving the bus at the gates of the pedestrian precinct, she tramped through bizarre-shaped dusty vehicles to the street. The people didn't like it much when winter's floods spread that sludge of turd and greedy microbes over their living rooms. But they blamed — illogical creatures — *the storm defences themselves*. Everywhere in the world river cities had to live with these preparations: eyesores, expensive to maintain, much resented. You could not persuade the public that one catastrophe did not cancel out another. They were frightened of earthquakes and volcanoes now, not the new deluge. Ah well, thought Ellen. It's all fashion if you ask me: the fashion in disasters. What next, I wonder?

The New European Office was on the site of the old Westminster Hospital, which had been razed after a sick-building incident twenty years ago. She scowled as she approached the round-shouldered building with its yellow and blue glass walls. The gaudy naivety of modern architecture offended her. She pined for the angular, serious cityscape of the last century.

'Legoland,' she muttered aloud, enjoying her own tetchiness. 'Cars that look like telephones. Daft, I call it.'

The door to her exile had a handwritten notice pinned to it: 'STREETS FULL OF WATER. PLEASE ADVISE'. It was getting mournfully dog-eared.

The World Conference on Women's Affairs (WOCWOM) had been in session for two solid years. It was physically located in Krung Thep, Thailand. In Krung Thep, Ellen Kershaw and her assistant spent every working day. She was not an eager delegate. Ellen Kershaw, the arch-Anti-Balkanist, detested the very concept of *women's affairs*. But she had made a false move in a skirmish now forgotten. Her enemies had pounced on her error and Ellen found herself in video-conference exile. Though her physical presence in the host capital was not required, she might as well be locked up on Mars. Her constituency affairs were being handled by a locum. In the daily life of European politics she could play no part until the conference ended, whenever that might be.

It was a point of principle to stick close to London office hours. She arrived in KT soon after one their time, leaving ten hours later to return to evening London. She maintained that to shift further would damage her young secretary's health. Outside corporate rule, the status of non-time-located work was low. Ellen was not going to have the two of them looking like machine-minders. They didn't miss much by logging on late. There wasn't much to miss.

Robin Lloyd-Price was sitting in deadspace eating his breakfast and reading the *Bangkok Post* on the tv. He was a long thin boy, with slick fair hair and a fresh pink and white face, like a child in a Gainsborough portrait. He reminded Ellen of a highly polished toy, but she smiled when she saw him. Before the disaster she'd only been amused by Lloyd-Price, who, transparently, had hoped a spell as PPS to a stern elderly socialist-feminist would take the heat off his active private life. Two years as cellmates has to make or break a relationship. To her own surprise the old socialist had grown very fond of this product of ancient evils.

'Something's happened,' he said, with his mouth full. He had real public school manners. Quite disgusting, Ellen thought them.

'Oh? What?'

'The aliens have landed.'

'Pah. I thought you meant in KT. Might have known better.'

'I do. They touched down first in the USA. They arrived at Bang Khen at six a.m. local time today in a spaceplane that has since vanished, looking for the government of the world. Poonsuk announced it about half an hour ago. I have the release here. Want it up yours? They hope to talk real estate.'

'Oh, they do, do they?'

'They're telepathic.'

'Who says so?'

'The US air force.'

Ellen made a derisive noise.

A tap on the door and the maid came in with Ellen's tray: one of the brown mice who run in and out of all the offices of Westminster regardless of imaginary geography. This mouse had today acquired a white cap with streamers, also a frilled apron that wasn't part of her uniform.

'They don't show up on radar. And they have some kind of empathic total control over earthling computers. They landed in the Aleutian islands, they've been living in one of the closed towns in Alaska, exercising their hypnotic powers over . . .'

Ellen frowned at Robin, and offered thanks for her coffee and brioche. 'Sarah,' she remarked, as the maid hovered, streamers agog. 'Is that cap satirical?'

'Yes, ma'am.' The child bobbed a sly curtsey.

'I'm glad to hear it. You may go.'

Ellen settled at her desk. As part of their freebies they had a virtuality set (single) whereby they could 'really' walk into the streets of the watery city and enjoy a range of tourist entertainments. Robin had played with it for a while. Ellen was not interested. She found the Multiphon, the video-conference interactive translation chamber, sufficiently irritating.

Maybe only Thailand would have actually built the thing: for show, for fun; in commitment to the curious Thai ideal of libertarian formality. Everyone has a right to their own language, their own funny little ways. It was an attitude that had enabled them to hold the world at bay for centuries. But Ellen bristled. Reasonable people did business in English. Those who had historical reasons to resent this (eg the French), lumped it. All that powerful simultaneous translation hardware was so much proof of the half-baked woolly-hat-anarchist ethos of the WOCWOM.

This was not a virtuality. Ellen's senses sat in Westminster, looking into an array of tv screens and listening to a headset. She watched on mainscreen (just now) the view the tv public saw and saw herself, if she looked closely, sitting there in the EC block. But she had no illusion of astral travel except, maybe, a brief moment or so of vertigo at the end of some particularly long ten hours. The session was more populous than usual, more ersatz astral beings and more flesh-and-blood bodies too. Stats running up a subscreen told her that the 'press gallery' was packed. That didn't mean much. The world's news-gatherers browsed this sort of thing automatically, and then threw it away.

There were no aliens on show. An Australian factory inspector had the dais screen – the floor, as Ellen still termed it internally – reeling out statistics of effectual imprisonment, of starvation rationing, of 'immorality' (he meant lesbianism) in ex-Japanese production hives, *these enforced convents of young women and girls* . . .

The immaculate Poonsuk Masdit, convener of the Thai National Women's Committee, lay tiny on the dais beside the giant face of the Australian. She was on her couch: it must be a bad day.

Ellen searched around the chamber, a manoeuvre which caused her desk on the mainscreen to revert to a telltale holding image of an empty chair. Curiosity wasn't private in the Multiphon. Looking, as it were, over her own shoulder, she saw that there were faces in the USA block, in the desks that had been empty for a long while. Now *that* was interesting. She requested a release on the subject USA delegation. It didn't appear. The Multiphon's ingenuity was spent in tv effects and language handling. It was not a reliable secretary.

A spokesperson for the Multiprod hive (speaking from Melbourne) countered the inspector's information, showing that the young ladies indoors were actually *healthier* on their restricted diet.

Maybe it sounded more convincing in Vietnamese.

On her lap below the console Ellen shuffled a pile of papers and multicharges, a tiny sample of the documentation she was supposed to study. Here was something about numbers of young women in service in the UK. There were government charts proving that the movement towards 'resident domestic work' and away from 'qualified employment' was innocently chaotic, with no underlying linear trend. There were the raw figures, with another story. There was a report on the fate of servants fired for getting pregnant: the children, illiterate and fatherless, penned in nominal 'schoolrooms' while the ageing 'girls' sweated in the UK's own production hives. The nations of the old 'Third World' were always pushing this sort of stuff, making sure the conference didn't forget that abuses happen everywhere. Ellen grimaced impatiently. The woman question was certainly a world-wide scandal, but this talking shop wasn't the solution.

If there were factory girls running riot in the alleys of Liverpool, I suppose I'd be more enthusiastic, thought Ellen cynically. There'd be votes in KT attendance, then.

But the riots were in Karachi, Lagos, Jakarta, New Delhi – in monstrous outback glasshouses with names like Black Stump and Lizard's Knee. (Though why on earth they should be frightening! Such tiny sticks of flailing arms, hampered in tattered mummy cloths: such shrill and feeble defiance.) Ellen sighed. Even an army of mice can be alarming, because it seems so unnatural.

The WOCWOM annoyed her because, lifelong feminist as she was, she knew how that sexual-politics label obscures the real issues, to the advantage of the enemy. This was basically a conference about global labour conditions, which the employer nations did not feel obliged to attend. You could see it at a glance. The crowded blocks belonged to India, Pakistan, parts of the Middle East and Federated Europe, ASEAN and Oz and Africa. The real powers in the world, China, the Pacific Rim, the corporations, the USSR and the EC, didn't need to be here. They could have as much influence on this affair as they wanted through their clients, the 'protected economies'; partners in energy audit trade-offs. Today, as usual, Ellen was alone in the EC block.

At least you couldn't blame the Americans. They were too busy with their internal affairs. Or, rather, they had been. She tried for her release again: nothing available.

Funny how things turned out. The '04 was supposed to be the great environmental catastrophe, God's punishment for the human race's misdeeds. Thirty years on and it was plain to see the really significant thing was that Japan had achieved the age-old dream. China and Japan became one. And, my goodness, didn't the world feel it! The important world, that is – balances of power and so forth. Surprisingly little had changed as far as the powerless were concerned.

Ellen pushed aside the butterfly wings of cosmic order, mangled into nonsense by the Office of Statistics. 'Innocently chaotic', indeed!

'Robin, my lad, I can't be bothered with this. From now on, don't take *anything* out of the hopper. You watch. Give it a year or two and every reform fought for in the great Krung Thep Wigwam will be down the toilet. There'll be nothing left but a few scraps of legislation so obvious and minor they were passed without a murmur.'

Pity for the mouse army pierced her: thoughts of her own people, lost generations, beaten down in the service of King Cotton. She heard the cynicism in her own voice. It depressed her.

She straightened her shoulders. 'Women are the poor of the world,' she announced. 'The last working class. They're causing a ruckus now *because* they're getting stronger. We can't help them, we can only cheer them on. You can't stop struggling. But while you're at it you have to remember you're only a symptom, not a cure. Progress imposed politically is never worth anything.'

'Then what is?' grumbled Robin gently.

'My revenge. Let's have the horoscope.'

'"Plan your day with care,"' said Robin, tackling the *Bangkok Post*'s English with aplomb. '"This could be a disturb week, so you will need to think carefully about what you want to do. It could be easy to be saddle with a bad bargain. Also, you may believe rumours that are unfounded. Stick to routine jobs if you can."'

Now that was what Ellen called proper international communication: disrespectful, casual, perfectly intelligible.

'Good. The techs over there will make sure we have a quiet session. Hand me some real work.'

Robin did as he was told. He was accustomed to Ellen's blunt manner. She meant no offence. He watched her, a dumpy old lady with more than a passing resemblance to the late Queen: the same crumpled jowls, the same unchanging hairstyle (defiantly dark, in Ellen's case), folded in rigid waves that didn't seem to have stirred for half a century. Robin's friends pitied his plight. He took the sympathy, finding it useful, but loyalty to Ellen had been a calculated decision. He was young, he had time to spare. From now on he was well in the black in a certain system of credit. He was the boy who was safe to have behind you in a foxhole. These things matter.

There were less tangible benefits. *Ellen is my Hermit*, thought Robin, *a passionate Gamesplayer if he ever had the time. To earn what she's got cost her too much, and she's off the board. But in her service I'll gain enlightenment without being battered to bits in the process.*

Outside in Westminster, the 'Autonomists' who had manoeuvred Ellen into jail were up to their usual tricks. Ellen began a hostile perusal of certain documents in the private files of a prominent Little Englander. She knew that the boy found her lawless tactics highly entertaining. She ignored his silent, amused attention for as long as she could.

'Well, what's up with you?'

'Don't you want to know about the aliens?'

'What aliens?'

'The ones I was telling you about. They've been taken to see the Queen, Poonsuk said. No one in the chamber knows what to make of it, but *I* don't believe Poonsuk ever plays the fool. No blague, ma'am. I think they're here.'

'If this is a wind-up, you young monkey – '

She returned to KT. Revenge is musk and amber, but she liked to be teased by Robin. There was a stir in the chamber. Empty chairs sprouted as video-conferencers searched for better camera angles; realtime bodies pressed to the aisles. A troop of girl soldiers, beautifully turned out, entered Ellen's view. In their midst there were several people in light brown coveralls. They marched towards the dais, towards their own image on the screen behind. Censorship was breaking down. Odd figures scurried, machinery and trailing cable became visible. In Westminster Ellen's headset roared like the sea in a shell: Babel reborn. The techs were probably planning to sue the stargazer of the *Bangkok Post*.

'. . . in the interim, the Aleutian visitors will speak from the USSA,' quacked the Multiphon, suddenly reduced to the blatting tone of a novelty domestic appliance.

Ellen's request finally came back, in print on one of her subscreens. *Delegation Name change.* The release you have requested . . .

Mainscreen view swooped to the çi-devant USA. More brown coveralls winked into existence there. For the first time, she saw what the fuss was about.

'Apparently there were three landings,' said Robin demurely from his own desk. 'One in a country near the Cameroon, I've forgotten the name. One in Burma . . . I mean Karen, up beyond Chiangmai, one in Alaska. The Alaskan group seems to be in charge.'

My dear, you look very odd. Good heavens, what have you done with your underwear?

Ellen clutched her ear as if an insect had bitten her. Aliens! Suddenly there was nothing available but a close-up of the dais. She saw a senseless heap of brightly packaged objects. Lace-trimmed handkerchieves. Velvet jewel cases, tvs with global translator facility and zapback, a group virtuality set, suits curled like crisp black pupae around the desk; a blanket of vatgrown sable: all kinds of expensive and nasty giftables.

'Beads for the natives,' said Robin's voice in her headset. 'What d'you suppose they want in return? Hawaii?'

Ellen muttered and slapped keys, to no effect.

'Get out and switch on the telly, Robin. You'll probably find out more that way.'

The Multiphon pulled itself together. The chamber reappeared with the Convener on the dais and a slender, elderly gentleman in a black kimono seated beside her couch.

'The government of the world,' said Poonsuk.

Ellen's mail box was flashing merrily. Naturally. She was the only EC delegate in the chamber. Conscientious out of the habit of a lifetime, she had often been the only delegate in the chamber from the whole White North. She watched the flashing from the corner of her eye, the signal slowly taking on delightful meaning. She noticed that there were empty desks, dishevellment: some delegates seemed to be in a state of emotional collapse.

Scraps of précis wrote themselves up on a subscreen. The old man in the kimono was the visitors' go-between. He was a Mr Kaoru, retired businessman living on a private estate in the tiny State of Karen (not to be confused with Karen state, next door in Federal Burma). He had been acting as host to one of the groups of aliens. The Aleutians (the Multiphon appeared to have decided that Aleutia was the name of the alien planet) had agreed they would all accept his extended offer of hospitality.

(What? she thought. But surely they've been in touch with each other –)

'Kaoru is one of those bloody *noms de guerre*,' Robin provided. 'This Jap is up to no good, if you ask me.'

'Ex-Japanese, please, Robin. We're in livespace. Accidental rudeness is a daft waste of ammunition.'

On the BBC, the inevitable series of dying swan acts: heads of state crying, *well, I'm fair gobsmacked*. And the arcology at last, heap of slum dwellings in the northern wilderness. The alien-lovers, converts of a new religion: incoherent losers with drug-coarsened faces, radiant; mutilated.

What must they think of us? wondered Robin.

And the story was grabbed, caught hold like flame, ran from one domain to another until some fresh bulletin trashed it or it flared through the billions. Robin was withholding judgement. Wary amusement seemed the appropriate response so far. He felt comfortable in the mode, could reside here indefinitely. There was no need to rush towards belief or disbelief.

Ellen noticed that today the United States of America had become the United Socialist States of America, and nobody in the world had a thing to say about this remarkable event. She wondered what kind of omen that was for the future. She wondered how long it would take for the rest of the building to remember Conference Room 27/2W, and come beating a track to her door. Oh, this was musk and amber indeed!

Was that a man or a woman loping up to the ceremonial lectern at the World Conference on Women's Affairs? It was nothing to anyone, at the moment, what these supposed aliens did for sex. But everything this odd-looking stranger said might mean worlds. The first words spoken in the darkness of a new creation.

'Robin, my lad, pay attention. If this isn't the start of a tom-fool advertising campaign, things are looking up. This is *change*. And what's more, you and I are going to be very much sought after before five o'clock this afternoon.'

iii

'Izzy was in advertising,' said Johnny. 'In-house, persuading one bit of the corp to look at what was going on down the hall, that sort of thing. She couldn't do it from home. Price-sensitive material, not allowed to leave the building. It wasn't a great job – '

'Rows and rows of pretty young ladies, pouting by numbers.'

'Yeah. But we'd always been sure Izzy wouldn't give up work, and we were lucky she could get a job with a Seimwa peripheral – the bastard CofI clause, you know. Bad news for a lot of marriages. When I was on a trip Bel went to daycare. Otherwise, I looked after her.' Johnny cleared his throat, rolled over and looked at the ceiling. 'Bella was the best thing that ever happened to me.' He laughed. 'I have to be careful who I say that to. Rampant male in charge of helpless female child!'

'Don't worry,' said Braemar. 'I'm very tolerant.'

A doubtful pause.

'I'm joking,' she assured him dryly. 'The sexual exploitation of children does not come within my shockingly broad definition of permissible behaviour.'

But a lot of other things did.

Johnny lay alone on his cot in the room at The Welcome Sight, thinking about Braemar Wilson and the alien. The partnership prospered. Johnny met the alien in the Royal Botanical Gardens, which were in the grounds of the pagan palace. They were gently dull, the arranged greenery and the rather limp fountains suggesting a quiet plaza in an unfashionable mall. It was a setting that Johnny found reassuring, and 'Agnès' felt the same.

She never again seemed frightened, or quite so young as the first time. She never mentioned his daughter again. He was grateful for that. She talked about her home planet, its blue sun, its tiny moons, the parkland and the cities and the protected wilderness. As on earth there was a fairly large proportion of desert, but it did not encroach. She told him about a trip to the seaside when she was a child. The sea was a long way from where she lived now, she missed it. They had perfected global climate control long ago. They had no population problem: she found the concept puzzling.

She had no objection to the camcorder, which Johnny set up before them on a tripod. She was obviously familiar with this kind of technology, in some form or other. But she did not easily grasp the idea that the human race wasn't telepathic: it seemed to her that what Johnny knew all earth's people knew at once.

Once she wanted to know what an old guy was doing who shuffled along and set up operations by the path with a needle and a cigarette lighter and a spoon. 'Agnès' became uneasy in the course of Johnny's potted history of the drug wars.

<Is mountain climbing still illegal?>

'What do you mean?'

<When people go out into the wilderness. Out on the steep rock, where it's cold and the air gets thin and if you fall you may die. Is that a crime?>

He reassured her, and changed the subject as soon as possible. It was hard to resist the temptation to describe a tolerant, compassionate culture like her own, where everyone was free to live exactly as they pleased; and yet tenderly protected. But he was not ready to go into the things she would find out if she stayed, the bad stuff. He was taking things slowly.

She was covered with vermin, and grossly unselfconscious about dealing with them. Which gave him an insight into the nitty-gritty of starship life, and made her seem more human, not less; cabin boy on the *Santa Maria*.

Except that there was no *Santa Maria*. There were three landing parties (Brae had the facts right); there was no mothership. Agnès became evasive when he asked to see the vessel in which she and her companions had arrived. Eventually, she admitted that it had vanished. It would rematerialise when it was needed again. He gathered that the journey from the home planet had taken a matter of hours. She couldn't (or wouldn't) tell him more. People in the other parties could possibly provide tec-spec. Agnès was in constant contact with them, but not by technological means, nor means that Johnny could share. Sometimes she'd stop, 'break transmission', and get that inward look; and he knew she was communing with her friends.

He asked her to point in the direction of her native star in the sky. Could she show it to him, if they met on a clear night?

That was a trick question. Johnny knew the state of play on habitable planets. He knew that this teenage cabin girl had made an unimaginable journey.

Agnès laughed. <You're kidding. No one could possibly see it from here.>

He had a feeling that anything Agnès said in his mind could be taken at absolute face value. So maybe the star she hailed from was further even than he'd suspected, out of reach of any form of detection beyond the light-cone. It could be taken for granted that they had faster than light drive of some kind. Wormholes, some way of tying knots in the galactic spaghetti. This was no surprise. It was a truism that the aliens who landed, whoever they were, *had to be superior*. Or else we'd be visiting them.

On the playback he tried to see his alien with innocent eyes. It was odd to see how her lips didn't move. At the time, the experience of talking to her seemed so natural he didn't notice things like that. It made him feel queasy. The global audience had better not react the way he had done the first time. He pondered over how they'd get past the initial barrier of disbelief. One cannot prove telepathy on television. Tissue samples would be the real proof, but that suggestion ran slap into what he'd have called a taboo, if Agnès hadn't seemed far above such human twitches. But everything would be fine, so long as she agreed to let them use the tapes. She'd almost promised that it would be okay very soon. Very soon, Agnès the alien would make her first tv appearance.

He and Braemar played with the hoax option, using it against each other. But he knew that she knew that he knew; that what they had here was Johnny's life, his freedom. His hands would start to shake whenever he thought of the value of those interviews.

Without Braemar he couldn't have done it. He couldn't afford to buy even a flat-lens camcorder on his pension, and there was no market for antique books in Fo. If there had been, he'd been too sunk in misery before Braemar arrived . . . He owed her.

But Johnny was the one who had the contact.

The Welcome Sight had suffered an influx of Polish construction workers and become rather rowdy. It was early morning, but the muted roar of an all-night party was still coming in from the compound.

He sat up and reached for his bumbag. He smoothed out the crumples and stared at the picture of Bella. His own face looked back. Izzy was there too, and other generations. But he saw mostly Johnny – in the set of those unfortunately rather teeny black eyes, the width of her brow, the mouth. The natural timidity which he had bullied into an eejay's bravado. That ineradicable look of sweet-natured honesty which was going to be a lifelong trial to her; and a decided asset.

He revisited Upper West Side: a quiet wintry street, swept and neat, below the partition's windows. He held a sobbing baby in his arms in the purple light of a snowy afternoon. Bella's been poking her fingers through the *shoji* screens again, a cute but infuriating trick. Every time he yelled at her it hurt like hell, but comforting her was so exquisite. My God, this is appallingly addictive. Here is where it starts, the feedback system, the whole pain and pleasure loop . . .

I'm doing this for you, babe.

The skin of his mind crept. He could stand the bugs in her hair, the gap in her face. But the other stuff! He could amuse himself with pseudo-scientific notions of how telepathy might be achieved, but nothing made sense. He was like some ancient chemist rambling in the wilds of unknown toxicity, Marie Curie catching herself a cancer along with a Nobel Prize. The alien used his own manner and tone to speak without words, used phrases that had no place in her flat, formal English. She was in his head; what was she doing there? And why Johnny? Possible developments occurred to him: none pleasant.

He lay back on the grey sheets that smelled of Braemar – vanilla and roses, and the musk of sex. Repetition had blunted his sense of her astonishing generosity. She liked to live dangerously, that was it. She was a wicked woman. She didn't understand that to handle that cam – after what he had been – hurt something deep inside him. She was teaching him to live with his disability, to accept that he was never going to get better. He could hate her for that. But her preferred means of intimate protection, sliding over him, so cool. Her sex closing around him: pump, pump, *explode*. Now that was totally unproblematic.

To talk dirty and live chastely had been natural to Johnny. It was the image: I act tough because I do a tough job, but you can invite me into your home, America. My hands are clean. Johnny buried his face in the pillow, groaned with delight. He was supposed to be taking her out for breakfast. She was late.

Her phone lay on the bed, where she had dropped it. Braemar sat looking at the inhabited shell. The almost-living thing in there was a computer. A thing that accepted information, processed it and passed it on. This version, which was not animal, vegetable or mineral, despite its nicknames, was no advance on the best of etched crystal in its capacity for 'fuzzy' logic and human-like neural connections. But it was fast and robust; untroubled by power surges, dust, magnetic storms or solar flares. Best of all, it could rebuild itself in situ if strange impulses came along that needed different pathways. 'Incompatible', the computer people boasted, was a word that had no meaning for the blue clay.

Braemar didn't care about coralin's wondrous properties. She had none of Johnny's reverence for the Machines, big or small. But she wasn't immune to superstition. Inexplicable things happened. A phone could deliver messages twenty years old, tell you on its own account that your mother had just died . . . The global network could be haunted.

It's alive. It bit me.

Alas, no. Not this time. The news was real.

She chose the red dress with the tight bodice and full skirt. He had accused her of bringing these outfits to Fo just to drive him wild. It was true, of course. He might as well get the benefit. She applied make-up. As she leaned to the glass she saw her scarlet breasts lifted and offered like parted, inflamed buttocks. So cheap, these pretty clothes and things, so lovely and cheap. A sensible female executive tries not to think about where it comes from. The poor south, the live-in sweatshops in her own back yard. But fear nags, and fear has its remedy, older than humanity. When in doubt: present.

If the Eve-riots continued to escalate, young Johnny was going to have trouble keeping his trousers fastened on the smarter streets of London or Paris or Strasbourg.

The clamour of Fo came up through her open balcony doors. No air-con before noon: L'Iceberg conceded so far to the idols of the times. She stood in front of the mirror. One more time. It had been no trouble, none whatsoever, to keep him thrilled to the core. Poor Johnny! A mixture of guilt, contempt and remorseful affection stared her in the face. She usually had herself in better control. She altered the surface, without further recourse to paint. There was nothing left but a costume and a mask.

The costumed clownette will save the world. If no other reason makes sense then for your sake, you idiotic child.

Now to return the young animal to the wild, none the worse for his adventure.

She met David Mungea in the street. He was due at a development meeting with Ex-Mitsubishi (Civil Engineering), and was bound for Fo's conference studio. She walked beside him, edgy as always when alone with any man except an acknowledged lover.

'What shall I bring back for you from Flanders? A wreath of poppies?'

'I'd prefer chocolate.' Her eyes flirted for her. 'And make sure it's cocoa, none of this "nature identical" rubbish they try to sell me in Fo. What will you tell them this time?'

David was Johnny Guglioli's ally over environmental issues. When he was very drunk he tried to convince Johnny of this, with little success. But it was true. In the Asaba of the future, if David had his way, people would travel by foot, a few by tilt-rotor. Non-freight traffic would go down the light lines. Freight to remote areas would be by airdrop, *faute de mieux*. What could be more virtuous in this less-is-better world?

David grinned. 'I'll think of something. We Africans must be pragmatic. To save our future we must use what we have, not what we don't have. And one thing we have plenty of – '

'Is bribery and corruption. David, you are shameless.'

'Yes. However, there are no more roads.'

She laughed. The minister ogled her high fashion in purely

friendly appreciation. 'How about your business? Is the therapy working?'

Braemar sighed. 'Oh, yes. It's working fine.'

Johnny sat on his bed, barefoot. His face fell.

'Hi, David.'

'I must go,' said the minister. He bowed theatrically over Braemar's hand.

'That dress is disgusting,' said Johnny affectionately. 'I'm surprised Mungea didn't tear it off you in the street.'

'I'll be frank with you, so am I. I'm constantly amazed at the stunts I get away with. I lead a charmed life.'

'You're late.'

'Someone called me.'

She shut the door. The room was sticky and ugly. The staff at the St Maurice were more tolerant than Johnny would credit. He was misled by the catch-all paranoia of the poor. At L'Iceberg they wouldn't have thrown out a paying guest's *homme libre*, even if there was a slight risk of his leaving marks on the data processing furniture. But Johnny was more comfortable here.

'I'm not hungry,' she said. 'You tear it off.'

It was magic sex. It had been magic from the start, and it only improved: this time more than ever a headlong, seamless passage from intense arousal to explosive completion. He was getting better at lasting her out, too.

When the fun was over he lay exhausted, her face in the hollow of his collarbone. Overhead, the sleepy drumming of the rain. The works social was quiet at last. He missed his net. He had liked to stare up into it, but she said it stifled her, had insisted on an electronic bug killer. She simply could not understand how he felt about *any* overspending: no more than she could understand how he felt about quarantine.

Replete, as always he became restive. It was probably only abstinence (and innocence!) that made sex with her seem so great. She was too old, too cynical, too conservative. She had never properly explained what she was doing with a deadly weapon. At the best estimate, she was only interested in the aliens as a route to big money. They each held tape copies of the interviews, but the maker was hers. Braemar's position was immeasurably stronger. He'd be a fool to trust her, and he didn't.

'Braemar, we've got to talk.'

She propped herself on one elbow, her face appearing softened by loose hair, make-up the prettier for being a little blurred. He was suddenly so glad she was there that his suspicions vanished.

'I'm afraid,' he said. 'Brae, I'm getting truly scared. A voice on a phone proves nothing. *Maybe they do have Bella.* And I don't know what Agnès is doing to me: how she's changing me.'

Braemar tucked a fold of the sheet between his sticky body and her own. 'Johnny, trust me. You are not becoming a telepath.'

The tone, motherly and jeering, instantly flipped him back to hostility.

'Okay Ms Wilson. Let's be nasty. I'm starting to feel pretty strange about this partnership, too. We fuck, but are we even friends? You don't believe anything I tell you, and I know there's a lot you're not telling me.'

Running feet came pelting down the dirt-floored alley to Johnny's door. It flew open. Two ten-year-old boys, half the hotel's junior management team, burst in. They yelled with laughter and leapt backwards, covering their faces. Behind the kids was David Mungea.

'David,' Braemar adjusted her sheet with composure. 'You're back soon. Where's my chocolate?'

He spread his hands, looked into the empty palms with surprise. 'It seems I left it in dreamland. Gone in an instant, in the twinkling of an eye. My friends, I didn't mean to disturb you so dramatically. I was passing, and I thought of two people I knew who were not near a tv. The aliens have landed. We are no longer alone with God in this universe. They are in Krung Thep at the Eve-riots conference for some curious reason. Better still, my two newshounds, some of them are also in Fo.' He was very amused. 'So now I know how the milk got into the coconut, eh? You should hurry to the studio, but I'm afraid you won't be alone.'

His retreating laughter sounded loud and clear above the children's giggles. The bastard.

Braemar slipped off the bed and began to put on her underwear.

'Don't look like that, Johnny. David doesn't mean any harm. A scooped paparazzo is funny, that's a law of nature.'

'You too,' said Johnny. 'You fucking knew.'

It was a shot at random. He wasn't thinking clearly, he was too angry. His great plan, in ruins, was revealed as an absurd fantasy. She pulled the red dress over her head. When her face emerged it had withdrawn into icy distance: no more his partner in lust, hardly even an *acquaintance*.

'Of course I knew something was up. It's obvious in those interviews. Agnès wouldn't let us put her on tv, but she was expecting things to change any day. I heard the news a few hours ago. There didn't seem any point in spoiling our last date.' She put on her shoes and flicked open her phone. 'I'm going home now, Johnny.' She made a little social grimace. 'This must seem brutal. But Fo's no longer the place to be and I can't afford to wait for you to fix your travel. Look me up when you're in London. Any time.'

She didn't, to his profound regret, have the balls to try and kiss him goodbye. If she had, he'd have throttled her.

The night, when it came, was almost starless though the sky was clear. She crouched in the fringes of a patch of tall vegetation which her mind called 'a small wood', and stared into the awesome void. Darkness in this context meant precisely *not* empty, but that was one false perception that she had not mislaid en route. Other illusions had deserted her: *flatness, up, down*. Her weight didn't seem changed, the dark horizon was wide, but she held on to things so as not to fall into the sky.

Beside the wood, in this dark, dark night, there were steady, rhythmical noises. She believed the rhythm must be accidental, but groping around she stumbled upon a square-cornered barrier. Faint light emerged from the walls of a broad ditch. She watched as two large beasts came abreast of her. She couldn't see much detail, but something moved after them along the lipid surface below the towpath: they were pulling a barge. She was afraid there would be some kind of people and ran away. She imagined someone marching up with a torch, the beam catching her white blobby buttocks. She ought, of course, to step forward boldly and announce the triumph of her race: *I come from far away, I come in peace* . . . Well, maybe another time when she was feeling more competent.

She sat hidden in something like long grass and giggled to herself: *ci sono canali*. It seemed vastly, hilariously appropriate. She was not a sensual person, her life was in her mind. She huddled, knees to chin, and various sensations that she had not missed built themselves into existence. Cold, prickles, bruises. The air that she was breathing began to taste strange.

She closed her eyes. That almost starless void. Its few clear lights.

Peene opened her eyes. She was safely back in her cell. That was what people called her room, for its monastic simplicity. No visitors had been in here for a while, which was fortunate. The quiet movement of equipment over here was nobody's business but her own. However, she didn't care to be laughed at. She lay still for twenty measured minutes by the clock, which she'd moved so she didn't have to shift her eyes to watch it. Then she carefully eased herself free of the foam and got up.

It was cool in the room. She put on the dear old kaftan that served her for a dressing gown and sat for a while, then went to her workstation. *Where was I?* This was the ticklish part, for she could bring back nothing except memory. She drew pictures, shifting pixel by pixel until she had an identikit image, in depth, of the sparsely furnished sky. One can't just *go*. One has to be heading somewhere. She had chosen her destination advisedly from a small set of possibilities. She had the 4-space coordinates of a relatively minute area to contain her search for a match. The rest was number crunching. She let the program run and went to look out of her window.

Across the campus a pair of radio-telescope dishes stood small in the distance on their spiderweb limbs. They were not functional. Earthbased telescopy, in decline anyway, had died a death after '04. It might recover, now that the skies had calmed. Maybe people would start again from the beginning. Peenemünde liked that idea. There should always be a place for the human eye and its serendipity.

Astronomy was her passion, not her business. She had to be devious in accessing the space telescope 'Cannon', and the machine time for her processing, or someone would notice and ask questions that she didn't want to answer. Which was partly how she came to be up so late – though on this occasion she'd been working through a night and a day, forgetting everything else. Campus road lights and broken cloud drowned the summer constellations over the Prussian plain, and not a soul was stirring. Which was odd, because there were several non-time-located projects on stream. Everybody but Peene and a few other eccentrics loathed non-time, but loathing was usually kept within bounds. It didn't extend to wild-cat strikes. She shrugged and went back to see how the crunching was getting on.

In forty minutes (stolen in seconds here and there from a big

machine busy on other work) she had her result. She screen-
dumped the final image and aligned it with her identikit.

Nunc Dimittis, Domine.

Peenemünde wept, and blew her nose. The sweetest joy on
earth transfigured her pudgy face.

> Lord, now lettest thou thy servant depart in peace:
> according to thy word.
> For mine eyes have seen thy salvation,
> Which thou hast prepared before the face of all people.
> To be a light . . .

Peene had no intention of 'departing'. She was no saint in this
respect. The glory that she saw ahead was not God's alone. Fair's
fair. He'd had this wonderful game, this lovely trick to chuckle
over for eternity. But those first tears were selfless naked delight,
sufficient in itself.

She blew her nose again.

'It's nonsense,' she muttered. 'All nonsense, self-deception and
– and *pseudo-science*. In the morning, I will see why.'

The smile broke out again: certainty of certainties. She padded
barefoot to her kitchenette and heated up some sweet rolls and a
jug of cocoa. Feeling suddenly hungry she added cheese and jam
to the tray, carried it over to her single easy chair and switched
on the tv. The screen had been blank for the past day and night,
since before she began this last experiment. Which was not un-
usual. It was a symptom of Peenemünde's eccentricity that she
was content to live for hours or even days with the curtains
firmly pulled over that essential window.

She was probably one of the last people in the world, excluding
the terminally poor, the terminally sick, the mad and babes in
arms, to discover what had happened to planet earth.

She sat opening her sweet rolls and listening, cutting hunks of
cheese and spreading jam on them. Finally she just sat, staring,
her mouth open. A race of telepathic superior beings has arrived
on earth, by some unknown means of faster than light transport.

'Oh,' she said. And in English, with a lightness she did not feel,
'*That's torn it.*'

People thought of Peenemünde as unworldly, because she was

held to be very clever and she had no small talk. In fact, like most shy 'unworldly' geniuses, she was as entrenched as any other human being in the mire of getting and spending, status and renown. She sat there munching, full of helpless rage. She wanted to kill someone. If no one else offered, God would do very well.

4: Uji

Clavel, (who had been Agnès) sometimes found himself lying in the dark, scarcely aware that he was awake, listening. The noise ran through him: irritating, melancholy, trapped in a never-ending repetition. There was a street cleaner stalled below his window. He would wait hopefully for it to fix itself and go on, until at last he remembered that the sound was the river at Uji, and he was far from home. Then he would roll over and touch his guardian, listen for the breathing of the others. Count them as if they were still in Africa. At least no one was dying tonight. In a hollow of fragile security, with walls of grieving sound, he would sleep again.

In the early morning he slipped out of bed and went to change himself. He never wore underwear in the daytime now. Dust covered the white pan of the shower and of the water closet in its cupboard. Clavel wanted to try everything. But even his long-suffering guardian rebelled at the idea of water sloshing around in their changing room. Standing naked he drew a fingertip along the inner rim of his bellyfold and flicked the wanderers it gathered on to the thickest dust.

<Eat – eat!>

It would be years before this place was hygienic.

The sanitary bin was full. The local excretion pads, provided by their host, were adequate but bulky. He carried the bin to the waste consumer in the kitchen beyond the end of their wing. The house at Uji was one long main block with wings jutting from either end and various smaller buildings connected by covered galleries. The garden of combed gravel around them lay on a bed of air. Clavel took a short cut to the kitchen: the garden let him pass then shifted itself like a throat swallowing; smooth again, differently smooth.

<Thank you, little stones. That was pretty.>

He fed the waste consumer, which had been built by Atha, Rajath's commissar, and patted it. <Good machine, eat up.> Clavel had no talent for infecting metal with self. But the gesture, habitual tenderness towards the self-pervaded world, was deeply ingrained.

The ordinary digestive workings of Clavel's people did not produce bulky waste. The natural consequences of eating local style (with or without underwear) had horrified everyone else who'd tried it. By the end, the African party – apart from their captain – had been reduced to cow's milk, a vaguely medicinal brew which was the nearest Fo could provide to recognisable food. Now Mr Kaoru had hard food delivered to the helipad, and the kitchen staff processed it in a fermentation vat. Only Clavel persisted in following local custom.

<What is the point in coming all this way . . . ?> he protested.

And heard the good-humoured, jeering chorus finishing for him: <To act as if we're still at home!>

He filled a bowl with rice, prepared specially for him in water in the local way. <The poet is eating without underwear again!> It was true he found the exercise slightly alarming. <You'll ruin your digestion>, was one of the more sensible protests people were making. Clavel lifted a shoulder to the dubious amusement that surrounded him. Carrying his bowl and chopsticks he wandered on. To provide entertainment was part of a poet's business.

In the room at the end of the evenside wing, Rajath's wing, Lugha was curled up on the polished floor engrossed, a study band around his head. He scrambled to a more dignified position.

<Oh, poet. Look at this.>

Clavel looked. Without the band he saw only flat coloured patterns squirming. Local script trotted along below.

<What does the squiggle say?>

Clavel squinted. <That's a picture of an atom.>

Lugha was irritated. <I know what it means. What does that stuff *say*? Make the noises.>

'Deo . . . xyri . . . bonucleic . . . '

Clavel found it easy to match the sketched signs with the formal speech. The difficulty the other formal language users experienced bemused him. Don't any of you dream? he would ask.

The small one had lost interest, anyway. 'It is about the fundamental elements. They only recognise five. No wood, no metal, only milk and blood and water and fire. Folded together in their pairs, and breath for the transfer. Clavel, why do the people want samples of our tissue? I asked Mr Kaoru and he told me to consider this information here.'

Clavel chewed rice and peered. The romance of fundamental physics stirred him: water and blood and fire!; but his understanding was slight. He tried to share the sharp mind's fascination with those dead images.

'I thought you said they knew more than us about complex physics. Well, if they've only identified five bases that's okay. You were worrying about nothing. You get too anxious.'

The poet and the sharp mind were drawn together by their obligation to formal language, but there were barriers that couldn't be breached. Lugha didn't try to explain. He contented himself with a superior shrug.

<Why are we refusing? We've not been going around in sealed suits the way they do. They could scrape us up from anywhere.>

The drop into normal conversation was abrupt enough to be insulting, but Clavel saw that Lug was seriously curious, a compliment from the expedition's know-all. He squatted on his heels, running a hand over the child's flank. The grooming gesture stirred a tiny exudation, from Clavel's skin and Lugha's. The child added a scant, accepting nod, for manners: <yes, share my space>.

<However you alter a wanderer you can't make it into a weapon against its owner, or any member of the owner's nation. That stands to reason, doesn't it, because the first thing it would attack would be itself. Weapons are built from dead tissue, from unaware flesh. That's what we're being asked for.>

Lugha was ridiculously naive about human relations. He stiffened, nasal pinched with real shock. <That's awful. Are we at war, then?>

<Hm . . . All trade is war, we say. Not necessarily, kid. It's called exchanging hostages. You'll understand it better when you're older.> He was teasing. The person who lives only to learn would never understand this mystery.

Lugha frowned. <But they don't have wanderers.>

<Rubbish. Everyone does.>

<They don't.>

Clavel looked around the room they were in. It was another shrine like the big one in Fo, from which their images had been sent to the seat of government. The walls were banked with screens and desks, cases full of records, niches in which lay headbands and handholds like the set Lug was using. The equipment was familiar enough, but incredibly ornate and various. Lugha was fascinated by this place. The rest of them, even Clavel, found Uji's wealth of fabulous occult toys somewhat eerie. Practically every room had its own shrine. They'd been forced to move most of the sacred furniture; it was too much. He remembered the mad saints of Francistown. They too lived surrounded by ghosts, ruled utterly by commands and portents from the spirit world.

But surely nowhere in Francistown had been as empty of life as Uji seemed. Everything they touched was dead. Except for Mr Kaoru only images came near them, most of the time: ghosts on a screen.

<This is a sterile environment, child. That's why there are none of their wanderers about. We're in quarantine.>

Lug gave him a withering look. <They don't. You'll see.>

He pulled the band down again, small horny fingers were lost in flabby gloves and thrust into the box in his lap.

<Go and sing your lovesongs somewhere else. I'm busy.>

At night the whole valley was filled with the sound of water. By daylight the mournful babble retreated. Clavel followed it through the gardens and past the trail that led to the helipad. There had been a ground access road when they arrived, but Kaoru had advised them to have it blocked. The heap of earth piled in the cutting was already thickly furred with greenery.

The cottage used by their benefactor was hidden in the grove of trees that surrounded the helipad. He came and went very discreetly. Clavel was the one who saw most of him. The wandering poet would glimpse that slim figure sitting on the rocks or under the trees in a dark stiff suit, like a slightly embarrassed piece of statuary; and they would talk informally. Clavel had made a Kaoru record. He didn't actually want to do this. Clavel, intensely religious in his own way, was embarrassed by the conventional rituals. But he knew from Johnny that it was the polite way to make friends.

Kaoru puzzled them. His welcome was a different order of mystery from the behaviour of those holy lunatics in Francistown. In a way he'd acted as one hoped one would oneself, if visitors from another planet arrived in the garden. He often said that their arrival had filled an empty life, and there was no reason to suppose he lied. There was clearly a tragedy in his recent past. But there was also the quarantine, so quietly imposed. There were bound to be other areas in which he'd favour his own people: the mystery was that he declined, formally or informally, to acknowledge this conflict of interest. They must take him at his own estimation until they knew better. He was a shosha-man, a broker helping business relations along. The term 'honest', associated with that expression, was a local joke.

Clavel delighted in their humour; so dry, so neat.

A stream fell down to the river through stands of feathery green and over carefully placed rocks. It tumbled recklessly from pool to pool. Clavel sat beside it in a favourite spot, knees reversed, with Johnny a close and comforting presence.

And God said, let there be a firmament in the midst of the waters, and let it divide the waters from the waters. And God made the firmament, and divided the waters which were under the firmament from the waters which were above the firmament: and it was so. And God called the firmament Heaven . . .

It was strangely moving, that some poet of this planet of free running waters should describe a situation he could never have known. To recount the verse gave Clavel goosepimples. The skin of his forearms budded and wept small chemistries. A faint breath of Clavel slipped through the weave of textile and entered the air.

Farmland began beyond the valley: fields which produced mulberry (a textile); and cow's milk, the medicinal fluid that was produced by a large material being. The quarantine zone was extensive. Nothing natural, not the simplest commensal, moved in those fields. And what lay beyond?

The park in which Uji manor stood was large. It didn't seem polite to ask whether it was Kaoru's private property, or if recreationing locals had been forbidden for the duration. But the poet felt trapped. There was a world outside Uji which he had barely glimpsed. And would not see again, until Rajath and the rest were satisfied.

Rajath, who had been Guillaume. As a compliment to their host, they had now taken formal names in his favourite ceremonial language (different again from his own formal language; these people were so elaborate about everything).

Rajath, then. He was a part of Clavel, a mundane appetite that must be appeased before the poet could concentrate on wonder. He was also a very irritating person. Rajath had come out of their long argument during the separation with entirely a different opinion from Clavel as to how things had been left between them. That was always the way. Comparing notes you found that he recalled a totally unfamiliar conversation: and with such wide-eyed innocence . . . Clavel had not been pleased to discover that he was supposed to be coming to this inventive person as an abject suppliant, begging to be taken in. If anything, it was Kumbva (who had been 'Eustache', to 'Agnès' in Africa) who had the right to declare himself dictator. Kumbva was the one who'd found this place, and met Kaoru. But that open-hearted person had no interest in such distinctions: and Clavel loved the engineer's detachment. He wouldn't want to erode it, even if he could.

So Clavel had made the best of things. He had added some suggestions of his own, inspired by his conversations with Johnny, to Rajath's trade-war tactics. He and his crew were in a much better position as a result, and they had a substantial stake again. But he'd been too clever for his own good. The locals were now so impressed that Rajath thought he could make the killing of all time. He couldn't decide where to start. He dithered, tipsy with greed, and the poet remained a prisoner.

Leaves, rocks, sunlight. There is nothing new. We are always at home. Clavel started at the sound of motion, distinct through the white noise of the stream. He looked up, and met a bright eye peering through the green. Tiny piping notes came from the thing in a high register of fury. They had brought no commensals with them from home. They ought therefore to be alone in quarantine. They had been promised that these 'material beings' were harmless, but it was extremely hard not to react when something with the half-alive presence of a weapon came rustling out of the bushes.

Everything was so familiar. This could be any park, in any city: and then along came a reminder of the awesome truth.

Clavel knew that none of them had left home before they came together at Uji. Poetic remarks of this kind annoyed the self-declared dictator mightily, but it was the truth. They had been living in the margins of their own adventure, habit of mind blurring experience and refusing the evidence of the senses. They were *inside* the adventure now: and Clavel was afraid of what it was doing to them. For so long at home they had been one nation. Opportunities for lying, cheating, stealing, had been limited. Fear of weaponry played no part in most people's lives. Here, things that had been hidden for generations began to be expressed: lost memories that would have been better left unstirred.

Clavel perceived the trickster and wise but lazy Kumbva chatting in the character shrine below. Rajath jeered at the poet's distaste. The notion that certain kinds of human behaviour 'should' disappear forever was absurd, he said. <*We are what we are. There is no future, no past . . .* >

The bird flew. Clavel pondered. He felt that he'd gone too far in the help he had given Rajath. He needed a new intuition to restore the balance. It should be something that would make the locals look like less of a pushover. If the person who can never resist a profit saw his easy pickings threatened, that would concentrate his mind and get the tedious business dealings settled.

The air was populous as in Africa, but there was nothing truly alive in it. Clavel wondered exactly how the quarantine was achieved. Had he seen no skin-wanderers on anyone in Fo? He couldn't recall. How does one see, taste, feel, an absence? <They must have life,> he told Lugha. <They have houses, clothes, food, tools, plants. How else? By magic? One can't eat the dead.>

He slipped a finger inside his collar, picked a wriggling iota and considered it for a moment: the microcosm of all complexity, all being. And ate himself.

He curled down in his niche, withdrew from his companions. They said he was singing lovesongs. Let them say. Uji was enough of a prison. Clavel would not be teased out of such sweetness as he could enjoy here.

People had told him that the infatuation would pass, that the reality was physically impossible: and he had half believed them. But time passed, and 'Johnny Guglioli, late of New York City' became more real to him every hour. The poet gazed on the stream.

Johnny's presence became as real as the water. Johnny was here in the rocks, hunched up in the angular way of these people, who never forgot their bipedal dignity. <I was too brash, and so then we were both too shy,> Clavel told him. <I should have had faith in myself. A poet is still a poet, at fifteen. My talent is intact: to know the truth and tell it.>

The memory of that bungled declaration made him bare his teeth and shudder.

<But it can't have been so bad. You came back to me. We talked hour on hour. We didn't say a word of love, but we both knew what was happening. What else could those awkward generalities we exchanged possibly hide?>

<Yeah,> agreed Johnny, shrugging. <It's fucking weird, but you're right. You are my truechild. All of me but the me that speaks aloud knew it the moment I saw you: that's why I was so incredibly scared.>

<You don't hate me, do you, for explaining to the others those things? About the – um – 'ftl drive' and so forth? I know I kind of took advantage of you . . . >

Johnny laughed. <All trade is war. All war is trade. That includes love, why not? How not?>

<There are stories of lovers placed the way we are – >

<Yeah, I know. Serving different interests, showing off to each other with the wittiest, meanest moves. But those stories tend to end sadly, kid.>

<I've never been in love before,> said Clavel. (It felt like the truth. Lying down with people, even marriage, meant nothing beside this meeting of souls.) <You and I have never met before, not in any age of any world. The sad stories are the sweetest. I want us to have the best.>

The years had not seemed long. He had been absorbed and happy, engrossed in the purpose of becoming himself. It had been a time of learning, incident, rebellion, of coming arrogantly into knowledge that no one could match: as arrogantly letting dead ends slip by and dwindle, until the very entrances to those pathways were lost.

Scale shifted, different sets of rules came into play: the pattern was the same. Clavel remembered dimly, as a lost purpose hundreds of years in the past, that one reason he had joined this enterprise was to look for childhood's end. He sat by the stream, entranced, gazing on himself through his lover's eyes.

He had heard epicures say that this was the best part of a love affair. Love returned, but undeclared. Physical separation could be so exquisite, at the right juncture. Each of you acutely conscious – so that it stung like a bruise, like constant half-arousal – of that other self in the world. He was amazed at the power of the experience. But why shouldn't it seem all-important? This is the event, thought Clavel, that makes sense of the whole cosmos, the infinite reflection on reflection. And he burst into speech, such a speech as he had promised Johnny when they talked together on the garden seat in Fo.

'Self of my self, parent of my heart.
If I reach out in my mind's world, you feel that touch
wherever you may be.
'I lie down to embrace another, my kisses go straight to you.
'For no one can share pleasure, it belongs to the Self alone.
I can only come to you, I can only be with you, sleeping, waking,
living, dying, always. Your mouth is in my cup, my claw is in your
flesh . . .'

He couldn't go on, the words stirred him beyond endurance. Clavel got up abruptly with burning cheeks, and only recovered composure several rocks downstream. By then it was too late: the mood was broken. He walked on, in a kind of isolation he had only known since Fo.

One of the pools was occupied. Maitri, who had been Benoit in Africa, lay there contentedly, knees and head and shoulders rising from a mass of soapy bubbles.

<I could get used to water bathing, so long as I don't have to do it in the toilet. My dear, you've been singing love—>

Clavel bared his teeth. He sat down beside the pool. <Stop policing me! All of you!> Young shoulders lifted and fell spikily. <You're making the water dirty with that soap. You should be more careful.>

<Nonsense. There's plenty more where this came from. Look at that sky. Look at the clouds.> Maitri squeezed his sponge reflectively. <I know how you feel, baby. You feel as if this Johnny

is as much your self as one of the little creatures that creeps about
eating the shed cells of your skin. You imagine he's a secretion of
your glands, and that you are Johnny's likewise and would die on
any other flesh.>

Clavel's firm presence set into childish sulks. 'Do not laugh at me.
I'm not mad, or vicious. It is not impossible. Look at those pictures
Lugha is reading. These people are built of atoms. They are part of
the natural world. We all know stories of strangers who fall in love,
and it turns out they are not strangers. Their love is proved by their
sharing wanderers, like you said. That can happen, why not this?
Chance never gives up, you know. The probabilities get smaller and
smaller. They cannot vanish.'

Maitri gestured lazily. <Please, let me off the speeches. The same
chance that occasionally brings someone unknown into the world?
Do you mean this boy is insane?>

<No! Just that a̶ ̶d̶ents do happen.>

Clavel's attention turned to the sharp one's study: proof positive
that this beautiful coincidence was possible.

<All right, I concede. Humanity is a state of things, not a
peculiarly shaped object. That you should have found someone
very like yourself so far from home is only grossly improbable.>

Clavel's guardian sighed. It was seductive to have his baby back,
but disconcerting to have Clavel, on whom one was quite
genuinely dependent, gibbering like this.

The baby shrugged broadly. <Don't worry, my dear. I'm not
completely mad.> He frowned, cupped hand over his nasal.
<Friendly one, have you considered? They might be busy fooling us
while we are busy fooling them. Our sharp mind calls their science
clever, but one might as well say it doesn't add up. Maybe it's an
elaborate fake. Or else, they may deceive without meaning to, as
we did in the beginning.>

Maitri laughed at that. <Until you explained how we could do
better on purpose!>

The laughter was wrong. It jarred on some complicated poetical misgivings. Maybe Clavel had made his contribution to the
scam knowing it would snarl things up. Because, for indecipher-
able reasons, he was *afraid* to go free and find the beloved
Johnny . . .

The information came in a burst so choked that even Maitri

found it hard to follow. He sat up, wincing on the shifting and bony pebbles. <I didn't mean to upset you.>

Clavel stood, sharply. <I'm going for a long walk. That should please you all. I know you like to laugh at my eccentricities.>

<Pure one, wait!> cried Maitri. <Don't forget the> "priest conference." <Come back in time to change!> Too late. That young person, oh, forever young, had already vanished again into a tumble of boulders.

His guardian was left squeezing bubbles and brooding. Here they were, a tiny group of quarantined traders who could hardly remember how anything was done – and Rajath bent on embroiling everybody in a scam that looked increasingly dangerous. Everyone needed Clavel, the backwards-pulling, the *reluctant power*, to cog the wheels of that other's energy. It was Maitri's fate to be the one that Clavel needed. And what happened? Instead of making the poet wake up and take notice, he found himself arguing with a teenager about true love.

He wondered gloomily if it would have been easier if his ward had been born a boy. Such shifts were not unknown. Maitri and his lover were both masculine types (not, he hurriedly added, that they took a lot of notice of such parlour games!). It might have helped. He shook his head. Impossible to imagine his Clavel different, even in the most trivial respect.

In the character shrine at Uji, Rajath and Kumbva ate breakfast together. Records for each member of the expedition had been brought from home. The tapes had been preserved through every adventure, even when the living subjects had not survived. One of the first things they'd done when they were all at Uji was to set up a proper chapel, with display equipment made over to use the local dead-power. None of them was particularly religious, except Clavel in his own peculiar way: but in this ghost-bothered world it seemed like self-defence.

An excerpt from Rajath's story was playing. A child born in poverty, trekking through swamp and forest to the big city to claim his greatness; sleeping under the stars. Neither of them was watching, but it was an episode that Rajath found reassuring. It conjured up the best that he knew about himself.

<What I can't understand,> said Rajath, spooning his gruel with

habitual verve. <Is how they came to be expecting us. And you, your experience was the same.>

The food was in fact terrible, tasteless mush. Atha couldn't seem to get any variation from the local hard stuff.

Kumbva chuckled. <It wasn't us they were expecting. It was some other, important people.>

Rajath agreed. <A fine case of mistaken identity. Thank goodness – thank you, oh pure one – that we realised our position in time.>

Rajath had made no speeches in Francistown, there had seemed no call for them. It annoyed him deeply that it was Clavel, who didn't even care, who had come up with the idea of making formal announcements that were outright lies.

He sucked his spoon, dropped it; and made a speech. 'Let me try this on you. Today, when the priests come, one of them insults us. We require compensation. We take it in the form of property rights. We sell at an immense profit and take home the loot.'

Kumbva raised an objection. <Sell them their own again? With respect, my dear, they were not impressed by your first attempt: those gifts. I liked the real estate idea from the first – one knows how that market behaves, everywhere. But why complicate it? Time is cheap. We have generated some excitement, people will pay extra to buy what we have owned. We have only to trade our goods for land, wait, sell; and take our profit home along with enough curios to dine out on for a lifetime.>

The African party had lost most of their trade goods in the crash, and traded the clothes on their backs, practically, just to stay alive. The others had fared better. But Rajath insisted that the stores of toys, textiles, deadware, rare ores, were to be kept under wraps. He was convinced that the expedition could do better without them.

<And besides,> mused Kumbva, weakening. <Where's the insult to come from? They adore us. To be fair to you, they do ask to be cheated.>

Kumbva could see as clearly as Clavel how horribly it might go wrong. The chance of much greater gain, for himself and his household, was sufficient to offset the risk. But he made a cautionary speech: a rare outburst from the person who always takes life easy.

'Just be careful, Rajath, for all our sakes. When two strangers meet neither of them knows what to believe, and the advantage goes to the boldest liar. But no one likes to be made a fool of. One trick too far, and respect could switch to hostility in a moment. There is a whole planet full of them. We don't know how many. And we are scarcely forty.'

<Everybody expects me to have ideas,> grumbled the misunderstood leader. <So I do, and what thanks do I get?> He scowled at Clavel, who was sitting out in the garden hating him. The sting of the poet's disapproval was a constant goad. He hated himself for caring. Clavel didn't care if Rajath lived or died. <*You exaggerate*,> murmured Clavel. Kumbva ran his nails across the other's neck muscles. <Ssh. No one hates you.>

He acknowledged the touch with a tiny nod, calming under it.

<What I want to know,> said Kumbva, picking and eating, <is why do they keep threatening to strip search us? Quarantine I accept. It makes things easier: sterilised machinery is easily reinfested. But what does the colour of my backside have to do with business? I think they're crazy.>

Rajath took the other by the shoulders and turned him to the screen. <Look at that,> he said. <Look at me, risking life and limb for the bauble reputation. Shall I show you yourself? You are crazy, my friend. We all are. That's why we're here.>

He laughed. <Anyway. I'd rather be crazy, than go home and be known simply as one of the chumps who went on a camping holiday and forgot to take a spare lavatory attendant.>

It was unfortunate. The African and Alaskan crews had both had casualties, in both cases the losses including that most important person. Even now Kumbva's artisan couldn't provide for them all. There had been some embarrassing moments. Such are the joys of an obligation to the adventurous life.

i

Braemar took her companion's hand and stepped neatly down.

'I do admire a woman who can dismount from a field tilt-rotor gracefully.'

She accepted the compliment with a smile.

It wasn't such a feat as it might have been. A passion for much strapped and belooped overalls seemed to be sweeping the world of ladies' fashion. It was the quarantine uniform, designed by the Karen government as a compliment to their guests. Gentlemen could wear their own clothes, so long as they didn't mind having second-skin sprayed over the material. Every inch of flesh covered in anti-contaminant film, every head decorated with some form of bug-eyed 360: the journalists were a fearsome sight. Pity the aliens, faced with this monster crew.

The precautions came late in the day, from the earthling point of view. Certain alien artefacts were at this moment defying analysis in secret somewhere, after passing through several hands. Other objects were known to have vanished into private collections: who could tell what picnic debris still lay festering in the West African soil, or in the remote Aleutian islands? But they were necessary. The Aleutians were supposed to be sensitive about physical interference, and no one wanted to upset the superbeings. Not a flake of human skin, not a single hair would contaminate their enclave, and not a mote of Aleutian tissue would leave.

Even through plastic film the air was miraculously sweet after Karen city. The party passed through an ornate stone gateway of old Balinese work and into the pampered grounds of Kaoru's retreat. A single survivor of the old teak forest towered like a sentinel. There were artful grottos, a 'ruined temple' in the distance, some charming animal sculptures by the water. The house stood on the riverbank. Metallic dragonflies hovered around the visitors as they descended: a fanciful reminder of Kaoru's security system.

In Africa and in Alaska search parties swarmed over the landing sites. Some were nominally scientific, some frankly amateur. They were all hunting for the secret portals, doors in the air through which you could step across the galaxies, or into another lobe of the multiverse. Braemar was not a believer. She still found herself staring with unnatural attention at certain portions of the fine lawns, at places where odd shadows seemed to fall from nowhere and the air seemed to shimmer. Uji's press releases dwelt on the complete security of this valley. They stressed that the aliens were safely contained and no threat to anyone. This was nonsense, if anything the Aleutians claimed was true. The rest of the invasion force could arrive – here or anywhere – at any moment.

Braemar walked sedately, thinking of the time of the '04 when the whole world (the whole tv audience) became expert on the mechanics of plate tectonics and the behaviour of molten rock. You would hear people talking in the queue at the chip shop about the importance of an angle under 60° between compressed crystals in the crust, about oceanic ridges and superheated plumes. Your landlady at the pub would explain the unregarded warning of the great Californian quake that never was, the grim precedent of those huge ancient molten flows in Southern India, which (didn't you know?) were the real reason for the death of the dinosaurs.

When the aliens were news it was Outer Space, and exactly why faster than light travel is supposed to be impossible (for lowly earthlings). The remains of various space programmes had been caught napping, for Outer Space had been out of fashion for so long. But a flurry of activity discovered nothing new about a wholly anecdotal but now famous cluster of ufo sightings; and there was not a sign of any mothership lurking in orbit. Everyone knew about that. Everyone knew about the lack of 'habitable planet candidate systems' in this neck of the galaxy. Housemaids could recite to you the 'best guesses' at the 'actual distance in light years' that the aliens had travelled.

No one was interested in the American Socialist Revolution, but a Californian database called SETI leapt into the news. People in the chip shop queue discussed Clavel's 'blue sun'; and tried to explain to each other the meaning of the expression $E=mc^2$.

The alien planet was beyond reach of human knowledge, the ftl vessels had 'vanished' until they were needed again. (The USSAF was supposed to have had some footage of a landing, but the tape had mysteriously disappeared.) The aliens, no longer hot news, settled in Mr Kaoru's upcountry retreat where their host (their keeper?) invited favoured members of the media to attend occasional open days.

By a ridiculous accident, the visitors had decided that the Eve-riots conference was the seat of earth's government. It was in session at the time, and nominally at least as inclusive a gathering as the UN. The mistake had been allowed to stand. It was convenient, it gave the real governments a breathing space in which to make up their minds how to react. There was little danger that the visitors would discover the deception. They'd shown no interest in the conference. They'd announced – through Mr Kaoru – that they'd like to have some human company and named a handful of Eve-riots delegates.

The chosen few had been quickly coached in anything SETI knew about xeno-anthropology and related topics: ('We were shut up for a weekend,' reported Robin Lloyd-Price. 'And forced to peruse an inordinate quantity of science fiction.'); and left to invent the rest. They didn't sleep at Uji. They came up from Karen and stayed all day, six or eight of them on tours of a fortnight at a time. They didn't use recording equipment, in deference to alien custom. When they came away, they reported their observations to SETI, supposedly without omission. But there was no surveillance equipment in the manor – Kaoru and the 'government of the world' policed each other to keep it clean. So in strict evidence no one knew what went on inside, apart from these specially staged open days.

The Uji-watchers were still *talking*. Yet their allegiance had shifted, you could feel that in the press releases.

Braemar checked off faces. The British pair, Ellen Kershaw and Robin Lloyd-Price – the slick boy who turned any question you asked into an oh-so-British joke. Dougie Milne from the USSA, and his assistant Martha Ledern. The skinny old Vietnamese, Vu Nyung Hong (Chas), with his ethereal looking compatriot Rosalie Troi – who was actually his niece, and some kind of RC cleric.

Milne had been a psychotherapist before the Revolution. Rosalie Troi was deaf, birth-defected stone deaf and too poor to try and get it fixed. Braemar had tried to quiz her on the way up, but Mother Rosalie scorned her halting BSL. Braemar gathered only that in Rosalie's opinion alien telepathy was perfectly genuine. It was *not* a sneaky form of sign language. Ledern's was an interesting face. That girl had been an urban terrorist (not to mince words). Had the aliens really chosen her, or had she been slipped into the pack?

The watchers could keep their secrets. Braemar didn't mind if the team found her hostile. But she had not come to Uji to play *what is it we aren't being told?*

The 'Agnès' interviews were still in her possession. She had made no attempt to rush them to the world's tv screens. Johnny Guglioli might be touched by her fair play, wherever he was, but he'd be wrong. Since the day the aliens asked to be taken to earth's leaders the game had changed. In this round she needed to look like a virgin.

The visitors walked, followed by a giggling group of filmy local girls pulling the tiffin trolleys (the aliens didn't eat earthling food). No ground transport was allowed here; and only recording equipment that had been vetted, no other tech, not so much as a phone or a wristwatch. And definitely no live transmission. No one questioned these restrictions. They came under the heading of 'reasonable precautions'.

Braemar shuddered. An image of the tampered convertible in Africa came to her, mysteriously horrible. There were no extras in the group either: no discreet plainclothes police or bodyguards. No muscle, no weapons and nowhere to run to should things get nasty. The path was smooth but Arthur, the man from the BBC, solicitously took her elbow. He'd fixed the invitation, of course. An independent hadn't a chance of meeting the aliens on her own account. She looked up at this rather blowsy, jowly specimen of English middle-aged manhood and leaned a little more sincerely on his solid arm.

There would be no violence. Never had been until now.

Kaoru was waiting in the main hall of the manor house, a quiet figure in a dark, old-fashioned suit. He greeted his guests distantly, then retreated to the back of the room. Those who were welcome to pursue him knew who they were, and no one else had better dare.

Mr Kaoru, sometime wheeler and dealer for a Japanese trading house, was adept at fanning up a smokescreen of prestige.

Ellen Kershaw, senior nursemaid, made a short speech reminding everyone they should have used 'the facilities' before they left the helipad. No one had yet revealed what the aliens did with their digestive wastes, but they didn't understand the human version. They would become uneasy if someone left the audience for no intelligible reason. Lunch would be served in the courtyard. The Aleutians didn't like to watch humans eat.

Karen waitresses began to circulate with trays of the local hooch. There was no further structure to the reception. The aliens were at their ease: sitting, lying, curled on the floor. They wore the now famous dun coveralls decorated with the now famous random touches of local colour. They awaited the onslaught, unconcerned and magnificently informal as tigers in a zoo.

Arthur slipped off to join the fringes of Kaoru's court. He'd been here before: he knew the form. Braemar's mouth was dry, palms wet. Her certainties deserted her.

'Agnès' on video had seemed approximately human. So did the fright-mask characters on the sparse tv coverage of Uji life. The soothing illusion vanished in this hall. She saw baboons dressed in clothes. She saw mobile animal faces, lined and puckered by such emotion, such experience that she felt like a flatworm. She wanted to laugh and point like a child at a pantomime, but she also had a terrifying urge to drop down on her knees. She had been warned about the Aleutian *presence*. She refused to value the reaction, but she could not suppress it.

We don't know how they shit. Or even if they do. That was the measure of human helplessness.

Whereas we believe they can read our minds.

The days of video-conference travel were over. The Aleutians' attitude to telecommunication was curious, a rich field of study, but certainly it was impossible to network with them. One must be physically present. Ellen Kershaw and Robin were based in KT now, moving up to Karen city whenever they were on tour at Uji.

Ellen's hopes had not been realised. A year after the event, the Aleutians had something of a cult following but they did not command attention in Westminster or Bruxelles. She and Robin, picked out by the aliens for reasons that still weren't clear, had been removed from exile into exile. To her own great surprise, Ellen found that she didn't care. It was a privilege to be here.

The hall, incense-scented and cool, dropped its shadows around her: home. The media people spread out slowly. Rajath, 'the pirate captain', came over with a smile – bared teeth, the same modified aggression.

'Thank you for letting us bring Sarah,' said Ellen. 'This will be something to tell her grandchildren.'

She and Rajath were old friends. It might eventually transpire that the 'talkers' were not in charge. Maybe they were highly trained mediators, or crazy pariahs. Like naturalists following a baboon tribe, the team handed out personalities that made some kind of sense; genders, too.

Sarah, the same brown-mouse maid whose ironic costume had once amused Ellen in her exile, bobbed a nervous curtsey. She was keeping house for Ellen in Krung Thep now, and in Karen city when Robin and Ellen were on tour at Uji. She had conceived a passion for the aliens. Ellen was glad to have been able to make the child's dream come true, even if it pushed a few noses out of joint. The maid had been a godsend over the past months – self-effacing, cheerful, miraculously efficient.

Rajath swept an extravagant bow. He took the child's hand, perused her face. He turned to Ellen. 'Never give a sucker an even break!'

His manner suggested a mixture of knowing amusement and wild panic. Ellen laughed, though she'd no idea what the joke might be. Rajath's moods were always infectious.

Sarah did not laugh. She looked for a moment as if she might scream and run. Some people did react that way. But she controlled herself. Rajath crooked his arm, proffered a dun-clad elbow.

<Come, princess. Honoured, I'm sure. Let me introduce you.>

To her credit, young Sarah accepted the alien's gesture without starting or squirming. Brave girl! But Ellen had every confidence. The Aleutians were always well-intentioned.

Rajath's gnomic utterance was typical. The ones who spoke aloud seemed to share Humpty Dumpty's robust attitude: words mean what I say they mean. They could handle any language, but they had gravitated to English. But they spoke in proverbs, sometimes they made no sense whatever. The term 'Aleutian' was a case in point. It remained current, because when asked the real name of their planet, or their native country they replied with enthusiasm, 'Aleutia!' The names by which they were known were of the same uncertain provenance. They had emerged from a succession of alternatives: Rajath had been 'Duke' at one time; also 'Hanuman'; Lugha had been 'Coyote'. The SETI database had called them 'Sanskrit-like terms', which was exciting for those who believed that the human race was a lost tribe of some great galactic race.

Visitors who came to Uji on days like this were bemused by the silence, and disappointed if they didn't hear voices in their heads. In fact, human experience of Aleutian telepathy was a fugitive thing. Most Uji-watchers had never 'heard voices'. Yet at the end of a day here Ellen would not be conscious of any absence. They said: 'We are always talking to you, and you are always talking to us.' It was true. She could never catch it happening, but there was constant communication: and she was not excluded.

One learned not to scorn the daftest theories. Not even Rosalie Troi's idea that they were honest to God holy angels. Not even Kaoru, whose motivation was the barmiest of the lot. Ellen's secret was her joyful feeling that if these were superbeings everything she'd ever fought for was vindicated. It seemed so right that the possessors of such advanced technology and awesome power should be above all *socialists*: interested in each other, concerned with each other; a true community.

If Rajath was an angel, he'd have to be the unholy kind. They called him captain because he behaved like a leader, but the 'pirate' part was pure anthropomorphism. She watched fondly as he waltzed away with her maid's hand tucked in his arm. Where had he picked up those gestures? Fred Astaire! It only wanted the top hat.

She looked around to see what the day's hazard was doing, and beckoned Robin with a nod. The freedom of the press is sacred, but Ellen had an old-fashioned conviction that one can and should keep the sacred vermin under control.

'I want you to watch that woman with the dark red hair. Braemar Wilson.'

Silence became a habit at Uji, but Robin did not seem averse.

'Don't get any daft ideas, she'd eat you alive. Just be ready. She's up to no good.'

'What's she likely to do? Throw acid? Claim indecent assault?'

'Something on those lines. She won't find any news here unless she makes it. And she's not the type to waste a journey.'

On that historic day in Krung Thep, Rajath had spoken in fractured proverbs. *We come in peace, bearing gifts Don't look us in the mouth Let me shake you by the hand.* But it had seemed clear that the Aleutians intended to initiate trade. There had been guesses at exciting waste-disposal techniques, genetic material for superefficient food plants. Nothing had yet transpired. Nor did the aliens justify their existence in other ways. They couldn't be interrogated and they wouldn't be vivisected. The Uji-watchers were beginning to feel both protective and defensive.

Near the centre of the hall a fountain plashed in a massive terracotta basin. Braemar leaned casually on the rim of the pool. The Aleutians had an *alien attitude* towards water. They didn't like indoor plumbing and considered the sound of the river a miserable irritation; she'd seen something about that.

That's what people like, that's what sells a programme. For aliens to have the response to human things that makes sense from them – that is to say, no reaction at all – does not work on tv. (She was thinking about work, work and money; and the lens that watched her act might be anywhere.) Was it feasible to make sense of this trip financially? She had to pay off the Karen government, and then pay to have her maker 'processed' (which meant vetted for anti-alien bias) by the soi-disant 'government of the world'. Another cut for the ASEAN IPB; maybe twenty per cent to a tv agency . . .

She touched the control on her wrist, flipped her view to check her own appearance. She was looking all right, she thought. With the ease of long habit, she was looking exactly like someone thinking about money.

A dun-overalled figure appeared in the left rear quadrant of her field of view. It was different from the others. A body was evident under these clothes: lumpy hips and breastless torso.

Beyond the fountain bowl stood a glass case, taller than a man, ribbed in gold. The Itchiku kimono, from the Symphony of Light sequence: one of the three still physically in existence. Aitatabu.

Clear water, mountain calm. The glorious colours of autumn drowned in stillness. She walked over to admire: it joined her.

'Do you find this work of art beautiful?' asked the human.

'Yes.'

'Could you tell me what it means?'

<I'm helpless in front of other people's poetry,> said Clavel. <It is the explanation of itself, don't you see?>

'Speechless with admiration? Well, that makes sense.'

Braemar knew that this was Agnès, now known as Clavel. She had been careful in Fo. As far as she was aware, Johnny's alien had never seen her. But if telepathy was real, then Agnès-Clavel had 'seen' the inside of Johnny's mind, and maybe 'seen' Braemar. If so, too bad. She was here because she had to be here, just as in Africa. Clear water, mountain calm. It *cannot* read your mind. Braemar couldn't imagine why she was feeling so nervous. She had nothing to hide.

'So you are his friend.'

The alien spoke. Braemar was too shocked to know if its lips had moved. The alien too (was this imaginary?) seemed paralysed by its own boldness. Braemar desperately tried to look like someone thinking about a beautiful art work.

But the alien was on another tack. 'You're right,' it said, grinning. The sound was definitely real this time. 'I saw you working it out. You're gonna have a tough time trying to make money out of this trip.'

And Johnny Guglioli stood there: rueful, unforgiving.

The shock was awful. The ghost vanished into the planes and angles of the alien mask.

Braemar laughed. 'You won't believe this, but I'm not here to make money. I wangled my way on to this guest list out of pure curiosity.'

The alien smelt vaguely yeasty. They looked at the kimono again. Braemar's confidence strengthened. All perception is perception. Even a telepath (*doesn't exist!*) has to have prior assumptions; and looks no further if the evidence seems to agree. If it knew her, it knew her only through Johnny's eyes. She was safe enough.

The terror (which had no basis) receded, was replaced by an intuition – strange enough in its way – that Clavel was herself quite anxious to change the subject.

'Excuse me, sir,' said Clavel at last. 'Mr Kaoru?'

No words formed in Braemar's mind, no expansion. Kaoru, what? The Uji-watchers probably had not told these people anything. They were amateur slaves of a Californian database whose theory of how to meet alien intelligence was substantially defined by twentieth-century tv shows. Thou shalt not impose thine ideology! Or even thine simple general knowledge.

Kaoru was sitting at the back of the room in a big English club armchair. A handful of eejays from China and the Rim clustered around him, along with some corporate employees and her own man from the BBC. The Chinese carried their hardware like unwanted bouquets. They were, of course, diplomats and shouldn't bloody well be here but the 'government of the world' wasn't going to argue the point. The ICI party in their dark suits, streetwear of a bygone age, looked like members of a monastic order. As perhaps they were. The Dominicans of the new Christendom, where money is a God grown old and respectable, the days of red sacrifice over: a public institution. That's the way it happens with us, Clavel. There's just so many approximate spaces into which the approximate pieces fall. The old ex-Japanese was not attending to business. He sucked at a gold filigree inhaler, probably medicinal, and gazed dreamily at something far away and very dear.

'So you want me to explain Kaoru? Well, here goes. Thirty-odd years ago something terrible happened to your sponsor. Do you have earthquakes and volcanoes on your planet? Plate tectonics? I won't attempt to explain, but it was spectacular. Great cities were destroyed, mountain ranges exploded, the islands they stood on vanished under the sea. A lot of people died. Kaoru's problem is that he should have been among them. Does that make sense?'

Clavel's mouth and nose space had changed shape.

'Some kind of sense,' decided Braemar. 'Now comes the best bit. Afterwards a legend grew up that a handful of the people had escaped in a secret spaceship. Mr Kaoru thinks that you are those people, or rather, paradoxically, their extremely distant descendants.'

<Is it true?>

It did not speak. No. Do any of us really speak in casual conversation? Approximation fills the spaces: each fills in the other's part. But how could an *alien* play that game?

'About the spaceship? I doubt it, but there may be some truth in the rumour. As for the rest, well . . . you tell me.'

<But why didn't he tell us?>

'You want to know why he didn't tell you this himself, I suppose. He's afraid you'll burst his bubble, of course.'

Johnny was right, the invasion was terrible. It felt like hot wires (it isn't happening!). Amazing that the Uji regulars thought telepathy was wonderful, a rest cure for the mind. Maybe not so amazing. They were picked out: the animals most amenable to training. But revulsion didn't protect you, she found. She felt a shadow of the old Japanese's hunger, of Johnny's faith. The epiphany which she knew was within herself, was not born of alien nature but of human need, came rushing over her, nearly irresistible. Save me or kill me. Do something wonderful . . .

'Clavel, there are many things your minders won't tell you, not because they mean to deceive but because you're supposed to know without asking. You should bear this in mind. What happened to Mr Kaoru happened to all of us. Do you have post-operative shock in your country? This organism has recently suffered a profound insult. We lost a great chunk of our notional financial capital, among other inconveniences. Imagine you've arrived in Europe, say fifty years after the peak of the Black Death. Can you grok that in its fullness? Can you feel the psychic effect of such a swathe of death, the economic shockwaves of the massive resettlement? On top of what was happening in quite the normal run of things in Bangladesh and the Sahel? No, of course not. Well, we tucked the evacuees in somehow. Things were pretty tight: they still are. Our concerted psyche took a massive jolt. We're not quite ourselves. People will believe the wildest tales, for a while. But we're getting better. *Don't you fool yourselves about that.*'

'All's fair in love and war,' said Clavel.

It had not been listening, but watching. Watching every quiver, not of her facial muscles but of some inner surface.

'Excuse me. I see someone I have to talk to.'

Braemar fled.

Out of the main hall, in the shadowy gallery, she found a double-leaved door – across the join three bands of some kind of resin. Braemar started as someone came up behind her.

'What's in here?'

'Their dead,' said Ellen Kershaw. 'Some of them were injured in the crossing, in ways beyond these people's medicine. It is the Aleutian custom to seal a funerary room, dry out the air and leave the bodies to desiccate.'

Ellen reported what she'd seen, which was all anyone could do since the Aleutians did not explain themselves. It sounded, she decided, pleasingly authoritative. Wilson shuddered conventionally.

'Gruesome.'

The room next door was open and dimly lit. Ellen followed her into it. A group of multiscreen desks sat huddled together, talking to themselves.

The human team called this a 'taboo' room. The aliens didn't call it anything, out loud. It would have been less surprising if the telepaths had ignored mechanical communication. They had remained in contact with each other, mind to mind, spread over the globe from Karen to Alaska. Some believed that they were in contact in the same way with their impossibly distant home. What could they make of these jabbering peepshows?

In fact their attitude was more complicated. The 'government of the world' had provided delegate facilities for the visitors, in the early days when people still thought in terms of a charade kept up for possibly hostile invaders. The Aleutians said thank you politely, and then quietly moved everything in here. They left the desks permanently running, perhaps out of good manners. Occasionally Aleutians had been spotted making brief, almost furtive visits.

There was another room, the one the team called 'the ship's log' where Aleutian audio-visual records and display equipment were kept. It was special too, but in a more relaxed way: likewise Kaoru's magnificent library. Sometimes several of the nameless would be found there together, engrossed in some ancient movie-drama.

It was the conferencing facility that caused the problems. No one knew whether the aliens were aware of the real status of the assembly at Krung Thep. Most likely they couldn't care less about gradations of earthling authority. But they called the world through the screen 'the land of the dead'. They tolerated 360 cams: *recordmaking* was a familiar and acceptable activity. But their first participation in the Multiphon had been their last. They wanted nothing to do with interactive tv.

It was alarming, Robin said, to think someone might have introduced them to virtuality gaming on their travels. They'd probably have been so appalled they'd have instantly blasted the earth to flinders.

Ellen didn't want Braemar Wilson in here. She knew what this room would look like on television. She could feel it in her bones – the insult, the rejection. All these human faces, human voices, pushed away and ignored.

Braemar gazed around. 'It seems our visitors aren't interested in tv.'

They sing and dance, thought Ellen. They have their own instruments, and the nameless sing without words. They make pictures, they play games. They find each other endlessly absorbing, they don't need artificial stimuli. She knew better than to say anything out loud that was remotely critical of the sacred screen.

'Their visual-record technology is curiously close to ours. You must have heard of the "ship's log", which has given us our glimpses of the Aleutian home planet. But why should they be interested in our squabbles? They don't have wars, nor any kind of organised violence, on their home world.'

There had been a massacre at a camp of young female construction workers near Islamabad: Central European migrants undercutting the local skilled male labour. The Women's Affairs conference was deciding what kind of slap on the wrist it should despatch to Pakistan, egging itself on with footage of dead Bulgarians.

Braemar had fled in panic. She ought to get back to the main hall at once. She told herself she was being useful here, since she'd trapped the chief nursemaid. She knew Ellen Kershaw of old, had her down as one of those idiots who thinks boats shouldn't be called 'she'. She bore the woman no ill will, but if you need to engage someone in conversation it's useful to know how.

'Ms Kershaw, Ellen. You miss your conference desk, I'm sure. It must be pleasing to see how many women are here today.'

Ellen grunted warily. 'Young women with careers in the media. It's hardly new.'

'My goodness, no. But I can't say I envy the mothers among them. I recall too well the childcare guilt and panic that goes into one of these trips.'

'Some children do have two parents.'

Braemar laughed lightly, and nodded at the massacre scenes. 'What do you make of the alien attitude to gender politics?'

Ellen was furious. The 360 cam that ogled her like a second little head beside Braemar's face had a vision field, a 'light shell', that included most of this room. There was no way she could escape with dignity. For a moment she was recklessly inclined to rely on censorship: but that too could be a gift to the media monster.

'We humans tend to perceive gender in them, but the Aleutians don't respond to that line of questioning. We have no idea how they reproduce, you know.' She smiled, putting the sex-mad media person in her place.

Kershaw, old-maid socialist, saw brotherly love and no nasty sex. Even Poonsuk Masdit, a person you had to respect, spoke reservedly about 'medical possibilities'. She was dreaming of a cure for her mysterious wasting disease. Braemar was suddenly angry. They were blinded by privilege, all of them here. There was no way of warning them. Nothing could make them see a *new race* of *superiors* through the eyes of the powerless.

'No gender. I see. But they have a rigid caste system. Isn't it true that most of those here are slaves of the dominant few, with no existence outside their hereditary tasks? Isn't that right?'

To the corrupt everything is corrupt. Ellen was morally certain that Aleutions didn't *think* like that, but Wilson could smear anything. It was absurd to jump to conclusions. What Uji needed was time, and patience of a kind that humanity seemed to have forgotten.

'Ms Wilson, I'm afraid you're ahead of the project. We have no firm basis for any interpretation of their social behaviour.'

'There's no firm basis for anything, is there? All right then, tell me this. If they don't mean to stay, why did they bring the children?'

Ellen set her jaw, tried to loosen it again; drew breath. 'They have some form of belief in reincarnation. The children are here because they are considered to be important people. Does that offend you, Ms Wilson?'

'They came here in ships nobody has seen. They don't understand tv, they don't have any normal machines, they spend their time doing ritual dances. They're supposed to speak English, but what they really do is mimic a few phrases. They've been described as magic savages. Would you say that's fair? We come to meet the superbeings, we find ourselves staring at performing animals. Ellen, would you mind telling me who called you up and recruited you to the Uji team?'

The Aleutians didn't make phone calls. Everything was negotiated through Kaoru. But he was no puppetmaster. Anyone who spent an hour here, with an open mind must admit that the Aleutians patently understood everything. Kaoru operated the way they all did, on intuition and trial and error. There was nothing else in the face of this enigma, the unresponsive other.

There is a classic test of self-consciousness: does the creature recognise its own face in a mirror? The Aleutians would fail. They did not look in mirrors, had put away the few they found at Uji, reckoning them even less useful than tv. Humans would fail, too. A human would fly at the beast in the glass, immediately recognising an enemy.

'Ms Wilson, if you insist on using the methods of tabloid journalism – '

'Is that supposed to be an insult? Do you despise my audience, Ms Kershaw?'

Ellen's frustration with this smiling, painted hussy was on the point of explosion. She was saved by the pirate captain, who came swaggering in. They wouldn't let people disappear alone, or in ones and twos. They didn't like it.

Rajath glanced at the screens and briefly covered his face, an oddly human gesture before the broken bodies laid out in the dust.

Then he stood, hips spread in a gruesomely exaggerated cowboy pose, and pointed his fingers at them.

'Bang, bang! Get off my cape!' He loped forward, peered at another screen, turned to Braemar. <Don't you find it odd that your government is so obsessed with a single, poorly defined personality trait?>

He put a long, powerful arm around each of them. He smelt like a stale dishcloth. 'No fighting in church?'

A journalist interrogated Kumbva. 'Do you believe in the paranormal?'

'Does a frog croak? The paranormal is my stock in trade.'

'But you are an engineer?'

This alien was built like a bear: both bigger, and thicker in the arms and legs than most of them. He had a waistpouch made of plastic cowries tucked into one of his sleeve loops. He pulled it out, stowed his hand in the bag and made puppet-mouths at the clustered eye fastened by the journalist's ear.

'You cannot be serious,' said the alien, and walked away.

Maitri had brought out a recorder. He had often thought of taking minor orders, and felt quite at home at a 'priest conference' (or 'press conference' as they seemed to pronounce it). Besides, it seemed only polite when so many people were recording *him*. Rajath hadn't come here to sell religious impedimenta, so he could hardly complain.

A local cleric came up and boldly touched the gadget. The baggy brown box slung from the alien's shoulder felt like rubber. The eye-band was thick and opaque: a rubber blindfold.

'What is that?'

'It's a secret,' said the plump one confidently.

The priest, or deacon or whatever he was, seemed oddly disconcerted.

<It's very sad,> Clavel's master at arms confided in Rosalie. <Did you ever know a couple who were truly 'twin selves'? Even you and your lover, though I'm sure you're very happy. But my partner's elder ward is obsessed with the great romantic illusion. You know the sort of thing: 'Marriages are made in heaven'. Do you know the boy he's fallen for? Could you speak to him?>

The alien spoke English: *marriages are made in heaven*. Rosalie Troi did not read lips well, but the words were clear. She tried to read the meaning. It spoke of the meeting between two races. Its face and body showed a parental concern, a slightly mocking anxiety; above all the alien spoke *personally*, as if it were speaking of the meeting of two individuals. But there was doubt, and that chilled her. Might the human race be found wanting? Speak to me clearly! she signed. Mind to my mind!

<But I am!> protested Maitri's lover.

Douglas Milne missed Lugha, the demon child, who for some reason had not appeared today. He had to content himself with the nameless Aleutian, identified as 'Rajath's cook', who was, Douglas believed, Lugha's parent. From what Douglas could gather, Lugha was considered as exceptional as he would have been on earth. The nice thing was it made no difference that his father (mother?) was a lowly, mute hereditary servant.

Douglas laid picture cards, squatting on his heels beside the alien. Aleutian child, human child. Aleutian adult, human adult. Human adult couples, showing affection. Human mother hugging baby. The humans were modestly clothed, in deference to the Aleutian taboo against nakedness. Douglas laid sequences.

Where do babies come from?

The nameless alien showed signs of interest.

Milne was always impressing on the others the dangers of interpreting their non-verbals in human terms. But you had to start somewhere.

'I guess you must love Lugha very much, he's a great kid. I suppose it was absolutely necessary to bring him along?'

Nameless picked up the mother-baby picture. He touched the mother's eyes, drew the line of her tender gaze to the baby's face. Any human on earth would respond to that as a lovely, natural picture. Nameless seemed disgusted.

'The mother shouldn't hold the baby?'

Nameless gave Milne a direct, dignified look. There was a widespread superstition in the team that with full eye contact they could read you right down to your bowels. Douglas held his ground. Nameless laid an arm across his belly. That gesture *might* mean parenthood (motherhood?). The other hand repudiated the look in the human mother's eyes.

I love my baby, nameless might be saying. But not like that!

Intrigued, Douglas tried to advance the embracing couple. He pointed to the male human, pointed to nameless. The alien put together male human adult, human child. Eyes, nasal, mouth became loose and tender and greedy. It was tempting to read his grimace as deliberate miming of emotion: of sexual, romantic love.

Douglas regarded those who heard voices in their heads with kindly suspicion. The Aleutians communicated between themselves telepathically. Anything else was fantasy. But he had his inexplicable moments and this was one of them. Nameless was saying one should not fall in love with one's own born child. One fell in love with some *other* baby.

The alien took the cards with what seemed distaste, and dealt out adult with child, adult with child: made the sex face. He crouched back with a smug, superior expression. He seemed to think he'd delivered an important lesson in decorum.

Douglas was excited. The Aleutians made no sense on this subject, the few body scans that had surfaced were blurred by clothing. The current, inevitable practice was to consider them male/neuter, though one or two – 'beautiful girl', 'the poet-princess' – were universally regarded as feminine.

'You have sex with children?'

The nameless had lost interest.

Robin had been told to watch Braemar Wilson. He saw her approached by Clavel, the one they called 'the poet-princess', and stopped worrying. No visitor had been known to resist sustained contact with a talker. He assumed a casual pose in one of Kaoru's priceless Hepplewhite armchairs (no easy task, but his bones and the chair's were close kin, they belonged in the same century), and watched the reception. There was an atmosphere this session. The nameless were eyeing each other, moving around the room like teenage louts shaping up for a rumble. It might be just one of their games. It might be an attack of Uji-paranoia on his part, but he rather wished that Sarah wasn't here.

He was still sitting there when Braemar (he'd missed her exit) emerged from the gallery with Ellen and the pirate. Good, he thought. That's under control. But a sense of danger remained.

Rajath sat with Braemar on a fine Louis Seize daybed. He stared at her 360 avidly, like a monkey about to reach out and grab. He made a long arm after Ellen, who was walking away.

'Sorry, sofa. Do you mind three?'

The aliens were devout animists. They talked to furniture, treated their gadgets like pet animals. Reincarnation, animism, their strange response to certain technology – Wilson was right. SETI considered it quite likely that the Aleutians were not in charge: that the *real* superrace, source of the ftl, had yet to reveal itself. This wasn't an idea the alien-watchers wanted to share with the global audience.

Ellen sat down uneasily. The pirate captain was up to something. She could feel it pricking in her bones.

Braemar leaned forward, with a teasing grin at Ellen. 'Mr Rajath, do you really know everything we're thinking?'

The alien scrumpled his nose hole. He twinkled like an old queen enjoying some obscure *double entendre*. 'When a stranger leaves the room, he disappears.'

Johnny's alien crossed the room in front of them – like a sulky enchanted princess, like a baboon infanta.

'What about Clavel? Can you read Clavel's mind for me?'

The knowing look vanished. Their eyes were dark, the brow bone above rimmed not with hair but some other kind of dead, scaly tissue. There was an epicanthic fold, brown iris, round pupil; slivers of whitish cornea. They were human eyes. One could say the same of an octopus. Eyes are defined by the behaviour of light. A hole opened in jelly.

'They that have power,' he said, 'to hurt and will do none. Who do not do the thing they most do show. Who moving others are themselves as stone. Unmoved cold and to temptation slow. They rightly do inherit heaven's graces and husband nature's richness from expense. They are the lords and owners of their faces, others but stewards of their excellence.'

Passion came roaring through the stiff enunciation, a blast like physical heat. Admiring, bewildered, hating his own admiration: he spoke the words as if he'd thought of them then and there. She was transfixed.

Ellen was jealous, downright jealous. The tension building up, in Rajath and all around, barely penetrated her resentment.

Sarah was sitting beside the alien called Maitri. She'd taken out her workbag, and the crazy thing was that looked *natural* to these rich fuckers. What else would a maid want to do when she's meeting creatures from outer space in the flesh, but sit sewing other people's underwear? You're not supposed to be curious. You're not supposed to be a person. They don't know that you can play games in the arcades and have a life, a wild life, netting with strangers who only know the *real* you, not the one in uniform.

Stitch, stitch, stitch. Her hand dipped neatly in and out.

Braemar Wilson had ignored Ellen Kershaw's maid, never glanced her way through the briefing and the journey. Which was ironic, since these two were here on much the same terms. Perhaps that was why the smart Ms Wilson had kept her distance. Rajath had now placed her where she could hardly miss the girl. Sarah was busy with her mending. The alien beside her seemed fascinated by this ancient earthling craft.

<You're discovered,> said Maitri to Sarah. <Why don't you surrender? Honour is satisfied. Please, don't do anything stupid.>

It didn't make sense to keep on sitting here. He felt an idiot. But every time he tried to make a move Rajath hissed at him from across the room (or even from outside it), <*Don't you dare!*> The dictator insisted there was no actual danger and he was probably right. But it was easy enough for him to say.

He noticed gloomily that his ward was in public with no underwear again.

Sarah hated darning. But Kershaw hated throwing things away, and Sarah respected that. Most of the rich people she'd met were fat hypocrites in the green department. Kershaw wasn't a bad old cunt. She was what you called a real lady, in the jokey cant that went with Victorian costume and curtsies.

I can do it, she told herself, eyes down and needle whipping. I can do it. They won't hurt me. They're harmless. She remembered what she'd been told. Pretend you're acting innocent in front of a bunch of MPs.

It'll cause a big stink, of course, if I get fingered. And poor old Kershaw will be in the shit. But there's no such thing as telepathy.

The monster stroked her arm, and heaved a sigh.

A louse crawled out from the collar of Rajath's suit: a red bug about half the size of a matchhead. Braemar had a sudden intuition. This was the moment. She reached out to groom. They'd been shown how it should be done, in case anybody dared. She felt bone and muscle arranged with unpleasant wrongness. The alien moved like a cat being stroked. He was almost purring. She took the bug. That wasn't in the manual. It had no legs, it oozed between her plastic coated fingertips.

Outrage erupted! Braemar felt the silent explosion: she was so tensed up it was seconds before she realised she was not at its centre. The sulky infanta shot across the room, changing shape in flight.

She was wolf by the time she reached the sudden mêlée of nameless around the other couch, and pulled out of it the earthling servant girl.

Someone screamed, loud and human.

'I didn't do nothing!' wailed Sarah. 'It was an accident!'

'No,' said Clavel.

Plump Maitri stood dumbly there, sucking his wrist.

The hall was caught in a moment of paralysis. The group around Mr Kaoru turned faces. One of the inner sliding doors opened. A small figure came in. Its trunk was covered in a dun quilted leotard. Its arms, legs and face were coated with tiny wriggling spots of colour. It came into the centre of the group and performed a slow pirouette. Changing colour in brilliant patterns rippled over its eyes and mouth.

Another human screamed, furniture tumbled.

Douglas Milne spoke quietly to his assistant. 'Martha, will you go and see about lunch?'

'Yes, sir.'

When Martha Ledern slipped outside, the Karen girls were nowhere to be seen. She hurried away from the main block. The naked sky frightened her. She had seen little of it in her life. She had to bite on a back tooth to convey the emergency message. *Help! Trouble!* Only Dougie knew that she carried this alarm, but dammit it would be *insane* to have no recourse. She was trying to blank her mind.

An alien appeared from nowhere, one of the nameless. He took her arms. Another forced her jaws, thrust a rubbery gag between them. Shrugging apologetically, they ushered her back indoors.

The aliens took charge, silently. Sarah's needle was clean, apparently she'd wiped it in her panic. They eviscerated the maid's workbag and found the other needle, which was hollow and filled with Maitri's blood. It looked red enough to be human.

The media, coralled by Aleutian nameless, muttered in terrified amazement. Braemar Wilson was somewhere in there, probably one of the idiots who was still recording – for what good it would do them. Confronted with evidence that her maid had *planned* the theft of Aleutian tissue, Ellen felt hopelessly ineffectual. She protested wildly that the little girl probably just wanted a souvenir and found room for fury that Wilson, of all people, was witnessing this catastrophe.

Kaoru and his small audience stayed where they were. Ellen's own common sense told her it was useless to appeal to the ex-Japanese. In his place, she'd stay out of this.

'Robin, look after Sarah. I'll talk to Rajath.'

The pirate captain had retreated to the fountain, was surrounded there by the group you might call his 'servants'. Ellen blustered and pleaded. Rajath shrugged, grinned nervously, folded his arms in embarrassment: such human signs. It was no use. The Aleutians were going by a rule book unavailable to the humans, and there was no room for discussion.

Robin Lloyd-Price whispered, 'Don't be frightened, Sarah. We'll get you out of this.' He could have strangled the kid with his bare hands. Was it possible that Ellen had planned this trick without telling him? They were ruined. Off the guest list. It was worse than that. *The honeymoon's over.* He saw terrible consequences flowing. They have immeasurable resources . . . He knew that he had no idea what he'd been saying, making soothing noises while the kid's skinny brown hands clung to his.

The aliens moved like crystals in a kaleidoscope, making patterns of shocked outrage: a progressive sequence pointing to an inevitable conclusion. They moved like one thing. Douglas Milne remembered the day in Krung Thep. He felt again the first naked dismay when he realised that the aliens were not only vastly superior to humankind but . . . but *alien*.

They took Sarah from Robin.

<Be brave,> Robin heard Clavel saying. <Do you have a lover? Think of him, have him be here with you.>

'*She's thirteen years old!*' Robin cried.

Maitri's lover, master at arms, brought in a long flat box. The humans had never seen it before. Its contents were not mysterious. The humans saw the alien select a narrow-bladed knife. Maitri and Clavel held Sarah at the shoulders, two nameless spread a sheet of some translucent material. The master at arms ran his hands over Sarah's breast, chose his entry. The knife went in so accurately there was hardly any bleeding from the front wound. Sarah tumbled. The master at arms showed his clean hands. Silent as Aleutians themselves, none of the humans moved a muscle.

Clavel laid the wrapped body down gently, and moved away, showing his clean hands. Maitri made a speech.

'He had other things to do in this life, but his obligation was stronger.'

ii

At such an extremely awkward moment, it was natural to take refuge in dance. They danced *The Bones of the City*, just as they were, without changing clothes. After the first figure Rosalie and Chas took hands and walked the next. Then Dougie came around to the singers and joined them softly. Finally even Ellen and Robin made some attempt, though at the best of times Ellen was a barely passable dancer.

The local party left after that. Mr Kaoru saw them off and came back to the hall.

'You may need advice,' he said. 'Please call on me for anything.' He bowed and left them.

Lug came in, a rather sulky Lugha, decently dressed.

The cosmetic wanderers had been his trade goods, an ingenious notion because it took up no space and he could replenish supplies indefinitely. Cosmetics were so short-lived that people were always wanting more. He had confirmed his suspicions, but he wasn't pleased. Going by the locals' reaction to his demonstration, he was not going to make his fortune.

<You see. Told you so. They don't know what wanderers are. They don't have any.>

There was a burst of slightly hysterical laughter.

<Little one, you are so small-minded. Will you never learn to pay attention to what's happening for others?>

Atha's demand was absurd. Lugha could not learn to be other than Lugha. But a child's guardian was often the last to accept that. They had a story about it here, the 'hen' who rears the 'duckling'.

More laughter: but everyone was terribly uneasy.

The locals had imagined they could get away with murder, because Sarah wasn't personally known to any of the Aleutians. In fact, the Aleutians had spotted what was planned at once. The weapon thief – the usual kind of tearaway, blazing with bravado – had given himself away. They had decided, more or less unanimously, to pretend they didn't know what was happening. An 'outrage' like a tissue theft was exactly the excuse Rajath needed for his plans. To cover them against claims of malicious inaction, gentle-mannered Maitri had been detailed to try informally, to dissuade the local hero . . . with the inevitable result.

It wasn't the sort of thing you expected in a room full of clerics, but nobody blamed the locals. To attempt to steal tissue was a nasty trick: but then, it was an equally nasty trick to lead them on, knowingly, until the deed was actually done. In such a situation no one can claim moral advantage: and even when the deed is done or someone makes a speech about it, the tactical advantage could go to either side. If that second needle hadn't turned up, the Aleutians would have been the ones looking very stupid.

So far, everything had seemed fine; it seemed a lucky turn of events. But the aftermath had been alarming.

The Aleutians had replied to Sarah's crime with a conventional, bargaining-counter 'expression of deep outrage'. But the locals had not responded in kind, formally or informally. They didn't accept Sarah's death as fair, they refused to admit their sharp practice. They had suddenly become openly hostile, angry and disgusted. There had been no formal announcement of reprisal, but it was obviously going to be a rough one when it came.

What did they expect? If you bring weapons into play, then people will die. It's hardly the end of the world.

The meeting was a free for all. Points were noted in a random jumble, out of which a course of action would have to emerge.

The friend of Clavel's local lover had been the least able liar in the hall. Clavel wanted Braemar's generous admissions struck out of the evidence. He was overruled. Braemar's own people must know he was congenitally honest. If they didn't want advantage to be taken they should have kept him away from Uji.

Kumbva wanted to know (again), <How can they believe that we travelled faster than light? They know the rules of the dead world at least as well as we do. They know what can't be done. Is their 'belief' maybe a double bluff?>

<They're in the market for miracles. And they've seen our character tapes,> explained someone. <They believe we're the whole expedition. Think. It would be very strange indeed if exactly the same forty people had arrived here as had set out generations ago.>

In the new mood, everything that was odd about the locals looked suspicious.

<Formally, they tell us there's only one nation here, "the human race". Yet their government is tied up with a shooting war. More lies.>

<Of course they lie about it. Wouldn't you, if you were dealing with a trade delegation? Several of them have admitted to me, informally, that the war is real. What I don't understand is that they say it is between "masculines" and "feminines". That must be some kind of cover-up.>

The Aleutians found the local obsession with this personality-trait duality a huge joke. The funniest thing about it was that the locals at Uji (and in Alaska, and in Fo) *didn't seem to know the difference.* They were as oblivious to the masculine to feminine spectrum in themselves as the most rational Aleutian: as someone who would never dream of having their profile worked out. But sometimes it seemed they could talk about nothing else!

<There are two nations,> explained the poet. <One bears the others' children for them. They get called 'Feminine'; and the obligate-parasites 'Masculine'. Like the 'Purples' and the 'Flowers' at home, remember?>

People remembered. Long-buried memories of this kind were coming back to everyone.

<It's a local joke.> Clavel shrugged unkindly. <Why it should be considered funny, I can't imagine.>

The avowedly masculine element in the gathering fell on him with catcalls. Clavel, much amused, refused to retract.

A division into parasites and childbearers was another peculiarity to add to their obsession with religion, their promiscuous mingling of formal and informal language, their horrid food. But the variation of human traits is wild and wide, even within a single nation. It wasn't for nothing that an executioner searched each body before he struck to find how this particular heart was placed. Kumbva put their collective opinion into words.

'It takes all sorts to make a world!'

For once it was Rajath who brooded, unable to join in the byplay. He could talk of nothing but the main concern; this frightening abyss that had opened between them and their trading partners. It must be turned into opportunity.

He had been delighted to find when he arrived on this planet that his talent for foreign formal languages, after long disuse, was still intact. It annoyed him that he couldn't get hold of the inflection as well as Clavel, but he was in control. Still, these locals *cheated*.

<How is one to know when somebody means to be taken seriously if they don't reserve the dignity of the spoken word for those occasions?>

Rajath hurriedly retracted before the majority of his friends and dependants could start beating him around the head.

<Of course, you're perfectly right. To speak out loud is not especially dignified. It's to put an end to process, block equivocation. Idiotic, really. But sometimes one must pin things down. Otherwise we'd never know what was going on.>

Everyone jeered. Rajath's talent for creative interpretation was a tolerated scandal. The trickster was unabashed.

<At this point I'd like to kill Kaoru, because he knows too much and he's seen too much. But I don't see how to get away with it. He's not likely to do anything to offend us, unfortunately.>

Atha had been uncomfortable since the locals left. <You'd better kill me too,> he confessed sadly. <I can't remember, Rajath: I can't remember what is a secret and what isn't.>

Lugha hugged his guardian and glared at everyone. <He didn't do any harm. Don't we all get tired of being offered the feelthy pictures? It's an insult. Do they still think we'll break down one day and name a price for the things?>

Lugha was told by several persons to moderate his language. What happens when people lie down together is not to be discussed. Clavel's lovesongs were bad enough, but a poet couldn't help himself. The small mind, that can only hold knowledge, was under no obligation to talk dirty.

Rajath was getting ready to speak. His eyes darkened, his whole face glowed. Rajath the beautiful was never so lovely as when he was deep in greedy mischief.

<Our sharp mind is right: they have no wanderers?>

That was agreed to be proven. Only Brhamari, Kumbva's physician, refused to be convinced. <If they don't have wanderers, then how did they come to call this> – he slapped the polished floor – <a wanderer? When, as they know well, it wanders scarcely at all from a fixed track.> Brhamari nodded, ineffably pleased with himself. <That is the application of science!>

His point wasn't taken. <The doctor is an idiot,> they agreed, with varying degrees of tact. The doctor bristled and withdrew into a huff.

Kumbva was intrigued. <What are you getting at, oh great dictator?> Out loud, he added: 'Do you remember my warning?'

Rajath dropped from Kaoru's chair. He made his speech.

'I have a plan. Okay, we went too far with our expression of outrage. We can't take it back, so we'd better frighten them before they start thinking of revenge. They are angry? We must be twice as angry. Their lack of wanderers is a card up our sleeve. Our artisans have proved how easy it is to convert their machines. I will need help from Lugha and Clavel and Mr Kaoru. Meanwhile, there'll be no more visitors. No more fooling around. We're going to get down to business.'

Clavel had opened a sliding wall and sat propped against it staring into the evening sunlight, his legs gracelessly asprawl. He considered the character shrine, and the room that held the dead: both stuffed with hoarded trade goods. In the evenside and the dawn wing, the other captains' quarters were cluttered with small luxuries from home. He reviewed his own remaining possessions and those of his crew, and admitted defeat. A few scraps of souvenirs, and a carton of baby things that had once been a locker in the cabin of the lander.

<If I had anything to sell, I'd go out and sell it and put an end to this stupid game. But since I haven't . . . >

So that was that. Conversation became desultory.

Samhukti, Rajath's chaplain, pondered the revelation that Mr Kaoru believed himself to be part of their nation: and rejected it.

Rajath's young partner, Aditya, recalled the time in Alaska when the locals had nearly tried to force him to betray his rich lover. He longed for another taste of adventure.

<Divinely lovely one!> sighed Rajath. <If you could love me I'd give up all my plotting.> The next moment, he was puzzling over his latest scheme. <It won't be so easy to mingle with the locals, now. Better go in disguise.>

Maitri, extremely glad to have seen the contents of that hollow needle secured, began to relax. He wondered mildly: <Why is a recorder called a 'secret'?>

Kumbva fetched a laptop computer and pored over it with some of his people. Clavel glimpsed the calculations: like thickly textured cloth, shifting in and out of detail. Kumbva's signals master kept track of faraway deadware by occult means only he and Kumbva could understand.

<If we are forced to communicate something formally, it will be a very sudden decision. We must always be ready.>

Clavel was depressed. Eveybody had noticed, even those who had least use for words, that the poet had refrained from making a speech, and therefore was certainly reserving his options in some way. They heard him withholding agreement. They tolerated, accepted, imposed no sanctions. The Rajath mood had prevailed over the Clavel mood, in Clavel as much as anyone. And yet people were anxious, anxiety gone underground. Aditya expects drama, Kumbva gets ready for an emergency.

He considered the status of the spoken word among his own people: meaning which made him a kind of holy fool and Rajath a fascinating troublemaker. What did words *mean* to the locals, who seemed to use them so freely? Nobody cared. Nobody else but Lugha wondered what the locals were made of. And Lugha didn't really care. <We're here to trade,> protested his companions. <Why worry about the nature of the raw stuff, if you can put it in the vat and it comes out food?> Maybe they were right.

But the river spoke to Clavel of Johnny. There'd been a lot of grumbling about the locals' 'dishonesty'. How long could Clavel go on deceiving his other self?

It was late in the evening. The meal had been prepared and served and the kitchen made tidy. Lugha was in the character shrine with the other children learning to be himself, learning (as far as Lugha could learn) to know his companions: the meaning of a certain person's gestures, the consequence of an enmity, the myriad tiny lessons of history.

Atha slipped into the other shrine, and covered his face. He knelt in front of the images.

Feminine people, according to the lore of Atha's kind, are the people who'd rather work through the night in the dark than call someone who can fix the light. The kind of people who chatter when they're exhausted and go to sleep when they're happy. The kind of people who can't live without being needed but refuse to need anything from anyone. Masculine people, on the other hand, can never leave well enough alone, break things by way of improving them, will do absolutely anything for a kiss and a kind word . . . One could go on, but it was hard to imagine what such an idle, gossipy game could have to do with what he saw in this screen.

Atha had assisted at the more conventional religious services in Kaoru's character shrine. He had attended *Tampopo*, *Diamonds Are Forever*, the NBC serial of *Genji Monogatari*. He knew, therefore, that these were people just like himself. He accepted that most of his companions didn't believe in magic. But Atha wasn't one to scoff. He had seen some strange things, in his time. He could try at least to give solace to the dying, to comfort the grief. The cook closed his eyes. His skin wept, invisibly. Go, little Athas. Hurry to this place, wherever it is in the real world, and do what you can.

iii

Karen city. The premier hotel had the kind of defective aircon that is infinitely worse than sweat and a fan. The chap from the BBC didn't know that 'five star' means nothing good in a grubby industrial town of the South: he wasn't much of a traveller. It wasn't Braemar's place to tell him. She lay in a long cane chair gazing out at the lights of waste plant that churned on through the night; lights of boat-bars and floating markets that bobbed on the waters of the Kok river. The stuffy room stank of incinerated chemicals.

The alien child aswarm with coloured lice had been bustled out of sight pretty sharply. How thoughtless of the kid to burst in on an execution like that! She wanted to think about that weird apparition: what did the bugs mean? But she was afraid to think of anything that had happened at Uji.

The chair was vat-grown rattan, quite a nice piece. The room's furnishings were surprisingly good and up-to-date. One should always notice the pleasant things.

She felt as if she was suffocating.

'What will happen?' she wondered aloud.

'I haven't the faintest idea. Maybe it will blow over. After all, one little *kaffir* servant girl. We cannot expect them to share our notions about the sanctity of individual human life.'

Arthur was nervous, and his tongue unguarded.

'Um. One can trust Kershaw and Lloyd-Price. And the Viets. Absolutely heroic, the way they joined in the cabaret: could be they saved our lives. But I worry about those pinko Americans. A covert alarm, my God, damned idiots . . . Then there's Kaoru, whatever his bloody game is. And your lot, Braemar. You could have the glob-pop up in arms. Can you resist that?'

'Ha. If I had anything to show.' She tipped her head back in the chair. 'Oh, what an irony. Frankly, I'd love to see the Nips back. If they were still here, I believe I'd be able to replace my maker without remortgaging my house.'

The Englishman's bulk shifted on the bed. 'You think they can make the confiscation stick?'

'Want to bet?'

Braemar stared at the lights on the dark water. How contented the Aleutians were in that valley. They didn't miss the wide open spaces of freedom. Kaoru's chopper pilots were fairly tight-lipped, but there had been a giggling reference to *incontinence pads* . . . Containment, yes; of every kind. They were habituated to it. But what was the use in stringing telltales together? People would go on gazing at the emperor's new clothes.

Kaoru had sealed Uji. The innate prejudices of the Women's Affairs conference had worked for him: not to mention that cretinous Californian database. No interference! As a matter of etiquette, we mustn't take so much as a flake of dandruff. But no one said it was serious, everyone told you the aliens wouldn't hurt a fly. Well, now we know. If we touch a hair of them, they'll kill. That had been the unspoken truth behind the sweetness and light up there, all along.

Think about something else.

What about Clavel? Johnny's alien. Who embodied the 'Purity' sonnet, and who drove her chief wild with reluctant admiration. She found herself surrendering again to the attribution of gender, maybe merely from weakness. It means something, generally, when a young woman is reluctant to pronounce the name of a young male acquaintance. Think about her, think. A bad thing happened. Forget it. Remorse does no good.

The meaning of actions. Physical assault: to draw blood. To draw blood is an act of war. The meaning of words . . . They use the spoken word like decoration, the icing on the cake: they don't need it. Read minds? No, not in the traditional sense. But what they do instead must take some fancy wiring. Maybe they *are* superior, not in any comic-book way but insidiously, hopelessly.

Stop it. You know that trap.

On the hotel room tv, an Uji archive tape played. Lugha the demon child sat on the polished teak floor at Uji with Douglas Milne. Douglas tossed a coin: a small disc as near to the notional *fair coin* as could be honed from metal. 'Heads. Tails, Heads, Heads, Tails, Tails, Tails, Heads, Tails, Heads.' Lugha's voice was a faint sound. He giggled just like a child. What did that kid use for the connection between eye and brain? A cubic mile of coralin? She wished she dared tell Arthur to switch it off.

'I sense you're not smitten?' said the Englishman, uneasily jovial. 'It was a nasty incident, but personally I still foresee great things between us and the Aleutians.'

If you let him, Arthur would soon convince you in a hundred subliminal ways that whites, especially the men, are inevitably better, brighter . . .

Sometimes, just sometimes, there was a kind of satisfaction in the clairvoyance that haunted Braemar.

Somebody passed below, singing: a Japanese folk song that had been a global hit about ten years ago. 'The crows have wakened me/By cawing at the moon/ I pray that I shall not think of him.' The single voice was reedy and uncertain.

> *I pray so intently*
> *That he begins to fill my whole mind*
> *This is getting on my nerves*
> *I wonder if there is any of that wine left.*

'Shall we go to bed?'

She sat beside him. In the confusion and panic of getting out of Uji the forms had been observed, more or less. Her skin was sore from the decontamination. The itch of loneliness was stronger. She let him handle her breasts, but put a finger to his lips.

'Ssh, don't say a word. I want to pretend you're somebody else, do you mind?'

A pound of flesh, yes. Brae always paid her way. But not one drop of blood.

Rajath and Clavel visited Mr Kaoru's cottage.

Its single room was strikingly different from anywhere in the main house. The floor was square tiled in slick grey, the lighting was fiercely white. There were photographs on the walls: flat, monotone images of a kind the Aleutians had seen nowhere else. In an alcove stood deadware machinery which was also strangely styled. The screens carried columns of squiggle, no figurative images; and nothing was moving there. Neither of them had been inside the cottage before. They felt that they had entered a very solemn shrine; knelt and covered their faces.

Kaoru had been about to rise to greet his guests. He remained, half seated and half kneeling behind his low desk, the dark, full sleeves of his housecoat sweeping the floor. Kaoru's face was very old, the skin crumpled and reamed by a thousand lines of decay. None of them were the sort of people who knew much about old age, but maybe it was because his physical features were so closely written that they felt at ease in his company. They could read the impacted grief in that face, as if it was acted out on tape; and the wildness that was so reminiscent of Rajath. They could imagine encompassing the person within alongside their certain knowledge of each other.

Rajath explained the plan. He demanded, in compensation for Sarah's heinous crime, several tracts of real estate which must be evacuated and the deeds handed over. They hoped that Mr Kaoru, who was in no way to blame for what had happened, would help them to draw up the necessary instrument.

Clavel converted this into correctly inflected speech, while Kaoru listened, head bent and nodding occasionally. At the end of it he looked up, and his quiet amusement was eloquent.

'And will the invasion force now arrive?'

Kaoru drew aside the polished cover of his desk. He opened an atlas and turned to a projection of the globe. He handed Rajath a light pen.

'Perhaps you'd like to mark the areas. I would suggest you favour the temperate latitudes, between thirty and forty degrees. Avoid volcanic regions, but give yourself plenty of coastline. Conurbation would present problems in the long term.'

'But for maximum irritation,' murmured Clavel.

'Quite. Also, you'll find it hard to avoid them entirely.'

Rajath drew a square on the southern half of America, another near the tip of Africa, a circle on West Africa for Clavel's sake. He kept the marks small. He didn't know the exact scale of this simulation, but he had a vague idea. He didn't want to appear greedy.

In the end he settled on seven portions: one in each half of America, two in Africa, a piece of New Zealand, a piece of western Europe and a piece of somewhere between Europe and China. He knelt back on his heels. Kaoru enhanced each area and brooded over the tiny hologram detail which meant nothing to his visitors. He was moved to justify the ragged corrals, but on reflection restored Rajath's original lines.

He smiled, looking past the ebullient Rajath. 'You could call them "treaty ports". Or some such name.'

Clavel's joints crept, urgently desiring flight. Scribbling over a planet like that was certainly funny. Why not laugh?

He had felt close to Kaoru in their quiet talks: the old man reminiscing about the weary years in business, his mind dying all the time. When he had learned Kaoru's secret, his instant reaction had been delight. Of course! his heart had cried. That proves it. That explains how I can be the same person as Johnny. The story was undoubtedly nonsense, Kumbva and Lugha had immediately told him so. But it made sense to the lover.

But the steely sense of family that Kaoru expressed, along with that odd formal speech, made Clavel's blood run cold. The disaster that Johnny's friend had described had no doubt been *done to* Kaoru's household: such things don't just happen. Even so, Kaoru's attitude was alarming. Did all of them on this planet treasure injury like Kaoru? It was a worrying thought.

He realised there was no question of 'breaking Kaoru's bubble'. Even if it had been expedient to explain that nobody remembered anything about a secret spaceship: how would anyone dare?

Rajath admired the dangerous future in his own scribble, quite unmoved by Kaoru's horrible hints. They were still very alike!

Kaoru printed SPOT sheets. 'These won't be up to date,' he apologised. 'That's the price one pays for genuine isolation. But a matter of weeks makes little difference, unless some natural catastrophe intervenes. This planet is like a mouth of old teeth; constant tinkering does no more than rearrange the damage.'

'Oh, I know exactly what you mean!'

Rajath did not. How could teeth be 'old'? He was making a joke, one they'd heard often.

'Mr Kaoru,' cried Clavel. 'Revenge is so embarrassing, afterwards. Your good times will come again, and then you'll feel so stupid. Why don't you wait? Everything will turn out right.'

Kaoru had come around the desk. He presented the sheets, beautifully bound and sealed in clear plastic. He patted the air near Clavel's cheek, as if petting a favourite grandchild.

'Little American.'

'Why have you lived on so long, so alone? Old age is hateful.'

Kaoru retreated. His eyes twinkled. 'On the contrary, I find that it is like coming out of prison. An old person like me can do . . . ' He paused, savouring: 'Almost anything he likes.' He considered. 'You are aware, I presume, that your trading partners consider *themselves* to have been seriously injured, and may be uncooperative. Have you made plans to cover that aspect of the situation?'

They shrugged: of course.

'I wonder how you will justify your actions.'

'Self-defence,' answered Clavel promptly. 'We have been attacked by the very people we trusted. We are few and vulnerable, it is natural we should make a show of strength.' His nasal contracted wryly. 'There are always justifications. We assume they'll have their own moves.'

'Quite so. But it is often better to reply first. Will you be needing transport?'

Since Clavel's idea about faster than light travel came into play, Kumbva had declared the landers must vanish. The

engineer said that anyone with talent like his own would be able to
see exactly what they were.

'Yes, please.'

They retrieved their shoes from Kaoru's tiny porch. Clavel helped
the door to close. It would have closed itself, the gesture was mere
good taste. Rajath forgot to be irritated by this poetical over-
sensitivity. He acknowledged that he couldn't have managed the
interview alone. The garden was hot and bright and still. Clavel
screwed up his eyes and thrust his fists to his temples.

<Oh, what must it be like, to be so alone!>

Rajath regarded him with amused sympathy. <Wait long enough
and you'll find out. Everything must happen.>

<Will I? Tell me, action man. Suppose we went back to the house
now and found . . . The cooks are in the kitchen. They're cross
because they don't like cooking hard food for me.>

Rajath shrugged agreement.

<Suppose we went back and found the cooks in the hall playing
Go? What would you think?>

<What should I think? I'd think we made a mistake. You *are* an
odd person, poet.>

He followed Rajath back to the house, stepping in his faint prints
over the laminate emerald turf. If the world were to fall apart, one
would know it had never been whole in the first place. But it does
not. An atom is the smallest material unit of Self. False: the division
is unreal, a necessary fiction. The world remains indivisible,
though we can only think of it in pieces. Therefore the wise among
us, those we call our dependants, spend as little time as possible
playing the nonsense game of finished thought, of formal language.

Clavel felt like someone trying to look into his own eyes: pull
them out on strings of wet tissue and turn them to face each other.
The image was sufficiently painful.

The sunlight touched his hair, the feathery plantings called
'bamboo' whispered. But nothing was awake out here: every blade
of grass was lifeless, separate, empty. How did they *do* that? Up
ahead, Rajath laughed. It was impossible to alienate him or disgust
him, however hard they both tried to dislike each other. It is one's
own mind that one argues with, grumbles at, reproaches. The
whole is inescapable.

Inescapable, he promised. *Indivisible*. And shivered.

*

They left the valley in one of the supply helicopters, and transferred in the hills above to a more highly powered vehicle. It delivered them, in the middle of the night, to a very cold airstrip that seemed folded in solid darkness. This was called Bhutan, the tilt pilot told them. Mr Kaoru had once kept a house here for the young people who enjoyed the winter sports. The Aleutians wore borrowed great coats. The pilot of the jet that was waiting brought out a tripod, set it up and stood back.

'I am sorry about the cold,' said Kaoru, from the land of the dead. 'Another penalty of retirement: this is my only long-haul plane. To purchase another, or to bring this one to Uji, must have caused comment.'

They bowed. Clavel had schooled Rajath and Lugha. 'We humbly thank you for your honourable support!' Kaoru vanished from the air.

The pilot bowed to the box, wrapped it in black silk and tucked it inside his jacket. He folded the tripod.

'There are mountains behind you,' he said, 'six thousand metres high.'

Rajath and Clavel nodded. They might have known there would be mountains. Deep: they heard, not high. Lugha went to the jet, reached up and tapped its metal flank.

'It seems very . . . dead.'

His teeth were chattering.

'Get inside, you dangerous character. We have a lot to do.'

The Uji-watchers sat around in deadspace in the proudly named 'conference facility' of their hotel in Karen, staring at Kaoru's exquisitely presented document. The team from that fateful day had stayed up here, waiting. KT had achieved, so far, media silence on the Sarah Brown disaster. Poonsuk had been furious at being dragged into an affair of confiscated material and silenced journalists, but she'd held the line.

'This doesn't enter the net,' said Ellen Kershaw briskly. 'I'll talk to Rajath. Kaoru has misunderstood him.'

She saw Kaoru as the villain: he had been manipulating events for his own ends all along.

Someone ran in from the studio next door. 'Come quickly! The pirate's in the Multiphon!'

Each of the six flew to a desk in the hotel conference studio. The desks were only twin screens, had only Thai and English: it had never mattered before. The chamber must have been half empty when he started. It was bursting out in faces: but there was only one voice.

Rajath spoke from the taboo room at Uji. He had blown the Sarah Brown story already. Printed précis ran up their subscreens.

The team in Karen were bewildered. Aleutians didn't understand interactive tv, hated it; wouldn't go near it. But Rajath handled the screen like a veteran. His personality leapt out at them, entirely present.

'No! Don't imagine you can apologise and forget it. You have pretended to trust us. You trust no one. You are liars, cheats, thieves. Do you think we don't know this? We know the truth about each of you. None better. You declare war while pretending peace, building weapons in secret when you know it is against the law. Why do you only speak to each other through the dead? Why else but because you fear to be found out in your lies? Very well, if that's the way you want it. In ten days from now those areas we have designated must be sterilised and handed over. Remember, we have undreamed-of powers, immeasurable resources. We shall punish cruelty and reward obedience!'

His figure seemed to grow, dominated the whole chamber. The idealised brown and blue turning globe, which closed a major speech, struggled under his outstretched hands. The dais screen went blank.

'That's Kaoru, Kaoru put him up to that,' muttered Ellen stubbornly. But her voice was shaking.

There were no scheduled flights to the USSA from Thailand. It took Douglas Milne five days to get to Washington. He belonged to the generation that had abandoned jet travel. He had travelled to KT by boat, under clean solar power and sail. He felt he was sinking back into the filth.

The geophysical catastrophe of '04, that wiped the Japanese islands from the sea, also marked the point for the USA where the slide from prosperity turned into an avalanche. Japanese enclaves sprang up in many places. But the Chinese phenomenon was more than that. Japan and China became one, an entity with no particular friendship for the US; and the hungry giant began to call in some debts. The economic and environmental disasters worked together – not instantly, but through the next decades. Johnny Guglioli was one of the many post-holocaust babies who had no conception of the sense of horrified loss that benumbed his elders. He was able to work for a limited good – a better deal from his feudal lady – without envisaging the task of rebirthing a nation. There were others, with bigger ideas.

In '24 a Hispano-African lady called Maria-Jesus, a motel cleaner, took one of the rich to court for 'illegal domestic surveillance'. She didn't do it on her own. The image of this poor woman, neither young nor pretty, being spied on as she brushed her teeth or changed her sanitary tampon in her miserable partition was supposed to push buttons. It did. 'Illegal' surveillance was an accepted fact of life, and an irrational sticking point for a nation addicted to subscriber soap. No matter. The case grew massively, over years, until there were millions out on the streets shouting for Maria-Jesus.

There was a lot of flailing about at the end: so that, ironically, the final flip-over was a right-wing coup. But that technicality was already lost in history. Socialism (of a kind) had triumphed. It would have been the story of the century, wonderful movie-drama, if the aliens had not arrived.

Rajath's speech devastated everyone who heard it. The superbeing had spoken at last, *de haut en bas*, as they had been longing for him to do. He opened up vast pits of guilt and fear. Robin Lloyd-Price recorded that he remembered the feeling from prep school. The relief at having been found out, the desperate longing to be punished. By the time Douglas Milne reached the President, most of the world had seen the pirate's speech: and the punishment had begun.

The first thing he saw when he walked into the Oval Office was a huge painting, in oils, of Daniel Ortega on his white horse.

Carlotta stood beneath it. She was heavier than when he'd last seen her, *much woman* in a ribbed maroon silk suit and magisterial heels. Her dark hair was combed back, held at the nape with a clasp of silver. The parrot was on her shoulder and she was feeding it with sunflower seeds.

'What's that? Some kind of *memento mori*?'

'If you like. Can you live with it?'

She was the age that people are when they stop being young and before they hit the wall, so long as they can afford health care. Impossible to say more than that. He remembered her differently: young in anger, old in poverty.

'No,' she said. 'I will not be looking for excuses, in a few years time, to put the gilt braid on my cap and groom my grandchildren for stardom. I begin as I mean to be remembered: a colourful figurehead. Don't you know, Douglas, the successful Revolution' (she pronounced it the European way, soft in the middle) 'is when afterwards everything is almost the same as before? Only a little notch better.'

She touched the parrot's feet: it waddled down her arm. 'Pirate, put the shells in the bin, please.'

'*Okay, sister. Anything to oblige my sweetheart.*'

Douglas hated that bird. It made him (he was quite aware of the subtext) feel redundant. Carlotta walked around the desk and he sat – collapsed – facing her.

'What's going on?' he asked piteously. 'Is there a – a bodycount? I've seen nothing, only the tabloids on the plane: obviously doctored stuff.'

Carlotta looked at him wryly. 'I wouldn't be too sure. No, there's no bodycount. The thing's too random, too many panic reports.'

Three days after Rajath's speech there had been a report in the UK tabloids about a horrific freak occurrence on infill work alongside one of the old freeways. It was juicy stuff: delicious cuts of rampaging bulldozers, earthmovers with bloody teeth, mangled human limbs. The world's lowest form of tv newslife used no eejays, no human sources. They grabbed health-and-safety records of bloody accidents, and doctored industrial mishaps into horror-shorts. This was well known. It was twelve hours perhaps, a long time, before the world understood that this incident was unenhanced reality; and connected it with the alien's promise of retribution.

In England, a team of smart civil engineering machines turned on their supervisors and passers-by. In France, there was mayhem in one wing of a large modern hospital. In Pakistan, part of a refrigerator factory had come to life and killed its whole complement of machine minders. That one was recognised as perhaps the first outbreak: it had been happening before Rajath spoke. Others came to light; and it was still going on, mainly in South Asia. But, as Carlotta said, it became difficult to sort out a clear pattern.

In terms of the numbers of dead, the incidents themselves were nothing to the mortal dread they inspired.

'You had to come back in person?'

'I'm not a telepath. Rajath convinced me not to rely for long on the kinds of communication Aleutians don't like.'

'Well, you were wrong. The videophones are still working. So far it looks as if we're clean this side of the ocean.'

Douglas put his face in his hands and groaned. 'Coralin – '

On the day that the aliens had announced themselves in Alaska, there had been mysterious failures in USAF information networks. The collapse traced back to the Copper Ridge base. The timing of the damage was such that its extent would never be known. A lot of data had been destroyed, mangled or mislaid in those few most turbulent days of Revolution. Because this failure involved coralin hardware, it had been treated with special secrecy. No party in the struggle wanted to start a panic about QV infection. It was only later, after things calmed down, that people had realised the obvious connection with the aliens.

In the nascent USSA the Aleutians were widely regarded as real, supernatural angels. At the same time, the Big Machines were revered with an intense religiosity. The revolutionaries, when they understood their dilemma, had taken a calculated risk. They said that the 'demon child' had supernaturally understood in an instant how to use an earthling computer terminal. They didn't say anything about the trail of damage.

'This is our baby, Carlotta. We knew, and we did nothing.'

'I don't see how it would have helped to blow the whistle. We did nothing because we knew there was nothing to be done. Did you hear about the French hospital? Seems the Aleutians don't like sick people any more than they like tv.' She examined an imaginary blemish on one wine-dark nail. 'Well, maybe they can fuck up anything. Maybe not even a screwdriver is safe. But I tell you this as a friend, Dougie. If you have money in the blue clay, in my country, get it out now.'

They can take over our machines. What are we without intelligent machines? Douglas knew what kind of hospital it had been. Gene-therapy: longevity and fertility. Robotics and re-frigerators. The aliens were attacking the sham of the slowdown.

When the two other parties arrived at Uji, there were some injured with them. They were put in a room by themselves. Medical aid was declined. No one found out what happened. Milne had been foremost among the non-interventionists. If they know how to die, he remembered telling the team, I hope they can teach us.

So now the teaching had begun. He shuddered. Stop that.

'If we could cut through the panic,' Carlotta was saying, 'the smarts for the English roadplant were newly air-freighted from South China, a short jet plane ride from Thailand.'

Dougie grimaced. *Air-freighted robotics*. There it was again, the crime and the punishment . . .

Carlotta scowled at him. 'Oh, come on, Dougie. This isn't deathrays from the Overmind. They got out of Uji and they *did something*. They sprinkled poison dust over a few robotic plants: whatever. If we could trace a South East Asian connection for all the metastasing, at least we might cut them down to size.'

'Oh, God. What are we going to do?'

'Douglas, how would I know? You tell me.' She stared at him. 'Do you know we're about to go to war?' Her hands with their blood-red nails spread on the desk top, a gesture of strength. In her eyes a sweet, bleak tenderness: mother to the world. 'It's going to be ugly, ugly. I am proud of that. I am proud to know that the boys of our United Socialist States will make terrible soldiers, that they can't cope with that role without going crazy.'

The fast editing didn't repulse him. He admired her. Most likely nobody would lift the room's record of this hour, most likely the war with Canada didn't mean a thing any more. But her whole internal life, he thought, must consist of savouring and polishing these phrases and gestures. Good for Carlotta, if she could keep it up 'til the end.

He was glad she'd stayed in here, in this public space: governing from under the red light. That was the right way. The last time he'd been in this room there'd been sleeping bags scuffed about, microwave on the floor surrounded by spilling cartons of food debris. Things were more organised. He noticed that a lot of obtrusive Big Machine presence had departed along with the frowst. That was one of their aims: to slacken off an unhealthy obsession. And they'd had so many other good purposes. It had been working, too. Beginning to work . . . But he had given it up gladly to go to Uji. Regret, regret. If Carlotta could read his mind right now, she'd think he was crazy. Or hypnotised, possessed.

She recalled him to the present. 'So what was worth the plane fares, Dougie?'

He was recovering. He'd been on the verge of fugue all the way from Krung Thep. 'Rajath is not their leader. He's a . . . a hat, as the Japs used to say. There is a leader in there, you can forget Kershaw's egalitarian fantasies. He may not be on earth.'

'Or she.'

'They don't have "shes". But we can do business with Rajath. "Okay, call it off, what do you want?" Give him a blank cheque, claw it back in the process of negotiation.'

Carlotta sighed at him. Suddenly he knew why she seemed so calm. She'd given up. 'When there was time,' she said. 'You stupid bastards didn't tell us you were in trouble. Now there is no time.'

She gave him some paper and went to the kitchenette. 'Are you hungry? Coffee? I could make you a sandwich.'

'Mortadella!' shouted Pirate, and jumped from the keypad with a great rattling of chain-mail grey wings.

He read the fax, and felt the blood drain from his face. 'Where'd you get this from?' he breathed.

'Peking. Isolated line. They've recognised us, you know.'

She came back, leaned over his shoulder. 'When Mr Rajath gave us the orders about his real estate, he seemed to think we'd know what he was talking about. He doesn't know everything, does he? But there's somebody up there at Uji a bit more public-spirited than you or Martha.'

'Kaoru.'

'Of course, Peking couldn't keep something like this from their clients. Pakistan – a nuclear state, you'll recall – doesn't care much for this suggestion here. Or that word the alien used in his big speech . . . "sterilised".'

Douglas whispered, 'Oh, God!'

'The nest must be burned out.' She laughed at his expression. 'That's not me speaking, *tonto*. That's the wrath of Islam. The Chinese seem to think it's worth a try. I don't, but I'm only the President of the United States. Who am I to tell people what to do?'

She handed him coffee. 'I can't help you. I'm sorry. Your mercy mission has failed.'

She was so calm. 'No,' said Douglas. 'That's not why I'm here. I want you to do something, and I felt I had to ask you face to face. The Aleutians, you see: they know us. We have a chance to make a deal. We have to have the right to deal with them.'

The President was silent. She blinked twice, then smiled for her public. 'Ah, I understand.' She laughed. 'Oh, Dougie, those damned aliens. This is *not* the way I planned to go down in history.'

Ellen Kershaw tried to work. The summer rains had begun, the damp air smelled of jasmine, and rot, and methane/alcohol.

These beings are bipedal, they are marginally lighter (at one G) than humans of similar size, have less bodyfat; marginally cooler body temperature. Possible air sacs against the spine, a bowl of belly between the hips that might contain a longer gut than ours. Stereoscopic vision, omnivorous dentation: what looks like our tooth enamel, a rooted tongue. They find human food distasteful, but at some recent time (in our evolutionary terms) they ate much the same way as we do. But they are not naked chimpanzees.

The hair isn't hair. It handles like – shell? Like brittlestar tentacles, or *the legs of a dead spider.* (They were wary of human touch, but someone had managed to collect that vivid impression and it was faithfully simulated for Ellen's fingertips.) Something marine, a tang of the cold seashore in that weed-bundle hair, pumice skin, those lumpy, rocklike joints. They could be spiritual cousins of the original Aleuts, the Amerindian tribe that gave its name to those cold islands.

What about sex? Douglas's fantasy about the Aleutians as obligate paedophiles was nonsense. The Multiphon chamber had mostly been populated by middle-aged men with about thirty per cent of middle-aged women. There weren't many youngsters. It was so simple. Aleutian pairing crosses a generation. The Aleutians had picked out the few 'normal-looking' couples they could see. This explanation had leapt out at them when they got together on Dougie's breakthrough, before the ultimatum when it had seemed that the Uji project could be saved.

Ellen moved through the stacks of SETI's library, no longer taking
books from the shelves: haunted always by the Aleutians themselves. They would find this snatched information so ludicrous.
Their complete disregard for the rituals of first contact wore people
down. What did it mean? You cannot know us . . . you infants,
insects.

She had tried to fight for their innocence. She had insisted that
their execution of Sarah was not what it seemed. To a people who
believe sincerely in reincarnation, death is not such a terrible
punishment. Their horror at the idea of flesh or blood being
removed from them had to be taken into account. But then Rajath
spoke in the Multiphon. That speech had had a bleak effect on
Ellen. She saw the same old political monster mouthing the same
old threats: interest dressed up as principle, the same old story. She
was not afraid. A vision, a foolish dream, had been destroyed. That
was all.

She exited from SETI, pushed back the headset. The good people
were gone, no better than the rest. By a stupid accident the alien
invaders had studied the minds of a woolly-hatted bunch of
conciliationists under the impression that they were getting the
measure of the whole hive. They had made a big mistake. More
than likely, planet earth was going to pay for it: because Pakistan
would make her air strike. No one could stop that.

She and Robin were invested as plenipotentiaries of the Westminster government. If need be, they were empowered to speak for
the whole EC. The WOCWOM had become more popular in the past
year, but it was doubtful if the Aleutians would recognise video-
delegates; and difficult to rush more bodies from Europe to
Thailand in the present circumstances. It was unfortunate that the
two lonely champions of the gold and blue banner were pariahs in
the Multiphon, and couldn't hope to prove their innocence. But it
didn't matter. The government of the world had failed to achieve
closure. Poonsuk Masdit had been forced to inform the Aleutians,
via Kaoru, that their demands were rejected. And to warn them, as
politely as possible, that if they didn't vacate the Uji valley before
the term of their own ultimatum, Uji would be burned out.

There was nothing else she could do. The Islamic states were not
going to crack, not with China behind them. The ultimatum was
running out. No more flights in or out of Thailand, no big boats. At

the moment no one would trust their life to any kind of computer, whatever it was made of. Little fleets of manual-rigged prahu were doing a great trade ferrying refugees down from Karen.

Poor Poonsuk. What a terrible and meaningless end to the conference meant to better the lot of those mouse armies of helpless women.

Klong Ruam Rudi, still low on the pillars of the hotel's garden at this season, was full of eerily quiet traffic: the splash of poles and oars. She could hear hymns being sung. The church of St Saviour blazed with light on its concrete island. In the room next door the Thai girl who'd been looking after them since Sarah died was praying, on her knees before a tv flanked by pictures of the Queen and of the Virgin Mary.

'You don't remember '04, Robin. People think they're so important. So many daft idiots, convinced our little messes had altered the working of the earth's crust. It was terrible, the way people leapt at the idea of Gaia's Punishment. This time at least it's true. If we do get blasted to bits, some of us bloody well deserve it.'

Robin said nothing. He did not want Ellen to know that he was one of the 'daft idiots' this time. She was iron all through, the unshakable idealist. He was jelly at the heart.

The fans clattered to a halt. Robin started back from his desk with a gasp of alarm. His nerves were playing tricks.

Ellen shook her head. 'Only KT grid trying to scare us.'

Robin laughed, nodded shamefacedly. 'Kaoru's doing wonders with this evacuation. He's obviously been planning for years to turf the Karens out.'

Ellen had taken to wearing make-up, for the first time in about forty years, he guessed. The Multiphon fuzzed everybody into blooming infancy. It was the way Thai tv did things, but they'd been having to face other lenses in the last days. It was a shock to see yourself *au naturel*, on a diet of insomnia and adrenalin. Old-fashioned powder had collected in Ellen's bulldog jowls. He had thought of offering her something more efficient, but she probably didn't know he used cosmetics and she would be shocked.

The power returned. Ellen and Robin made no pretence of getting back to work.

'I can't believe it,' muttered Robin. 'I can't believe it. Why don't they just leave?'

But they stayed. Maybe they didn't believe the insects would carry out their threat. Maybe it took time to set up the ftl. No matter. In two days the superbeings would die. Not even the Pakistan government believed they would go unavenged.

When the ultimatum came, no one knew what to do. Rajath's plan did not allow for such a drastic raising of stakes. Eventually Clavel and Rajath went to the cottage again, in a very different mood. It did not occur to them, no more than the first time, to contact him mechanically and make sure he was there. Without realising it they treated him as one of themselves. They were right, there was no need. He was waiting.

Kaoru did not explain that the real governments of the world had intervened; such clarification would have been distasteful and pointless. He did not tell them that he himself had leaked their demands to those real powers. There was no need. The Aleutians believed in their hearts that whatever one earthling knew, all knew: Kaoru understood that.

'I assume, excuse me, that you are in some form of communication with your "planet"?' He stressed the word minimally. He would never spell out the truth he strongly suspected. 'And that people there command large-scale weaponry? Please do not mistake me, only a "show" is called for.'

Rajath was horribly at a loss.

<No,> Clavel told Kaoru. <Nothing like that. We know, at home, the kind of mess we're in down here: we know the kind of thing that's happening. But we are private adventurers here, you see. This expedition doesn't have big backers. It is marginal.>

He made a speech. 'I'm afraid not. Aleutia has no "standing army".'

'Ah, I see.'

Kaoru became very silent. The harsh bright room gathered around him, a shrine and a tomb. The figures and letters on the screens stood frozen in the moment of their death.

'And your preemptive encouragement?'

Long ago in Africa, in an emergency, Maitri had used his legendary power over big dumb mobiles to tame one of the local vehicles. Cars, even the meanest brutes, always loved Maitri. Lugha, in Alaska, had found it easy to get a computing colony-creature to do what he wanted. In those days in their minds they had not left home. It's bad form to tamper with someone else's commensals: but tempting, in a competitive situation, if you can seduce some dumb creature. That was why the quarantine had seemed so natural.

Clavel knew now that these feats had been exceptional. Some of the local machinery could be reached: most of it could not. Most of it was utterly mysterious. He didn't understand. They had used their discovery that *the locals don't have any wanderers*. But a deep, lingering conviction remained, even now, that things could not be as different as they seemed.

Clavel found that only formal speech would do, though it was hard work in this situation.

'It's like this. We have nothing from which to build actual weapons. Don't you remember? That's how this began. Lugha – a series of Lugha's smallest wanderers – altered the processing of some colony-animals of yours. I mean, of the locals'. Well, some people got hurt and died. We didn't exactly intend that. We assumed . . . well, commensals *don't* attack their own natural kin; not where we come from. We thought we'd cause a bit of mayhem.'

<Maybe an accidental death or two,> murmured Rajath, the irrepressible.

Kaoru was impassive. 'Will the effect continue to spread?'

'Lugh's not an artisan. His wanderers will not incorporate, they will die. The colonies will go back to the way they were before, unless we go out and dose some more.'

'I don't think that would be wise,' said Kaoru. 'You are, then, completely without resources?'

Rajath crouched on reversed limbs. He looked at Kaoru's withered hand, lying on the desktop. It wouldn't be impossible to start building now. He was sure that those who would count the cost would do so willingly. But the request that Clavel *could not* think of making wouldn't come from him. Once the weapons are out, no one gains. Tears of frustration brimmed his eyes and glistened in the dark of his nasal. The steps that had led to this situation looked so innocent.

'If all of you here died?'

Clavel bowed his head. <We didn't know you people were so rich. We can't afford these stakes. Maybe we would have to respond

in kind, but it would be disastrous for our whole economy and horrible loss of prestige for everyone involved.>

The old man listened to the speaking silence.

'The Americans have a saying,' he remarked. 'In the country of the blind the one-eyed man is king. Please accept my apologies, I had forgotten how very far that is from the truth. Please excuse me further: you must surrender most abjectly, or else give up hope of doing business and leave at once. Any attempt to set terms will only make these people more obdurate. I blame myself,' he added. 'I should have made sure I understood your position before we tried to bluff them.'

Kaoru's disappointment was a bitter reproach. He had been carried away by Rajath, people always were. <We should be the ones to apologise,> said Clavel. He crept up to Rajath and rubbed his hunched shoulders. <Cheer up. This is very embarrassing, but the worst will soon be over.>

<Will I have to talk to the dead again?>

Rajath was afraid to talk to the dead. They all were. At home, priests and monks dealt with that. Your occasions were recorded. If you had done wrong or done something marvellous you would make confession, and it would be processed into a tape for your record. But no one talked to the images! How could you talk to someone, without sharing their breath? Clavel reflected that there was nothing to fear. These people were as far away dead or alive. A vision of a whole world *uninfested* flickered through him, but found nowhere to rest.

<I wish you hadn't used the word "sterilised". That was a major insult, reminding them of their disability. I'm *sure* I never told you to say that.>

The great dictator sniffled. Rajath was always like this. He truly never knew his schemes were going to collapse, and he truly never meant any harm. It was moral idiocy, but somehow lovable. Clavel relented. <No more talking to the dead. Formally or informally. It hasn't brought us luck.>

Kaoru bowed very deeply as they left, acknowledging a presence that he'd felt bound to ignore on other occasions. He took out a can of glass cleaner and a duster, and began to polish his relics.

The open space between the National Assembly and Dusit was full of people. Many of them were defending tripods: friends and relatives hovering over or looking out of box screens, like tiny invalids carried above the jostling crowd. The streaming dusk was full of lights, water puddled ominously underfoot. The drastic and splendid measure the Thais had taken, of deliberately flooding their capital, had eased their problems for a while. But the water traffic fumes had began to build up, and in heavy rains the dikes that protected the National Treasure Area were awash.

Douglas had trouble getting through, though the crowd was completely docile. They knew who he was. His black face was sufficiently bizarre in this city. People kept pressing things into his hands. By the time he reached the doors he was laden with jasmine buds and tiny gilt Buddhas.

He was back because the Multiphon was still trying, fighting to achieve closure: though the Pakistan Air Force might well be on its way already. It was 26 June 2039; 2583 by the Buddhist calendar. Not yet quite a year since the aliens announced themselves in Alaska.

He found his desk, and Martha. They embraced, hugging hard. He gave her a jasmine garland. 'Carlotta's planning a war,' he said: as if the Aleutians were right, and communication isn't real unless you can feel each other's breath. 'She's living in the past.'

'Can you blame her?' Martha gave a gasp of laughter. 'These fucking superbeings, they've ruined our parade.'

'Any word from Kaoru?'

'He's staying up there.'

Doug nodded. It was what he'd expected.

'He sent a special message for you and me. He says he doesn't hold us responsible.'

'Huh?'

'For the Manhattan Project, I guess. Who knows?'

So this was what it felt like to be dying. It made you *raw*, in a way he couldn't describe even to himself. And yet you went on talking, reacting, living, right to the end. He entered the Multiphon and checked around, briefly greeting friends: the team. There were the Brits. No reproaches. This was too big for recrimination. Poor bastards, it could have happened to anyone. Everyone's been under pressure to get some goods.

(Hi Robin, Hi Ellen.)

Everything went dead quiet, for no discernible reason. There were plenty of astrals, he noticed. By this point no one was worried about offending the Aleutians. The Multiphon became for him its screen-self: a great assembly, a hall full of people, each of them equally present. All of them in here, and the billions outside. They were one entity. He was dying, he could do what he liked. He took Martha's hand and willed himself part of that being. Every one that wants to live, push on this balance, *push*, with all your hearts . . .

Ellen Kershaw was simply feeling tired. Uji was a lost paradise, one more in a long line. Aleutians and Earthlings both – their capacity for turning away from joy appalled her.

Then something happened. Poonsuk took the screen, began to speak. She looked dazed, stumbled out a few half sentences: listening to and watching something going on elsewhere. Ellen could not hear a word, but she thought that she was being told that Uji had been destroyed –

Six Aleutians walked down to the dais, and then more and more; the infants were being carried. Two of them got up by Poonsuk. They wei'ed to her, then they began to take off their clothes.

Naked, they remained human as angels. No nipples, no navels, no swelling breasts – idealised, ungendered bodies from a stained-glass window. Ellen shook herself, and managed to see what was really there. The exaggerated hipjoints were bone and muscle, no swaddling flesh. Each had an identical line of shadow in the groin: a vertical dimple, with a darkness of fur or loose scale more or less marked at the lower end. They simply stood.

'Oh my sainted aunt,' said Ellen Kershaw softly. 'Naked into the conference chamber. I can speak Aleutian. Robin, do what I do.' Resolutely, she stood and began to unfasten her skirt.

Douglas saw what Robin and Ellen were doing. He began to do the same. The infection spread. The humans undressed. Some eagerly, some reluctantly, some as if entranced. A wave of awkward, fumbling dance went around the hall, the video-conferencers undressing too. Peace, they said, peace, with naked flesh unarmed, unprotected. It was extraordinary how easy it was to communicate, to understand each other. How ridiculous that they'd ever built this crazy 'Multiphon'.

Poonsuk Masdit, head and shoulders on the speaker's screen with the brown and blue earth in a starry sky behind her. She was still looking and listening elsewhere, hearing voices in her head.

'I have an announcement. Ms Nazarene Rahchan and Mr Chen Juntao are empowered to speak for the peoples of Pakistan, and the People's Republic of China-with-ex-Japan. We have achieved closure. We are the government of the world. And we are empowered to make peace with our honoured visitors.'

The chamber filled with sobs and laughter. Such scenes, such extraordinary scenes, yelled the voice of some eejay in the press gallery. He was not immune. His voice was naked as the day it was born.

'We are here,' said an Aleutian, 'to make peace. We don't want anyone to get hurt. We have so much to offer, if only you'll be our friends.'

Did he or she speak? In English, aloud? Whatever he or she did was understood by everyone. The chamber exploded in excitement.

Douglas Milne felt himself *deliberately* let reason and caution go: let the wild delight, the pride, too, of meeting beings from another planet rush through him as if *this* was the moment of first contact. He grasped Martha's hand, and the hand of the nearest other human being, and bellowed out – 'Arise!'

> 'Arise! Ye nations of the earth
> 'The day of glory is at hand
> 'Stained with the blood of martyrs shed . . .'

The anthems battled, embracing, stumbling together, finding, like the naked bodies, a remarkable degree of basic similarity. 'The Internationale' won out, except for the Oz contingent who went on roaring 'Waltzing Matilda'. Singing people poured down from the desks, the Aleutians spread into the crowd.

'I would also like to declare,' yelled Poonsuk's voice, above the babel, 'the conference on Women's Affairs is closed! There are no women or men here. We are human beings!'

Ellen was muttering through her teeth, '*Keep your head, lass, keep your head when all about you* . . .' This is drunk driving, she thought. We've gone mad. We'll be sober in the morning, and there are still terms to be made . . . But the good people had been restored, their virtue intact. The Aleutians had sued for peace when they had no need to do so, when they had the earth in their power. And here, in this assembly of the powerless, the first act of the first government of the world had been to answer them with generosity and trust.

They didn't let me down, after all! Her eyes were stinging. This time, though every other brave beginning in history ended in grief, this time it might be true. One world! If the Aleutians could achieve that, even for an hour, what else might not follow? She grabbed Robin's hands. Hope and promise! Never deny them. Never, no matter how many times you've seen them fail.

Extraordinary scenes. At Uji Kaoru blanked his tv and sat watching the emptiness for a while. It was dawn and the coverage had been thinning out anyway, beginning to scrape the barrel for new bursts of emotion.

He went outside and dragged from the space under the cottage floor the ruins of one inflatable, two others neatly packed down and in much better condition. The outer surface that remained was chequered black and white. It bore signs in places of a sloughed carapace that had been consumed by Aleutian waste-disposal bacteria. He hauled the three together in the rain on the stone terrace in front of the cottage. It took a long time. He laced the heap with liquid and laid a fuse. Kneeling a prudent distance away, he set a light. The fire travelled, there was a gasp of vanished air: very little sound or visible flame.

He had no doubt that when they desired to return to that 'planet' of theirs, his protégés could grow themselves new vehicles out of whatever trash came to hand. This destruction of the evidence was by way of reparation for the poor advice he had given. He hoped and believed that they would now do well: accepted as equals, respected and successful in their own right. But he knew that he could hold off the curious world no longer.

He went indoors again, and sat thoughtfully at his desk.

In the time of the catastrophe each person had made his or her own choice. Some had chosen to die. The diaspora had Kaoru's respect, but he was not one of those who could accept another country, not even China, in the place of his own.

'I will never know,' he said at last.

He dreamed of an immeasurable voyage, extraordinary changes. Time is not the same out there. The future can revisit its past.

'Nor will anybody else. I can believe what I please.'

Out of his desk drawer he took a sword and a dagger. He had bought them at an auction. He had never had any right to own them. He looked the blades over, and shook his head.

'If not then, then not now.'

He reached into the front of his kimono, and carefully peeled a circular patch of translucent plastic from over his heart.

He opened the door to the garden and lay down beside it, his head pillowed on one arm. He watched the summer rain falling on green and quiet groves.

7: AT THE GATES OF SAMARIA

i

Johnny had a job shooting steers for a real meat business. His employer, a Mr Hargood, ran three hundred head of Sussex Reds on a farm outside London, partly on reclaimed freeway land. There had also been a stately home turned conference centre on the site, but a typhus variant had ended its career. Johnny walked the cold February pasture with his trusty sporting rifle. The gun was forty years old and an excellent piece of equipment. He used the sights to identify his numbered victims, and stalked them casually as they browsed on the other side of a fence. Beyond the ruins, pasture merged into spindly woodland where Mr Hargood kept pheasants. The herd was used to people with guns.

Kapow!

The last animal collapsed, without fuss. The others barely looked up. It was a depressingly corrupt arrangement. He felt like the secret police. *Keep your heads down, brothers. Don't rock the boat. You want to be fed and get your vax, don't you?*

Mr Hargood leant on the gate beside Johnny and grunted appreciatively. 'I knew you'd do, John, the first time I saw you pick up a gun. At least he knows one end from the other, I said to Mrs Ruthie: unlike our local aspiring cowboys. And the Youros are no better.'

'My daddy wanted me to be an accountant.'

He went in, skimming over grey grass, and forked up the beef. The herd drifted out of his way, unconcerned. He backed out, changing the dappled forklift's skirts to wheels for the track. Mr Hargood was on foot and required a lift. Johnny ticked off the dead animal on his dashboard spreadsheet, and blinked slightly at glimpsing the day's price for the meat.

'Fancy a bit of a bonus, John?'

'What's it taste like? Is it worth what the nobs pay?'

'Not to me. I prefer the regular stuff.' He gave Johnny a reproving glance, aware that this didn't sound good. 'I'm not squeamish, mind. Farmers don't get romantic about their food. I go for the taste. It's good for you, though,' he added, with conviction. 'I'd take it for my health if I could afford it.'

Johnny mildly despised Hargood's affectation of poverty. But it was the British middle-class disease, as natural to them as breathing. He waited in the gleaming farmhouse kitchen, where the Hargood's child was teasing the cook and a young girl in spruce uniform was fervently cleaning knives, until Hargood's wife – Mrs Ruthie – delivered a tepid, squashy parcel. 'Wrapped with her own fair hands,' remarked Hargood. 'I can see I'll have to watch out.'

The meat was folded up neatly in ersatz rhubarb leaf (the living, breathing, foodwrap), as if he was a real customer. Life with the Hargoods was a tonic. His cruel loss meant nothing to them. A rational human being who would work out of doors, with his hands, shedding blood, was simply pure gold. He was a valued associate.

He travelled home on the tube, empty at first but filling up as the houses thickened, the video-band chattering softly at the strap-hangers. A veneer of civilisation slipped away. He enjoyed the wary glances at his rifle case, and his own consciousness of the bloody parcel in his bumbag. He stretched his legs in as manly a style as the cramped space allowed, and smiled aggressively at his opposite neighbour. I do a dirty job, ma'am. And I do it well.

The train dived into its hole, into the warren of London.

Johnny had come to roost in England for a variety of reasons. After Amsterdam and Vienna, London was the home of expatriate America. He had little in common with the present émigrés but he'd made London his base because of the language, before the Revolution and after he gave up the medical circuit. There was probably less stigma here for notifiables than anywhere else on earth, and such indifference to the Big Machinery that QV was rated no worse than a typhusoid. The average Brit barely knew that a 'living' material had taken over from etched silicon. He would get asked, 'But isn't a computer virus a kind of programme? How can that infect a person?'

Then he'd been trapped by history, since those B-movie days last June. His pocket money stopped the month afterwards. Seimwa's assets had been seized: and had turned out to be pure virtuality finance that vanished when exposed to reality. The USSA made a commitment to maintain pensions like Johnny's when it started raiding the rich. But they axed him, practically the next day (with sincere apologies), as part of an austerity drive.

There had followed a period when the last remains of his old life seemed to slough off him, almost painlessly. The last of his privileges vanished with the last of his fame. Nobody cared about the eejay with the QV any more.

Izzy's number was changed. She didn't let him know. He found out from the embassy: and she'd moved, too. Their relationship had become more hostile. She claimed she had to protect Bel from the taint of his politics, which was pretty funny. They both knew Izzy's superstitious dread of the QV was the real problem. He didn't pursue her.

The loss of Bella faded, a scar that he would touch sometimes and wonder how it got there. He discovered one day that he'd lost the 'Agnés' interviews in a box of books that he'd sold as a job lot when he didn't have work and was liquidising a few assets. It seemed like fate. The aliens were as distant as Mars, and he preferred it that way.

When he first got back, he'd tried to investigate Braemar Wilson. He took her commercials out of the library. *Death and the Human Family*, *Home and the World*, *The Safe and the Sacred*. They were tacky, but surprisingly good – he discovered with regret. Her original name wasn't in the public file, nor her date of birth. She'd been married once, to Nirmal Anand Datar; had two children, a boy and a girl. The boy was dead, so was her husband.

It had always seemed to Johnny, coming from his protected environment, that people in Europe got sick and died at a ridiculous rate. The news was constantly full of plagues and epidemics. It was an illusion. People died just the same at home, outside the cleaned-up citadels. Still, her losses sobered him.

He took the lozenges that he'd confiscated to his doctor, a somewhat shady young man who did Public Health work as a front for more lucrative activities.

Jatinder handed one of them back in a slip of plastic at Johnny's next visit. 'It's not peppermint. There's a castanospermine, interferon; a lot of trace things. She's had a serious premature cancer, I'd guess, and is on this stuff for life.'

Jatin looked embarrassed. All doctors are Americans at heart, the man was ashamed for Johnny's friend. 'Yes, I'd say she's a controlled cancer. She's also not getting any younger. But could be in very good shape, considering, with one of these personally tailored concoctions.'

'Has she been very sick?'

He knew that she used onei, the cannabinol analogue Youros called 'the ladies' drug'. He'd presumed it was for pleasure, but clinically onei was a rehabilitator.

'Don't be downhearted, Johnny. Look, you should sit where I sit, trying to make babies out of people with genetic values like dog dirt. To have a big one and live means the main systems are high class. Go on driving your old car. She won't let you down.'

'I'm celibate, you know that.'

Jatin leered cheerfully. 'Of course, John. 'Course you are.'

Johnny'd been hoping for some tabloid story, an explanation out of a cheap thriller for the way he'd been treated. But if there was anything in Brae's medication unknown to earthly science, Jatinder wouldn't be the one to find it. It was too late, anyway. He'd lost interest. She was no engineer. Even if he'd passed her something, it would never reach the heart of a machine. She had used him, she had ditched him. She was still trying to get near the aliens; he glimpsed her efforts. She was welcome to them.

Something profound had happened to Johnny in Africa. It had taken time to work through, but it was complete now. He was grateful to Braemar Wilson and the alien, both. He was no longer a broken piece of Johnny Guglioli the eejay. He was someone else, commonplace and humble but whole again.

The train stopped. Johnny woke up and piled out, avoided the attentions of the helpful guards who never had enough seniles and disables to keep them happy. Checked his pass through the manual gate: lots of people did that. Ran the barrage of beggars and musicians in their package-taped pitches. The smell of London enveloped him (the train smelt of citrus-based antiseptic); acrid, slightly faecal, oxygen starved, mysteriously cosy.

He lived on the Gray's Inn Road, a locution which was strictly accurate: like most roads in central London it had been whittled down to an alley by new housing. Johnny navigated the tiny footways through the chill and dusky undercroft of Holborn Infill, where ancient hardbacks could still be found stacked in the back of plastic-wrapped booths. The wind was bitter. He burrowed into the ramshackle pile of hutches that was his building, attempting to hang on to the daydream he'd been enjoying. Hargood would make him a partner. He'd get in touch with Izzy, send money for fares. They'd live in the country, Surrey borders, near the National Forest. Bel would have a pony. No harm in wishing.

He had an active fantasy life. Braemar featured in it too, but those dreams weren't convenient on the train.

'Aren't you going to check your mail, Mr Guglioli?' whined the concierge. She held the end of her sari modestly over her brow, one corner clamped between her sparse yellow teeth and dark with spittle.

Johnny turned resignedly to the booth. She read everything that came in. It must be a nasty of some kind. He snapped on his gloves. Gone were the days when he'd rather never touch a keypad than make this humiliating, telltale gesture. Plastic exam gloves were no sure barrier against the QV – if it was there. But the new Johnny kept the rules, without any fussing. It was easy enough to humour this paranoid old world. As Braemar used to tell him: you can have quite a normal life.

In New York before the Revolution there was one number and it was your slave brand, but at least it covered everything. He groped around his various homemade mnemonics, fighting the terrible urge to enter a code that would make the Post Office forget how to spell the letter 'e'. He didn't often get mail.

The concierge cackled maliciously. 'Not there, Mr Guglioli. *Private* mail.'

There was a white envelope for him in the dusty, empty pigeonholes. Which explained the malice. She probably hadn't managed to pry it open.

Just as in Fo he had to live like an aristocrat, the only tenant with an en suite. It was a sad drain on his finances. But even Brits (supposing they were respectable enough to live indoors) wouldn't share a toilet seat with a notifiable. His shabby room was the biggest in the flat, even after the capsule bathroom took its chunk. Mrs Frame, the landlady, preferred single working persons – single meaning male, no children. The rest of the building was the same, which suited Johnny. He had a micro for drinks and takeaways.

Strictly no cooking. He would give his bonus to Mrs Frame. He wondered what she'd make of it.

The girl brought in a plate of buttered toast and a pot of tea. She lingered, telling him about Gerald-ji Jones, a tv personality who was walking to Sri Lanka to celebrate the aliens' tour of Europe. It was 'for world unity', explained the child, fired with vague enthusiasm. She had only one hand, the left was a small lump fringed with buttons of very pink flesh. She habitually kept the lump tucked on one hip, elbow out, to conceal it – which gave her a rakish air.

'That's nearly the end of your butter ration, Mr Johnny. Shall I ax Mrs Frame can you lend some?' She gazed passionately at his envelope. 'Aren't you going to open it?'

Johnny had never been able to understand people who lived through others, even when it was his job to provide vicarious thrills. But Mrs Frame's girl's hunger was so candid he couldn't disappoint her. He opened the envelope carefully.

'It's an invitation.'

'Oooh! It must be someone important getting married!'

He held out the card, forgetting she couldn't read. It didn't matter. She dumped her tray, got it in her good hand and stood there saying 'Oooh!' and examining it in rapture while Johnny stared ahead of him in amazement. I don't want this, he thought. I have my daydreams, I have my toast. I'm *happy*.

The reception was in the Barbican. The white-gloved receptionist punched out a lapel for him. Come and meet the aliens. The aliens have landed! The start of their first European tour. It had been weird to see those headlines on the street corners with his square of archaic virgin pasteboard in his pocket.

There was a live chamber orchestra playing behind a black curtain, the musicians outlined in crimson below their visuals, mathematical aurora of vibration. There were big stands of greenery, elegant red brick pillars. The aliens were far away. He glimpsed those theatre nurse uniforms through a frieze of sober evening wear. The English Prime Minister, that utter nonentity, was up with them, along with some real celebs. Those who couldn't get near or didn't dare clustered around the courtesy monitors, as if the other end of the room was at the other end of the world, and watched the main event interpersed with Grade A filler. He stood with his glass of nasty champagnoise, watching Carlotta and that parrot: and wishing the President of the USSA didn't look so much like a novelty cabaret act. He didn't know what he was doing here, except that to stay away would have been like an insult to Mrs Frame's girl.

He saw Braemar. She was wearing shalwar khamiz, Asian ethnic costume of tight pants and a loose tunic in silver, lime green and mauve. Her hair, still that dark mulberry red, gleamed through a silver veil. He didn't have a desk or a phone on which to raise the guest list of a party, to sus out whether it was worth his lordly while. But he had known she would be here. What he hadn't been prepared for was a sudden, excruciating intuition. No one knew that Johnny Guglioli had done the first ever alien interview. Someone had wangled him this invitation, someone from the past. It must have been Braemar.

He retreated to the bar, where he couldn't buy a drink because he should handle a cashcard with gloves and in this place he was too embarrassed. So much for the new Johnny. He could smell the soft, wet heat of night in West Africa. He felt an awful nostalgia for the sheer high-strung misery of that time.

Braemar came in: saw him and did a swift u-turn.

A heavy Brit in royal blue slumped beside him. 'Bit of a crush, eh?'

The man was BBC, it said so on his button. A political journalist, no eejay: the kind who thought knowing about the mechanics was beneath him. Johnny used to detest those guys, and let them know it. This one was, thankfully, a complete stranger. He was also very toxed.

'Let me buy you a drink, uh, Johnny?'

The man flipped open his wallet and waved it at the barman, who removed a card and reached over impassively to swipe it through the customer's side of the cash register. Johnny grinned wryly, but took the beer.

'Polish?'

'Good guess. I'm American.'

The sarcasm went way over this guy's head.

'Aha. The USSA. That explains the fancy dress.'

'I suppose it does.'

'I see you're interested in our Samaritan.'

Braemar had been trapped before she could get out of sight. The drunk jerked his head at her. 'Barearse Wislon.'

'I thought she was British.'

He laughed. 'I thought you Americans read the Bible. Our Samaritan, she doesn't quite worship on the right mountain. But she's generous when a chap's in need. You'll be all right there.' The heavy man winked roguishly. *'Une demi-mondaine toute complète.'*

'She's a what?'

'But of course!' The man rolled his eyes. 'Money doesn't change hands but what else would you? A professional woman, always requiring favours. She's careful, mind. No penetration, not even with a clingie. All good clean fun.'

This was painful, if flattering. Johnny could only shrug, and wish he hadn't taken the man's beer. The drunk downed his whisky and shuddered.

'They scare me shitless. Sorry to bother you, uh, Johnny. I was there, you know. I saw them kill that girl. And we did nothing. Our minds were controlled. Now everybody's like it. They permeate the air, they're everywhere. You ask Barearse. She knows.'

He pushed himself off the bar and lumbered away.

Johnny moved, too, before another lunatic could appear. He was surprised there were still people who felt like that about the Aleutians. A waiter stood in his way, proffering a tray that contained neither glasses nor canapés.

'Mr Guglioli?'

He took the white packet cautiously. It was heavier than the first. He opened it, and found he'd been given a message that he could not read without help.

'What is this? What am I to do with it?'

'I don't know,' said the waiter, interested and fearful. 'I was just told to deliver it.'

'Who — ?'

'Well, them.'

The man became even more uneasy, and melted into the crowd.

Johnny wished urgently to know what was going on. He put the envelope inside his jacket and headed, with determination, for the guests of honour.

'Johnny.'

Braemar was in front of him.

He stood staring at her. The changed costume, different manner, had a strange effect. All these other people thought Braemar Wilson was beautiful in some conventional way: regular features, good skin, slinky body. They were wrong. The thing that was beautiful was *Braemar* (good grief, what a discovery), looking out of, defining, whatever disguise she chose to affect.

'It's good to see you,' she said.

'Oh? I don't know why. You found your way on to the guest list without my help. Don't waste your time, Brae. The other whores will be turning all the good tricks.'

She nodded, accepting his rage with the sad, humble look that he remembered so clearly. He stood there, shaken beyond bearing by her eyes, her breathing presence.

'Did you get me invited here? What's this about?'

'The party? I think it was arranged for you, Johnny.'

Johnny's mouth dropped open.

Braemar took a card from her case, wrote on it with a tiny gold pencil. New Things, Inc. He remembered the Planters Bar.

'Come to see me. There are things you need to know.'

He could see the theatre nurse uniforms. The celebrity cluster was shifting, moving into livespace for the public part of the evening, the speeches. An alien smiled: not at him. He saw the baboon mask break out in teeth below its dark centre, and remembered 'Agnès'. Braemar had slipped away. He saw her graceful figure veiled in colours of a moonlit garden (lime green and mauve! Surely only Braemar –). She was coming on to a Royal Society laureate. He heard her laugh, it sounded totally false; it hurt him like a slap in the face. Abruptly he'd had enough.

He sought out a washroom, shut himself in a cubicle. He couldn't read what Braemar had written. It was in Italian. He infuriated himself by trying to spell it out and failing. He took out the other thing again. It was still a passport, apparently a valid European passport belonging to John Francis Guglioli, USSA citizen. Media person, self-employed. It said nothing about his being subject to quarantine regulations. The concept was downright nonsensical. When he used to chase ufos to ease the pain of exile he had travelled like toxic waste, plastered with special clearances. Nowadays he had no use for travel documents of any kind. He turned the rectangle of charged plastic around, a monkey with a strange toy. What does it mean? He felt like a counter in a game, a helpless bundle of pixels. Someone had picked him up and stuck him on the board again, he didn't know who or why.

He realised that the covering note had somehow not been delivered . . . to his mind? He sat on the toilet seat, face lifted, waiting for visitation.

An image flashed on him, but it had nothing to do with aliens. Carlotta in front of the new flag: the deep, blood-red flag with the silver stars. Some of that blood was mine. I sliced my wrists, I let my life run out. He saw the inevitable camera eye peering down at him, circled by its coy message *for your protection*. He jumped up on the seat with an inarticulate yell, and flailed at it uselessly. Viva Maria-Jesus!

Ex-eejay QV victim in toilet incident . . .

The thought of burly security persons with nil revolutionary sentiment brought him to his senses. He scuttled out of the washroom and fled, hugging his bewilderment, into the cold streets of the warren.

He phoned her. She didn't have a videophone, which surprised him. He wouldn't have put her down as an anti-tech of any kind. Her voice sounded brutally familiar.

She lived in a whole house, south of the river in opulent New Cross Gate. No infill here. There were trees growing through the sidewalks and private cars along the kerbs. A repro minicooper, bright red with willow-green detail, gave off an aura that he could not mistake. Beyond, a plain white electric van was pulled up. Johnny could see the profile of the driver, and the flicker of a changing page of newsprint in his hand. He was intrigued.

He stood on the pad in front of a battered doorman. The screen remained blank but a distorted human voice emerged. The door was opened by a teenager who was clinging to the choke collar of an enormous black and tan hound. The girl's eyes were big as saucers, rich brown: eyelashes like sooty forests. She was wearing an *ich bin ein Bangladeshi* teeshirt.

Woof! Woof!

'Shut it, Trix. Come on down. We're trapped in the kitchen, the housebox is bust.'

The basement kitchen was huge, poorly lit and festeringly untidy. It smelled of sloppy domestic recycling fighting with something viciously hygienic. On a counter by the door sat the kind of house control box to which Johnny had been accustomed since childhood. Six keys were hooked on its side, the screen showed a holding pattern of floorplan. Whatever was wrong wasn't obvious.

Braemar sat at a long table that was strewn with the remains of breakfast wearing a drab grey woollen khurta and leggings, her face barely made up. The dog went to sit beside her, head higher than the tabletop. Another woman in bunchy striped skirts was scrubbing pans at the kitchen sink. A small boy (by the clothes) of around two years old was sitting on the floor. The girl with the unnaturally enormous eyes stepped over him as if he was a puddle: but Johnny was immediately attracted. He and the baby stared at each other, measuring up.

The girl ogled him. 'I'm a decommissioner,' she said.

There was a shrine beside the housebox: a gaudily coloured sonar map of the sunken islands, Honshu in fragments along the black pitfall of the trench; the bright lipped lava flows.

'I think about the atoms in my reactor, nothing else. I don't even chant. It's a quantum effect. The decay of an unstable particle is suppressed by the act of observation. D'you realise, people all over the world have been maintaining the Zeno phase in the nuclear reactors down there for thirty six years? It's mostly the Japanese, of course, led by the scientists who ran the decommissioning before the catastrophe. The Japs wrecked themselves trying to make things safe, you know. That project cost five million extra lives, they reckon. Ikata, Fukushima Three and Tokai Three were so supersafe they were programmed to decom themselves, and they did it. That still leaves . . . '

She ran out of breath, paused to count the terrifying undead on her fingers; ran into difficulties and changed the subject. 'Have you got a job?'

'I shoot cows. Um, steers. For a real meat company.'

'Yecch. That's disgusting.'

'Someone's got to do it.'

Braemar laughed. 'Kamla, aren't you supposed to be studying that Dimbleby-Gorbachev interview?'

Kamla pouted.

'Get upstairs.' Braemar reached over and jabbed keys on the crippled box. 'And I want to see the tape on your tv. Within three minutes . . . Ionela – '

The Balkan-looking woman crashed another antique cooking utensil on to a toppling pile, leisurely removed her apron and made for a door which must lead to the yard – garden – beaming widely at Johnny on the way out. She did have rotten teeth.

When they were alone Johnny sat down, closer to Braemar than was actually strictly comfortable. He wished to demonstrate that her body didn't scare him any more. 'You run a tight ship, ma'am. Congratulations. How old?'

'Fifteen. Billy's two.'

Their manner seemed coolish for mother and daughter, probably because of the baby. Fifteen seemed young, too, though he hadn't noticed the daughter's birthdate on file. But he wasn't going to probe. Personal interest was nil, this was strictly business. He'd had time to adjust. Maybe, with the slightest encouragement, he'd have fallen sobbing into her arms. He knew he wasn't going to get it, and he didn't want it. Only a fool loses more than one safe world in a lifetime.

'So, how's life treating you, Johnny?' She smiled, the old provocation with the sex leached out.

'Oh, you know.'

'Slow horses and fast women?'

He grinned. He liked her cheek. Pitiless as ever.

'You've settled in London. You should have let me know. Is Robert still with you?'

'Living on borrowed time.' He was amused at her attempt to invoke past intimacy. 'My landlady doesn't allow pets. The day will come when she'll discover his box and I'll probably *betray* the poor little bastard, pretend I found him by the toilet and was about to turn him in.'

'And, let's see. What are you reading?' She peered at the title of the ancient volume that was weighing down his jacket pocket.

'*A Separate Reality*.' She thought this was hilarious. 'Castaneda? *Johnny!*'

'What's wrong with that? "To see beyond the surface of life" . . . I like that.'

Oh, this was cosy. The old friends talking over old times. Let's forget completely how those times ended. How British!

He took out the white packet and laid it on the table.

'Exit one drug-crazed lady in red, enter the *distinguée* Asian matron who never touches anything stronger than seltzer and never leaves the house without a veil. What d'you really look like, Brae. Can you remember?'

She leaned across and took the packet, took out the passport and looked it over. She lit a cigarette. 'I take it you want to know what this means? I can't tell you, not yet. But I think you'll find it's real. Or "nature identical", I suppose I should say. I think you can look on it as a kind of taster. A promise of what you might gain. Clavel, who was our Agnès, remembers you.'

Braemar Wilson was the anti-Aleutian pundit. He'd seen that developing and appreciated the tactic. She'd had one terrific piece of luck, but otherwise the aliens story was a tough one for an independent to crack. Presentable opposition, however, was something the aliens' promoters were short of. Her hostility, one could assume, was pure marketing. This lady would surely have nothing to do with a small group of crass extremists called White Queen – rumoured to be British-based – who were busy trying to convince the world that there was something bad, dirty, evil lurking up there at Uji.

But Johnny remembered a certain night: a journalist with a deadly weapon. The drunk at the party had been scared stupid, and he'd said, 'You ask Barearse. She knows.' Johnny regarded the respectable Ms Wilson curiously. His eejay's nerves were twitching.

'What's going on, Brae?'

She put down her cigarette. 'I don't know.' She hesitated, apparently wondering how far to trust him. The cigarette started chewing itself to ash.

'You were there for the Sarah Brown incident, weren't you?'

Braemar shook her head. 'Her name wasn't Brown. Girls like Sarah don't have fathers. When they take on maids at Westminster they allocate surnames in rotation: Jones, Brown, Patel, Kelly.'

'You know something about her?'

She changed the subject. 'Nobody knows anything. Nobody knows about you, Johnny. The aliens have never told anyone, because they don't understand a contact that involves only two individuals. I think Clavel maybe does, but she has other reasons to be reticent. You're still special, Johnny. We could still have our story on the front page.'

He didn't react. He'd expected something like this.

She touched the passport. 'Your contact isn't with the tour, but this shows she's trying to get hold of you. What about it, Johnny? Shall we go into business again? I've always wondered why you didn't try to capitalise on what happened to us. Couldn't you think of a way? Or were you afraid to open old wounds?'

Johnny gasped, thrust the heels of his hands against his temples. 'Shit! I never even asked myself! My God, it must be a post-hypnotic suggestion. Galactic conspiracy!' She waited for him to tire of the joke. Johnny dropped his hands, and stared at her coldly. 'You dumped me because you thought you could get the stuff without having to share. You've found out it's not so easy to get real close, and you want me back. You must be fucking *joking*. I'm not buying and I'm not selling. I lost the tapes. I don't want to know any more about aliens than I see on the tv.'

He slapped the false passport. 'You got me invited to that party. You probably mocked this up yourself and had it handed to me as some kind of crazy lure. You're wasting your time.'

The baby had been in and out from under the table, muttering and driving a little red and blue dustcart around. He chose this moment to come barrelling on to Braemar's knee. She laid her cheek against the mite's soft, dark hair.

'What if the superbeings could get you back on stream? Have you heard from Izzy recently? Does she still send pictures?'

It was nice that she remembered his story so well.

'That's cruel, Braemar.'

'I'm a cruel person. I thought you knew that. Cruel and sentimental, like James Bond.'

She put Billy down, went to the dishwasher and rooted out a beaker. She filled it with juice. The child said thank you nicely and returned to his game. There was a window behind, where greenery crawled in pots and trays. Braemar stood with her back to the light, her lovely face obscured.

'Okay Johnny. I won't bother you about the aliens. But can't we be friends?'

A tv at the end of the room came on. *The Times* masthead: it must be one o'clock. The lead story was about Eve-riots across the USSR: a heaving mass of bodies in the streets of some comfortless breeze block city where dirty snow lay about.

'Silly fools,' said Braemar. 'There is a state of affairs, it is the way things are. The men give the money to the women, the women bring up the children. The less any woman tries to mess around with that arrangement, the happier she'll be.'

Johnny laughed aloud. 'Do you really think that's about sex?' He jabbed a finger at the violence. The screen, which was a good one, seemed to gobble the space around it. The sight of a boot hitting a face made your blood pump, it was truly horrible. 'We're running out of land and food and money, Brae. Okay, we don't know much about the visitors, but we certainly need help from somewhere.'

He leaned back, looking at the floorplan on the monitor. Big house. Big dog, too. There were Public Health regulations which implied her pet must be more ostentatious even than it looked. That drunk had known what he was talking about. She was nothing more than a high-class, self-publicising tart. Knowing Braemar, she'd probably hired the police rig to impress her friends.

It was nothing to Johnny how she made her way, but there was a mystery about this woman and the aliens. It had been bothering him since Fo: and probably, against his better judgement, he was going to try and get some answers.

'Is that a real dog?'

'She's an antisense. She eats but she doesn't shit. Isn't that wonderful? Doesn't come on heat, either, lucky girl. She's based on a pedigree Doberman bitch called Keymer Sunburst Orange, but I call her Trixie.'

'Hardwired?'

'No, I trained her myself. *Attaque!* Trixie, *attaque!*'

For a split second his blood ran cold. The engineered monster leapt to its feet: and crashed on to its side, legs in the air, whining.

'A true female, you observe.'

Johnny hoped she'd missed his moment of panic. 'Very witty. And if you tell her to roll over?'

Braemar slowly grinned. 'Then she dies for the queen.'

'I'll remember that.'

She released the dog somehow, it resumed its heraldic pose.

Johnny stood. He looked at the housebox. It was ancient, years pre-coralin; and never updated. 'You've been plugging your phone into this, haven't you? You shouldn't do that, Brae. I know it works, but it's a false economy. The blue clay kind of humiliates your silicon, you have to rig up some objective distance between them.' He sighed, slipped the passport into his bumbag and slung the bag on his shoulder. He couldn't fix anything, not ever again.

'You're leaving? Damn, I didn't even offer you a cup of tea.'

'I have to go to work. Invite me. I'll try to fit you in.'

Kamla got pregnant for the first time when she was twelve. Braemar was the one who found her, comforted the blood-spattered guilty child with whatever nonsense came first to hand. *Don't be absurd, God doesn't punish babies, it will just go back in the queue* . . . Six months later she was pregnant again, and defiant. So Braemar had taken her in, earning the undying hatred of Kamla's mother (but that had happened before). A teenage girl, neither clever nor specially pretty. Naturally she wanted to have a baby. What other prize was within her reach?

Johnny's response to the Eve-riots was childish. Of course it was about sex. There was nothing in this world that wasn't about sex, unless it was about money. And of those two, which came first? The chicken or the egg? Braemar's fear of men, bone deep (never acknowledged anywhere but inside herself), seemed to her completely rational. She was convinced that President Carlotta felt exactly the same. But their dominion was a fact of life, if not *the* fact of life. One doesn't fight facts. One puts them to use.

She sat with her chin on her hands.

She had left Johnny alone since Africa, never tried to trace him. But here he was. Fate had brought him back: fate and the aliens themselves. She couldn't, in conscience, refuse the gift a second time.

She wondered if he had really given up hope of returning to his old life. Good for him, if that were true. What he'd lost did not exist any more, and he was young to have learned that lesson. Maybe he was merely sulking: Achilles in the alley. But no matter why he'd chosen to vanish from the media scene, he was still ridden by the demon curiosity. She could use that. She would find a way to help Clavel and Johnny, be a fly on the wall at their reunion.

She chuckled: a wry, half-silent breath of laughter.

Had the boy never been in love, that he couldn't read the alien's message?

He didn't like Braemar Wilson much, and who could blame him? But he was lonely as hell. He would be back. Braemar smoked another cigarette and savoured the pleasures that were promised her for another while. To have him in the same room again. To make him laugh. Treasure.

Kamla came down and heaved a theatrical sigh of relief. 'He smelled of blood. What do you want a jobard like that around for?'

'He gives terrific backrubs. What do you think?'

Kamla giggled dutifully. Naturally she didn't really believe that adults had sex. Especially not elderly members of her own family.

'Nani, can I borrow fifty 'cu?'

Braemar flashed a glance of awful warning at the forbidden word. 'No you may not. *No more cosmetics.* You'll thank me later, when your friends are growing moustaches and melanomas.'

Braemar tapped softly at the green baize door. It opened. She was in a laboratory of many ages. At the small, bright, modern end the scientist was at work. 'Come and look at this.'

A passage opened up before her, between benches of curious shaped flasks, retorts, gruesome creatures wriggling in jars, coloured flames. The scientist showed her an array of tiny sausage filaments that shimmered with different, delicate patterns.

'Look at this. Here, and here. These strands are from daughters of the same cell. Do you know what that is? Of course not, why do I ask? That is Cairns-Hall mutation. The cell shapes its own future by producing some protein tailored to process any chemical stimulus I provide. Here you can see it happening in the temporary single-strand. There is testing going on. They are thinking about what they do. Full-blown Lamarckian evolution, that's what you see. And more. The ability to create a function to deal with a situation.'

The scientist believed that she'd invented this peremptory 'mad professor'. She was blissfully unaware that to those who knew her outside she was exactly the same as in life. The real person also hated personal contact, loved to network because of the power it gave her to switch you off.

'Would this happen in the brain, Clem? Could it work on something like a – a talent for languages?'

The scientist hissed in disapproval. 'Everything has a chemical origin. Why not? Maybe. Though there are difficulties. Unless they have some mechanism I don't know of for exchanging genetic material . . . But at the moment we are studying alien tissue, not fairy tales. Please try to concentrate, your highness.'

'Sorry.'

The scientist hummed on, forgetting her own admonition instantly. 'Evolutionary timescale, pah. Your body, highness, is built of dumb animals and vegetables. What could grow into the "you" called mind is switched off nearly everywhere. Imagine, gracious highness, if your whole body was teeming with cells that could behave like this, another glandular system; and every one was – I can't be sure, but something like *you* – a vehicle of your will. You could shed skin cells that would be tiny factories. They could keep you clean, like the colony that was mother to my world in here. Or tools. Take a few cells, offer each a different stimulus, add some waste plastic and maybe some turds: your intimate servants grow for you a cine-camera.'

'These mobile factories. Are they harmful?'

'To humans? Not so far as I can tell.' Clem's voice smirked. 'But I can't say for sure. Give me, oh, maybe three hundred thousand humans and permission to kill half of them. Then I guess I might be able to put on the aliens' packet "harmless to your health".'

'What *are* they?'

The scientist chuckled. 'They are big colonies of protozoa.'

Braemar was not impressed. 'Yeah, like the rest of us.'

The scientist had pronounced, once and for all, that the alien invasion was not an 'enormous hoax'. But she had produced no useful information. Some of her confederates had wondered if the aliens might melt if they stood out in the rain. She'd refused to research this and turned down several other such hopeful notions with unconcealed contempt. She declined to discover a devastating allergy: to housedust, or common salt, or planet earth's peculiar amino acids. She went her own way. The scientist was playing. She liked being the centre of attention. And she knew that none of them had the power to question her.

The problem was academic. Since the Sarah Brown affair, it was not possible to announce to the world that alien tissue had proved to behave like normal biological material, not the flesh of angels. There'd be global panic if anyone heard of what was going on here. The telepaths presumably knew everything, if they *were* telepaths. They had not yet descended in fire and thunder on the scientist's hideaway. But maybe this was another example of their august mercy.

'Come over here.'

There was an open-topped tank, the depth within split into two. A multicoloured animal moved in each space.

'On your left you see simulated yourself: a human cell. On your right, the alien. By the way, this really is you, Brae. I stole it from you, ha ha ha. You don't mind?'

'Um.'

'This here,' (the focus moved) 'is what we call the nucleus. In here, the chromosomes of your mama and your papa are bound together. What God has joined and cannot be put asunder: the chymical wedding that is you. These little pieces are the mitochondria, traits here come from your mama alone and do not recombine. Now, see the alien.'

'It looks the same.'

'Wrong.'

It was sometimes a good idea to be wrong. The scientist's tone brightened perceptibly.

'You should never think in those terms, gracious highness. I do not call this – stuff – this big untidy cluster, this kittenball of bases DNA. I call it "alienDNA"; aDNA. There is no mitochondria-analogue: and there are other very great differences.'

'Sorry.'

'There is an extra altered phosphate group, an extra hydroxyl group, making in all seven bases. There are different hydrogen bonds from human DNA, which means a different configuration within the cell. It's impossible for an informed observer to call these two the same.'

'Oh, I see.'

'But the greatest difference is this. You will know what "everybody knows". That most of our DNA is – still – apparently useless information. That is not the case here. Yet not all of what you see is used by this individual. Not hardly any! The cell is a schizophrenic, it is in a terrible mess. Suppose in the nucleus of one cell of yours is one person. Guess how many *separate individuals* live in here? Guess!'

'Three?'

'Between three and five million. Approximately.'

'Oh.'

'Each of them maybe as complex as you or I. So far as one can tell. Highly concentrated, very conservative, very acquisitive individuals. I suppose, since they have no power to become new by recombination, they dare not shut down anything that might one day be useful. It is crowded in there. But don't worry for Mr Alien. The snake pit is doped. I would say there is a chemical event – analogous to our "moment of conception" – forever deciding which of the strings is expressed.'

Braemar seized on a word that suggested something concrete. 'Do you mean you know how they reproduce?'

'I can guess how they don't. How can I put it? This alien had no daddy.'

'Parthenogenesis.'

'Ah, long words. If *I* had a baby which had no daddy, that would be parthenogenesis. Leave aside scrappy random mutation, and external effects like the conditions inside my body, that baby would be me. If this alien had a baby. Well. There's no reason I can see why it should not be a little Mr Alien. But there are many more chances that it won't be.'

The sexless, disembodied voice became dreamy.

'The most incomprehensible thing about this universe is the fact that I can understand it. Alien, but not . . . Of course, the bases have to be like ours, still it's so remarkable: so near and yet so far.' The image in the tank changed. 'This is human adenine, the fiery humour. Touch it, put your hands on, touch your own anger.'

Braemar ignored this. She'd been boobytrapped in here before. 'Isn't it vanishingly unlikely,' wondered Braemar, 'that they should be so like us? Surely that means they maybe *were* human, a very long time ago?'

The scientist laughed. Ha ha ha, Clem's usual mechanical cackle. 'When the galaxy was seeded by the Gods with humankind? Don't you believe it. The chemicals are God. They decide everything. But listen, don't you like my new joke? As you know, we are

made of the five humours: watery, fiery, airy, earthy, and the one
that Aristotleans called quintessence. Adenine is the base which,
in its functions, suggests aggression, appetite. Therefore, fire.'

'Um. Could we possibly get back to the Cairns-Hurt mutations?'

'Cairns-*Hall*!' The scientist must never be questioned. 'Listen, I
haven't any news for you, nothing that you can understand. Everything I say to you I have to talk in bad analogy, wild surmise.
This isn't easy work. I don't have a big fancy laboratory, I don't
have hordes of robotics. And these things keep dying. I cannot
make them build me an alien. I need that trigger, and where is it?
And then you ask me, "How does their telepathy work?" You ask
me, "Prove that what they did to the smart machines is not
magic" . . . Get out of my lab! Get out before I blow you sky high!'

Braemar returned to New Cross. She peeled off her headset and
gloves, pulled the printout and began to read, rubbing her brow and
chewing her lip. She found it marginally easier to make sense of this
stuff on her own. Her outboard monitor held nothing but a
government health warning. *You are entering a computer-generated environment. Remember that nothing you see or touch or hear
is real.* Too bloody right, when you were dealing with Clem
Stewart. Underneath, a message appeared: GET ME A FRESH ALIEN
BUD. FAILING THAT A WHOLE LIVE ALIEN. THEN WE'LL BE COOKING!!!

ii

On the stairs in the house in New Cross there was a picture that
Johnny didn't like. It was large and plain. It showed a kind of cot or
cradle standing in an empty attic. The grain of the wooden
floorboards was brutally clear, there was nothing else in the picture
but a shaft of light. The name of the picture was *Parsifal 1*, the artist
someone called Anselm Kiefer. It was a copy. The original, he
gathered, was fairly famous. To Johnny it always seemed that the
baby in the cradle (the baby suggested by the cradle) had to be
dead. He would avert his eyes, coming up the fine wide stairway:
remembering Brae's child who had died. Remembering Bella, the
scar that hurt sometimes when he was tired.

It was a time when the *küss die hand* chivalry of deep

continental Europe once more defined a woman's place. In middle-class society any grown-up, single 'working woman' was barely respectable, let her morals be pure as driven snow. But as the drunk had told him, 'the Samaritan' had her niche. Her smart friends would gather every Wednesday for an evening of refined karaoke and a little sedate role-play after supper.

The mood of Braemar's London had been set by the '04. There was no order in the cosmos any more, only the shocking certainty that *anything can happen*; and a proliferation of fortune-telling theory. People were waiting for the next global disaster, because catastrophes were normal now. It could be another massive lava flow. Popular science said the '04 could well have marked the start of a totally devastating series. But anything would do. The neighbour star that goes nova and floods earth with killer radiation, the giant asteroid on a collision course, the new and unstoppable mutated virus, the Night Of The Living Dead . . . This was the world that had abandoned movie-drama and stayed away in droves from the holo-films. Animation, cartoon emotion, was the favoured artistic expression. Dramatic realism was too slow, too ordered: completely unlike nature.

Johnny would meet the Ride of the Valkyrie as he came up the stairs, and find Elmer Fudd in his Siegfried helmet chasing Bugs around the drawing room walls. He would hear the Samaritan's guests discussing popular new releases: *Things Can Only Get Weirder*, and *The Death Star Hypothesis – Still More*. Apparently the aliens had arrived instead of something worse. But Braemar's friends were not grateful on that account. There was plenty of cocktail-party enthusiasm for 'White Queen', for the gang's tv flyposting, and their letterbomb campaign: the kind of support that starts, 'While one can't approve their tactics . . . '

He allowed himself to become a fixture at New Cross Wednesdays through that spring and summer. He never saw Arthur of the Beeb there, but he met the rumoured successor: Pierre Larrialde, the Basque diplomat who had no tickets to Uji but did have a lot of money. Larrialde was one of the boldest anti-Aleutians. Perhaps the Basque felt he had nothing to lose. He was a controlled TB, feverbright eyes and horribly skinny.

Most of the regulars were the same kind of obnoxious rightists. They thought it was smart not to believe in QV because maybe there was some connection with the aliens' 'superpowers'. They loved to cross the room and shake Johnny by the hand as a kind of obscure sideswipe against Aleutia *and* socialism. He would stand around, listening to the cut-glass Brit middle-class voices and wondering which of these fat cats were the real terrorists.

'White Queen had a very good point there. The KT conference is playing into the hands of people who've been hacking away for years at the very roots of national sovereignty.'

Johnny was quietly eavesdropping one night when a hand landed on his arm. He found beside him a tall, skinny old bloke with floppy white hair, who gazed at him wistfully. 'Mr Guglioli. You like the KT idea of "one world", I suppose?'

'Don't see much wrong with it,' agreed Johnny. His expression must have given him away. The talkers moved off, oblivious. The old man forgot to let go of Johnny. 'What exactly is it these White Queen people are afraid of?' Johnny asked. 'The Aleutians seem like good guys to me, now we're at peace.'

The old man blinked, in slow motion, so for a moment he seemed to have fallen suddenly asleep on his feet. 'They call me the White Knight,' he murmured. 'No, indeed you're right. There's nothing to worry about, for your generation. Or even maybe the next. That's why it takes great concentration, great clarity of mind to be afraid. Are you afraid?'

'Not me,' said Johnny. 'I come here for the cartoons.'

'Ah yes, the cartoons. The implications are serious,' sighed the White Knight. 'We have entered a post-literary world. We cannot record detail: *there is too much*. We must resort to diagram and algorithm.'

Johnny nodded politely.

'In the cartoon, we abandon the Quattrocento. We no longer peer through the lens of Alberti. We no longer experience story as a dream, centred on the self. The frame is decentred, the illusion of "realistic" depth is eliminated.'

Classic Animation, with its armies of slave labour, was revered over here. The intelligentsia missed no chance to rip into digitised realism. Even the auteur of the famous, award-laden *Red Chrysanthemums* was no hero in Europe. It was politics disguised as aesthetics. The day Eve-riots hit the big studios the computer-generated stuff, with 'quattrocento' illusions intact, would have its artistic licence back instanto.

Johnny didn't bother to say this. The old guy was the type who doesn't listen to a word: he knows the interviewer is a kind of spacer bar. Besides, the real subject of this conversation was not cartoons.

'And yet, you see: there is exactly the realism of our situation. In a classic cartoon, if you fall in the water there are always sharks.' The White Knight waited a moment, as if hoping for some response to his cryptic come-on: then patted Johnny's arm and wandered away.

The alien circus had returned to Uji after an impenetrable progress through the European capitals. The baboon faces were everywhere, hazed towards humanity, the open hole blurred into a flat nose with wide nostrils, the jaw smoothed to vertical. Since they'd decided against blowing the world away they'd become fantastically famous. They were more respected than the chairman of Du Pont, more popular than the most adored Balkan royalty. A startling number of global tvsponders not only believed that earth would be under alien rule within five years, but also felt this was a good thing. Negotiations over a modified version of the famous 'real estate deal' continued. The visitors were staying.

Kamla was an impressionable girl. She despised him for a while, then she started flirting. Catching him alone in the kitchen, she slyly pushed a science fiction comic across the table. There was a small bump under the film-sealed antique paper.

'What's this?'

She rolled her big eyes and thrust out her chest. Another of those messages about population strained over her plump breasts: DONT BLOCK THE EXIT. She was also wearing a Natural Death Movement headband. He wouldn't be surprised if Braemar encouraged the illiterate teenage mama to dress like this. It was her idea of fun: a walking one-liner on the absurdity of any attempt to shift human nature from its crazy defaults. He hurt himself trying not to laugh. Or trying not to cry. Those monstrous eyes were still like enough to sting him.

He pushed the gift back. 'It's books, not comics. I don't think you can afford it.'

Braemar herself never recalled those African nights by a single glance, or word, or gesture.

He went to the beach with them: with Kamla and little Billy, and Kamla's brother, a slender arrogant ten-year-old in prep school uniform. It was his day out, but he didn't seem too thrilled. This visit was obviously one of those dismal 'treats' that helpless children have to endure from their relatives because they don't know how to say no. Johnny felt about twice lifesize and cast himself as the hulking minder. He lurked along several paces behind his employer's family, kicking the desolate shingle. The sea off East Sussex was officially no more polluted than it had been forty years ago. It was grey and scummy, and slithered rather than lapped along the grimy pebbles. The women and the baby retired to a heap of concrete knucklebones. Johnny and the boy, Piers, chucked stones.

'The Normans,' said Piers, 'came up here.' He pointed to a line of office blocks that showed above the sea defences. 'And we were over there, up on the hill above the field that got called Senlac. It was farther from the sea in those days. We'd come rushing back from walloping Danish Harold at Scotch Corner, and everyone was simply wiped out. But we had to fight.'

Oh. Those Normans. The beach's name had meant nothing to him.

He looked down at Piers: the boy's milky coffee skin, with freckles two shades darker, the hatchet profile that could have been copied straight from that savage old she-eagle of Pakistan. Irish grey eyes, nappy chestnut hair in aspiring dreadlocks. There didn't seem to be a scrap of native flesh in the brilliant mosaic.

'The Saxons, you mean. You don't look much like a Saxon, kid.'

The boy stared, the way the British do: placidly, totally dismissive of the foreign worm. 'It was still us.'

Johnny thought of Larrialde. *I will not endure to see my country once more overrun.* The blind simplicity of these territorial urges. He hated Larrialde. You could bet Larrialde never worried too much about the infection he was spreading, callous bastard. The image of Braemar in a cloud of eau-de-nil taffeta, whispering with her sickly patron under cover of the music, came into his mind, sharp as life. It choked him.

And then she turned, and she looked at him and smiled. *Come on in, Johnny. Join us in the preemptive resistance movement.*

Well. He'd known all along, really. He'd known since one night in Africa about the general outline of Braemar's hidden agenda. It was still hard to believe. The secret truth seemed so banal – so unsophisticated, so unlike her.

It was late. Johnny was babysitting. The Marmunes, who lived in a 'grannyflat' out in Braemar's yard, were busy people. Kamla had a date. It was natural by now for Johnny to do favours like this. The housebox came to life. The keys were working again. He saw her groping in her purse. She let herself in and came downstairs with Trixie loping after her. The dog, to Johnny's relief, always stayed in the front hall when Brae wasn't around.

She'd been at *The Times* studio, cutting chat for one of their tabloids. She was wearing the new season's fashion. For reasons the White Knight could probably expatiate at length, the Frock World's response to Aleutia was a retreat from frank outlines: a flimsy, fragile, misted-up appeal. Braemar wore a scant apple-green tunic and silk leggings under a many-layered jacket of white muslin. She looked lovely, exhausted but lovely. Sometimes he would re-member the outfits she used to wear in Fo, and it made him feel slightly ridiculous.

'Somewhere out in orbit,' she grumbled, 'there is a ship. A dirty old, battered old, cramped old multigeneration spacehulk. That we could have built last century, technically, if anyone had set their minds to it. The fact that no orbital junk-tracking has spotted it means nothing. It is black all over, invisible to radar, heavily shielded. And they're maintaining radio silence. I never said they were idiots. Just liars.'

'The Lagrange nodes?'

Johnny had been to space, so she couldn't win on this topic. He watched her wondering what actually happened at a 'Lagrange node'.

He put her out of her misery. 'You know, the comsats inserted in the lunar plane when the US and the USSR space stations did their famous weightless-fuck: joined up at the hip and we were off to Mars. The sats are still functional. Funny they haven't picked up *anything*.'

She blustered. 'Well, even if . . . It's a great big ocean out there, easy to miss a thing that size.'

She was right and didn't know it. Johnny smiled in a superior way. Braemar ran a jug of filtered water and stuck it in the oven. 'Sorry I'm so late. Coffee?'

Johnny was surreptitiously checking his bumbag. The tube stopped at nine o'clock. He would have to take a taxi and haggle in pounds sterling, the daily struggle of the streets. He hoped she wouldn't notice, but Brae was on to the flicker of green like Robert homing in on a pinch of sugar.

'Johnny, dear, is that a twenty I see?'

'Yes, ma'am. And it is mine. All mine. For once in my life, I am going to be able to make change. This dirty, greasy, stickytaped fragment will be one small personal triumph over the grim misery of twenty-first-century London life.'

'I'll trade you two fifties.'

Fifty pound notes were relatively common.

'No market.' He pushed the note firmly out of sight.

'But I'm paying for your taxi.'

'If you insist. I still keep the twenty.'

She laughed. 'Watch out, you're becoming naturalised. Did you hear all that about Peenemünde Buonarotti?'

Buonarotti was a German physicist. She was known as 'the first genetically engineered genius'. Surrogate womb, two certified genius donors. Her parents – purchasers, more like – had given her that atrocious name to represent the pinnacle of Western European civilisation. Amazingly, something had worked. Ms Nazi-Rockets-and-Renaissance-Art was a prodigy: plenty honours, plenty corporate funding. But she was famous nowadays chiefly for having declared that she didn't believe in aliens. That the super beings were frauds, and she could prove it.

The White Queen gang was trying to make something of the fact that nobody had heard from Peenemünde Buonarotti recently. They had bombed her corporation, challenging them to produce their dissident. Buonarotti's employers were unimpressed. She was a very private person, they said. If she didn't answer the phone, that was her choice.

Of course, Braemar hadn't been officially speaking for White Queen. She just happened to be interested in the gang's activities.

Johnny gave her his *humouring the madwoman* leer. 'Whoops, sorry. Forgot to tune in.'

She put coffee in front of him, began to hunt the housebox for the afternoon's post. She found the bills. 'Ah, look at this. *How hard it is, to eat another man's bread and to climb another man's stairs* . . . That's Dante, you know. Bless the man, he puts things so well. Do you still have your Dante?' She turned, cheerfully despairing. 'My *maker*, Johnny. They took my maker. I can't work, I'm reduced to whoring around tabloid chatshows. I can't even mortgage my soul to replace it until the buggering "world government" is good enough to admit I'm never going to get the old one back. My nice frocks are product placements; we scarcely eat in this house unless I can lig it somehow.'

'Aha, it comes out. Your real reason for persecuting these unfortunate extraterrestrials.'

She didn't laugh. Suddenly, wrong-footing him completely, she was serious. She shook her head. 'No, Johnny. I'm not interested in revenge. Anyone who has ever injured me is going to die. A satisfying proportion of them, if I was taken that way, in lingering pain and humiliation.' She left the box, sat down at the table and rubbed her eyes. 'How tired I am, I must look such a hag.'

Buried moments. He remembered how she'd seen him talking to that drunk, and walked away. It was Arthur of the Beeb she'd walked away from, the man who got her into Uji. He wondered about the price of cutting those letterbombs. How did she pay the tubercular Larrialde? He couldn't help it, his imagination would stray to the weird things Europeans did instead of copulate: *safe sex*. When he was a kid, that was the dirtiest expression he knew.

If you have a friend who is a whore, and you realise you were once a trick she turned, first you hate her. Then you get used to the idea, and accept that you were probably asking for it to some extent. But he would never believe she had screwed him purely for business reasons. She had saved his life by an act of peerless generosity. Nothing could ever take that moment away, or tarnish it entirely.

They did not ask each other awkward questions. This big empty house told Braemar's story: of a failed matriarchy, the family that should have been. He wondered sometimes about Nirmal Anand Datar. There were no pictures of him, none of the children, either. But he didn't ask. Nor did she pry into his own shabby life. They were two lonely people together, comforting each other.

'Kaoru suicided,' he offered helpfully. 'I've often wondered why. Have you tried to make something of that?'

'Hardly merits the word. He was over a hundred years old. He simply stopped taking his medicine.'

'What about the minders? I heard Robin Lloyd-Price was only at that KT conference as a result of urgent evasive action. Been putting it about a bit, making himself cheap. It was a while ago, but maybe you could dig up his promiscuous past?'

'I'll pass it on to my contacts. They might like that.'

This was the way it was. They kidded along, and Braemar was never going to admit she was a hands-on terrorist until Johnny asked her straight out. Whereas he wasn't going to ask, because he hadn't yet decided what he was going to do about White Queen.

'It never troubles you that the whole of the rest of the world has a completely different opinion of the aliens?'

'It troubles me. If I say I don't believe in magic, and there must be a rational explanation, they tell me they're not human. If I say they came in a multigeneration ship, nothing we couldn't build ourselves if we put our backs into it, they tell me that's not possible. The ecosystem would clog up and die, and anyway the cosmic rays would get you. God give me strength. We believe they travelled ftl because it says so in the stories. That's the only reason.'

'That, and the fact that the Aleutians told us so. Why would they lie?'

'*Augh*. Why wouldn't they? There's nothing like a good lie to win friends and influence people. You can't believe the whole world could be so fooled. Imagine this: the USA and USSR, poised for forty years on the brink of destroying human life. Was that a fantasy? It was real. Then, pouf, it was gone.'

'Clavel convinced me.'

He was annoyed then, because she'd lulled him into mentioning Clavel-Agnès, that whole experience which they both knew was out of bounds. He moved into the attack before she could take advantage.

'For one moment let's be realistic. Something's over, yes: and it hurts not to be the crown of creation any more. But *they are superior*. It sounds corny but face it, we have to trust them, we have no choice.'

'Oh, certainly we should trust them. They only want to take over a few smallholdings, shoot a few turkeys. How many treaties was it, Mr Americano? Two hundred and fifty-two? Have I got that right? Johnny, I know they don't mean us any harm. They don't have to. It's historically inevitable. If they're superior, that means we're inferior. Right? If we're inferior, then give it a generation or so and there'll be Aleutians in our jobs, Aleutians in the White House; and two doors to every leisure centre; two kinds of life.'

He recognised the classic Wednesday evening whinge. 'I think you're a damaged human being, Brae.'

'The White Queen,' she said, 'is a character invented by Charles Dodgson, a nineteenth-century mathematician who was intrigued by nonsense theory. You may have seen an anime. The White Queen's peculiarity is that she screams before she's hurt. To save time.'

'Thanks. I'm familiar with the works of Lewis Carroll.' He leaned back in the chair. 'You're up to your neck in this vile reactionary business, aren't you, Brae? Letterbombs and all.'

She nodded.

It's always a shock when a major suspicion is finally confirmed.

She broke in on the silence, before he could decide what to do next. 'I'm not a terrorist, Johnny. But our reaction to the Aleutians is dangerous. It's mass hysteria. It is madness for us to treat them like gods. They're few and we're many. I think they hoaxed us quite unintentionally at first, and now they're simply playing up to our fantasies.'

'Oh, sure.'

'They aren't telepathic. They just think they are.'

Johnny choked, spraying nature-identical coffee. 'I think you're on drugs.'

She poked a seedy dishcloth at him. Johnny pushed it down-wind and mopped himself with the sleeve of his jacket. She leaned forward, fired up. 'Listen to me. Babies don't learn to speak in order to communicate. They get on perfectly happily without words as long as they're with people who know them. Am I right?'

'Uh – '

'When you say you "know what someone is thinking", and you're right, is that telepathy? Gesture, body language: when you know someone well, an educated guess. That's what the Aleutians have. Imagine living in a silent movie. You know silent movies, Johnny?'

There had been a vogue for them a few years ago. He knew.

'The pictures tell a story. The plot's a folk tale, which everyone can follow without much help because everybody knows it already. There's a lot of emotional detail, sheep's eyes and visual gags, and occasionally a title, a few words carefully framed for emphasis. *That's* how the Aleutians communicate.'

'Doesn't make sense. They'd keep on fucking up all the time.'

She was ready for that. 'You know, people used to look at gibbons swinging through the trees and think, how amazing, what perfect acrobats; how is it they never fall? Then one day someone did a survey of gibbon skeletons and found bones that had been broken and mended over and over again. They fall all the time. It's simply that, statistically, swinging works well enough to make sense. The Aleutians have been here for – how long? – and they remain convinced we operate the same way as they do. Does that sound like "real" telepathy to you?

'The truth is, their theory that we're linked by this "Common Tongue" of theirs has only worked once. And it was with you. Do you see what that means? You and Clavel together, you could change the nature of this meeting of worlds.'

Johnny had not found out anything new by hanging around Braemar: no details. He still didn't know what to believe about the invitation to the Barbican, or the false passport. But he kept on coming. Perhaps, in a twisted way, he was drawn to White Queen. He found himself, alarmingly, wondering if he could sign up – with reservations. It was the old, vanquished need to be part of the main event reasserting itself.

She was overstating the case. There had been others who heard the alien voices in their heads: in Alaska at the start, and sporadically ever since. Johnny was only interesting because he was within Braemar's reach.

A single lamp stood on the table, echoing summer twilight. Braemar's arms and throat glowed through layered muslin. How beautiful she looks when she's lying, he thought. He smiled, and put aside the dregs of his coffee.

'I still love the way you talk.'

'Thanks. But I'm trying to recruit you, hadn't you noticed? What do you say?'

The babylistener function on the housebox sighed and muttered:

billy was restless. Kamla's shrine glowed. At the other end of the room someone was walking around an expanse of grass in Argentina. The first enclave was being readied.

'Why didn't you tell me any of this in Africa?'

She groped in the litter on the table for her cigarettes. 'Does it matter? I'm being as honest as I know how, here and now. To you the aliens look like saviours. Okay, maybe you're right and I'm wrong. Fine. But you must agree that we need to know them, to reach them. And you are possibly the only human who can do it.' She grinned at him. 'Well? What's the verdict? Will you join up or turn me in? You could try telling the tag outside, for a start. *Habeas corpus delicti* . . . I keep throwing corpses at him, but it's almost as if there's a conspiracy to keep White Queen out of the courts.'

Johnny was frowning. 'You were at Uji that day when Sarah Brown died.'

Braemar sensed danger, but couldn't see how to avert it. 'I was there.'

'The attempt to steal tissue was a White Queen stunt. Has anyone ever stuck that on you? I'm right, aren't I?'

She knew where he was heading, he saw the flicker in her eyes. She took refuge in messing with her cigarettes. 'No one made the connection. I think the Westminster government still gets the blame. I was Sarah's backup, supposed to cause a distraction. The idea was that I acted hostile and she acted demure. When she accidentally stabbed an alien with her darning needle I would throw some kind of wobbly on the other side of the room. It was a stupid stunt.'

'I'm glad you admit it. In effect, you killed that kid.'

'We didn't know they'd kill her. We had no reason.'

Johnny shook his head. 'No use, Brae. Anyone who takes up terrorist action of any kind accepts that their life is forfeit. You knew.'

She stared at him, silenced: abruptly pulled away from the grip of his eyes. 'We got the goods, anyway.'

She hated to think of it. The feel of that squirming thing in her mouth. No idea what it might do to her.

'Don't try and tell me you got something out of Uji.'

'A bug. You remember, Clavel was covered in them. We have one of those. It's not really a louse. It's a mobile scavenger colony, their way of keeping hygienic.'

'Are you making this up?'

'The decontamination was rushed. No one asked me to open my mouth. Then I hid it in my first-aid kit in a glob of wound-dressing jelly. Got it back to London in perfect condition. Our scientist was over the moon. So much better than blood, she said. The telepaths didn't notice a thing. It was as easy as shoplifting.'

Johnny said nothing, staring at her.

'So you see, they are not angels and we can prove it. We have a sample of Aleutian tissue under analysis.' She took a breath. 'I suspect they shed living cells, like that thing only much smaller – and maybe somehow "conscious" – into the air around them, constantly. I don't think that makes them "telepathic" in our supernatural sense of the word. It's not psychic power they use, it's a kind of very intimately informed guesswork. You and I can speak Aleutian, Johnny: "Common Tongue". But the physical difference makes them able to trust their guesses, while we can't trust ours.'

She finally lit her cigarette, gazed at the flame.

'People will tell you duality was invented by a chap called René Descartes. It's nonsense, we were always like it. We have our persistent fantasies that everything is one, man. But our experience has never borne that out, never. I look at you, you look at me. Something passes from my eyes to yours: well, that can't happen, because the space between is "empty". No action at a distance. That's our predicament. We are alone. Even when we speak or touch each other separation remains what we believe in, it's our default state. If we lived as I think the Aleutians live, in a kind of soup of tiny emissaries of ourselves, then where would we have fixed the borderline?'

Still he didn't speak.

'The old tapes are nearly useless, they'd simply look faked in this climate. But if you and Clavel could do it once, you could do it again. I don't know. The mad scientist says their basic chemistry is very like ours. Call it convergent evolution, the anthropic principle, or what you will. Maybe a few of us are somatically, semantically nearer to them, and you're at the top of the scale. What you have is *precious*, Johnny. A piece of this enormous story belongs to you by right.'

He didn't say a word.

'You could learn so much. And she wants to talk to you. Why

d'you think she sent you a passport, of all things? She wants you to come to her.'

Not being an Aleutian, she didn't know how much trouble she was in. His silence could mean anything.

'You killed that kid,' said Johnny. He slammed his hand down on the table. 'I thought you were in this for the money. I knew you were into alien-bashing, even the letterbombs, but I thought it was a career move. I never dreamed you were *serious*. You are *sick*. You were trying to get evidence that they have poisonous blood or whatever racist nonsense: and in effect, you caused all the deaths after that incident. You are *crazy!*'

She tried to keep calm. 'Whatever we did had to be invasive. No one was going to get away with "accidentally" taking a rubbing of Aleutian skin. We'd been told they were good and gentle people, Johnny. We believed that. We only wanted openness.'

Johnny stood up. His hands were shaking. He stuffed them in his pockets. 'Oh, no. You don't catch me with the same bait twice, Ms Wilson.' Outrage made him reckless. 'I'm supposed to be a sucker for exotic sex, so you want me to fuck the alien for you, pick up some dirt from her pillow talk. Thanks very much. But no thanks. Those aliens are the people who could save my life, clear my name. I don't expect you to rate that. But the world's starving. London's packed like drawers in a mortuary. The planet's bubbling with toxic waste. We need their help.' He stabbed a finger at Kamla's shrine. 'At least your idiot niece is *trying*.'

She had been close to them. Locked in her crazy obsession she had not been touched. Braemar was the one who was unreachable, unable to conceive a truth obvious to everyone.

'What a bunch of mindless fascists! Do you realise what could fucking *happen*, to *all of us* if they find out what you've done? Just because *your* life is so dirty it is not worth living . . . You suicidal, murdering whore, you hate them. You hate everyone.'

He stormed out, blundering over Trixie on the way.

He emerged from the tantrum several blocks away, outside the neighbourhood incinerator. It was after midnight. He'd be lucky to find a taxi. He felt a fool, and almost turned back to apologise: but no, he would not. White Queen was far more sinister than he had guessed. There was something ugly, deeply ugly, going on and he didn't want any part of it. A false idyll was over.

iii

The Aleutian Affairs office in Ruam Rudi was about to close. Martha and Robin were hanging around the lobby, talking quietly. They would be going out together as soon as the access light went off. Ellen sat at the duty officer's desk. The sight of Robin's rosy Gainsborough fairness beside the glacial American blonde jarred on her: a poor colour combination. But at least their arrangement, however far it went (she did not enquire), kept the boy out of worse trouble.

Chutima brought the last freight mail delivery. There were always presents for the aliens: clothes, food, music and home movies, even long and rambling handwritten letters. Robin and Martha followed her in, idly curious. It was Robin who identified the suspect package. They were off guard at Ruam Rudi. The terrorists usually preferred to bomb the corporations, whose public offices were traditionally fair game.

'Quick. Put it in a bucket of water,' he joked. He made to toss the packet into one of the fat earthenware pots that flanked the office door, Ellen's treasured blue lotus. They were real jars. ('Please,' said a polite notice, in English, 'remember the flower and the jar are real here.')

A chemical tag ripped. A big glistening bubble leapt into existence and flowed swiftly into the centre of livespace. Inside it a fisheye street scene. Glimpses of bygone fashions, curvaceous old motor cars and wide, sprawling boulevards. Music. Fading. 'It's May the tenth, nineteen forty,' the bomber's disguised voice told them. 'Whitehall, London. The Panzers have cut through the French cavalry at Dinant.'

A silhouette. A bulky figure stood looking out of a tall window into the unseasonal heat and dust on Horse Guards Parade. 'I hope it is not too late,' muttered Churchill, chewing on his emblematic cigar. 'I very much fear that it is.' He turned around. 'Remember "holosell"?' he rumbled. 'Rip the tab for your free gift, and suddenly there's a walk-round image of a three-piece suite filling your front hall. How vulgar! *Everybody* wanted that kind of advert outlawed. So we were told. When it was put to the tvsponders, *everybody* turned out to be *la bourgeoisie*. Ordinary people loved it.' The

Churchill cutout grinned like a schoolboy. 'Holosell died a natural
death. The letterbomb lives on, because the people want to know.
They understand that this is the only way that outlaws like me can
reach them. With the news that no one else dares to tell.'

He appeared to touch the bubble skin. 'Clever, isn't it? A hollow
sphere with a boundary of rearranged air, the molecules arrayed to
form a reflective surface. 360 camrecorder technology is a wonderful thing. It's a pity that no one will ever know. The Aleutians don't
like our media gadgets. The whole telecommunication web is
dismissed to their sidelines, they're not interested in anything
we've learned. No one will remember this incredible age. The
pathways will close, the limbs of *our* science and art will atrophy. I
wonder, will relics ever be found by a new human civilisation, on
the other side? We can only hope so.'

The mournfully pompous tone of this distorted gibberish enraged
Ellen so that she could hardly speak. But speak she must. In public
hours this office was routinely sampled by every newsagency on
earth. She must assume this scene was already on tv somewhere:
soon it would be everywhere. A letterbomb cannot enter into
dialogue. The tactic was to challenge the ghost, disarming a potent
illusion.

'Mr Churchill, you greatly underestimate the intelligence of the
modern public. "Ordinary people" are well aware that our visitors
are *aliens*. We understand very little about each other as yet. SETI
informs us that it will be generations before – '

Churchill became a woman, a famous personality who'd been
dead for barely the requisite thirty years.

'Once upon a time, we had a thing called the "collective
ideology". It protected us, kept us from understanding things we
didn't want to understand. You people have SETI. You're afraid to
get close to the aliens. So SETI tells you to keep away. You're afraid
to refuse their demands, so SETI tells you to do whatever you're
told.' The embodiment of well-groomed authority paused.
'Frankly, I think you're losing your grip. In *my* day, a database was
a reference tool, not a pagan idol.'

The bubble collapsed just as the access light went out.

'Sorry,' said Ellen. 'I walked into that one.'

Martha snapped gloves on and dropped the remains of the packet
into a baggie. The gadgetry was already melting. It wouldn't tell

them much. They could identify the private studio that produced the bomb, but it would be boobytrapped to hell, a raid a pointless gift of more coverage to the bad guys. She stared at the place where the bubble had been, psychic habit having turned that patch of space into a blank screen. 'The White Queen has an eejay in the band now.' She scratched her armpit ruminatively. Her white-blonde looks went with the mannerisms of a hoodlum.

'You mean Johnny Guglioli,' said Ellen. 'The young man who made an appearance at one of the gigs on the European tour.'

'Yeah. He's good, always was.'

No one had found out how Johnny Guglioli had tapped into the guest list for the Barbican reception, what it was that had been delivered to him there; or by whom. The aliens' minders had been fully occupied trying to keep tabs on their superbeings.

'One of old Seimwa's artistes with an imaginary disease. And an aging meeja courtesan. No great loss to their families.' Martha locked hands and pointed an imaginary pistol. 'I think we should take them out. Applied with care, assassination works.'

'I never know when you're joking,' said Robin admiringly.

Chutima, the elderly Thai woman, and Ellen Kershaw eyed each other.

'How can she be so sure?' murmured Ellen.

It was known that Braemar Wilson had been a founder member of the anti-Aleutian group White Queen. The usual line was that she'd been traumatised when she witnessed the death of Sarah Brown. But Ellen remembered that adamant hostility coming off the woman in waves before anything went wrong. It was eerie. Of course there were risks: everyone accepted that; and basically everyone trusted in the Aleutians' good will. But what did Wilson know? What was the secret horror that everyone else had missed?

i

Clavel left the SS *Asabo* at Liverpool and made his way to London. He didn't know what had gone wrong. He had waited and waited. But Johnny didn't come to the Devereux fort.

He had not worried about his appearance, the last time he was in Fo. He was *Clavel*; and people either knew that, or why should they be interested in the shape of his features? But he had learned to be a stranger. He could not stop himself from naming himself a stranger with every breath. People would notice, they would look, and they would see one of the famous Aleutians. He wore a mask. No one wondered at that, it was a common gesture.

Aditya had given him some jewellery to sell, fair exchange for the delight of at least a minor scene with Rajath. He discovered that the value of 'Aleutian artefacts' had soared: which in itself should give everyone something to think about. Rajath's real-estate scam was more than ever pure greed.

It was a long way to London and the traffic cripplingly slow. In the dark he pulled out of it to rest, along with many other travellers. He lay in his car, too fiery to sleep, his body crawling with excitement. He stared into awesome distances: that vast ocean, vast sky; the tiny stars that had never seemed so far away. He thought about all the starry banners in the locals' assembly hall.

He had tried to have a conversation once with Douglas, the Dark River (in the Common Tongue, Aleutians named him *sad one*), about local formal names: Ellen, which meant *Shining*; her true-child *Bright*. So many stars, so many people who were seen as forms of light . . . what did it mean? But Douglas didn't want to talk about it.

When he arrived at the city perimeter he left the car and walked. He walked around for days, surrounded by the two nations. Clavel had believed they must be defending separate territories in most places, coming together only to parley in elaborate ceremony. That was how it looked in the dead world, and it fitted what he remembered of the conditions of a shooting war. But in this city the enemies lived together, as in Fo. He hoped for their sake the fighting wouldn't reach them. It would be dreadful: hand to hand in every house, every street.

His escape from Uji had been easy enough to organise, using the resources of the dead Mr Kaoru. But he was very much on his own here. Nobody had any helpful suggestions, except the strong one that he should not sell anything more. He ate the food that other people left on their plates; and slept where he tired. He asked everyone he met if they knew where to find Johnny Guglioli. There might be more efficient ways of tracing an individual, but he didn't want any fuss: and time is cheap.

He only realised after several days that he was becoming terribly, terribly sad. He had no reason to be unhappy. He was an explorer again, and he would soon be with Johnny. But a pall of grief filled his air, crept into his pores.

At night Clavel ran four-footed. Once he curled up in a dusty doorway, out of the wind, and heard a few people singing dolorously.

Were you there when we crucified our lord?
Were you there when we crucified our lord?
Oh, sometimes it causes me to tremble, tremble, tremble,
Were you there when we crucified our lord . . .?

He did not catch all the words but the meaning flowed through him like water: shame and loss and never-ending sorrow. It was as if every story in the shrine of the singers had been mutilated in the same way, cut off at a nadir of misery and defeat. Clavel found himself weeping helplessly. But the tears were mysteriously sweet. He didn't want to stop, he wanted to go on weeping for ever.

He found a system of tunnels, guarded by the dead. The dead trains alarmed him more than Kaoru's jet plane. But there were maps on the walls and written signs everywhere, which made life a lot easier. He began to cover the map methodically.

The tunnels were randomly dark and bright, packed and deserted. The mask became unnecessary. The people who rubbed against him, jostled him or hurried by accepted him as one of themselves. Some liked him, some didn't, some gave vent to irrational bursts of hostility. Nothing was strange.

He went into a canteen and walked around the tables. He ate a dish of rice, sopped it with reddish bitter sauce he found on another plate; finished up with a kind of cake. It was no particular hour outside on the platform. There was a ghostly half light over everything. A heap of clothes shambled by, and called to him hoarsely.

'You're low, you are!'

Clavel suddenly realised why this tunnel world was so reassuring. But he couldn't refuse. He and the ragged man sat down.

'I need to eat and I can't afford to pay.'

'It's low. Dustbins, I've done dustbins. But not straight off someone's plate.' He patted Clavel's thigh. 'You've got to watch that. You stop worrying about what people think of you, and it's the downward path. I've seen it happen.'

'Don't worry,' said Clavel. 'I'm not going mad.'

Something started a rush on the transport and bodies began to sweep by them. So many faces, drawn and miserable. This grief had been all around him in Fo; at Uji whenever the locals came to visit. He had not been able to feel it until now.

'Can you read?' asked the ragged man.

Lugha had worked hard to assimilate the written language. There was no struggle for Clavel. He had learned once that everybody dreams, but only those who use language can describe the state to themselves.

'If you're a poet,' he said, 'you don't just remember dreams, you remember *how dreaming works*. You can do it in the daytime: mapping from one set of states of affairs to another, so that there arises this thing called "meaning". I couldn't tell you "how", no more than I could tell you straight off exactly how I put one foot in front of another. You don't "how" it, you do it. You can do it with suggestive abstract patterns as easily as with shaped sound . . . In fact, you can't stop. It's because you and I are addicted to the thing called "meaning" that we use words, and have responsibilities, and people who depend on us.'

'Ah. What's it say up there, then?'

'Marble Arch.'

'Ah. D'you believe in God, miss? We're all part of God, did you know that? Every man and woman, part of one great whole. This life is a moment, a tiny step on the way. We're animals in our bodies. We don't matter, except for the spark of something that carries on. Something divine. 'Scuse me, miss. I'm on the wrong line.'

He gathered himself up and headed for the stairs. Clavel followed him, but he was soon lost in the crowd. Clavel was moved, profoundly, by the confirmation that these people were no different flesh. Sorrow was the missing link. That bottomless sorrow to which he had no clue held these people together. It stood for them in the place of living wanderers. He walked on, stirred and elated: singing softly.

Were you there when we crucified our lord . . .?

Johnny went a little mad after he ran out on Braemar. He knew she didn't deserve the dirty names. Or if she did, then not from Johnny. He couldn't claim she'd tried to entrap him. It was nobody's fault but his own that he'd fallen in love. He wanted to go back and explain. But she didn't want to know: and in fact the whole can of worms opened by the suggestion about Clavel did not bear explanation. So he went crazy instead.

Assailed by homesickness, he sat in his room watching rewired *Sesame Street*; and fretted uselessly at the bowdlerisation of Oscar the Grouch. He would actively seek out Carlotta and the parrot, and yell advice and comment into his one-way tv control. He told her to make friends with the aliens. They were telepaths, he would remind her. They'd met a few dippy East Asians and a few paranoid Youros: they thought that got through to everyone. Remind them we exist, he shouted. Ask them in, invite them back.

He cleared his room of the anti-Aleutian debris he'd picked up: personally carried a heap of paper and charge plastic down to the incinerator and saw it fried to vapour. He felt better when he'd done that. How could he expect Clavel to come and save him if the ether around him was poisoned with blatant hostility?

He would wake up in the night feeling slimy, filthy. This used to happen in the American hospital in Amsterdam, when he was trying to get a clean test. His therapist talked to him about the connection between his different losses: communion with the machinery, sexual intercourse, social intercourse. The doctor advised frequent masturbation. Johnny would have to learn to enjoy self-love; and fight the self-hatred that might lead to violent behaviour. If he was going that way, he'd have to be put on permanent medication.

They were not easy on you in that place. In principle, they believed in non-committal quarantine. In principle they even believed in Johnny's innocence. But the responsibility was awful, and they let you know it.

He began to dream about the future. It was a good place. It was like a big, big ecocyclic mall, very safe and full of pretty greenery. Kids with ridiculous make-up raced around. There were some babies – welcome and much loved, not stealing anything from anyone. He would wake from one of these dreams feeling peaceful and reassured. He knew that none of the people in the dream mall was exactly human, but he felt okay about that.

The end of August was hot and grey and windy: fever weather. He had less work to do because people were not buying red meat; and therefore less money, but he wasn't going to starve. Idleness was more of a problem. It was a dull day in early September when he hallucinated for the first time. The alien looked at him out of the entrance to Holborn tube.

He crossed the street and found a newsagent dispenser shouting headlines at the rush-hour traffic. He inspected the machine all over: screen, masthead menupad, grinning delivery drawer. He had to buy a paper before he was convinced it was real.

It was the experience that he'd had in Fo, uncannily mimicked. Far too exact a copy to be anything but fake.

He went for his six-week medical and said nothing about his problems, suffered the objective sampling with the stoicism of despair. There was nothing wrong, according to Jatinder. Johnny had always known the man was a careless crook. He didn't need a doctor to tell him what was happening. The QV disease, which he had almost forgotten, had caught up with him. His mind had begun to rot.

Johnny's room had a window. It looked into the airwell between his building and a buried nineteenth-century façade. There was another window opposite, barely a metre away, grimy glass intact under a lintel of blurred stone flowers. It was closed off inside by a partition wall. There was a trompe l'oeil effect: Johnny's lit room was reflected there at an oddly convincing angle. He had often caught himself thinking he had a neighbour. When he started hallucinating he kept moving his bedscreen over, so he wouldn't imagine an alien in the reflected room. Mrs Frame's girl, who considered Johnny's view of the airwell a magnificent amenity, kept moving it away again.

The rains started early that year. Everyone was pleased. The cycle of feast and famine had already become traditional: no water for months, then gulp it until you choke. The old native English felt cosy about it, dreamed they were lording over the plains of India again. My God, the heat, Carruthers . . . Johnny had absorbed something of this feeling. The night the monsoon broke in earnest he felt calmer. He lay in bed listening to the storm, thinking of great London steaming gently as it drowned. Londoners would have to resign themselves soon: become amphibians or get away from that tidal river.

Braemar claimed that the way people reacted to the Aleutians was a meaningless hangover from '04. People had believed that the disaster was a 'punishment'. The Aleutians were interpreted the same way: it was nonsense, mass hysteria.

She was wrong. The punishment was real, and still going on. Poison seeping into the Pacific, teeming artificial cities in desert places; too much for the world to bear. He was being punished himself, for the wild excesses of twentieth-century technology. That was why the alien swam up in his rotting brain. He closed his eyes, sick and miserable. He had always known, deep in his heart, that no one could corrupt the NIH. If the Big Machinery said so he was infected, never mind how. How long would this foreplay last? You get confused, can't tell the difference between two years ago and yesterday. First you forget what you had for breakfast, then you forget what the word 'breakfast' means. How does a person cope with the onset of premature dementia?

\<Johnny, let me in.\>

The voice was so convincing that he got up and went to have a look. The alien was out there in the wet dark, clinging to the other windowsill. 'I can't!' he shouted. 'This window doesn't open!'

It fumbled in its clothes, then leaned and reached out with one clawed hand across the airwell. The glass melted. There was a pungent smell. The alien clambered, joints all wrong like a giant bat, and tumbled into his room. It was Clavel.

<What a storm,> she said. <Do you think there's something wrong?>

'Yeah, there's a fault. We're trying to fix it, but it's kind of endemic.' He was naked. 'Excuse me.' He pulled on his jeans. He brought out a towel and handed it to her.

She buried her face, scrubbed vigorously at her hair.

He reviewed the new situation, feeling drunk with relief. 'You're real, aren't you, Clavel.'

She dropped the towel. The dustmask she'd worn for disguise still hung under her chin, sopping. The dark centre of her face didn't look so bad in real life. He was kneeling in front of her, she reached out and grasped his upper arms and *stared*. What a gaze! He was grateful for her understanding.

'You have to travel incognito now you're famous, I can guess. Thank you, Clavel. I don't know why you're here, but *thank you* for being real.'

She knelt, joints turned the human way round again, dripping on to Mrs Frame's turf-effect rug. 'You didn't come,' she explained helplessly. 'So I came to you.'

He was entranced. He gazed at the creature from another star, staggered by the impossible abyss that lay between them. The wonder of her presence was far greater than it had been in Fo, because she was accredited now. She wasn't a fake or a figment of his eejay's imagination. She was genuine. He reached out a tentative hand. Immediately, she grasped it. He felt the weird texture of her skin, saw the trimmed claws, counted the fingers, stroked the thick horny pads that would make her fist into the foot of a running beast.

Clavel, her dark epicanthic eyes fixed on his, bore the handling without protest. She drew a deep, shaken breath. He realised he might be distressing her. He laid her hand down gently, and went to fetch the passport.

'Why did you send me this? You sent it, didn't you?'

She lifted her shoulders: the gesture that reached her eyes, much more like a smile than her bared teeth.

'Jivanamukta made it for me. One of Lugha's people. Oh, I've been begging, borrowing and stealing to get us back together. Most of my own artisans died, you know. Why didn't you come, Johnny?'

The easy spoken English startled, and almost disappointed him. She was dressed in Karen street clothes, dark embroidered breeches and a batwinged linen blouse; a sash wound around her muscular waist. The clothes were deeply grimy as if they'd seen months of wear. She was carrying a small daypack, Asean make.

'Never mind. I came to you, there's no difference.'

She shrugged out of the wet straps, and produced a bottle of clear brown liquid without a label. 'It's whisky. We copied it. Three of your months old, I promise. I wanted to bring you something.'

She looked up at him very solemnly, the nasal space pinched in and a corner of a sharp white tooth chewing at her lower lip.

Mesmerised, Johnny brought two beakers: dispenser cups that he rinsed out and reused until they split. Mrs Frame's precious crockery was always returned to the kitchen. He was back in the game after all. Stuff Krung Thep, Johnny Guglioli's on stream. He thought of Carlotta: of home and freedom.

'Shit, I can't make a record.'

Clavel showed teeth. 'I ought to tell you, Johnny. I should have told you before. I don't reckon much to organised religion.'

'Neither do I.'

He could understand her English, but he didn't know what she meant. He'd have *invited* her inside his head, if he knew how.

'Will it be okay if we have a recorded session later?'

<If that's what you want.>

He grinned. 'Great. Thank you.'

She poured the whisky and they drank.

Clavel swallowed the spirit carefully. He had taught himself to manage open beakers, dipping his face and tipping his head quickly back. The false warmth running through and through him couldn't stop the shivers.

He felt the intimacy of the quarrel within himself. Clavel had as much Rajath in him as anyone else, still as keen on the loot. But things would get dangerous, and things would get ugly: he could see it laid out. It was Clavel's curse and blessing, this capacity to be frightened at a distance. What harms us ever harms us now. What harms any part of our self is still injury.

And sure as Johnny is myself, this world is part of us.

'I want to tell you everything. No more kidding around.'

Clavel's teeth were chattering so he could hardly speak, not from cold but from excitement. How to proceed? It must be true. He truly had never been in love before, because he'd never felt like this. How do people manage to lie down together in this state? (No! He really – *go away* – he did not need any advice.) He laughed, showing his violently trembling hands.

<I want to get out of these wet clothes!>

'Oh, of course.'

Johnny brought another towel and Clavel stripped to his underwear. Johnny's eyes followed his every move with a candour that burned. The selfishness of love burns clear through the body. My claw is in your flesh. I will lie down with myself. Now, they thought, Clavel and his lover, half out of their single mind with lust and pure spiritual joy. *Now and here, myself and I . . .*

Johnny knew Thai 'Mekong' whisky: brewed in a fortnight, but civilised stuff, not much stronger than beer. He was halfway through his drink before he realised he'd been fooled by the universal translator gadget. This was not Mekong. It was something very soft and very potent. Johnny wasn't much of a drinker. He looked into the beaker ruefully. At least it wasn't eating the plastic. He was in Fo again, taking unknown risks. But the kid wouldn't harm him. He'd always been sure of that. She'd gone very quiet. He was afraid he'd offended her modesty by staring at that breastless torso, the weird dropped shoulders; great V of sliding muscle wrapped where her ribs should be. Her damp and scanty dun undersuit showed every detail.

<How you've longed for this,> said Clavel. <I'm the one who can give you what you most desire in the world.>

Johnny was shocked at having his need stated so bluntly, by the voice in his head. It was like getting fingered by the faith healer. Hey, you there. You in the back row, with the crippling fatal disease!

'You know about that? I guess you do. And you can help me?'

<You must *do* something,> said Clavel. <I am as ready as I can be, without a sign from you. I'll *die* if you don't touch me.>

The alien was shuddering visibly. 'Huh? Oh, yes.' He held out his hand. That seemed to be what she meant. Two half-naked bodies, a sticky smell of yeast. Briefly, the accusation he'd yelled at Braemar crossed his mind. *You want me to fuck the alien for you . . .* But he wasn't going to risk his incredible prize on account of petty squeamishness. She was such a kid, this alien. Quite harmless. She used his hand as an anchor, and pulled herself into his arms. The closeness must be part of it, skin against skin.

<My wanderers are hiding,> Clavel told him. <Because I'm so scared.> She reached into her bodysuit-thing, brought out a hand crawling with blood-coloured lice. They glistened. Johnny stared, too disgusted and fascinated to move a muscle. The arm around his shoulders drew his face down. She began to kiss at him, the way a cat kisses: thin, stretched lip and an edge of tooth. She touched his nipples, traced whorls of hair down to his belly. She pressed the bristling hollow of her nasal cavity to his face, at the same time trying to reach the louse-covered hand into his pants.

<Kiss? Do you not kiss?> She touched his nose. <Your – your *this*. It gets in the way.>

He was paralysed with astonishment. A mad voice inside was still asking quite seriously *how much is the cure worth?* But then he tried, gently, to get away: and found he couldn't. This was beyond a joke. Clavel shucked off her underwear. The naked chicken-skin baboon crouched over him. It took his hand and buried it to the wrist in a fold that opened along its groin. The chasm inside squirmed with life. Part of its wall swelled, burgeoning outward.

'*Ah –*'

The baboon clutched his wrist and worked its bellyfold up and down, its thighs slipped along his hips. It wasn't female after all, but a kind of hermaphrodite. Something slid out of the fold: an everted bag of raw flesh, narrowing to a hooked end. It was enormous. Johnny felt a jolt of horrible arousal, like the affectless clutch in the groin he'd get from a glimpse of violent pornography. Clavel's eyes were still fixed on his, *still sweet and childlike*. Suddenly, he lost his nerve completely. He struggled and protested, still attempting to laugh off this gross and ludicrous social error but inwardly totally panicked.

The alien didn't know what he meant, or didn't care. It descended on him. He tried to scream. He could not. And this was what he had always feared, why he had run from Braemar. Stark horror! This was how it was always going to end. The faith

so close to fear, wonder so close to terror, betrayed him utterly:
stripped him, robbed him and flung him out, meaningless, into a
bursting vacuum.

  <Johnny? I love you. Please, Johnny, don't make me stop – >

ii

Braemar, mistress of signs, never worked from home. She was
unavailable for phone-in interviews. She held on to the enhanced
status of mobility: you won't make plug-in bonded labour out of
me. But on a night like this she was glad enough to shut the
mortuary drawer behind her.

Billy was crying. Kamla was fast asleep in his nursery with her
head in a box tv, her dreams awash with advertising aimed at
people sixty years or so her senior. Brae left her: she'd wake and
grizzle if you took the thing off. She changed Billy's wet pyjamas
and bedding. The poor little bugger then wanted to chat, he
probably hadn't had a word out of his mother all day. But she
stonewalled on that. One has to keep the limits clear.

Fed Trixie. The smell in the kitchen was vicious. Braemar had
refused to buy a gimmicky 'robot' that Ionela wanted, and this was
the Transylvanian revenge. Ionela, drunk on nouvelle consumer-
ism since Braemar shipped her tribe over here, had decided it was
her Christian-Sustainable-Developmentalist duty to make do with
just one cleaning product. The evil woman had been caught using
toilet cleaner to rub up Braemar's antique furniture.

Domestic robots don't work, and they make one look a vulgar
fool. But the peasant craved toys, craved any kind of power.
Braemar could remember going through that stage.

She had been to her pharmacist. It was lucky that the poor
devoured patent medicines, or undead monsters like Braemar
would be in trouble. There were hardly enough of them to support
the surviving illicit dealers. Nowadays, everything was bloody
legal and the quacks (Braemar didn't believe in doctors) never
prescribed anything but electricity. If you broke your leg they'd
give you a course of ECT.

She ought to eat. There was nothing in the larder but a dish of
potato mash smeared with baby saliva, and the end of a carton of
egg. She poured it into a dish and stuck it in the micro. Eat
sparingly, keep calm. Maybe you'll live for ever.

Trixie followed her to the drawing room. The wall panel had
defaulted to a river scene, green and moony shadows. The room's
floorlength windows were wet and black, the glass set to let in no
light and reflect nothing. She thought she would use no more
loony tunes, that was getting stale. She would move on: maybe
Alison de Vere. She walked around tidying things. Stopped in front
of a mirror and preened. That's a pretty woman still, in her pretty
suit of peacock blue and gold thread. She felt how the love of
lovely things would grow on her as other pleasures receded. She
would become a dragon buried to the eyes in her musty hoard, like
granny in the old house (so long gone) in Nairobi.

Outside in the wet dark there were rows of glistening tended
vegetables that Braemar would never see on her table. No one can
change their nature, she was not a giving sort of person. But it was
mysteriously soothing, a secret indulgence, to let herself be robbed
blind by the Marmune tribe.

She woke up the tv and checked a few headlines. The bouncing
rouble. Korean concern, will New Zion once again bale out
Moscow? The failure of New Zion: overcrowding, Eve-riots,
trouble brewing. How strange it was to see the human world going
on so complacently. She had an urge to reach into the illusory
depth and shake someone by the shoulders.

Once the newspaper barons owned the tv stations, it was
obvious that the papers would take to the screen. The tabloids and
the quality dailies and the weekend sections: faxed to your breakfast bar, on the street corners; and dominating the multiscreen in
the living room as well. Once again, money achieves the inevitable. What else but a 'newspaper' could carry enough conflicting
viewpoints to satisfy the twenty-first century punter?

What was less predictable was the way the rest of the tv
withered away. There was the BBC (or similar) for worthy projects and Westminster: and that was practically it but for the news
in a myriad forms. News and commentary; people scarcely wanted
anything else. There was enough horror, enough drama, enough
art, enough pathos there for anyone – certainly enough fiction.

She had done a minor commercial about this trend: *Death of a Sitcom*.

It was against Braemar's principles to buy Indie tv. if anyone wanted her to watch their self-indulgent rubbish it had to be free. She rifled through the current codes that had come her way . . . Thinking about the absurdity of keeping Kamla in education. Thinking about the incredible barrage of human diversity tapped by that space hanging on her wall. Johnny Guglioli's world view was so different. His planet earth was the citadel of New York: a beleaguered fortress waiting for the cavalry. So young. How could he see the world that Braemar believed in? Always more problems, always more solutions. *It's just the normal noises, Johnny*. We don't need any help.

She was at a low ebb tonight. She remembered sweating in the hotel room in Karen with the scared pig of an Englishman. It is true, she thought. I sent that girl to her death. Johnny's right, there's no way back to civilisation from here. She was afraid (*afraid?*) that she had pushed Johnny too hard the other night, deliberately. Probably she had meant to drive him away, anything rather than drag him farther into this business. She closed her eyes. There he was. The dignified young American, so self-possessed among her second-class celebs: and shabby enough to satisfy Thoreau himself. *Beware of any enterprise that requires new clothes* . . .

Well, he was gone and White Queen would have to think of something else. Try again, fail again. Fail better.

That's the whole story, she decided wearily. That's our best case. And wondered why on earth it seemed so important that the fake superbeings shouldn't complete their takeover.

She opened a window. Took a few drops of onei, set the decoder to read an antique tape of *Miami Vice*, set the sound filter to block out the ambient noise of London and the hifi to sample the rain. The air was soft and damp as night in Africa, and stirring with natural music, *musique naturelle*.

Trixie quietly went over to the bin, chucked up her dry owl pellets and came back to the nest of cushions, settled her muzzle on Braemar's knee with a contented sigh. The Annie Mah dress with the glow-worm skirts . . . Braemar lay in a waking dream of idealised memory, pure epicurean pleasure.

'Get up.'

Johnny Guglioli was standing at the open window. He was drenched to the skin, and he was pointing a hunting rifle at her.

'I'm going to kill you.'

She keyed out the hifi. Johnny had no shirt under his jacket, his feet were bare in plastic sandals. Water streamed from his loose hair. He looked terrible: his mouth slack, the lines of his face wiped away. The house key was in her hand, power to do all sorts of things, but her mind wouldn't work.

'You set me up!' he screamed. 'You did it. You damned whore you're going to die. *Call off the dog.*'

The Doberman was trotting towards Johnny, tail swinging gently.

'Basket, Trix.' Braemar stood carefully, heart thumping, the onei leaving her in a rush of icy chills. 'What's going on, Johnny?'

He sobbed. He jabbed sideways with the rifle, a cheery Gallé cat flew and shattered on the parquet. He turned and cleared the rest of that table, swept the pictures above it from the wall and stabbed and trampled them, using the rifle like a bayonet.

She was wondering how far it was safe to preempt him, to humiliate herself ahead of his orders. She was wondering how long the rot had been spreading, if there was anything left of Johnny in that slack shell. Should she undress?

His wet hair flew in his face. He tossed it back, and smashed some Tyrone crystal. 'Your police bodyguard's gone.'

'I know. They're on strike.'

There was nothing else he could reach. He pointed the rifle at Braemar again, his hands perfectly steady. She looked down it, ideas spinning uselessly, with a dry mouth and loosening bowels: and suddenly became exasperated.

'Oh, who cares? I'm sixty-three years old. I'm tired, and my complexion's past praying for. Go ahead. Shoot me. Make my day.'

'*Sixty-three?* You said you were forty-seven.'

She laughed. 'That was two seasons ago. Forty-nine isn't smart this year. Go on, Johnny. I'm far too much of a coward to kill myself, but I'd be crazy to turn down an opportunity like this.'

The rifle wavered. 'The alien broke into my room,' he whispered. 'It raped me.'

'Raped?'

He bared his teeth. 'It – they're hermaphrodites.'

She began to walk towards him. She walked 'til the muzzle of the rifle was touching her breastbone. She took it from him, and carefully restored the safety catch. Johnny let her do it. He sat down on a swan-backed chaise longue, expensive copy of a gloriously decadent Regency original; dripping over the watered silk.

'How do you tell?' he asked. 'You use onei, you must know. How do you tell if you're dreaming?'

'Try continuous memory. If you can string the course of the day together without waking yourself, then however bad things seem you are probably awake already.'

'I can't do that. I can't even remember how I got here. It's the QV, I'm going.' He began to sob, heels of his hands thrust into his eye sockets.

'I don't think so,' said Braemar. It was true, she realised. She genuinely would rather be dead than watch Johnny succumb to the subtle poison his body might be carrying. Rather he killed her first. But with profound relief, she knew that it had not happened. He was sane. She touched him: quickly drew back when he flinched away. 'Tell me?'

'I was feeling weird. I was having dreams about the aliens' planet, watching tv round the clock and shouting at it; and I don't know. Generally going crazy. Then I saw her in the street. Of course I didn't take that seriously. Tonight she broke into my room. Clavel. She'd sneaked out of Uji on her own and got to London passing for human. She told me some "artisan" made the passport: they can do a lot of things we've never guessed. I was completely off guard. She told me she was going to reveal everything. Just what you've been saying. How they're not superbeings, how they've tricked us. And then – '

Silence. He stared and stared, his eyes like bruises.

'You said rape. What does that mean?'

'*What I said*. What d'you fucking want, Brae?'

'No, I don't want a blow-by-blow account.' She broke off, electrified: pity turned to iron in her voice. 'But you'd better be ready. Other people will.'

Johnny looked around, maybe for the first time aware of his surroundings. He ran his hands through his hair. 'What a mess.' He shuddered. 'I'm sorry, Brae.' He wiped his fingers on his jacket, looked at them, frowned and wiped them again. 'They're gone.'

'What?'

'The bugs. They were all over me.'

Braemar drew breath. 'Clavel? What happened to Clavel?'

'Clavel was . . .' Again his eyes stared, seeing monsters. 'They were all around me.' He grinned, a gruesome rictus. 'I don't think I shot her. Better check the gun. Clavel left, after . . . and then I don't know much what I did.' He made an enormous effort. 'Can I have a shower?'

'No.'

She got up, pulled on her house shoes, pulled him to his feet. 'Not yet. We're going to the police.'

The police station was on the edge of the infill. Beyond it ordered street lights died: a rat's nest of strung bulbs and jampacked lit windows twinkled. In front of it searchlights played. The police seemed to be dealing with a major incident. The road was full of people in fluorescent raingear holding umbrellas over 360s; rushing around with loud-hailers. Braemar stopped the car before she got too close. The confusion terrified her. So Johnny wasn't alone tonight. It was the end, then, the phoney war was over. She'd almost prayed for this moment: but she felt sick.

One of the rain-geared figures strode across her view, brandishing a plastic placard for the news screens across Europe.

Braemar laughed. 'Of course, it's the strike.'

She got out of the car. So did Johnny. When she looked around, he'd vanished. He was walking quickly back down the street. She had to run to catch up, her slippers spurting water.

'Johnny, where are you going? Come on, please, *come on*. You can't protect a rapist. I know telling people is going to be vile but that's not possible. One does not do that.'

He kept on walking. 'Sorry. Can't help you. My mama didn't bring me up to cross no picket lines.'

She grabbed his arm. He shook her off. She got in front of him, impassioned and righteous. 'Johnny, you can't walk away from this. You have been assaulted, physically and worse: treated with vicious contempt. Think, it could happen to others. And maybe the rest are worse than Clavel, once they drop the pretence.'

He stopped, shoulders hunched against the rain. 'You are insulting my intelligence, Brae.'

The rain fell between them, striking the pavement in hissing crowds. Above them a hoarding had shorted out. It fizzled and croaked an occasional loud blurred syllable, as if trying to call for help. A bevy of ringnecked parakeets huddled along the frame. They dived out into the wet at each burst of sound, sherbet green in the street lights, screaming an immigrants' lament for another city of trees and dust, where the rain was never so chill.

'Okay, forget the propaganda. What about revenge?'

Johnny sat down on the edge of the kerb, fists balled between his knees. He glanced back. The small crowd of picketers and their attendant newspersons had noticed nothing. After a moment, Braemar sat beside him. He forced himself to look at her. He was thinking of the first time, in Africa. He had told himself that night that this was the best sex there could ever be in the world. When it starts off so desperate, so *unstoppable* it is indistinguishable from rape. And then you find she wanted it all the time . . .

'I cannot do it, Brae. I just cannot.' He looked away. 'I don't know if the rape accusation would stand up. I wasn't in control of myself. She – it – didn't finish. I did. I was . . . Do I have to explain?'

'No,' said Braemar at last. She sighed, acknowledging defeat. 'You don't have to explain.'

She tucked the minicooper up to the kerb. It was raining hard. They sat in the brief refuge of its lighted shell.

'What d'you want to do now? Send for your mad scientist to take samples?'

Braemar shook her head.

'Oh, God, Brae. These little bug . . . lice things . . .'

'Don't, Johnny.'

'It knows where I live. It was watching me for days. And the others know too. I felt them: in her, in its mind.'

'Don't give yourself the horrors. They are aliens, remember. Biologically speaking, one of those cells on human flesh is a fish on a bicycle.' She took his hand, gripped it. 'Listen, Johnny. The Aleutians have done no deliberate harm to any human but Sarah and she, as far as they were concerned, was committing an act of war. They tampered with some machines and there were casualties. But by my reading those deaths were unplanned. Okay, they made some wild threats – well, everybody does it. They are not hostile. You can believe that. I believe it. She's not going to come after you again. This was a ghastly mistake.'

Johnny turned and stared at her in disbelief.

Braemar dropped her eyes. 'Yes, okay, I know. It's not my usual line. But I want you to be clear about this.' She sighed. 'Clavel's in love with you, Johnny. Remember how she called you "Daddy", back in Africa? They believe in reincarnation. A "Clavel" might be born in every generation. It's their big romantic quest, to find another edition of yourself: your "true" parent or your "true" child. I should have told you, but I didn't know how you'd take it.'

'Thanks. That helps a lot.'

She couldn't tell if he'd taken in a word. His tone was bitter.

'I'm sorry. I don't know how to say how much I wish it hadn't happened.' She hesitated. 'I think you saved me from making a very stupid mistake. A denouncement like that could have backfired badly. Can I offer you a bed for the night?'

He didn't answer. He was looking at the house. 'Is your housebox bust again, or did you leave those lights on on purpose?'

The lights were soon explained. The doorman had become a pale mess of shapeless plastic, spreading down the wall. It must have started on its anti-intruder routines before it died. The front door opened at a touch. They retreated.

'My God,' whispered Johnny. 'She wasn't alone. They were close by, watching. I thought that part was a hallucination.'

'How many were there?'

'Four, maybe five. They'd come looking for Clavel. I don't know if I saw them in my room, or if Clavel just knew they were near. We call the police,' he decided. 'And wait in the car.'

'They won't come,' said Braemar. 'And I have people in there.'

The silent hallway was empty. Trixie was lying at the foot of the stairs. Braemar whimpered faintly and dropped to her knees. But the antisense lifted its head and struggled groggily upright.

'Good dog,' whispered Brae. 'No licking! Bad girl!'

Johnny took her by the shoulders and put her and the dog aside. 'They're still here, I'm sure of it. I'm going to try and get my rifle. Stay close.'

Up to the first floor and not a sign. The drawing room door was open, the tv running its decor loop. The rifle was where they had left it.

'Got to check the children.'

She hurried to the stairs, the antisense silent beside her, Johnny behind. The aliens came out of the nursery. The landing was brilliantly lit, toys strewn about: the figures imposed on it seemed like anime. Their presence here, out in the human world, was so far from context they did not register as substantial. One of them was shouldering Kamla's boxheaded, inert body.

'Ah,' said this one. 'Clavel?'

There were four of them. The other three were carrying long-barrelled bulky firearms: human weapons.

'We are unarmed,' said Braemar quickly. 'Drop it, Johnny.' The rifle clattered. 'He's not here. We don't mean him any harm. You have no need to take a hostage.'

The aliens did not look at each other, but they seemed to consult. The one who was carrying Kamla put her down. 'Unarmed,' he said. It must be another of the Uji talkers. Braemar couldn't remember their names. 'What's that, then?'

Suddenly they made a rush, animal silent. Braemar dropped her hand from Trixie's collar.

'Roll over, baby.'

Trixie flew, teeth bared, making the horrible low noise of a big dog that means business. Johnny's rifle had made no impression, but now the aliens screamed. One of them fired, yelled louder as if panicked by the noise and fired again. Whoosh! Heat flared, Trixie dropped like a stone. The aliens swept past the humans, one of them continuing to yell like a banshee. They ran out of the front door and slammed it behind them.

The little boy had started to cry but he was barely half awake and was soon comforted. They put Kamla back to bed, still peacefully boxed.

Outside, the street was quiet. Braemar went with a torch to the Marmune quarters and managed to knock up Ionela's aged uncle, who claimed to have heard nothing and was nasty about being disturbed. They cleared up Trixie, and went back to the drawing room. Rain was blowing in through a window which no longer had any glass. Braemar stepped over debris to her cocktail cabinet.

'No one will have heard. This is a soundproof neighbourhood. Drink?'

'No, thanks.'

She sat down beside him, with the whisky decanter and a glass. Her business suit was filthy. There hadn't been much blood involved in bagging up Trixie's seared remains, but what there was had joined the smears of rain and dirt. The watered silk of the chaise longue, she noticed, was ruined.

'I am truly sorry about all this mess.'

'Some art must disintegrate.' She giggled. 'Hey, shall we phone the police now, and claim aliens smashed the place up?'

Johnny started. 'Oh, the taxi. I came in a taxi. I think . . . I don't believe I paid the guy.'

Braemar looked him over, and grinned. 'Don't worry about it. I expect he's feeling grateful to be alive.'

'Are you really sixty-three years old?'

She nodded, lightheaded with relief.

He calculated. 'Kamla is your granddaughter.'

'She is.'

Johnny choked. 'Do you know, she made a heavy pass at me?'

'Of course she did.'

It was hard to remember that the aliens had not personally wrecked this room. The devastation was so clearly the wake of their passage: an unintended blow, entirely without malice. Braemar gazed, counting casualties: and the last of them Johnny, wild-eyed, shaking, grinning with adrenalin, but somewhere inside how deeply, ominously *relieved*.

'I suppose you're ready to sign up now, aren't you, Johnny?'

'Yeah,' he said. 'Yeah. You bet I am.' A vengeful grin broke. He couldn't hold it. 'Brae, I feel so – ' He did not know how to start telling her. 'When you told me you'd got stolen tissue, I was so fucking *terrified* . . . And then Clavel came. I thought it – she – oh, God. I thought it was cleansing me of the QV.'

So many layers of shameful revelation: waking up sticky-wet in the night, burning those papers. Uncontrollable bodily functions, scared kid who talks big but never could stand up to authority. Believing in the Big Machines because he knew they could punish, believing abjectly in the aliens because he hoped they could reward. The revolting experience he'd had was no more than he deserved. Everything about Johnny Guglioli was small, stupid, unclean.

'*I wish I was dead.*'

'Oh, no,' said Braemar. She put her arms round him, hugged hard. Johnny went rigid for a moment, then piled into the hug fervently. He pulled back, looked her in the eye with lingering suspicion.

'What's this? First aid?'

'*No.*'

They kissed. He had kissed her before, but never been sure of the meaning. He'd beeen hypocritically shocked and secretly glad that such good sex didn't mean what it ought to, in young Johnny's simple philosophy. But context is everything. They kissed for a long time, the spark that crosses the gap. Came to rest finally, plastered against each other in a desperate pose that frankly admitted far more than lust.

'Why the *fuck* did you leave me like that in Fo?'

She pushed her face into the front of his sodden jacket, thumped at him with one fist, the other hand still clinging to him as if he was saving her from drowning.

'Anstandigkeit. Shit, I did not mean to do this.'

'Well, it's done now,' said Johnny complacently. 'What is anstandigkeit? Not that I care, so long as you promise never to touch the stuff again.'

She attempted to recover some composure, prised herself free. 'Decent behaviour. I didn't want to get you involved with the red-hand gang, so I wanted you to think badly of me. Anyway – ' She shrugged, offhand. 'There was the age thing.'

'You can forget that. Don't ever mention that.'

Braemar smiled. 'I won't have to. It will mention itself. But I'm serious, listen to me. *I don't blame the Aleutians.* What wrong did they do tonight? They had a right to kill Trixie. They saw exactly what she was: a weapon, nothing more. I don't blame them for anything, Johnny. I only refuse to see certain lovely things destroyed, lost and meaningless for ever, if I can by any means keep them alive.' She was embarrassing herself. 'Let me give you an example, dear cousin. I think the American Constitution is a truly, truly remarkable document. The Aleutians will not. They won't value it at all. I've no doubt they have their own equally touching notions. I don't mean we're better than they are, in any sense. I wouldn't hazard a guess either way. But if they stay, and things go on the way they are now, the Constitution goes down into the dust. Forever. Do you understand? I want you to help me to fight them, but that's the only reason why. Well?'

He studied her earnest face, fascinated. 'I'm allowed to sign up as an anti-Aleutian terrorist, but only if I do it for purely aesthetic reasons?'

She nodded.

What had happened to the cynical promoter of the status quo, the venal demi-mondaine? Where'd she go? She was here. Braemar didn't become any less Braemar for revealing that she had principles of a kind: a weird and oblique morality.

Johnny laughed. He shook his head. 'These sentiments appal me. Can't I just go out and git some gooks, and be sorry afterwards?' He glanced at the tv panel, still playing its chaste river sequence. 'Do you by any chance have a record of Jessye Norman on top of Mount Rushmore singing the "Battle Hymn of the Republic"?'

'Did she cut that?'

'I haven't a clue. It's an image I have, seems to suit the tone of the conversation.'

It was very cold in the room now. Braemar glanced around. 'Did you see my cigarettes? I suppose you'd like that shower.' She hesitated. 'I don't know what happened, and I'm not asking for details. But if you didn't want it it wasn't sex, whatever your involuntary reaction. It was common assault. She beat you up: forget about it.'

He was touched. She didn't need to be so careful. He had fallen into the firefight, into the zone he'd once visited like a second home. When the world is bursting into flame around you, you don't agonise over what happened hours, or even minutes, ago. You grab what the moment offers.

He had settled in London because it was where Braemar lived. She was his enemy, but the idea that he might bump into her one day did a lot to make life bearable.

'I've thought about you so much.' He touched her hand. The profound *rightness* of being allowed to touch her again warmed him all through, like the onset of a very strong and gentle medicine.

'In my lonely little room.'

Braemar took his hand and held it to the peacock blue khamiz, hard against the live movement of her heart. The vitality of that beat against his palm, through the silk, seemed to slow the whole world. He remembered the unbearable pauses of sex with Braemar, pools of exquisite suspense deep in the riot.

'Tell me,' she said. 'I want to know every detail, and then act it out . . . Do you think that's a tacky idea?'

'Awful. Let's do it.'

Trixie?

The synthetic Doberman had joined the spirit world. Her claws would rattle along the halls for a while, her smooth head would be an absence that the hand reached for. She would fade away: fade with the house in Nairobi, with steps and doorways of the past, ghosts that surround the body, layer upon layer.

Braemar listened. The fantasy clung to her: the disorienting thrill of having entered, *informed* the erotic puppet that was herself in his mind. Johnny was deeply asleep. She got up very quietly, pulled on the grey kurta that she used as a house robe. She had unloaded his rifle before they came to bed. She didn't trust her ability to comfort that much. If he woke his adrenalin-fuelled bravado would most likely have deserted him, and there might be hell to pay. Where was the gun now? She couldn't find it in the dark.

In the morning she would be back where she had been in Africa, but with a Johnny older and wiser (and so much more lovable). He might be recovered enough to be suspicious about the way she had let him off the rape exposé. She had never been tender with his feelings before. She'd been trying to pick a fight for so long. Why was she turning down this chance? She hoped he'd be too smart to ask. She did not want to spell out the answer.

You don't pick a fight that you can't win. You wait, and husband what advantages you may have for more covert action.

She crept down the stairs. Her drawing room looked horrible. The wrecked bijoux reproached her like abandoned toys. Since she was awake and prey to depressing thoughts she might as well clear up a bit. She moved into the room, picking up fragments. The Aleutian was crouching on the floor by the open window, so still and empty of presence it might have been made of wet stone.

It lifted its head.

Clavel lifted her head. Braemar stared at the alien. The moment might never be recorded in the annals of human/Aleutian relations: but this night had changed something for ever.

'Clavel,' she said. 'Your friends were here, looking for you.' A glance and suppressed gesture took in the wreckage. 'Please go. I don't want them back.'

'It's okay. We know where I am.'

Braemar had studied the scientist's wild results, and the African tapes, and the stuff that Uji made public, until her mind ached. She began to have visions – flaring from the discipline she didn't know to one she had made her own. That use of the first person plural gave her pause. In Aleutia, she wondered, did 'we' dig holes in the road? Did 'we' increase the gas bills, and predict the weather? Undoubtedly, yes. Ellen Kershaw would be thrilled.

Clavel noticed the wall panel, and recoiled like an atheist in church. 'It was a chapel. I am so sorry. Johnny was very upset.'

Her petty impulse to palm the mess off as the work of Clavel's friends collapsed. You couldn't lie to an Aleutian about another Aleutian. Was it possible that *Clavel* had had time enough to get to know the 'three to five million'? Some of them at least she knew so well that she needed no script, no update to follow the story. They are born again, she thought. They are born again and again, until everything they were has been developed to the uttermost: and nothing can happen that isn't expected and understood. Braemar stared, mesmerised, into eyes that had opened upon Eden before the fall. The human race is not so stupid, after all. It doesn't go down on its concerted knees for nothing.

In Braemar's world, it was widely accepted as proven that the brain chemistry and the individual were one and the same. But that Universe is its own fastest simulator. The whole mapping would never be known, the nature of the link maybe never pinned down. How does the genome 'be' a person?

'Is it true?' she asked. 'Do you *remember* being alive before? Are you consciously the same person, for ever and ever?'

Clavel made a cracked noise in her throat.

'Why is that funny? No, don't tell me, let me guess. There are schools of thought like the layered cities of the Indus failing to decide that question.'

She was being cruel. The immortal superbeing, presently a desolate teenager, couldn't guess why she was subjected to this philosophical taunting. She probably didn't even know in what relation Braemar stood to Johnny. Telepathy's no different from other means of understanding. It loses sensitivity under stress.

Clavel's dark nasal crumpled. 'Are you a woman? I thought I knew what that meant, so far as it matters. But the worst thing was I tried to *treat him like a woman*. What does that mean?'

Touché.

Suddenly Braemar was filled with pity. How does it feel to be a devout telepath, and discover in the midst of passion that your faith is empty, that the beloved has received none of your sending, that the world is not what you supposed? How does it feel to rape someone you love? She saw the horror in Clavel's alien eyes, and wanted to tell her how time seals over these terrible caesura; how life goes on.

Clavel still crouched, motionless. She was probably saying she knew about the healing power of time, thank you. Nothing reached Braemar. Telepathy does not exist. But to be immortal, and feminine, and unmutilated by the secret fear . . .

She struggled with the bitter envy, and with awe. These perceptions belong to me, she told herself. I'm imagining this. She's *alien*, that's all. Equal but different!

'I want to tell you everything,' said Clavel humbly. 'About the ways we've fooled you. I meant to tell Johnny. That is what I *meant* to do. Are you a priest? I think you must be. Will you make a record?'

Clavel is still dancing by the stone-age fire, still painting on the cave walls, still leading, by an aeons-past chance fall of the tumbling dice, her half-beast siblings in the hunt.

'No,' said Braemar. 'I don't want your confession. There's nothing you can tell me that I don't know already. Go away.'

Clavel knelt for a moment longer. She stood, she nodded sadly, and slipped out into the dark.

Johnny had a TENS bracelet on his wrist, an electronic sedative he'd accepted under protest. He woke up, anyway, to the sound of crying. He tugged the bracelet off, groped and found the switch on a bedside lamp.

Braemar's room was shades of straw, cornhusk, dove grey: softly swathed old-fashioned decor; little furniture. She was sitting at her dressing table, naked, head down among the armaments. She wasn't making much noise. He felt absolutely an intruder, but he couldn't pretend he hadn't woken.

She looked up when he was halfway across the room, and the tears stopped abruptly.

'What's wrong, Brae?'

She shook her head.

So Henny-Penny, Cockie-Lockie and Chicken-Licken set off together to tell the king the sky was falling. No one paid any attention. They knew Henny-Penny was a silly vain female trying to make herself important.

She wiped her face on a handful of ecru tissue. 'I feel so old,' she whispered. 'I look the way I do. But I feel as old, at sixty-three, as I ever thought I would.' She stared into the mirror. 'I am worse than old. I am dead. I am something that ought to be dead.'

Johnny crouched at her side and kissed her, gently. 'I won't let them get you.'

'Oh, Johnny. That's exactly what Trixie used to say to me.'

She pushed her fingers into his hair and pulled his face close against her small, soft breasts. 'I feel naked like an animal in a zoo. I think Aleutians are watching us. Let's get back into bed, hide our heads.'

She had changed, since Africa. He found her body as greedy but somehow less accessible, a more difficult study. Loving Braemar was going to be more work than being humoured by the lady in red; and the rewards less simple. But infinitely greater.

i

At Uji, the house and the stone garden were protected from the hill country cool season by an invisible mist of warmth. The Aleutians sat on the outer verandah, poking fingers through the veil into chill air. Kumbva, Rajath, Aditya were on fire with their adventure. Rajath's master at arms was calmer, but wore an air of quiet alarm. It had been unwise, scary, pleasurable and shameful. They couldn't leave it alone. The spectacle of themselves, brandishing those barbaric weapons . . .

<How I screamed!> cried Kumbva, with enormous relish. <I was so frightened.>

<How amazing,> marvelled Aditya. <I've known that I'm supposed to be brave and react quickly in violent situations. And look at that. I do!>

Undoubtedly Aditya had saved their lives by dealing with the terrifying weapon the householders had.

<Those teeth!>

Rajath groaned. He was lying informally curled, a scarf wrapped around his head. He pushed at the lovely one with a feeble, invalidish gesture. <Please. You're making me feel sick.>

It had been unnecessary. The truant Clavel had been quite safe, and the house his rescuers had broken into had been the home of a friend. The households of the bold band did their best to soothe and calm, aware that raw embarrassment was keeping the recount going, as much as anything. It would play itself out, the irritation would fade. There would remain a nugget of fresh awareness. Since Kaoru's death they had travelled round this planet with their local guides, meeting significant characters and everywhere the usual hordes of clerics. But they had failed to grasp the scale of this place;

or of its dangers. Their recent escapade had been a very different experience.

<That thing . . .> Aditya was still crackling. <So ghastly.>

They had put the sterile weapons back in the locker in Kaoru's cottage, where they had found them. Aditya's eyes gleamed. <Maybe we should wear them the whole time?>

Rajath groaned in disgust.

Kumbva put his cowrie bag on his head for fun and ran through the dusk up to Kaoru's cottage. He danced in the wet grass, spreading his arms – a purely feminine delight in ownership. Though their sponsor had chosen to die after the terrifying days of the ultimatum, they remained in many ways under his protection. He had willed the manor to them, with all its resources: a magnificent gift.

They had added some touches to the shrine; moved Kaoru's favourite possessions in here. The tape they had made of their benefactor played continually. They presumed the proper record was elsewhere. This was a meaningless fragment, but it seemed a nice gesture to display it.

Clavel was kneeling, stiffly, in front of the case that held the Itchiku kimono. His chaplain was with him but poor Clavel wasn't going to be able to make full confession on this planet, for the clerics had no resources.

Kumbva sat down and rubbed the poet's shoulders. He spoke of that horrible moment when Clavel had realised the truth: that Johnny's awe and hunger and terror – the perfect simulacrum of abject physical passion – was meant not for Clavel personally, but directed at the whole expedition.

Kumbva, who was never embarrassed by anything to do with lying down, considered this lesson about the locals curiously, measured it against incidents and remarks and was enlightened. But he dropped that topic under the onslaught of Clavel's enfeebled fury.

<Okay, okay . . . of course we mustn't take advantage.>

Clavel had behaved badly – persisting a long time after his only course was to make his excuses and leave. Dangerously, too, considering the locals' heated reaction to Sarah's death. Supposing Clavel's unwilling partner had kicked up a public fuss! The cool understanding of Johnny's friend, the priest Braemar, had saved a potentially explosive situation.

<It's not so very terrible. You can't admit it at the moment, but you have been actively seeking something of the kind. You were tired of your own virtue.> (Kumbva suppressed amusement.) <Perhaps at last you'll begin to grow up.>

He made a speech. 'You did no lasting harm. The notion of lasting harm is a childish fear. Throw it off. Think how you will feel about this a long time hence. Ask yourself why not now? Unless you plan to grieve for ever, remorse is nonsense.'

Kumbva left him.

Clavel knelt with closed eyes and saw the lights in the dark: orange and red and sulphur yellow, in serried ranks. You stare at them and stare, convinced that a phenomenon so huge and so regular can have no human meaning. Then you see that some of the tiniest orange lights are moving steadily. You are watching a procession of vehicles, far away but deep in the city's heart. So vast.

The others had followed him. On the night of the big storm, they were in London. They knew he was in bad trouble, so they came to Johnny's rooms. They had his address. Lug had found it in a local government written record. And when Clavel escaped them there, they followed Johnny in a stolen car, watched until Johnny and the priest left the house empty: and broke in to take a preemptive hostage. On the grounds that, after what had happened, the locals were bound to be demanding Clavel's hide. It made perfect sense to the four maniacs.

Clavel had found them wating for him in the park close to Braemar's house. They'd hauled the flier out of the back of the car and got it to unfurl. They were wildly excited: too excited to care what he'd been doing with the priest. It was dark, so dark in spite of the lights; and the air almost unbreathably moist and cold. Clavel wanted to die. He wanted the people of London to rush the park so he could die fighting. But no one came. London slept. The two nations refused to recognise what was happening. They stayed at home. They wanted grief, more grief so they could go on weeping for ever.

Clavel got up and left the cottage. If Kumbva only knew. But he could not be told. Around Clavel, the voices: whispering, shouting, grumbling, humming in quiet contentment; panting hard and fast in the greedy scuffle of lying down together. He walked in a cloud of witnesses, a slurry of other presences thick enough to chew. Always

there. There had never been need or reason to describe the way
they were there. But he could feel them tonight the way they
would seem to a – to *Johnny*. He was haunted.

Everyone was gathered in the 'tennis court', a large underground room where Kumbva and Lugha's artisans were busy
altering and refitting the somewhat makeshift new flier.

<We're going to call it a "shuttle",> announced Kumbva.
<That's the "human" word for a flier that crosses their planet's
gaseous shielding.>

It was the first time that Clavel had heard the formal word
'human' used in that way. Nobody else remarked on it. He
watched the group, and felt how confident they'd become in
handling the outward appearances of this strange world.
Meanwhile, Clavel had been wasting his time learning the inward-
ness. What he knew was so much more important. But it was
useless.

Everyone understood why Kaoru had destroyed the landers, and
it had been a wise precaution. But they needed more bodies. The
locals were almost ready to hand over the real estate, and it
looked suspicious to have so few settlers.

Clavel joined Kumbva and the trickster.

<Your luck won't hold. The lander will be spotted next time it
leaves here. The locals will track it, and know everything.>

Rajath shrugged. <No one caught us in "London". When people
are once convinced of a certain state of affairs they tend to stay
convinced, regardless of objective evidence. Besides, the
"humans" are credulous fools.>

Clavel stared at him bleakly. <You didn't come to rescue me.
You came to stop me from giving you away.>

But Rajath was far in the ascendant now. He made a speech.
'The mood at home has changed. As a nation, we were alarmed
when we first found this planet, distrustful of success after so long
without it. But planetfall and plunder was supposed to be the
object of the exercise. Everyone's had time to remember that.
There are plenty of takers now, eager for a piece of the action.'

Wrong, thought Clavel. We outgrew the false quest. We became
the Aleutians: wanderers, islanders, surviving cleverly on the
bounty of a cold and ungenerous ocean. It dawned on us that there
can't be a world for people without a people who fill it.

Nobody paid attention to the poet, least of all himself. He had not the heart to exert his influence, to unfurl that secret banner and employ the backwards-pulling power. He told himself it was too late. He told himself that the notion of lasting harm is a childish fear.

Maitri hugged his gloomy ward. <We're not shipwrecked any more. Of course we knew we could build again, but it's such a relief to have actually done it.>

'Are you real?' said Clavel dully. 'Or are you just a ghost in my head?'

Maitri was baffled.

They went back to Gray's Inn Road, where Johnny used the lobby phone to send a note to the Hargoods saying that he was taking a break as the work was so slack. They went up to his room, under the evil and fascinated eye of the concierge. It had only been three days, there was plenty of rent left on Johnny's key. The room had been tidied. The window was taped up with brown paper; that strange smell of cold-melted glass still hung in the air.

Johnny brought out Robert the Roach. The cockroach was crouched in the farthest corner of his plastic home, moping. The box was as clean as it had ever been. Johnny brooded over the life of this creature: barely eating, never 'sleeping'; built to survive indefinitely in a range of fearsome conditions.

Robert was one of the forerunners. If the earth got rich again his descendants might be galactic explorers, chitinous remote sensors for the humans who would never get there any other way. Without ftl, he wouldn't be more than a sideshow. Hey, isn't it two hundred years since anyone had a peep? Let's go smell out where Rob the Roach's ship is at.

The orthopteron scurried and clung to Johnny's finger, tasting him eagerly. It was supposed to have about the intelligence of a normal-type mouse. Johnny shuddered, remembering Clavel. *You have no wanderers*, she said. *Why don't you?*

'Must you bring that?' asked Brae. 'Couldn't we flush it down the toilet?'

'He might start budding, and then there'd be trouble. Besides, Rob and I go back too far. Love me, love my roach.'

He put the box in his pocket. He didn't need much else from this room. His books, a few clothes. He wondered if he'd ever be back. He had made a crossing, from Manland to Womanland, the river a convenient symbol in between. It seemed more of a transition than the day he'd married Izzy and left his parents' home. Basically, he didn't care what happened next. He didn't care if she went on servicing her patrons to pay the rent or to further White Queen's interest: he vowed that he would never enquire. It would be a long time, farther than he could imagine, before he got beyond the deep emotional need to get naked with her and fuck at every possible opportunity.

The narrow bed of his fantasies reminded him of Fo. Maybe to make love here would wipe out what had happened with the alien. The smell of melted glass poisoned a sudden rush of arousal. For a moment he wanted a specific violence, to fuck her without touching her. He could run out and get one of those all-over disposables favoured by perverts and hygiene maniacs. Force her to strip: break her open. He'd be sealed off, uncontaminated . . .

He sat down on the bed trembling, but hardly with lust. It was impossible to tell the people of earth the truth about their precious aliens. The truth was too vile. Things crawled, alive inside him. It was the filthiest nightmare, and it was real. He thought he would never again be free of this awareness of squirming life: on every surface, inner, outer, everything he touched.

Braemar saw that he was fighting horrors. She moved towards him, checked the impulse; picked her way around the miserable sticks of furniture to the other side of the room.

'Do you still have that card of mine, the one I gave you in the Barbican? I bet you kept it.'

He attempted a sneer. 'I bet I did not. I'm no sentimental fool.'

She found his bumbag on the floor, where it had lain untouched by Mrs Frame's staunchly honest girl. She rummaged in its depths and brought out the slip of green.

'You really don't read Italian, do you?'

The leather case of books lay open on the table where Johnny used to eat his toast. She extracted his pocket Dante: gave it to him open, with her card marking a verse.

> *Men che dramma*
> *di sanque m'e rimasa che non tremi*
> *conosco i segni dell'antica fiamma –*

He read the crib. Not a drop of blood remains in me that does not tremble. I know the traces of the ancient flame . . .

'I had been telling myself for so long that my fantasy had nothing to do with the real Johnny Guglioli. That if I saw you again I wouldn't even know you. But there you were – exactly my Johnny.' She smiled, sad and humble. 'I knew you'd never recognise it. Anstandigkeit was safe enough.'

He wanted a naked body, and she casually handed him a naked soul. What could you do with a gift like that? Except take it. And vow useless revenge on a world that gave this beautiful woman such a notion of *her self* that she'd hand it over like a bandaid.

She wore the Annie Mah dress and took him to the opera, to see *All Men Are Pigs*, a black comedy remix set in the eighties: in which Sharon bets Tracy that she can, with the greatest of ease, transform their two impeccable 'New Man' boyfriends into repellent chauvinists. Braemar thought it was very funny. Johnny found the farce painful and the music ridiculously mannered, but he laughed too.

Braemar planned to go to Germany, to track down Peenemünde Buonarotti. She wanted Johnny to come. They discussed this in the park on top of Telegraph Hill. Billy played in the sandpit, two feral wallabies hopped and peered from behind stands of blazing autumn leaves. Mortuary London lay spread below. Ninety-six per cent of the British population lives in the cities, Johnny recalled. People piled on people piled on people. The rest is National Forest, roads, food production: a mood of smug self-denial barely keeps the packed islanders sane. It was a poverty different from Africa's, but no less piteous.

'I expect it was Clavel,' said Braemar, 'who thought up the revenge of the machines. Remember how she used to feel about the market trucks?'

Johnny nodded. 'What *is* she to them?'

'A poet. One of their unacknowledged legislators.'

Johnny had been to Dr Jatinder. The news that Johnny had been engaged in unprotected sex, and thought he might have picked up an infection, didn't shock him. He took it for granted, the criminal bastard, that Johnny's partner or partners were not to be traced. It was a relief when the doctor found nothing weird. But Johnny was not convinced, he still felt polluted. He thought of Braemar holding one of those squirming things in her mouth, and her courage awed him.

The reaction to rape faded mechanically, like a bruise changing colour. He was in mourning for the cabin girl of the *Santa Maria*. And the Aleutians that should have been.

'I guess I ruined your best shot, Brae. I don't think we're going to do that interview.'

Braemar nodded, avoiding his eyes. 'No, I don't think she'll be back.'

He filled the red and blue dustcart with damp sand and trundled it up and down for Billy.

'D'you still think of Bella?'

'Yes.' He began to shape a sand tower. 'It doesn't go away, does it?' She had lost a child herself.

She took the alien-made passport from her purse. 'We'll use this. I've had a White Queen mechanic test it and he says there's no reason a stripe-scanner wouldn't accept it. With luck, we won't even need to try: we're not leaving Europe.'

'What if we meet a human being? Or a smart face-checker?'

The day after his consciousness-raising experience with Clavel, he'd have stormed Uji with a bowie knife between his teeth. He had calmed down. He had no intention of being left behind on this trip: but the QV problem raised its ugly head.

'I'm still officially rabid, remember. It makes no sense in terms of what's supposed to be wrong, but they can shoot me on sight if they catch me out of Greater London without any paperwork. Or lock me up for life in a ward full of chemotherapy refusenik child-molestors.'

Braemar grinned. 'No worries. We'll go to the Queen of Bohemia. She'll fix you up so the NIH itself wouldn't know you. You've started to feel constructive again, I see. That's good.'

Johnny poked windows into his creation with the stem of a dead leaf. 'Guglioli,' he said. 'A little spire, yes? You see, I'm not totally uneducated.' He looked up at her quizzically. 'The Queen of Bohemia. So I'm to meet one of the gang in real life. Does this mean we're going steady?'

The Queen of Bohemia operated from Folkestone, commonly known as E2:500 from its notional distance from Paris. The native leisure industry, the buried seaside, was now ten miles or so inland, recreated under cover. The Queen of Bohemia lived, apparently, in a massive old Victorian hotel block right on the cliffs. It was classy, inside. Johnny paced the sumptuous broad lobby, wondering about this White Queen hacker. He was not averse to the idea of another fabulously beautiful and loose-moraled Ancient Brit; and this was a fancy pad. Whoever lived here – especially some kind of renegade biochemist – could write her own face. And body.

The concierge was a machine. Braemar dealt with it, and handed him an optical pass.

'Ssh. The domestics aren't supposed to have visitors.'

Under the hotel it was stone passages, peeling paintwork, a damp smell of brine. Something, the sea or the plumbing, whooshed and gurgled behind the walls.

In the service garage someone was working alone, directing robotics under a piece of Italian exotica. The mechanic came out, pulling off a hear-and-do wire. The Queen of Bohemia was small and thin in baggy overalls with a big nose and goblinish mouth, much silvered straight black hair and narrow, Slavic-looking green eyes. Age, indeterminate: not young, not old.

Braemar introduced them. 'Clem Stewart; Johnny Guglioli.'

'Clem,' said the Queen of Bohemia. She held his hand too long. She had cop's eyes, if not something a little worse. 'I suppose you really are John Francis Guglioli. I remember you, bright baby out of the Letat vat.'

She had a slight Eastern accent.

'And I suppose you really are the Queen of Bohemia?'

'Of course. By practically legitimate descent. Come into the alchemist's den.'

The den was behind a false wall at the back of the garage. Most likely a few of the residents upstairs knew of its existence. Johnny recognised some of the equipment, which meant it wasn't new but it appeared to be in working order. There were pictures on the walls. They were the kind that have to be displayed in Brit pharmacies to warn people what over-the-counter gene-therapy can do. They seemed to be up there for fun. Johnny had seen the rise of this new criminal industry in New York: new means of threat, traceless murder. New faces, weird babies, horrible thrills. He felt slightly sick.

The troglodyte chuckled. 'My grandfather used to work for the government, my father too. He came to England after the eighty-nine revolution and reverted to an old family name. And I live – as you see. Bad blood will out, they say.' She preened, stroking her silvery hair. 'I could have any post, anywhere. Public or private sector, if you understand me. I prefer this life. It suits me. I'm my own mistress.'

She walked with a shamble, like a cowboy off his horse, into a den within the den. Beside an armchair with an embroidered linen headrest a glass case stood on a table. It contained a sword with an engraved blade and a display of rotting beige documents. She posed beside this set-up, waiting for Johnny's admiring curiosity.

'Clem's a direct descendant of Elizabeth of Bohemia,' explained Braemar. 'A daughter of . . . um, James the First and Sixth. James Stuart. Like the chap in the movie-dramas; but shorter. It was her idea that we should be royals.'

The hacker smirked.

'You've never thought of reclaiming the throne?'

She was delighted with this sally. 'Yes, yes. A royal secret policeman, queen in Prava. That would be a good joke, the kind that we Czechs appreciate. But let's forget about me.' Her tone gave Johnny to understand that she knew this wouldn't be easy. 'You are a new recruit, I understand. You need a new face, short term. So tell me about your allergies, and your bad genes.'

'You know about my bad genes.'

'Political disease is irrelevant. If things are otherwise, you can still trust me. I will not wake any demons.'

She led him from the furnished nook. Braemar stayed behind.

'Sit down here, Mr Guglioli.'

The foam of the chair had a bloom of age on it, a crumbling lichen. It folded around him. Clem donned eye protectors and dipped her hands and face in a spray tank. She yawned to spread the film over her mouth, then moved in. She took a scrape from inside his cheek, probed his cheek bones, eye sockets, jaw, like a blind woman. She got a lot closer than was strictly necessary. He could feel her breasts, nudging through the overalls: he imagined grubby underwear.

'Any dentistry?'

'Nngh.'

The headrest guided his face forwards into a black-mouthed funnel. Tiny fingers that he could not feel inched his death mask.

'Keep very still now, for me to take your picture. You can open your eyes. What do you see in there?'

He saw a mirror, virtually imposed on the darkness. As he watched the cheeks of the image bunched up, the bridge of the nose spread; the space between eyelid and brow narrowed. The chin grew thicker and square. Maybe this was Francis.

'It's not you, is it? Quite unlike anyone you've ever met. We concentrate on the eye area because, as you may have heard, there, the tiny muscles and the way they shape your skin is the place where people mainly identify identity.'

She released him, straightened up. She read him his rights.

'You realise, Mr Guglioli, that in gene-therapy the most minor treatment can have unforeseen and serious side effects, which may not be reversible.'

'Yeah,' said Johnny, feeling a frisson of terror. 'Yeah, yeah.'

'What do you prefer? Eyedrops, inhaler, paper flowers?'

'Paper flowers.'

The alchemist's box of tricks went to work. Clem folded her arms and gazed at her client.

'So, tell me,' Johnny said, not to be intimidated. 'How did it start?'

She laughed, ha ha ha, as if she was reading from a cue. 'It was a game, Mr Guglioli. A fantasy game of strategy. Who knows why we played together? Some common feeling that the people around us were aliens, and out to get us. I was a founder. I started the royal character names. Of course, that appealed to me. Braemar was the one who brought in the Lewis Carroll references. We have been around for much longer than any wire-tapper knows. We collected real information for our fantasy, and so we discovered the hypnotised Alaskans. There was a meeting, in network, of a few players who were suspicious that this was the real thing. We exchanged real names, we made solemn vows. We decided to play on: big board, and see if we could prove it one way or the other. Our game was called "The Aliens Have Landed" – very simple. One could play it any style. After the announcement from Krung Thep, we became "White Queen", and we settled on the preemptive resistance scenario. Oh, and it was not a fantasy any more. That's the whole story.'

'What's your total numbers?'

'Ha ha ha. The technique of the casual, impossible question. Of course, I won't tell you. But will disclose this for free: we will have more recruits soon.'

'Do you do a lot of your kind of work for White Queen?'

Her mouth stretched under the film. 'Personal "explosive"? Sick buildings? Traceless poison? I never touch baby-making, it is a dirty trade.' She shook her head. 'No, Mr Guglioli. This is the first false nose I have provided.'

'So what do you do?'

'Oh, mainly I am experimenting with alien tissue. I have studied their genetic material and discovered things that would terrify you.'

He kept a straight face.

She watched him with those bad-cop eyes. 'You don't like me, Mr Guglioli. Nobody does. But here you are, the good people: and you don't want me but you need me. I like that.'

The plant began to bleep. 'Ah.' She retrieved a sealed dropper tube. 'Your prescription, gracious sir. Take two at bedtime. Coming down, I warn you there'll be some haemorrhage. You and Braemar will make up something unconvincing about doorknobs.' She dipped her face and hands in the tank again, popped out the eye protectors: tugged at her brow and cheeks.

Braemar came over. 'All finished? Thanks, Clem.'

The two women embraced. Johnny saw that Braemar returned the hug with enthusiasm, but didn't relish it.

Clem squeezed his knuckles. 'Be careful, fellow traveller. Don't you hurt my crazy friend. Even if she seems to enjoy it, eh?'

So it was a game. A big-board game: lunatics out on the streets, creeping round invisible obstacles, heads locked in some frantically exciting unreality. The mini-cooper slotted in to E2. The Brits had slashed their road system and instituted punitive fuel rationing, but the freeways that were left were packed. Millions of addicts could always get a fix from somewhere for this filthy habit. Johnny couldn't feel superior. He was about to drive to Prussia, and Brae wasn't going to do that on her official sixteen and a half litres a month. He suddenly wished he'd never got involved with these banal, crypto-fascist losers.

They had to drive, through the road tunnel. It would be too much of a risk to try and get Johnny on to any plane or boat, and Braemar hadn't set foot on a train since the Frogs bought out BR.

'You're the White Queen: who's the Red Queen?'

Braemar grinned. 'Pierre, naturally.'

It was a nasty answer. The image of monkey-eyed Larrialde, furtively hiding a bloodstained handkerchief.

She glanced at him. 'What's wrong, Johnny? You know the scenario. When the wonderful white folk come along, the decent people are thrilled. It's only the mean, twisted witch doctor who plots against them, along with maybe good chief Mbongo's treacherous discarded wife. The proverbial minority of troublemakers.'

'Sorry. But your hacker gave me the creeps. How can you trust a woman like that?'

Braemar smiled sourly. 'Clem is not a woman. She's a man.'

So that was it. 'You mean, she's a transsexual?'

She laughed at the prim tone of his correction. 'I do not. I mean she's a man. Clem doesn't perceive herself as a female trapped in a male body. She has no plans to go all the way. Clem likes two sets of equipment.' Braemar glowered at the traffic. 'Men wearing frocks, men getting pregnant. Men growing tits. Maybe menstruating next. Clem's weird enough to try it. Makes me sick. You couldn't any of you stand the real thing for long, believe me.'

The venom in her tone surprised him. Braemar of all people was such a consummate female.

There was no break in the conurbation between Cinqcents and London. Mortuary towers heaved by. Johnny waited until he reckoned the irritable fit was over.

'Brae. Don't get mad: but is it *true*? Do you really honest to God have some alien tissue?'

'It's true.' She sighed, frowned. 'The trouble is: you've met Clem. I trust her as a hacker. You can use her stuff without a qualm. But when it comes to what she says about the aliens, I've seen nothing real. Genes. What is there that can't be faked, on that scale? What is there that you can see or touch? I don't know whether to believe a word she says.'

Clementina settled in hir armchair, still shedding tatters of biodegradable skinshield. SHe donned a headmask with a trailing lead, and watched alien molecules that were building themselves, delicate as snowflakes, from the outside in. Such beauty and such potential! Some day soon SHe would destroy the work SHe'd done, and the records. Roll on the new dark age. SHe found it obscurely but deeply satisfying that nobody in White Queen knew quite what to make of Clem the mad scientist. They had no idea what an astonishing piece of work SHe had done in unravelling the alien chemistry. But, oh yes, it was all true. Soon enough (but far too late), people would begin to understand the implications. Clementina removed the mask and sat gazing at the glass case, at the tarnished sword. SHe thought of a day which was most certainly coming; and hir goblin mouth puckered wryly. SHe fully expected to die, eventually, while fighting for the resistance. Yet it was ironic that the aliens should be what they were.

'New recruits. Plenty of recruits! But which cause is just? Which cause is mine? Ah, who can ever know?'

ii

Peenemünde was in quarantine. Or, rather, in the English phrase that better covered the situation, she had been *sent to Coventry*. The university would not dismiss her, because of the scandal. But they'd taken her work away from her. Also the teaching, though that was no loss to anyone; she was a terrible teacher. She missed her project. She missed even more the human warmth: a tiny trickle of input that she had not noticed until it stopped coming.

No one would talk to her. Literally no one. They would barely nod. Since Peenemünde had scarcely ever in her life initiated a social conversation, her loss was a strange one. She kept to her few well-trodden paths as before, sublimely unreactive: but most improbably nothing *ever* bumped into her. She ate in the canteen, alone, took the air at random hours, fed the ducks in the duckpond. No one came near. She could understand that her neighbours, down to the campus cleaners, would wish to avoid contact with her views on a certain subject. But they did not have to broach that subject, did they? Perhaps they did. All around her it was aliens this and aliens that. If these superbeings were so wonderful, Peene thought, it was surprising that they would bear such a grudge against the silly notions of a mere earthling. But university people judge everyone by their own standards.

In the early days there was at least the fanmail. There was a graduate student, a beautiful young woman, who became wild-eyed and hollow-cheeked in that period when *they* material-ised . . . sermonised from Krung Thep, turned some robotics into monsters, threatened to vaporise millions. She developed a crush on Peenemünde, to the extent of wanting to take her to bed. Peenemünde had no sexual orientation to speak of. She was quite helpless to refuse. It was a horrible failure. The young woman could have no true affection or desire for the fat and tongue-tied professor: and Peenemünde did not know how to behave at all.

Afterwards this woman became a fervent alien-lover. But her eyes remained the eyes of someone who sees terrible visions, painted everywhere on the empty air.

Peene ate in the canteen, comfortably overlapping the narrow bench. She had not yet lost weight on account of her troubles. It was around 2 a.m. local time. Peenemünde, because of the present timetable of her covert use of the Cannon space telescope, was far astray from normal day and night. It didn't matter, no one noticed. She saw a couple of strangers among the non-time people, a well-preserved middle-aged woman and her son, who did not look like her and was maybe some kind of gigolo. Throughout Federated Europe and the Community, budget travellers used the universities like the monasteries of old Christendom. It was someone's romantic fancy that had by chance survived. In theory they must prove themselves legitimate pilgrims of learning. But the service was not overburdened, so no one bothered much.

Like most unsociable people, Peene had unsuspected reserves of idle curiosity. She speculated about the couple until she realised that *they* were watching *her*. Especially the young man.

She froze up inside. The terrible vision painted on her air was of herself crouched on Inge's bed, quilt scrabbled around a mountain of flesh that seemed to have appeared from nowhere: the body that she never considered important. Inge's beautiful golden face gone sullen-angry, herself babbling plaintively, 'Don't be upset, please. Maybe we could watch some erotic television?'

Peene left the canteen in a hurry. They followed her. She broke into a brisk trot. There was no one in sight. Nor watching: campus security was a farce. Her own self-image didn't help. She knew she was not able to 'deal with situations'. At the entrance to her own building she gave up and waited, panting.

'*Gehen Sie doch weg,*' she said. '*Mit mir wollen Sie doch nicht reden, denn ich bin schwachsinnig.* Idiotica: *Ich bin eine Privatperson. Gehen Sie lieber und sehen Sie sich die synthetische Kristallausstellung an oder die bunten Kapellenfenster.*'*

'My friend speaks only English,' said the woman. She had put her hand, straight-armed, right across the keyslot. Her eyes were brutal. 'You believe the Aleutians are faking, Professor Buonarotti. So do we. We should talk.' To get indoors Peenemunde was going to have to wrestle with this slight, well-dressed woman with the eyes of iron. She could not do that.

'*Können Sie nicht schreiben? Gehen Sie und schreiben Sie mir. Es stimmt, dass ich das Telefon nicht mag, aber ich lese meine Frachtpost. Vielleicht antworte ich sogar.*'†

The pudgy-faced young man seemed angry, perhaps because he couldn't understand. The brutal woman shook her head. 'No. We have to talk. Face to face.'

So she let them come up to her room. They stared at her little 'launch pad' but they obviously didn't know what it was, which relieved her worst anxiety.

'Sit down,' she said, in English. 'Shall we have tea?'

She made tea, and laid out a plate of cakes. It pained her to part with them, but she knew her duty as hostess. It was the first time in years that she had entertained visitors. The ceremonies soothed her. The young man was nothing like Inge. No one cares, she thought. Nobody cares what I say, so long as I only talk to other fools. The crushing anguish of her loss suddenly pierced her through. To talk about the beloved, this is the great hunger of the bereaved.

They looked around the room. The man stared at her friends gallery, especially at the sepia image of a young man's face: a long, rather sad face with a straggling, youthful beard.

'Professor Buonarotti,' said the woman. 'My name is Braemar

* 'Go away,' she said. 'You don't want to talk to me. I am an idiot. *Idiotica*: I am a private person. Go and look at the synthetic crystal show. Go to see the stained glass in the chapel.'

† 'Can you not write? Go away and write to me. It's true I don't like the phone, but I read my freight mail. I may even answer.'

Wilson, this is Johnny Guglioli. We represent an organisation called White Queen. You have heard of us, I know. We have tried to contact you. According to the university, you have no office and they don't hold your private number. You don't use any of the usual bulletin boards. We *have* written to you. We've had no response. I appreciate that this is a diabolical intrusion. But we believe what you believe – '

Peenemünde shook her head. 'Oh no,' she said, again in English. 'I don't believe, Mrs Wilson.'

'Braemar.'

'Braemar. I know. They are not aliens, nor superior beings. It is not logically possible that they should be.' She took up her tea and a cake. 'Consciousness. What is it? It is the inscription in us of the nature of things. What is the nature of things? The virtual particles leap to and fro between existence and nonexistence, the neurons fire up incessantly, for any reason or none. Properly considered, consciousness like reality itself is neither a thing nor an event. It is a certain crucial arrangement of information. And that is what cannot vary. Essentially speaking there is nothing in existence that is not an expression of *the conditions of existence*. You have heard the expression, an atom "wants" to achieve a particular state; or that a calculation "prefers" to settle for one of a limited range of results. Why do we say that? Because what we experience as *motivation*, for instance, as *desire*, is not particular to humanity, or even to anthropoid apes, higher mammals, birds. When a thing becomes more complex it does not change, it only becomes *more of itself*. The human mind/brain is so large a version, and so indefinite, it is quantitively like the whole universe, much in little. Our awareness is the result: built of the movements of the void, as surely as my hand is built of flesh.'

It was a lovely feeling. Peenemünde couldn't teach and her lectures rambled, but she did enjoy having an audience.

'When I say that crystals "desire" . . . When a like-minded colleague says that a rat "feels" aggrieved and lonely, this is not anthropomorphism. It is rather a demotion of the human than a promotion of lower creatures; if you must. Men move through life the way their own spermatazoa move along a chemical gradient. However complex, in a certain sense *quantitatively* indistinguishable. That is commonplace, yes. But it is my job to see the commonplace with new eyes. The information that we call "self-conscious intelligence" can only be described as general, it cannot be particular. (It cannot be *analysed* at all. But that is a truism of modern science. Analysis of any kind is only defective description.) So you see. If we talk of "alien intelligence", then it must come from outside our set of conditions. But logically, there is no way in or out of the sum of all: of the cosmos, so defined. So, that settles that. Whatever they can think, we can think. They cannot read minds. Unless we can,' she added, trying a touch of humour, 'and have not happened to notice it. Whatever they are like, we are like it.'

Peenemünde saw a tiny glance exchanged, which hurt her feelings. At that moment she made up her mind to have a small revenge, through these two, on the ungrateful world.

'So you don't dispute that they are actually from another planet?' prompted Braemar.

Peenemünde shrugged. 'Beside the point. The truth of that's a question of forensics: not for me. Wherever they came from. Whatever their physiology – ' she drew a breath – 'they did not travel faster than light. That is *perfectly clear*. That is inherent in my axiom of self-replication. Only consciousness can travel faster than light, nothing whatsoever material. So you see, those little space planes, they give the game away.'

She finished her cake. They were waiting, mimicking attention but 'turned off', to see if she would utter some key word that would once more engage their gracious attention. She had faced plenty of newspeople of this kind. It irked her, just the same.

'Let me explain. A long time ago, before '04, there was an international space programme. There was Mars Mission: things were happening. My funding body decided that the solar system was inevitably consigned to nation and block politics, and that the adventurous should spy out the realms beyond. Corporations are different from elected entities. They can think in the decades, in the centuries. You laugh at the idea of ftl: my corporation did not. Distances in deep-space exploration soon become impossibly un-wieldy for anything that moves, be it matter, visible light, radio waves. This problem *must* be addressed if we are to get anywhere. Sometime, why not now? The project has been on a "back burner" for a while. But a few years, ten years ago, I inherited it. I have been paid to have ideas about materials that might co-exist, through some holes or tunnels or slackness in the weave of the universe into another place: materials gradiented like the shell of a spaceplane, to be in several states at once – both hot and cool: both "here" and "elsewhere". It has been essentially no different from work I have done on vat-grown machine tools, very prosaic.'

'And you found it?'

She had already forgotten the young man's name. But she knew the type. He would believe anything, if it was romantic enough.

'A metal-organic that will walk through the walls of time? No, I don't believe we will ever see it. But I have had a minor success. To trigger the vat-growing processes, we need to recover from nature *the information itself*. What happens if we have hold of that, but without any material form whatsoever? In that case we have a thing without a situation, *besides that elected by its own will*. Suppose it has one.'

She paused again, for effect this time. 'Unfortunately, I was not yet ready to publish when the Aleutians arrived. I could see no applications, and therefore I was reluctant to publish. One cannot have science without application.' She scowled. According to that axiom, at present Peenemünde Buonarotti did not exist. She stood up. 'Come, let me show you.'

They looked at each other warily; they followed like lambs.

'There,' said Peenemünde. 'My prototype.'

The couch, the workstation, the lightbox. She handed a sheaf of FOC photographs to the young man: and the Cannon's greater gift, faint brocades recovered from within the spectra of a handful of main sequence stars. These were the jewels: which Peenemünde, and Peenemunde alone, knew beyond doubt to be the signatures of planetary atmosphere. The woman, Braemar, she positioned before the workstation screen and set it to deliver pretty pictures that could do no one any good. She didn't trust the woman. She had met (discovered afterwards, with chagrin, that she had met) industrial spies with the same smell.

'The set of all possible situations is indefinite regardless of scale, but the calculations for a small domain are obdurately difficult. The experiment of "travelling faster than light" to the next room would not be convenient. The solar system, as we know, is not hospitable except on this planet. The information "I" might not survive any better than the physical. So I have been wandering far afield, from the very start. Of course, everyone knows that there are possible planetary systems, according to perturbation evidence, scattered throughout our local area. Now see these absorption lines.' She pointed, quickly, at the coloured barcodes. 'This, this and this are traces of planetary atmospheres. The scientific astronomy community still squabbles over the whole idea of these planets. I have reason to be sure. This, these show finer detail: and these are earthlike or nearly earthlike.' She shuffled the papers together. The young man was looking too interested, and the woman had left the pretty pictures and was peering at the couch.

'Is your operation expensive?'

She realised that they had no idea, and she could lie: but social incompetence defeated her.

'I use quite a lot of power, and machine time. There's a non-time corporate project in a block down the way. I take everything from there. Du Pont/Farben can afford it.'

Then Braemar Wilson turned to her with words that won the scientist's heart.

'You must really hate them.'

'The Aleutians?' The half lie came easy, since she knew it ought to be the whole truth. 'Of course not. It was the luck of the game. But now. Will you try? Then we would be three who know.'

That was funny, to see their faces. Really funny.

'If you were to make the experiment,' she explained slowly. 'Then I would feel myself in a position to make a public statement of my views on the Aleutian question. Already things aren't good. If I do that I might lose my place here entirely. It would be a serious step. But I am prepared to take it, if you will first show your good faith in me.'

They glanced at each other, and away. The young man, she thought, would spoil everything. Wilson was ready.

'What exactly happens?' she asked. 'And where's the rest of your lab?'

Peenemünde laughed. 'Oh, no. This is all you two need to see, and I have told you all you need to know. To you what happens is that you lie down. Sensors, they are positioned in the foam, trace the outline of your body. You have heard of Kirlian photography? The couch takes the kind of photograph savages fear. It captures your soul. You say to yourself: *I will go* to a situation that you have in mind. As if in a dream, the dream of early morning when you dream that you have wakened, you stand up. You have arrived at that state of affairs, not as a ghost but in the body that has been yours since before the world was made.'

'Made of what?'

Peene shrugged. 'Plasma. Which is built into the mixture as before. Hydrogen, oxygen, carbon; a little iron, other traces. I have never noticed any missing parts.'

'And then?'

'You stay as long as you dare. Quite long, after some practice. You get frightened and come quickly home. None of this room's time has passed.'

'But you have to aim yourself at an exact location of space-time coordinates?'

Peenemünde was aware that this was her weak point. She did not wish to confess to suicidal recklessness. 'Remarkably precise temporality can be recovered from the Cannon's data, with the right manipulation. And there is a certain flow . . . You may not have *the precise situation* in mind, but in the travel mode it may be you run through the sum of all possibilities. There is plenty of time for that, where time does not run away. Or it may be that for some immeasurable moment there is nothing that you do not know.' She remembered a detail. 'Oh, yes, and you must clear your minds before you lie down. Be still and calm. The soul must not carry excess baggage when it travels.'

'This is criminal,' said the young man.

Peenemünde blinked.

He'd found the cable taped to her window sill. Peenemünde had had to drill out a big chunk of the metallic frame to sneak it through. 'Look at the diameter of this. You're stealing on a grand scale, aren't you? My God, I bet you're siphoning off a small city's worth of juice.'

'My colleague and I have to talk,' said Wilson.

The young man was glaring at both women with indiscriminate and mysterious fury. Peenemünde noticed for the first time that he seemed to be sporting two blossoming black eyes.

'By all means. Please. But at five a.m. German time the Du Pont project goes to sleep. You will have to make up your minds before that.' She hurried to her kitchenette and came back with a soiled paper bag. 'Feed the ducks. That always helps me to think.'

Braemar Wilson turned back at the door. 'If the aliens didn't use your patent method, how do you imagine they got here?'

'Oh, it's simple. They have a multigeneration ship. It is roundish and dark, and shielded with a layer of water about five or ten metres thick between rigid mineral shells. They came in off the plane of the ecliptic, so that most of our hardware wasn't looking the right way, and they are hiding somewhere close in a parking orbit. I think they're probably behind the moon.'

The duckpond was something less than five hundred metres away, surrounded by shrubbery and a few trees. A non-time block, quietly blazing across the grey turf, drowned the dim globes that lined the campus paths. The ducks were wide awake and came purposefully across the water as the two humans approached.

It was very cold, the sky was sooty. There was a bleak east wind driving across the great plain.

'What went wrong, Johnny?'

He sat on the stone rim, absently tearing up stale bread. 'Did you see the picture gallery over her bed? Mahatma Gandhi was up there, Chico Mendes. The Chipko woman; Gaura Devi. Teresa of Lisieux. Teresa of Avila. The wispy guy in the middle was the face from the Turin shroud.'

Braemar considered him. 'That's some obscure recognition for a young newshound. I didn't know you were a Catholic, Johnny.'

'I'm not – ' He broke off, shrugged. 'It's an Italian name, isn't it? What did you think I was, a bloody commie?'

Braemar sat down, immaculate in loden-green jacket and breeches, moleskin stockings; a flash of amethyst silk at her high collar. They had been travelling for days, the elegant lady and the young man who did not behave like her son. It had been glorious: spiced by the excitement of Johnny's disguise. Taking risks together; and the moment of waking; and feeling so beautiful when people stared and wondered what was going on. Braemar wished she knew how to set about preparing herself for star travel. For of course the idyll (which would end soon enough) was built on lies, and she did not feel calm at all. One would have to be mad to ask for anything different. The quiet mind, like reality itself, is a fiction.

She looked at the water. '*Femme je suis, pourette et encienne* – '

'What?'

'Sorry.

> A woman old and poor am I
> Who knows nothing, I could never read
> I see in my parish church
> Paradise painted, where are harps and lutes
> And a hell where the damned are boiled
> The one frightens me, the other brings joy and mirth . . .

'Villon. He was a poet, a mediaeval loser: talented boy, but he came from the wrong side of the tracks and he never learned to behave. I'm no Christian, nor Hindu. But I want to do right in my own terms; and I'm afraid, in my own terms, of what will happen to me if I do wrong.'

Johnny looked at her, at last nodded. 'Yeah. Exactly. I don't know if I understand, but yeah . . .' He touched his sore eye sockets delicately. He had underdosed and was coming down too soon. His anger had been absurd. Big science and religion are one and the same, they fit the same space. He'd often argued that point with self-deluded 'rationalists'. Our God-given systems, the void-powered data God behind them . . . It's all the same, dumb awe and naive paranoia. Only fools ignore that dimension: no one gets much further than a mediaeval peasant.

He wondered if he would ever again have control of his emotions. He saw his own turmoil as a fractal of the response of humanity confronted with alien intelligence. The world's billions in tears, in lust, panicking, flying into rages.

'Why'd she give me drops. I *hate* putting drops in my eyes.'

'You must have asked for something else.'

'Huh?'

'It's the way Clem works. Looking-glass logic. I'm sorry. I should have warned you.'

In the cold light of daytime half a world away they hunched shoulders against the wind, uneasily silent.

Buonarotti's story actually supported the aliens. If her employers had been researching ftl for years – and it seemed so likely – maybe Braemar and Johnny had stumbled on the reason why the world's corps had been so hands-off about Uji. *Careful, chaps. They're quite possibly the real thing.* They'd come a long way to find only new hints that the world was right and White Queen was wrong.

'All right,' said Braemar. 'Forget the cosmic implications, and get to market. She's an amateur astronomer, we knew that. She's a double Nobel laureate. Both times she tried to boycott the ceremony and refuse the money, since you can't turn a Nobel down, on the grounds that the award system is corrupt. But her corp wouldn't have it.'

'I knew there was something weird.'

'A touch priggish, maybe. Those are the bright sparks who gave Henry Kissinger the peace prize.'

'Who he?' The bread was finished. He tore up the bag and scattered it. Ducks eagerly gobbled the fragments. He thought about the grotesque economics of last century's lunatic particle hunting, and wondered what the other-worldly Professor Buonarotti was doing, singlehandedly, to Germany's energy audit.

'The woman's a criminal. What if that side comes out?'

'For siphoning a few ecu from a Du Pont subsid?'

'A few millions, Brae. I know what modern power cable looks like. Okay. So we won't grass her up, because her parents were Nazis and she had a horrid childhood. But what do we get out of trying this trick, which doesn't work?'

'I don't know, but we either take it or go home with nothing. Buonarotti is an eccentric. She's probably just making friends. Maybe she'll cave in when we call her bluff. The point is we need her. She's a genius, and kooky too. People would love her. It doesn't matter if it's nonsense. No one in our audience will listen very hard. It is non-Aleutian . . . and, and a powerful idea.'

How easily, silently Peenemünde had exchanged 'time' for 'space'. Situations, not locations. The universe is a four-dimensional landscape.

Braemar saw her young self marching along behind the buggy, face a ludicrous grim mask, her daughter's wrist in a vice-like grip. The toddler whining, the three-year-old sobbing outright. There was no money for bus fares because she was saving it for her secret hoard, the escape fund. There comes a moment when the cooing and cajoling ceases and mother's real feeling bursts out in ugly savagery. The children are astonished, and no wonder, at this transformation. They scream and scream. They resist more than ever with the obstinacy of despair. You know what will happen, but oh, the delicious release of that first instant. I never hit them, she remembered. I never wanted to, except the times when I'd have killed them.

The baby was gone where nothing could harm him. But still she dragged on that little arm, taking vicious pleasure as the little feet stumbled to keep up. My daughter hates me, thought Braemar. If there was ever, in any possible world, a way to get back there and undo . . .

Buonarotti had shaken them both. Lucky Johnny, his life was so blameless he didn't have to take the implications personally. She sighed. It was so obvious that they had to take up the offer. But this baby, as he had once kindly pointed out, was a deal too big to be physically intimidated.

'I cannot bear many more dead ends.'

Johnny relented. He turned, taking the wind on his back, and wrapped his arms around her.

'Okay, honey. Where d'you want to go to?'

Braemar laughed, amazed that he hadn't thought of it. 'The Aleutian mothership, of course.'

The ducks, remarking to each other that there was no more business here, cruised away into the dark. Johnny pulled her to her feet, opened their two jackets and held her, close as they could be; her mouth against his throat. An incredible, wire-thin sweetness ran through him: an ethereal orgasm, following the same pathways. 'If it's not there, then I suppose we'll be dead.'

'Be serious. Nothing's going to happen.'

He eased back, and tugged the plastic box out of his pocket. 'Brae, if I don't get through, I want you to have Robert.'

Suddenly, they were both giggling. 'Supposing we're dreaming. Supposing we've gone into fugue?'

They began to walk, Braemar hugging Johnny's arm. He could feel her shivering.

'Listen, Johnny. If the timeostat goes on the blink. If you lie down on that couch, and wake up in your own bed yesterday, there's a pub called The Back of The North Wind, on Kingsway, the corner of Parker Street. I'll meet you there, eight p.m. London time, two weeks from tonight.'

'Who goes first?' asked Buonarotti.

They would toss for it. Neither of them had a coin.

'Age before beauty,' said Braemar: and lay down.

'We leave her.' The professor drew Johnny away. 'And wait a moment.'

As soon as she lay down she suddenly, all at once, understood why she and Johnny had been knocked off balance by Professor Buonarotti's far-fetched tale. Simply this: it sounded like being dead. It sounded like dying.

Oh.

Peenemünde was wondering about Ms Wilson's clothes. She herself travelled naked. But she'd judged that if she told them to strip they'd dig in their heels: *sure* it was a practical joke. Well, one would discover something new. Mr Guglioli's black eyes were in full flower. He stared angrily at her friends gallery.

'That's a fake, surely you know?'

Peenemünde shrugged. 'It's only a picture.'

'You shouldn't need any persuasion to join White Queen. These are human beings, aren't they? Do you want them to be forgotten?'

Peenemünde felt helpless. That was the media for you. Human beings? These people never, ever listen.

'Those who live by the sword shall die by the sword, Mr Guglioli.' It sounded futile, even to her.

Johnny glared out of bloodshot eyes. The cell-like little room was charged with meaning. The day and night he had just spent with Braemar refused to order themselves in memory.

'Have you done this before? Sent one person after another?'

She didn't answer. She didn't have to. Her face gave it away.

Death. In the unmeasured pause before extinction, she heard voices. The cooper bucketing along with its inimitable bone-cracking fervour. Johnny waxing lyrical beside her on the perils of continental travel. E. coli big as cats, threshing around the sewers of abandoned Lyons. Giant Friesians, the fabled carniverous superbright cows that roamed lonely heaths in Belgium preying on benighted travellers . . . Johnny loved it. He loved being in an adventure again, as long as there wasn't too much contact with slimy creeps like Clem. She would almost have taken them down to the Zone-E to amuse him; except they'd have looked such damn fools when they were picked up.

She heard herself explaining her different feelings: how immensely touching it seemed, this contaminated world. How she loved the cheery way people managed to carry on regardless.

Her husband was dead. She put a lot of effort into trying to capture another male, simply because she was afraid to walk down the street, to go into a room alone. She had to have one of them, hired to protect her from the rest. The hire price wasn't painful, the choice was wide. It was quite simple, ought to be easy. Walked into the bathroom and found one of them handling her little boy's prick while uncomprehending baby hands held on to his erection. OUT, she said. GET OUT NOW. Without rancour, almost laughing. What else can you expect, when trawling for a mate? Contamination exists, therefore one learns to live with it.

She really didn't blame the bloke. She had, a fairy gift, become immune to injury. She had been rescued from the victim's role for ever.

She opened her eyes and found herself sitting with her back against a smooth, slightly warm surface. She was naked. She had the mental aftertaste of a long and complex dream: her whole life had passed before her, no doubt. No sign of Johnny.

She looked down. She found that though her back was against a wall her body was hanging forward, unsupported in air. She was in a tube, there was no perceptible gravity. The light spread, diffuse like daylight through a skylight, from a blue band along the curved wall. The air seemed normal. The walls were knobbly in patches, with an irregular series of covered hatches that had an industrial look. She began to move along the tube briskly, hand over hand. She came to hatches that were open, hooked up to concertina ducting: she ducked under or clambered over. There were no people. She kept thinking that things moved in the knobbly patches on the walls; but never caught them at it.

A much bigger hatch stood open. There was a row of things like sleds hanging from or held down near (orientation switched, sickeningly) the floor of a yard. The cabs were hooked up to big spools of fine wire or maybe yarn. She could see no drivers, but she had the weirdest impression that the trucks themselves were staring at her. She averted her eyes and dived past. There was a door that opened before she bumped on to it. A small room. A section of wall facing her had shelves in it, small tools captured in containers; dangling harness. An office. There was fixed desk furniture. The configuration looked familiar at the corner of her eye: keyboard, screen, adding machine. When she looked at it straight it became meaningless extrusions. She pushed herself inward: lost control and hit the far wall. It opened. It was a deep cupboard. There were transparent floating bags filled with folds and folds of dun clothing.

It was then that the reality hit her – where she was, what had happened.

Braemar held on to the cupboard door with one hand and groped her way into a foetal ball. She took deep breaths. Shortly, she embarked on the struggle of dressing herself. No one interrupted her. She hurried outside into the tube, clinging and grappling. Soon she felt she was no longer clinging but hanging. The pull became stronger. Soon after that, she was walking. She found her way blocked. Between hand and shoulder height beside the panel that closed her way there was a sunken pad in the wall marked with a simple icon. She pressed, poked, laid her palm. Nothing happened. *I have no wanderers.* In desperation she *rubbed* it like the genie's lamp. The panel swept aside. Braemar stared at her potent fingertip, and began to giggle.

She found herself out of the industrial estate and there were people everywhere: litter and flowerbeds, long transports like buses; short ones like private cars. The noise was almost human, but without speech. There was a haze in the air that made her cough. Nobody had noticed her arrival. She put her head down, and moved briskly through the crowds.

Johnny held out his hands, and examined them.

'It's a virtuality!' he laughed.

He had been terrified, just briefly. When a bio-physicist, who is totally world class, tells you she's going to make you one with the essence of being, and she seems to mean it . . . Johnny was a sucker for that kind of thing, it was his secret vice. Lucky Brae. It probably hadn't crossed her mind that they ran a minuscule risk of finding themselves looking into the no-fooling face of God.

So this is faster than light travel. Science moves out another notch, and the supernatural retreats once more to some decently impossible realm. He didn't believe it. The place felt like a game, the inside of a game. He didn't know this simulacrum body effect. But it was a long time since he'd been into anything. Maybe it wasn't even new.

His heart suddenly jolted. He had let himself be plugged into a virtuality game, undoubtedly coralin based or it couldn't be this good. He had broken quarantine!

The reflex passed. There are no rules, he thought. I've crossed the river. I'm not a QV victim any more. I'm a freedom fighter.

And anyway, this isn't real: none of it. I am dreaming.

The dim and narrow passage had bulkheads in the sides. They slid aside as he came level, weight triggered, revealing ducting and cable knotted together in an inextricable, organic tangle. One of the closets held a row of hanging pupae cases which, when handled, disgorged the Aleutian uniform. He dressed. Further along, at a crossroads, he found a diagram on the wall which was evidently a local map. The maze of coloured lines was not painted or printed but integral with the metallic skin of the wall. It was fresh and bright. Johnny studied it closely.

He had arrived, by luck or omniscient judgement, somewhere behind the scenes of this game-world, dream-world. He decided he was in a system of maintenance tunnels. Eventually, without meeting any one, he reached a dead end: a round, pod-like room with an extruded workstation and chair.

The workstation had a keypad of sorts, and it was live. Johnny started to play with it. He discovered that he had to rub, not press or tap. Nothing in this environment was completely rigid: it was uncannily and not too pleasantly like stroking flesh. But never mind. He discovered that he was symbolically literate, and began to explore.

You are in the lymph system of the world, the screen told him. In one of many observation chambers, sensory cells. You may not have worked here before. You may be merely curious. You may be a child. Here is information.

Here is the world.

The icons cleared, revealing a two-dimensional picture. The quality was poor, about that of single layer video tape. He touched and found that the screen was not glass, but some kind of almost rigid jelly.

There was a rocklike lump hanging in the bright darkness of space. A dumpy oblate sphere, a blackened aubergine that looked as if it had been knocked into space-faring shape by Mother Nature herself. Against a steady curtain of stars small bright points tracked

in slow-motion busyness. He couldn't get any idea of the dimensions. He remembered Clavel had told him: yes, we have moons,
but only little ones. He was looking in at the blob from one of its
moons, then he was looking out from the surface. The viewpoint
tracked slowly. (If at real-time speed, the aubergine was enormous:
but he thought not.) He found himself staring at a white and grey
pockmarked giant's cheek. It filled a third of the screen. So it was
lunar day for Aleutia. Must be new moon on earth, he couldn't
recall. *Far side* . . . he breathed. *D'you see that, Brae? The far side of
the moon.* The recorded sequence didn't give any choice of
viewpoints. He could not angle the eyes out there to find that one
big disc of a star which must be burning: white light, white heat in
the blackness.

More?

More icons. He stroked one.

Here is the *planet*, our wandering home, in section.

More jelly-video. He began to flip back and forth.

Here is the food production and a lot of other stuff, carried out in
zero gravity by eccentric-looking robotics: no humans visible.
Here, on the other hand, is a city square where children play: a
park, a lake, gardens. Layers of living spaces, concentric shells of
them. Here is the proportion of living space, production, and the
gravity-gradient deserts that we don't use for anything much.

Clavel had told him all about it. The cities are enclosed. No one
lives out of doors, in the artifical outdoors which is actually *inside*
where we grow our food. Just as on your planet, there's a lot of
wilderness, which we don't use. Telepaths don't lie, they only
translate their terms. Aleutia is a space ship.

Johnny began to realise that he was looking at the truth. He had
taken a trip, of some wild kind, a quarter million miles through
space: and he stood in Aleutia. He felt sad and cheated and
exultant. Brae had been right, all along.

He tried to get the control pad to give him alien coordinates that
someone on earth could maybe pin down. The machine would only
go on with its set routines.

Some adventurous souls go out into the skeletal supports of the
cavernous shell to prove their courage or to look for God; or merely
to have an adventurous picnic . . .

More?

The inside of a big, big hall like a museum. There were cases of artefacts which he couldn't make out too clearly. Next to each case, a tv screen; some of them elaborately mounted. Every screen was playing: movie-drama or else frankly unreal animation. He couldn't get a closer look at any of the shows, but he was fascinated to note that at one end of the big hall there was what looked like a recording studio: glassed off, a few people in there moving around. He was taken in quite close, the values of light and angle silently telling that this was supposed to be important, or at least ought to be: reverence.

'What is this?' he whispered.

The icons were derived from a humanoid body. In icon the ship itself was a forked animal, not a hollow rock: with blood and lymph and guts standing for the various essential systems. He had been moved on from the 'mountaineering' sequence to the tv hall by rubbing a big rayed eye. That was weirdly easy to interpret. The Eye. The 'I'. He remembered Clavel, suddenly and intensely: covering her broken face in that gesture of deep respect. The Self is God.

Oh, it was eerie!

He was being shown their temple, an alien cathedral. Telecommunication has a supernatural significance for the Aleutians . . . he knew that. What happens behind the screen happens in 'the land of the dead'. They kept video-records about themselves in a place apart at Uji, and treated it as special. No one really understood why, not even his own favourite authority on Aleutian culture, (or if she did she wasn't saying). So the communications centre was a church of 'Self'. But here he stood, using their tourist information desk. The radio-room couldn't be all that alien.

'What about those moons?' murmured Johnny.

Here are our satellites. Here is a gap in the default configuration. One of our satellites is missing. No, it has gone walkabout . . . an eye on a stalk to peep around the big moon.

He stared at the screen. No one had ever caught the aliens on earth making or receiving a transmission. But there it was. In an emergency, the landing party 'telepaths' could phone home.

Was he awake or dreaming? He couldn't tell. But a brilliant plan slipped into shape. He could hack their coms. He could break their cover. Absolutely. This was the key. Here it was (the fuzzy air brushed across his face) . . . Power over the aliens!

Guiltily, he became aware of Braemar, of the way she was standing there quietly letting him have the fun. She seemed to like him to take the lead. And he felt he could do anything while she was around: that tender, enabling presence. He remembered the ruthless way she had made herself seem obnoxious, in Fo, to save him from moral danger. (Or something like that, some esoteric feminine reasoning that he supposed he would never understand.) Why was she so rough on herself?

There was a fantasy, it almost seemed her favourite, where she would say *no* . . . and *please, Johnny, no*; and softly fight him, all around the room. She'd introduced him to this in Africa: a close-quarters reversal of the teasing come-on she'd given him before. It was horribly exciting, so *completely against the rules*. For her, too. She would be frantic, teetering on the brink, when he had her down, got inside. It was a game they hadn't played this time, not after the Clavel incident.

But the thought of it started to give him an erection.

He was becoming hyper-associative. The thought of *doing his stuff* again was sexual, inevitably. Doing it to the alien. This hyper effect (not only in terms of sex) was one of the hazards of modern computer gaming, and one reason why he had never been crazy about it. Sane people only used this drugless drug for business meetings.

He stood back. 'You have a turn,' he said, like a child.

Of course, she wasn't there.

A brisk march down the spooky, off-real corridor restored him. He wondered if Brae was here at all, and how he could possibly find her. Things had changed while he was in the pod room. There were scrabbling noises, odd shadows. Things watching him, and following. In reason, he should have nothing to fear from Aleutian security. According to Braemar they would have no use for mechanical surveillance. But reason breaks down. Addicted gamers become classically paranoid.

He walked into a yielding panel, backed off, rubbed the icon and was suddenly plunged into a city street. He did a swift U-turn. Something grabbed him by the arm. He opened his mouth to yell: it was Braemar.

He hugged her exuberantly. 'I've been finding things out. And you?'

She only shook her head. She seemed overwhelmed, her eyes stared as if blinded. He hugged her again.

'Isn't this terrific? Oh, God. We've got them, Brae.'

The passers-by weren't taking any notice. He flashed on Clavel's experience in Fo. It's easy being an alien. He kept his arm around Braemar and drew her into the corridor he'd left.

'I've got a plan. Have you seen any maps? We're in the hub here. We're going to climb out into the scaffolding. We'll climb in again at a different level. The place we want is two floors up, near to the equator.'

'How do we get there?'

'Simple. We take a bus.'

They stood, heads tilted, peering. It was chilly out here, even so close to human habitation. The girders were vast beyond the scale of any human artefact. A dizzying landscape, impossible geology of struts and spars, sprang out and down through the dark air with no visible limits. You could see how venturesome young Aleutians would come to test themselves, and maybe break their silly necks.

The bus had set them down at its terminus, by which time they were its only passengers. The transition from living space to wilderness was oddly natural: behind them, the walled city. The edge of the wilderness was overgrown with bushes like giant clubmoss, very dark green; a kind of turf; several different flowering plants. There were no people about. Johnny explained his brilliant plan. He told her about symbolic literacy, and read her the information provided at the bus stop. Since the Aleutian public transport didn't take fares it would have been possible to use it for the whole journey. But that was a bit too risky. Braemar was very quiet. He had the impression she'd spent her time alone wandering vaguely in a state of shock.

'"Down" is out, remember,' said Johnny. 'Out to the shells. We don't want to get too far, just crawl around the outside of the living space and find ourselves another bus stop.'

They climbed into the rock web. Perception and perspective shifted. It became possible to see that they were crawling in a mess of irregular bracing between two roughly concentric spheres: under a convex curved surface, and over a concave far away 'floor'.

Goblin claws scratched at Braemar's attention. She looked around and around, and nasty things slithered away unseen. She was clambering through an algal bloom of memory, the air was full of fragments of her past, fragments of meaning. She had seen all she wanted to see, she'd had enough of Aleutia. But Johnny must have his adventure. She was afraid to cross him, downright scared of his anger although he was such a baby.

She was afraid at every step that she would fall out of this precarious reality into a spasming void where *anger* was the rock, *fear* the air, shame and guilt the space that held her. They followed spiderweb waymarks, integral like the maps. The rock-like metal or metallic rock was well worn. Mountaineering might be a minority sport, but they were using a popular path.

'Johnny? Do you think this is real?'

'I haven't a clue,' he said. 'It's bloody good fun, though. Wait a moment. Down is out: I think we have to turn here.' He closed his eyes, trying to orient himself by inner-ear balance: and instantly wailed, fell to his hands and knees.

'Wow. Don't try that.'

'I didn't get any video of the engine room,' called Johnny. 'But I think they're using the sun for power. That has to be it. Some kind of massive harvesting of the solar wind, of the energy skirts of each star as they pass through its domain. They're lost, you know. They must be lost. No one would have come out to this god-forsaken neck of a spiral arm on purpose.'

The whole primitive mechanism grieved him deeply. Somewhere in him there had survived the vision of Planet Aleutia: pure waters, rolling meadows, lovely little eco-malls scattered like dewdrops.

'They're no better than us, they're in the same fix themselves. How useless.'

He was parleying with the hyper-associating Johnny who was anxious for excuses, because he wanted to *shaft* the aliens in the worst way. The aliens had become somehow entangled with Braemar. Get down, you stupid animal. The battle in his mind/body was eerie and horrible. Brae mustn't know what was going on. She'd be terrified.

'On the contrary,' corrected Braemar softly. 'They've learned to run a world the way our world needs to be run. They're what we need.'

She touched the deep worn treads: hand and footholds, Aleutians went four-footed here. So old a race of wanderers. So ancient and single an organism. *I want that ship*, she had said, and here it was. But where was the proof of Aleutian equality? That was what she asked. Not that they be inferior. She only wanted them to be equals. Why couldn't they be equals? Why did she always have to be afraid?

Goblins crept behind.

'One consolation,' Johnny called back cheerfully. 'This is a spaceship. When we start climbing, *technically* there's a slight gravity gradient: we'll be doing less work – '

Then he fell.

He fell away from her, a blur of movement. She yelled and clung to the rock. He was lying below, about thirty metres under her feet, caught in the fork of two rocky branches. Frightened, but not yet terrified, she scrambled down.

Johnny rolled over. He was not unconscious, he had not broken his back. He was clutching, two-handed, at a red spring that rose from the dun cloth out of his inner thigh. Nicked the femoral artery.

'Can't . . . stop it.'

'*Yes I can!*'

She stripped off her Aleutian suit. It wouldn't tear, she wadded the whole thing: rammed it against the wound. The dun-coloured underwear, pocket in the crotch for their sanitary pad arrangement, hung off her hips and cramped her shoulders.

Oh God, someone help me –

'Stay calm, breath shallow. Don't move.'

We do not wake up, why don't we wake up? People have been known to die in virtualities. Known as the Huxley effect, it can happen quite easily. Until this moment she'd been half convinced she was really dead and this a dream of the collapsing neurons. It was a vision anyway: hallucination, wish-fulfilment. But she couldn't wake herself. Her heart was pounding. Johnny lay back, lax: breathing shallow, watching her from under half-closed lids with a faint, apologetic smile. He was unconscious. But he was still here. Aleutia remained solid and the blood kept coming.

Something moved above her. She didn't turn her head. It scratched around in front. She saw a little creature with a segmented chitined body and several clawed legs. Its head was marked like a face, eyepatched like a caterpillar.

It had a human face.

Something landed with a meaty plop. It hopped up on a single rear limb like a coiled spring. It had a row of eyes, human eyes: and two pairs of soft little baby hands.

More of them came, none larger than a squirrel. Some were very small. 'Go away!' she sobbed, her hands fixed rigid in the welter of Johnny's blood. But the goblin creatures came up close. They were all over her and Johnny, seeking for messages, before the Aleutian arrived.

Having made the injured intruder as comfortable as possible, the doctor returned. Braemar sat crouched against the wall in the lobby of the first-aid station, half-naked and bloody. The doctor folded himself up near her. He reached out a hand. The skin of his fingertips crept, dust motes danced in the air. No action at a distance in Aleutia. A trolley came up. The doctor took a blanket from it, and patted the machine: a magnified sign, Aleutian kindness to animals, of the endless chemical caresses that kept everything going.

The doctor wrapped the blanket around her shoulders. The blanket was alive, too – not to Braemar's perception but she knew its status from the way the doctor touched it. Everything was alive: rock, metal, food, tools. Everything was crawling with the infection of Aleutia: a world of flesh infested with the life of its people.

He made a short speech in the unknown Aleutian language.

He probably said, 'How did you get here?'

No answer.

The doctor began to explain something. The dumb show he used, the grotesque half-alive tools he showed; it conveyed nothing. It didn't have to. She was inside the Aleutian paradigm. She already knew what he was bound to say. She knew the story.

Your friend needs blood. It must be yours.

She shook her head, desperately negative.

He had expected this reaction. Stealing tissue is an act of war. He covered his face, the gesture of reverence. He tried hard to convince the stranger, not of his brood, that he wouldn't dream of taking advantage. He explained, perhaps, that he had made a vow: *I swear by Apollo* . . .

'No.'

Your friend will die.

No answer.

The doctor was patient, puzzled, but only mildly curious. Aleutia was such a small place. He'd certainly heard about the expedition, was aware that there was a habitable and inhabited new world on his doorstep. The arrival of a pair of alien intelligences in his own voyaging home left him unmoved. He wasn't even greatly interested in knowing how. The unknown had no chill for him, no thrill, no *numen*.

On a counter there were things growing in dishes: his houseplants, his pets, his children. Some had eyes that seemed nearly conscious.

Braemar had to explain. It wasn't hard, he was a doctor.

<I'm sick,> she told him, in the Common Tongue. <My blood might kill him.>

She hoped the doctor would manage not to tell Johnny what the problem was. Maybe he didn't realise it was supposed to be a secret. He gave her another suit. He regarded her still filthy body with bemused distaste, but she was too tired to try and explain. They didn't understand washing with water, and he probably didn't have any significant water supply. He sent her into the ward behind his surgery to explain.

Johnny's face was waxy yellow-white. A living coverlet was tucked to his chin, a thing clinging through it to his thigh, and another to his arm. Perhaps he had guessed what she had to say long ago. His eyes were closed, he was gone. Where's Johnny? Johnny's gone. She had quarrelled with her husband, one day when he was dying. She left the hospital telling herself that she would make it up tomorrow. But 'tomorrow' he'd fallen into the last decline, and never knew her again.

'I want to do right,' whispered Braemar. Aleutia was real as death. The knowledge that she'd gained while she was alone was hard and solid. She must get home and put it to use. But she wished it could end here, that it was herself lying there. She wanted to tell Johnny the truth, but she was too frightened.

His eyes opened. 'I need a transfusion. Do they understand? Brae, your blood's the same group as mine. I saw it on your passport. D'you remember, in Fo?' He was very scared. He made a bare attempt to lift his head. 'My kit's in my bag . . . Where did we leave our bags?'

He had forgotten where they were, and why, and how. He was in Africa, or some other of the earth's many desolations: dying because he'd taken a stupid risk to get a story. There were no chairs. She knelt on the floor by the pallet bed.

'The doctor's going to take a blood sample from you, and copy it. They can do that here, but he needs your consent.'

'Why? Why can't they take your blood?'

He didn't want anybody's help but hers, didn't trust any other.

'I'm sick,' she whispered. 'I have AIDS.'

Braemar began to tremble. Johnny sat up. His eyes, a moment ago sunken and vague, were blazing with outrage. He swung at her open-handed, he slapped her around the head. 'You *bitch!*' She tried to fend him off, he punched at her breasts, her face. He was on his feet, the injury forgotten. '*That was the most beautiful moment of my life, you filthy cheating bitch!*' Braemar cowered, he grabbed her by the shoulders, pulled her upright, slammed her down. He punched and kicked in a frenzy. '*No, Johnny,*' Braemar whimpered. '*Johnny, please don't . . .*'

She scrabbled at her clothes, trying to show willing, the only way she knew to save herself. Everything fell away.

A wet evening in London. The tiny alleyways of Holborn were packed, the gutters running and chuckling, the meagre little stalls canopied with waterproof sheeting: which was more degradable than it ought to be and melting in shards over the goods. From a bar doorway came the strains of somebody singing, over Bing Crosby's backing, *I'm dreaming of a wet Christmas*, and the shops sold blue and silver filigree: raindrop garlands, comical cards showing families Christmas dinnering on the rooftree in a waste of water. The three-month orgy had begun.

In the suburbs people would still be spraying frost on their lawns in late December, if Holborn was a mangrove swamp. In a country where everything good is always in the past, it's the poor who make fashion.

Johnny walked in the crowd, head down, fists in his pockets. Singing garlands, karaoke, headboxes, kids with talking clothes. It was hard to believe the noise level could have been worse fifty years ago. The Back Of The North Wind was a gracious retro oasis. It had a traditional painted sign showing a big tree against blue sky, some quiet children sitting in the branches. Presumably that meant something, to the British or some subset thereof.

People were talking softly at tables or along the bar. Brass glistened; there was a red carpet, quantities of dark polished wood. The unstoppable ooze of meta-Christmas had been kept at bay. There were no garlands. Indoors the ftl afterburn was still almost unmanageable. He could wade through the tables, he could almost see through the walls.

Braemar was sitting alone, her chin on her hand. He studied her face, the hollowed temples, brooding eyes, lips set fine and hard as a knife blade. Her snow-deep pallor, without a trace of English rose to warm it, seemed mythical, inhuman. She looked like what she had been to him: the embodiment of misfortune, ruin, grief. Brae, not the virus, had wrecked his life. He could have lived with the QV, imagining himself innocent.

The mask had worn very thin. Neither white, nor a queen: she wore the ironic title like an essential shadow of the truth. A woman can be a female impersonator. A smart Asian matron (he wondered what the real mix was; something more complex, certainly) can spend her life assiduously, subliminally, passing for white. But peel away the double mask, and she was so like himself – crazy, timid, stubborn: for ever throwing out a shell of smart ideas and fast talk to hide the terrified worm inside. Johnny smiled without knowing it. He had lost the lady in red, and found his lost child. And he consigned Bella, the little girl he didn't remember, to someone else's care at last.

They hadn't parted on the best of terms. He was afraid to face her, afraid to meet that mysterious look of humility which had once so intrigued him. He knew where it came from now: guilty eyes of a beaten animal.

Braemar watched him coming. 'You aren't limping, Johnny.'

'Not a trace. They do mighty fine first aid in Aleutia.'

He sat down. He looked at her, and looked at her. 'He used to hit you, didn't he?'

'What?'

'Your husband, I surmise. The guy who gave you AIDS.'

She looked at him, and away: down the years. Johnny felt like an intruder.

'You're right. I was a virtuous wife. I didn't know any better. And he used to hit me. Bourgeois Asians have mixed feelings about mixed race. He married me because I was fair-skinned and had some education. I married him because I wanted a house, and children. He wasn't a very secure person, or very clever. He came to resent – various things. He would beat me up, and then make love to me; and I liked that. I got to like the combination. He would fuck other women, phone me up from hotel rooms berating me for making him feel guilty. That wasn't such fun. But the whole thing was addictive. It is sickeningly pleasant to be always the injured party, to have someone perpetually calling himself names and begging your forgiveness. You can't know if you haven't tried it.

'One day I made up my mind I would make him take an HIV test, mostly just to humiliate him. It has always seemed as though I killed him, because he was perfectly healthy . . . and then in a year he was dead. Krishna died when he was five. Of AIDS. My daughter escaped. I've lived with it: HIV positive, symptomless AIDS as they call it now. It's not half as hard as you'd think. There weren't any quarantine regulations in those days, but there were awful ideas about how infectious you were. It was natural to keep it totally secret. I take care. I have never infected anyone, as far as I know. And I haven't ever been ill, so I never surfaced. There's my pharmacist, some medical records. But no one's ever tracked me down. I doubt if anybody but family knows, for sure.'

The AIDS virus protects against QV. HIV carriers can't catch or carry the mutated, distant descendant of the disease. It had been a dirty joke for him in the Amsterdam clinic. If you want it badly enough, Johnny: if you can get it up for a burnt-out, aged leper the ward is thataway.

'One day, I was going to Africa for White Queen. We were keeping tabs on people who chased aliens, and in those days you were talked about in my circles: the eejay with the QV. So I knew that Johnny Guglioli was ahead of me and I came prepared to make myself interesting. When I found out what was happening to you, I used the most effective counter attraction I could provide to keep you from getting hypnotised. That was the way we were thinking. The QV couldn't hurt me. What can I say? It seemed like a good idea at the time. The story broke, we thought that was the end of your significance. I left. And I kept away from you, until fate beat me down.'

Her face crumpled briefly. 'When you reappeared there wasn't going to be any more sex between us, because there'd been a change of plan and I had you marked for Clavel. You think I betrayed something that night in Africa, Johnny: but that was only the start. I've always been ready to use you, to do whatever was necessary for the cause. The one thing I *tried hard* not to do – after Fo – was to use you and fuck you at the same time. Because I do love you.' She shuddered. 'I always did, or very soon. The lightning strike was real, and I knew it was, and went on lying to you. I'm a ruthless person, Johnny.'

He smiled. 'Cruel and sentimental, like James Bond. You did warn me.'

'Well, you know the truth. Has it set you free?'

'Never.' He reached for her hands. 'Brae, I'm the one who should be grovelling. I can't – I don't know what happened to me – '

'Don't.' She pulled away. 'I lied to you, Johnny. In a language that we might as well call Aleutian, since we haven't a word of our own. It's not the words, it's not the signs, it's something between. I did a horrible thing. Not only that first night but again and again since then.'

'Then I lied too. In that same language. I'm not clean. Well, shit, maybe I am: but I've never believed it. The outraged innocence has always been a sham.'

He reached across the table again.

She looked at their clasped hands, sighed a long shuddering note of relief. 'Okay.'

The physical link grounded them, made it possible to talk about what had happened.

'Johnny, tell me. What do you remember?'

He attempted to pull himself together. 'I remember that you lay down, and when I next looked you were gone. At that moment . . . I can't recapture the state of mind I was in, but at that moment I seriously believed you were hiding behind the door, or in some stage magician's cabinet. It seemed like – okay, we agreed to humour her. So I lay down. Then I was on a big spaceship and various exciting things happened that seemed normal enough, if you know what I mean. Then.'

They had been where only the dead go. The nakedness of that experience was still near, a strain on his humanity. As soon as he let himself think of it, he was flung back into a state where everything that happened was so true it could never be forgotten or denied. The corruption at the heart of their love, the violence and treachery, was as vital as the love itself. He did not forgive her. What he felt was too immediate, too intimate: it was nothing like forgiveness, or shame. He would never leave the moment of mutual betrayal. He would live in it, wrapped in her arms, never want anything more.

He looked her dead in the eye, trembling. 'Then there was some psycho-drama. And I don't know how it ended. The return, I don't remember at all . . . Shit. I remember roughly we came back from Germany together in a car. But it is as if . . . As if I walked from that first-aid place into this pub.'

Braemar winced. 'Ouch, yes, I know what you mean, Me too. Johnny, I have to confess my abstract knowledge of physics ended with – um – the Brit version of Junior High nearly fifty years ago. I have the most kitchen-cookery understanding of telecommunication technology, nothing more. Peenemünde's explanation was gibberish. I know I wasn't paying close attention, but I'd stand by that judgement. I suspect she's one of those superbeings whose left brain shuts down when she's faced with ordinary mortals. Have you *any* idea what could have happened? In girl-childish terms, please.'

'Oh.' He screwed up his eyes and struggled. 'Nothing is real. There's the void. Reality keeps happening and unhappening all the time. She . . . We had to disappear in Prussia, because of local point phase conservation. She caught us phasing. We were annihilated, as normal, but remade elsewhere instead of here.'

'Can't you do any better than that?'

'Uh, no.'

'I am smarter than I thought.'

'*God*, it was horrible. I *cannot* see that experience catching on. Something's going to have to be done. People won't want to go to Betelgeuse if they have to launder their souls on the way.'

'If we were in real Aleutia,' she said. 'What really happened there? I wonder how our visit is recorded in that doctor's log, if he keeps one. But if *consciousness*, the self, has to be unpinned and reassembled, maybe we'd be shallow fools to expect any less disturbing kind of travel sickness.' She shook her head. 'I think we're overreacting. We're a couple of savages going berserk over the metaphysics of our first trip to heaven in the big silver bird. People will learn not to dwell on the culturally constructed meaning of what happens to the mind in ftl travel mode. Oh.' She picked up something from the chair beside her and put it on the table. It was the cockroach's mobile home. 'Some bad news. I hope you're not going to be too upset. I'm afraid Robert didn't make it.'

Johnny opened the box. There was no visible damage, but the indestructible roach was perfectly dead.

'Good grief. You didn't slip him something?'

'How could you? I didn't *like* the thing, but I wouldn't harm it.'

Johnny started to laugh. For some reason the dead roach, failed 4-space traveller, was irresistibly funny.

'There must be less roach nature in either of us than we imagined.' He groaned and massaged his eyeballs. 'I feel terrible. Physically, I mean. I kind of partly feel as if I'm still spread over the sum of all the possibilities. It's remarkably like a monstrous hangover. Studies will prove, I believe, that faster than light travel is extremely hard on the liver.' He dropped his hands. 'You realise we have to go back. The idea is unspeakably terrifying, and I don't know if I believe it's other than a hallucination: but we have to try.'

'I know,' she said, sombre-eyed.

He stood up. 'I'll buy you a drink. What would you like? Shall we get drunk?'

Johnny was at the bar. Braemar watched him, trying hard to regret that she had failed to set him free. The barmaid had a headbox on the bar. She turned from one of her sneaked moments with the miniature screen and pumped up the volume on the big one overhead.

IN BY CHRISTMAS! yelled a quality tabloid.

An insufferably cheery young male face dissolved into a turning geographical globe. The same character pranced beside it, diminutive now and making lewd play with a long pink pointer. The sedate elderly lady icon, which this paper used for its 'serious' news, popped up in the left upper quadrant. *The world government says that within the next weeks a new party of visitors will materialise. They will be settling –* '

'Settling!' remarked someone in the bar, over-loud.

Johnny turned. His eyes locked with Braemar's, a contact deeper than touch: no action at a distance. He came back and they began to kiss, a shocking display in this public place by the standards of the age. No one protested. It was the festive season.

11: BELLING THE CAT

There had been the European tour, the Asian tour, the North Asian tour, the South American tour. The Aleutians had seen everything. They had done some wonderful things. They had cleaned up Karen city. The Kok river held some of the purest, liveliest, fresh water in the world. They promised that they could help – maybe do away for ever – with the poison that seeped into the Pacific. But they, like their gadgets, remained sealed boxes.

Dubbed 'hox-tools' by SETI, a term borrowed from genetics, Aleutian gadgets were the symbol of Aleutia's presence. Their function could be identified through human analogy: camcorder, computer, food processor, musical instrument. But nobody had any idea how they worked. The lucky (or unfortunate) Karens were acting as the world's guinea pigs. Meanwhile, the enclaves moved towards reality. Rajath started talking about the arrival of permanent settlers, or at least that's what he seemed to be saying. At this point, some of the original Uji-watchers began to form a conspiracy.

Aleutian artefacts were still – in theory – being studied in Africa and in the USSA, but results were hard to come by. There were staffing problems, zoning problems. No one wanted to offend the all-powerful telepaths. No one wanted a lab that was doing that kind of work anywhere near them. There had been, especially in the USSA, violent protest. An early analysis of the effluent from Uji, completed before Aleutian-fever really took hold, only proved that the visitors were good at clearing up after themselves. There wasn't a trace of anything alien in the water.

It was Ellen who suggested that they should try to plant a bug in Uji manor. She argued that the telepaths couldn't care less about mechanical surveillance. If the idea was proposed to them openly, they'd probably refuse because of the 'supernatural' connotations. But if a bug was planted on them they wouldn't find it because they didn't care. And suppose they did find it, they would not react strongly to an illicit piece of 'deadware'. It wouldn't mean the same to them as the theft of a drop of blood.

The Ruam Rudi office communicated with the talkers by audiophone and fax. It was hard work, especially when there was a tour to organise. But Rajath, Lugha and Clavel, at least, could read English fluently by now. The poet-princess or the demon child would even produce an intelligible reply to a direct question sometimes, either written or spoken. Since the day Sarah Brown died, no human had been inside the manor house, except perhaps for Kaoru. No one got any further than the helipad. Supplies and assorted fanmail were delivered by Kaoru's staff, who were now paid by the Uji estate. The same team flew the Aleutians down to Bang Khen, when they came out on tour.

Ellen decided to let Robin pilot her. She did not trust Kaoru's servants. They arrived at Uji mid-afternoon on a still, cool day of the hill country 'winter'. When the sound of the rotors stopped, she thought she could hear the river. The tall hedge of trees blocked their view down into the valley. Two dun-overalled figures, Rajath and Clavel, came towards them. Three of the nameless ambled along behind. Ellen and Robin got down.

'So much for the world where physical location doesn't matter,' murmured Robin. 'They'll have us running up here with messages in cleft sticks when they've really got us trained.'

'Ssh!'

'Home sweet home!' cried Rajath, shrugging and grinning.

But his welcome seemed wary, even suspicious. Ellen steeled herself. 'We thought we might as well make the maildrop, for once.'

'It gets us out of the office,' added Robin affably.

It was hard not to stare about, trying to spot changes. Kaoru's security turned away a steady trickle of hopeful intruders from this enclave's perimeters. That much they knew in Ruam Rudi. The government of the world had access to some of Kaoru's system, as in the original arrangement, but the Aleutians had been on their own here for a long time. No one knew what they were doing. Officially, they only left Uji to go on tour. In reality, no one had any control over their movements. They could come and go as they pleased.

The humans handed over two sacks of freight mail, which the Aleutians accepted with mild interest.

'And I brought you a present.' Ellen offered a long jewel case to her old friend the pirate. 'It's only a funny little curio, it's of no great value.'

People, schoolchildren, institutions, were always sending presents to Uji. Ellen, remembering the Aleutian delight in random personal adornment, had had a necklace made up. It was composed of large beads in the shape of brightly coloured Beatrix Potter rabbits: twenty solid Peter Rabbits, each about ten centimetres high, spaced by smaller beads shaped like lettuces, carrots and onions.

'It's what they call Reverse Chinoiserie,' she explained. 'Work like this was very popular in Tokyo at the turn of the century.'

'Oh! How darling!'

The poet-princess came and leaned over Rajath's shoulder.

'He'll treasure it,' said Clavel.

The pirate captain suppressed a split-lipped grin, and shrugged broadly. 'You won't stay for tea.'

'No, thank you. We have to get back, really. But I hope you don't mind accepting the necklace. Remember, it's a personal gift from me. No one else.'

The majority of delegates in the Multiphon chamber would have been horrified at the very idea.

The heavy foliage of the trees rattled and shuddered as the tilt-rotor rose. Ellen looked down the Uji valley, stung by nostalgia. It was quiet enough in the cabin for conversation, once they were on their way. Neither of them spoke for a while.

There are billions, thought Robin, who believe the Aleutians are angels, or who ignore the Aleutians, or who try to use them for profit. They may be right. Everything may be fine, or everything may turn out to have been negligible. But I am inside the game. In forty years, perhaps, I'll look back and know that here I learned how to work, how to pay attention to detail, how to drive myself. For now, there is no outside. The Aleutians are all there is. His hermit was giving him some unexpected practical lessons. You could spend a lifetime in Brussels or Westminster without finding out how it felt to risk your life, deliberately, for a political end.

'Nothing to worry about, lad,' said Ellen firmly. 'They don't believe our magic works.'

Back on the ground, Clavel said, <I told you. They're uneasy about what's going on here. They want to know what we're doing: Ellen just said so.>

But Rajath was examining the necklace. <What a horrid object. What are these things with the long ears? Some kind of weapons? It's not my idea of an ornament.>

For a while the balance of opinion had been with Clavel, and caution. But a few nights after that, when the moon was new again, Lugha and the shuttle took flight.

Oh, we were scared . . . No one was going to grass up Brunhilde, but we were really scared . . .

Braemar curled on the couch in her workroom, a blanket round her knees, and watched the opening of the third act of *Die Walkure*. The warrior maidens trembled at the sound of Daddy's tread upon the stair. They would help Brunhilde as far as they dared, but they couldn't ratify her action. No one would share the blame. *Daddy will punish* . . . She could live with that. It was harder to deal with the *Daddy* in the heart, the small voice that sounds so like one's own.

She went down to the kitchen, where Johnny was working at the housebox terminal. She watched him for a moment from the doorway: his shoulders bent, his serene profile. She had never seen Johnny in this mode before, communing with the keys and the screen. He looked very happy.

'I'm going to Folkestone. I want to talk to Clem about something: might as well do it in person. I can't help you here. I won't be late.'

Braemar had written to Buonarotti, freight mail. The Professor had replied, with dignity, by fax. She would be happy to have a second meeting for the purpose of the interview Ms Wilson had requested. Buonarotti evidently wanted to make it clear that she wasn't going to enter into a clandestine correspondence. But her letter was discreet and sounded cooperative. Meanwhile, there were last-minute hitches over the Aleutian settlement. White Queen's contact in KT said there was something going on, new developments, people getting twitchy. There was still time for Johnny's publicity stunt to have effect.

Braemar thought of White Queen as a company of warrior

maidens. They were *feminine* in gestalt, whatever their gender, in the sense of being the opposition to majority opinion: the unregarded, the party that's always out of office. She was not surprised at their girlish reaction to this latest plan. She went to Folkestone, got herself briefed by the one shield-maid who could be of real use; and endured Clementina for a while.

On her way home she pulled the car into a breakdown layby, leaned her head on her arms on the wheel: heard Clem's unlovely voice hammering on her memory.

'These creatures are excellent Aristotleans. The body that gives birth is no more than a host, *le serment*: a mere pod.' And then again: 'Their society must be ideally stable. Think of our little new science of nanotechnology. Imagine the world where human beings have always been the chemical plants. Their physics is biochemistry. Their technology will consist of having learned how to dope these chemical plants, to change the food-preparing response, and the nest-materials–shaping response and so on. Think of how our capitalist mechanical devices mimicked hands, feet, jaws: machines to do the work of a hundred hands, eh? But do you imagine the person who weeps industrial processes from the pores of her skin rules the world? Oh, no, I don't think so. In that world there are "persons" who truly are hereditary servants, teachers, tin-openers, waste-disposers; whose self-image cannot be shifted by the revolutionary preacher. Almost as immovable as ourselves, indeed . . .'

The birthing body is a mere pod . . . What would the Aleutians think of earth's women when they understood human physiology? They'd think nothing of the question: no interest, so what? But those earthlings who had always hankered after Aristotle would soon be busy, with the supposed blessing of the master-race.

She recalled Clavel and Johnny in the Botanical Gardens. They were so alike, those two, the missionary and the journalist. Clavel had learned a lot from Johnny. And put it to subtle use, damn her. It used to make Braemar's blood run cold to think what a part those interviews had in the shaping of the relation between Aleutia and humankind. It was a game to Clavel. One couldn't blame her. No harm meant in the world, no notion that anything could turn out badly.

She took out a document that she was preparing.

Aleutian society is feudal and cannot 'develop' further. The species is not divided into two sexes but into an unknown number of broods. They distinguish some kind of psychological spectrum, which they have readily identified with our distinction between 'masculine' and 'feminine'. But it has nothing to do with childbearing, and no substantial link with erotic/companionate pairing. Each individual has the ability to give birth, each body contains, potentially, the whole sum of the brood's genetic variants. Something of the skills learned in a lifetime are incorporated in the genetic material, and changes pass into the appropriate variant throughout the brood, through their habit of ingesting each other's mobile cells. Individuals who are 'reborn' have the chemical memories of their past lives. They are in some sense immortals who also evolve. But substantially their attributes remain the same through all their avatars. Children are identified at birth (we don't know how) and discovered to be long-lost princes or long-lost dishwashers. They are taught to 'become themselves' psychologically by intense study of records of 'their' previous lives. They are entitled to the recurrent person's income, influence, and they take on that person's loyalties, dependants. Social mobility within a generation might be startling to earth's eyes, the sum of movement is nil . . .

She wrote in ink, on paper. This wasn't going into any kind of computer storage. Such a mass of her own small and precise handwriting looked strange, the exercise of an obscure hobby, like a needlepoint cushion. But there it was: one began to prepare for the worst. She returned the papers to their hiding place and sat, staring.

There was a star somewhere. No way of knowing how far away it was. Not a blue sun. Most likely a yellow-white sun, class G2V; why not? It had an earthlike planet in a congenial orbit with an atmosphere of nitrogen and oxygen, it had chemical mixtures that became fusions and began to grow: a thing called life. There are only so many notes, as Humpty Dumpty said. This thing called life did much the same things as on earth. But something was slewed. It might be the difference of a hair's breadth from the way things happened on earth: a tendency for the different chemical groupings to 'consider themselves' less as closed domains, more as areas of greater concentration in a single soup: constantly exchanging substance with their neighbours and – remotely – with every other *indistinct* entity in the biosphere. Only the breadth of a hair – but by the time life on this other earth made things like humans, it made creatures extraordinarily familiar, but absolutely alien. They had the same pie, but they cut it up on their own weird tangents to the lines that humans put there. Aleutians were a different answer to exactly the same question: an answer that covered the same myriad heads of possibility and came out, over all, with something that looked the same and that worked just as well – only better.

She thought about posterity, which was ridiculous but she couldn't help it. People would research the background and find out about Nirmal. They would say: Braemar Wilson identified the aliens – superior beings – with the man who made her feel powerless, who turned her into a pariah. Everything she did was in a sense an act of personal revenge . . .

Braemar felt a rush of impotent rage against the imaginary pundits. They would reduce her to a stereotype, ignoring the possibility that *Braemar Wilson* might be able to see as far into her own head as they: that she might be able to accept the complexity of her own motivation, and still go on and do what had to be done. She calmed herself, amused. If her motivation was getting ripped up, it would be because something had worked. It was a small price to pay.

She put the minicooper into auto and let the ratrun traffic carry her home while she sat there deliberately recalling the Uji tapes, the faces and voices of baboon-individuals who were as *human* as herself.

Johnny's confidence in the power of his eejay's stunt was touching. How far did he really, deep down, believe in it? She wasn't going to ask him. She had managed for a very long time to get by without having anyone she could entirely trust. It wouldn't be fair to try and change that now.

Johnny's plan was simple. Not easy, but simple. He was going to hijack an Aleutian telecommunication source and send a signal to some earthling scientific hardware – one of the few satellites that faced up and out instead of down and in. Once he'd got the hardware's attention it would relay his signal to earth to be picked up by the various entities that still monitored deep space information-collection. Johnny didn't know what he'd be able to transmit. Ideally, he'd end up talking to earth on video from Aleutia, but it didn't matter. He didn't have to identify himself, get personal, or say much. He only had to *be there*, a signal source where none should be, displaying the signs that SETI was supposed to recognise. The agencies that picked him up should do the rest.

Some of those agencies might not be trustworthy. SETI was in the hands of the alien-lovers. The corps, too, clearly had a secret policy. Separately or collectively they might well suppress sensitive information to earn credit with the aliens. If they got the chance. But there were others. Amateurs, hams, grabbers . . . Johnny knew that White Queen couldn't be alone. Where there are secrets, there are people trying to find them out. The pack was closing in on that ship: he could *sense* that, now that he knew himself what was going on. There might be earthlings who already knew the truth and were keeping quiet, there were bound to be others who were in the hunt. Johnny could feel the breath of pursuit. But he was confident. He had the edge over the competition (and what an edge!). He was going to be the first, be the one to bring the people the news.

He spent hours performing mental experiments with White Queen gamers: getting up to date on esoteric satellite-ham lore, trying to work out hypothetical alien tech. He tried, in the course of this, to sneak out of them more information about White Queen. They wouldn't talk. He got the impression of a touchingly minute 'organisation'. He wondered what they'd do with themselves once the charade was over, the alien cover blown.

Finally, he tired of studying someone's maniacally detailed diagrams of an alternate universe radio station.

He snapped off his gloves, scrumpled them in one fist: looked at them and laughed. As long as he was on earth he was keeping the rules: it was a hard habit to break. He wandered the kitchen, peered at the festering greenery behind the sink. He found a glass-fronted cupboard with a shelf of old cookery books. Opening one at random, he read the name of the owner neatly inscribed on the inside cover. C. M. Wilson. The paper was gold-tinged with age, ready to crumble at a touch.

He went up to the workroom to wait for Braemar. The decorators had packed up and gone home from the devastated drawing room, leaving a litter of spray-on protection, canvas sheeting, ladders, discarded bits of food. She'd decided to change the whole thing: a whole new look. It was late. The house was cold and gloomy. The bone-gnawing chill of British middle-class winter easily penetrated the meagre heating. Kamla and Billy were asleep upstairs, but the place felt empty. Parsifal's cradle faced him, conjuring vague terrors.

He discovered she'd been watching Wagner, grimaced in disgust and began to channel hop. The fresh edition of New Scientist had a report on the current energy crisis conference. Johnny watched idly, until his attention was caught by a question from the 'floor.' For a moment he couldn't place the face of this tvsponder, or that aged voice – interminably hesistant, but persistent as the Ancient Mariner.

It was the White Knight. The screen politely identified him. The man's name meant nothing, but apparently the ancient knight, in a previous life, had been a high-energy physics researcher. Johnny supposed it was good to have one of those on the team, if you were playing out an old-fashioned B-movie scenario about alien invaders.

He heard Braemar coming up the stairs: and for no reason he could fathom, quickly hopped back to the *Valkyrie.*

'As bad as that? Not even Patti Smith? I thought you didn't like Wagner.'

'I don't. Just killing time.'

He was on the floor at the side of the couch. She got up behind him so he couldn't see her face, but he could feel her mood. It might be simple fear of the next ftl trip, but she hadn't been very communicative since they made peace at The Back Of The North Wind.

'I was watching an energy crisis thing. I spotted our old friend the White Knight making his citizenly contribution . . . Want to see if he's still on?'

'Augh. No. I'm not in the mood for "slowdown" hypocrisy.'

Johnny killed the opera, and they were left with a blank screen. The afterburn of faster than light travel had a lasting bite. Whenever you think you've got to the bottom of heterosexual guilt another crevasse opens. He wondered what was wrong now.

He turned with his arm across her knees. 'What does C.M. stand for?'

'So you've been prying? Not telling you. A girl has to have some mystery.'

'Are you in the mood to talk about psycho-drama?'

'No.' She reached out, twisted the braid of eel-brown hair around her fist. 'I never will be.' Her fingers traced the shape of bone, the sealed box of secrets under the pelt of a warm animal. 'It's not worth worrying about. All that sludge down there, everybody's made the same.'

Johnny got beside her and took over half the blanket. 'The prospect of another psychic acid bath is not appealing, but don't you think we should get going? What are we waiting for?'

She slipped her cold hands inside his clothes, exquisite shock. 'You're right. Have I been making excuses? I'm sorry. It's just that I hate to leave my drawing room at the mercy of the decorators.'

It was an absurd excuse. It could be the truth. She had such an appetite for possessions, and maybe she would never see her treasures again. He knew there was more, but he hadn't the courage to go after it. He hugged her instead, abandoning himself to those wise hands.

The next day they set out for Prussia.

It was black night in Krung Thep, one of the Buddhist Days of Atonement when everything closed down, services were cut to minimum and people stayed at home to pray for the planet. The killing time, the hot season, was approaching. There would be the usual epidemics here in the city of angels and all over Thailand. People would die: the old, weakly children, controlled cancers and notifiables. The over-stretched medical services would make no attempt to stem those marginal losses. Their relatives would thank them tenderly for dying in the rites of every major religion. It was the same the world over, with varying degrees of hypocrisy. Don't block the exit.

A buzz at the door, a face on the entryphone. Ellen was slow to respond. She was watching tv and nursing a half-empty glass.

The bugging of Uji manor had worked very smoothly, but the results were disappointing. The necklace didn't catch anybody's fancy. Instead of wandering around the aliens' private space, it lay

with other earthling gifts on a table in the main hall. It saw
Aleutians behaving as they had always done. It transmitted
fabulously detailed images of the 'hox boxes', but couldn't penetrate their mysteries. There was, needless to say, little dialogue.

Then, suddenly, nothing.

It had been five days now. Not a sign from the Aleutians, not a
spark of life from the device. For those who were in the secret, these
had been five days and nights of controlled panic.

Ellen tried to blame the gadgetry. She had wanted something as
simple as possible, but she'd been overruled. Every Peter Rabbit in
the necklace was a mass of minute light sensors, backed by layer
upon layer of exquisite gallium arsenide circuitry – no coralin, of
course. Now that it had gone wrong, she could not help recollecting
that the work had been done by a Korean firm in KT which was
wholly owned by ex-Japanese.

The entryphone, in despair, took a large bite out of her tv picture
and put Robin's face in there. At last she opened the door.

He was somewhat informally dressed in a grey singlet and floppy
black shorts. His slick blond hair was dark with sweat. He had a
bulky garland around his neck of jasmine buds and mauve orchids.

'Come on,' he coaxed, with a big sloppy grin – most unlike Robin.
'A few of us are getting together. Come and party.'

There were two garlands. He peeled one off and held it out.

Ellen stared at him, questioning. Robin only grinned more
widely. She waved the garland away.

'You'll make me look like a dog's dinner.'

Their tuktuk cruised into a city not entirely dedicated to
penitence. Ellen sat back and blessed the coolness of the moving air
as they nudged through the barely lit traffic.

She was thinking of Sarah Brown. Ellen had taken care to identify
herself personally with the tampered present. There would be no
threat to millions this time. The culprit would be handed over
cheerfully, and Aleutian notions of personal responsibility should
contain the damage.

She didn't ask a single question. Robin admired her calm, and
fought the churning tension griping in his insides. He knew that
Ellen assumed she was going to her death, maybe not at the end of
this ride, but very soon. She might be right.

They crossed over the river to Thonburi, to an area where

nondescript elderly blocks were interrupted by whimsical *fin de siècle* fun-chitecture. The Ephemeral 'Sweet BeachBums', their destination, shared a building in the·shape of a water buffalo with a jazz club, some games studios and a small shopping mall. The buffalo's legs were built for flooding. Lifts and stairs passed through airlock-sealed bulkheads and there were rescue platforms at the beast's knobbly knees. The jazz club was in the belly. Ham Yon, the private club section, was on the same level further south.

The belly street had a transparent floor. Shapes moved blurrily below, as if the city down there was already under water. Since it was Atonement Day, the girl at the desk in the private ante-chamber was really present, to save power. She offered, confusingly, to 'switch herself off' when Robin and Ellen arrived.

Recliners, covered with pretty imitation handweaving, were scattered over the floor. Poonsuk was there, Douglas Milne, Martha Ledern, Vu Nyung Hong; and Tavit Burapachaisri, from the Multiphon technical executive. The President of the USSA was also with them. Tavit was in the conspirators' confidence. Carlotta's presence was so bizarre that Ellen, for a moment, thought her friends were merely watching tv.

Robin removed his flowers and set them on the floor. He adopted a languid oriental pose in which he was obviously un-comfortable. Ellen measured the room's emotion. Martha knew something, the others didn't. The air was thick with excitement and bewilderment. But not terror.

'I don't think much of your choice of rendezvous,' said Carlotta, peering out of the screen. 'I may demand a change of venue before I speak.'

The ephemerides, beyond a notional window that filled one whole wall, strolled and posed in a pretty scene which no longer existed, somewhere on the filthy city-swallowed coastline of the Gulf of Siam. Occasionally one of them would seem to notice the audience and smile.

'Carlotta, none of those things are human beings or ever were. They are fancy computer graphics, that's all. Boys and girls who sell themselves to an Ephemeral House lose absolutely nothing, in the opinion of this culture.'

'Hmph. There's no such thing as safe porn, Dougie. Nor is there any such thing as cultural diversity on moral questions. That's an exploded theory.'

Pirate let out a wild shriek, as if she'd pinched him. She probably had, some way.

'Sure, the ghost-whores are respected. I suppose Saowapua and little Sumanta are in the can somewhere, piling up their fees for the World Wide Fund for Nature.'

Saowapua and Sumanta were the royal princesses.

'We respect your reservations, Madam President.'

Poonsuk was having a benign interlude. Even now, despite the effort that this adventure had entailed, she looked stronger than usual. She lay propped on one elbow, physically alert. The non-Thai members of the group eyed her nervously, though there was nothing but cool politeness in her tone or face.

'However, an Ephemeral House is an unusually private place. No ordinary brothel could be allowed to be so private, for the safety of its staff.'

'And if anyone *has* moved in with us,' added Martha Ledern, 'the Day of Atonement will smoke them out.'

Martha was acting watchdog. She had a pocket organiser open, sliver screen unfolded; and was reading the relevant pages of Thonburi infra from the citizen information base. Normally, a hundred spies and grabhooks might have buried themselves in that teeming palimpsest of data and energy; but the woods were well thinned tonight.

She looked across at Ellen. 'The President called me up. As soon as I realised what she wanted to talk about, I fixed a private meeting.' They'd used Sweet Beach before. 'I reckon we're safe enough in here.'

Carlotta was unconvinced. 'I thought the guys we're afraid of didn't use machinery?'

'Telepathy? Oh, that part is not worth worrying about.' Chas spoke softly, and the old Vietnamese raised a wry smile from his Uji teammates. Outsiders were fools about telepathy, awarding the Aleutians with vast powers for which there was little evidence; and against which there was no possible protection.

'Okay,' said Carlotta. 'Let's get to it. I have a message for you people.' She slowly grinned. 'Well, now. That got you going. Wait a moment, though. Let me tell the story my way.'

One of the girls on the beach spread a towel and lay down, in her tennis dress and eyeshade. Another ephemeride began to give her a massage, western style. She slipped her hand inside the white pants under the frill of skirt and turned to smile.

Carlotta scowled. 'Can't you turn the damn thing off?'

'With difficulty, Madam President. It's advertising.'

Robin got up. He and Martha dragged a couple of recliners, and propped them over the offending area.

'I suppose that's better.' Pirate muttered a little, but the President relented. 'Maybe some of you guys are aware that there's a partly functioning space station in orbit. No one's been there since the Revolution, and I doubt if we'll be back for a while. But some of the equipment functions. Signals get picked up.'

In the glory days there had been a debate about destroying the station, purely as a gesture. But it would have meant problems with the Soviets, and no one knew whether there would be a fallout of QV virus; and some rebels had a sneaking feeling that half a space station is better than none. Things were left that way.

Space science had suffered heavily in the Revolution. The SETI installation in California was one of the few centres that had survived: and the USSA government had less rights in there than the government of the world. The story that Carlotta had to tell had come to her from the monitoring of could-be dangerous weirdos, and only after that from her own military. She was damned if she was going to sell these snooty Eurasians the image of noseless cultists with homemade backyard dishes clustered in worship . . . But this was delicate stuff. Carlotta considered that people who held 'secret' meetings should be debarred from public office as being of subnormal intelligence. She herself had given up believing in privacy about the same time as she lost faith in Santa Claus. She was dressed carefully in Mom-and-apple-pie teeshirt and denims. The shirt carried the cancelled rocket motif and that favourite anti-space logo SOMETIMES GOD SAYS NO.

It was a fine line, between shocking the anti-space lobby and revealing the humiliating nature of this leak. But the USSA wanted an entry into the Aleutian gameboard. They'd wanted one for a long time, but had to pretend otherwise because a tour was out of the question.

'Before we go on, I should tell you: the source of the material you are about to see is protected.'

The idiots thought they'd raised the alien planet. They didn't even realise that if you could get tv pictures from across the galaxy that way they had to be seeing Aleutia as it was twenty thousand years ago, or something.

She would ask the questions. A simple ploy, but it usually worked. Her eyes panned around the room. 'Exactly whose bright idea was it to bell the cat?'

Pirate shrieked at the sound of his favourite hate-word.

The group in Krung Thep was horrified.

The dataweb that wrapped the globe was a haunted place. Strange things happened there, even before '04. No one trusted it who could use cable. Had their signal misrouted itself out to the space station and back again to be picked up by the USS military? It was terrible luck, but all too possible. *I knew it*, Ellen groaned to herself. *Too much power. The use of excessive force is always wrong* . . . The prospect of death retreated, but not very far. If the President of the USSA knew that Uji was bugged, then it was all over. She knew what had to be done: right from the start.

'Mine,' she said firmly. 'Our kind of surveillance means nothing to them. I decided it was a mistake to leave them alone, and I had a device installed at Uji.'

Carlotta looked cynical. 'At Uji? Well, that's interesting, Ms Kershaw. But I don't think you understand. Let me show you some home movies. I'm afraid the production values aren't what they might be.'

Ellen's first thought was that an Aleutian had slipped out of Uji – for some reason taking the doped necklace – and was, or had been, on board a submarine. But that didn't make sense. The necklace was being worn, presumably. The point of view moved smoothly from a small corridor into a wide, bright passageway: the submarine became an indoor street. There were people, lots of people. They were not human. They were completely unknown Aleutians. Ellen felt her heart begin to thump.

The picture lost colour, distorted, reformed. There was a large hall, a standing crowd. The hidden eyes looked through the Aleutian crowd to a dais. *Lugha* was there: the demon child. He was *dancing*. Beyond him, a row of Aleutians reclining. They wore, the first time anyone in the room in KT had seen such variation, coloured robes over their dun suits. There was a delicate, stately music in the air but otherwise the hall was silent.

Carlotta appeared, over the picture.

'We know where this is coming from. We've traced the signal. We knew it must be a bug, because they've absolutely no desire for us to know where they are. They say they don't have a mothership. They base a lot of their effect on that, and what it implies. But this alien ceremony is happening in our own back yard.'

'Madam President . . .' Douglas could barely control his voice. 'We know you didn't grab these pictures from SETI. Does that mean the military are involved?'

'Dougie, I'm surprised at you.' She was puzzled at the level of their consternation. 'We have no "military", not any more. Not the way you mean. Our soldiers are people who happen to be prepared to give up their lives for the rest of us. And they don't waste their time watching High Frontier tv.' She grinned. 'So now we know what you've been up to. I can give you the exact location. I can give you the dimensions of the ship, if you need them; and some emission details that are highly revealing about its probable motive power. Congratulations, comrades. I don't know how you did it, but it looks as if we may be on our way to a different view of the Aleutian situation.'

Robin got up and crossed the room. He took one of the orchid and jasmine garlands with him. He offered it with a courtly bow, and a brilliant smile.

This time, Ellen didn't refuse.

The minutely tailored alteration to Johnny's chemistry had once more begun to fade by the time they reached the university's reception hall, where they must register as pilgrims. He had failed to overcome his resistance to the eye-dropping operation. The bruising made him nervous as well as making his face sore. He lurked in the background while a porter checked short-term campus service codes on to Braemar's keycard.

He recognised them, and was curious. 'You here again?'

'Yes,' she said. 'It's a game. We're playing *Thirty Years of War*. We're Swedish spies, pursued by Wallenstein's agents. And I shouldn't be telling you this.'

'Ah, gamers!' The man nodded in respect. Only the rich played the big board on such a scale: people with juicy contacts. One could hope something would rub off, if one entered into the spirit. He returned the lady's card with a flourish.

'Good hunting . . . No, good hiding!' He beamed, and added in gruff English. '*I never saw you.*'

Gamers. The magic word. You could do anything, under that explanation. But your enemies could use the same excuse.

The rooms they were given were in a nondescript block of student accommodation. Inside it had the drab nakedness of a provincial airport in the last decades of the twentieth century, the *high basic* as it was labelled by art historians. Along with the old-fashioned architecture, some of the puritanism of the old divide survived. The unmarried couple had been allotted, with no right of appeal, two single rooms. Braemar in a female students' corridor; Johnny in a male. They foregathered in Braemar's room. It had a narrow bed with a quilt covered in dull orange, a workstation that doubled as a tv, a capsule bathroom, a rudimentary food and drink dispenser;

and a fixed screen in the wall for rules, service bulletins and emergency announcements. This screen said, in German, English and French. *Dear visitor, please leave this room as you found it*. It cleared and said the same thing in Spanish and Hungarian. That was its whole repertoire. A window looked out over three rubbish skips, some rusty, half-dead conifer bushes and further bleak buildings across the greyish turf. Dusk was falling. The cold, inside the room, was intense.

Buonarotti wasn't accepting calls, but had left a message. They were to come to her room at three a.m. local time.

Johnny peered suspiciously at the service screen. 'D'you think anybody's looking?'

'Wise up, kid.' She sat on the bed beside him. 'Remember what happened when they tried to sell subscriber soap over here? *Ces gens ici*, they have a pathological resistance to the idea of minding other people's business.' She touched her naked temples; touched her wrist. 'Remember that night at the Devereux fort?'

They were in livespace.

He heaved a sigh. 'D'you think you'll get your maker back?'

'No chance. I'll buy a new one out of my fees for *How We Blew the Whistle on the Bug-eyed Baboons*. Out of my share, I mean. Sixty forty, net, wasn't it? I wouldn't rob you.'

'I'm suddenly convinced it's a trap.' Johnny's mood inclined to gallows' humour. 'She's going to get us into our Kirlian state, catch us in a vacuum tube and turn us in.'

'I suppose that's a risk.' Braemar began to laugh. 'But how could she manage it, without bringing down on herself the horrible fate of premature publication?'

'Actually, I want to give up the whole idea. I want to stay here with you. Here in thus fucking room, why not? We've a canteen box and a toilet. They won't let us die. We'll become a tourist attraction. Is the door locked? I'll seal it with my pocket flamethrower. Gimme your card, let me snap it.'

He was acting the cliché of the reluctant hero: Braemar resisted in the same mode.

'Johnny, my dearest love, you know better than that. The way we feel about each other is fun, it is exciting. But it isn't the meaning of the universe. There's a job that no one else can do, and we can't walk away. Our *weltanschauung* needs us.'

He held her hands. 'I'm the best audience you'll ever have. I'm all the audience you'll ever need.'

They fell from the imaginary stage into a long silence.

'I was in love with you once,' said Johnny. 'In my lucid moments, I would realise that I was done for. Most of the time it was play. We were separated by impassable barriers: of politics and beliefs and so on. I could feel for you as passionately as I liked, feel that terrific sexy pain without any actual danger to life, to futurity. I'm not in love any more. I just love you, it will never end. But there's the QV. You can live with symptomless AIDS: there are no controls for my disease. If the virus is really there, I don't have much future. Unless the Aleutians – '

He broke off, gazing helplessly. How beautiful he looks when he is lying, thought Braemar. She saw in the wordless candour of his eyes the images of an old woman dying of an old disease; and a brilliant young eejay with all the worlds of Earth and Aleutia before him . . .

'You still believe they're going to save you?'

'Save us. I don't believe. But I hope so. When we meet them face to face, as equals, we will be friends. I hope for that.'

There was room enough to make love on the narrow bed, not enough for easy sleeping. Johnny lay awake with his bruised face, the warmth of her body and an arctic margin of cold that crept along his side. He watched the wall screen flipping to and fro, and wondered why Spanish, why Hungarian? Something to do with horses? Maybe there'd been a conference of game builders, plotting to get Germany addicted to virtuality bullfighting. There must be an explanation. There was always an explanation for every knot and nodule of difference in the texture of the world. It might be right down in the hardware, the part that grows like a coral: except that unlike a coral it does not die when conditions change, it continually redesigns and cannibalises itself. He went into the coral world.

Braemar dreamed that she was carrying a child to hospital. The warm, round bundle in her arms was covered in cuts and bruises and sores. She could feel that some of its bones were broken, she could feel the freight of blood weeping into the body's cavities from internal injuries. Someone was trying to take the child from her and she kept crying *leave me alone we'll be all right, leave me alone we'll be all right*.

It was a nightmare, not the truth. She refused to dream it.

She was cutting a new letterbomb. It was designed with Ellen Kershaw in mind. One needs a focus. For Braemar, the bombing campaign had become a personal duel. She would insert images calculated to press buttons that the old battleaxe hated but couldn't disconnect. She liked to think that Kershaw knew exactly what was going on.

This one opened blandly with the resurrection of the East. Forty-year-old First World voices wailing in horror, *it's like walking into Auschwitz*. The witness viewpoint watched the scene change. The filthy smog and dead trees and grey-faced coughing children, looming up and washed away. The children running and laughing through summer flowers beside a great, majestic shining river. A young woman knelt by the water. Slav-white, sloe-eyed and gently serious: generic FE consumer product presenter. The image was left a little grafixy around the edges, in case it bore too strong a resemblance to some living ad-actress. She knelt and lifted water to her mouth. 'This river is called the Danube. This would have killed me, thirty years ago.' Reverent, sacramental swallow. 'With God's help we have saved our mother, water of life; and ourselves.'

So much for the purity of Uji's insignificant stream.

(Soft-centred lies! She could almost hear Ellen gibbering.)

The viewpoint followed the river (it was a different river) to a shingle shore. Braemar moved it there, in control. Gulls called: a wild, free sound. Strike up the Henry Wood Fantasia . . . *Anchors Aweigh*. (Come on, Ellen, you sentimental old thing, confess. When you were a girl it was stories of The War that stirred you, long before the flag was red and the fight for social justice. Those sickening old tunes of glory still get to you when you're drunk.) The child came around the blunt end of an upturned boat and found the men. They wore long soft boots, padded doublets, dark beards. They had the leathery, seamed faces and startling bright eyes of seamen. One wore a pearl earring. They sat at ease, but full of energy. 'Are we ready?' asked the man with the earring. ''Ware an' wakin', captain!'

Along the shore there began to be the sound of someone beating a little drum *rataplan rataplan*.

Churchill, Drake, Davy Crockett, Robert the Bruce, William Tell, Prince Diponegoro, Rama of Ayodhya. Braemar had no shame. She would enlist the lot. When she'd finished teasing Ellen

Kershaw, she could move on to Johnny's gallery. How about a skinny, bald lawyer in a dhoti? *Quit India!* (Arrogant, lecherous bastard . . .) In the frankness of her dream, Braemar smiled. Real-life heroes have this peculiarity, they are always the product of really shitty situations. Corrupt and dirty damaged human beings, one and all.

Something went wrong. Too much conscious reflection had hurt her control, but instead of losing reality the dream slipped out of her hands. The long-dead pirate, gallant defender of his island home, turned to the child with a living face that had no centre . . .

She woke in tears, the beat of the drum still sounding.

Buonarotti was nervous. Johnny assured her that no harm would come to the Aleutians. Nothing was going to happen except a harmless media exposure.

She would let them use her device, but she obviously wasn't happy.

Johnny wasn't happy either. This room, weirdly familiar, forced him to recall that he could not sort out their actual return. The events were in his memory, he could feel their presence: but lost, like the last moments before a concussing blow. An aura of unattached panic haloed Buonarotti's furniture, making the whole thing seem psychic again. There was no ship, he and Brae had never left earth.

'Is there something you haven't told us?' he demanded. 'Try to explain. I'd like to have the process clearer in my mind before we go out again.'

Peenemünde hunched on her spare little bed under the eyes of the saints. She twisted her hands between her knees. She hadn't offered them any refreshments this time.

'In your mind? Ah, well. Try thinking of this. Your mind, which is apparently contained in the box of your skull, and within the limits of your physical body, has almost no space inside it. Or else almost no time. When you attempt to isolate a thought from the matrix of *allthought*: to delimit a position for it, when or where, you find this is impossible. Breakfast, fear, a past joy, the solution to a mathematical problem: it is all contiguous. This is where we replicate the whole, the void and its inhabitants: the macrocosm, which is also "contained", in a certain sense.'

Johnny glanced at Braemar, who shrugged eloquently.

'Look,' Johnny said, 'I'm trying to change the course of history here. I'd welcome some support and reassurance. What happened when we got back to this room?'

Braemar noticed for the first time how blue the big woman's eyes were: and the pure gold of that massy sheaf of hair, done up in a drooping coil. She tried to imagine the genius as a statuesque Aryan beauty. No, those mild indeterminate features, lost in the big slab face, would never have been lovely. She realised that Peenemünde was staring at her: an irritating dumb reproach. The stare met Brae's eyes, and recoiled in fright.

'You came back. Frau Wilson first, then yourself. There is an infinitesimal drag: I said *almost* no time. A tiny difference is enough, it becomes magnified. One is in no risk of reappearing before one has left. I think you had uncomfortable subjective reactions?'

'You could put it like that.'

'Yes, it is an effect. It is important to remain calm, and to remember what you are doing. Emotional turmoil is dangerous.'

She looked petrified, and Johnny wondered what they'd done: in what state the two of them had 'reappeared'. Abruptly, he lost interest in investigation. Professor Buonarotti must know about the side effects of faster than light travel. *Her parents were Nazis and she had a rotten childhood.* She must have suffered her own horrors. She had claimed she could envisage no commercial application for her discovery. At that time it had sounded like a transparent cover for the fact that the discovery was imaginary. But maybe she was damn right.

'Okay, let's go.'

He left first, this time.

Braemar lay on Buonarotti's couch. The genius looked down at her. 'Please, don't do it.'

'Do what?' said Braemar. 'Johnny's the one who's going to change history.' She grinned. 'One sword must do the deed. And Siegfried must strike the blow!'

Poor, ineffectual Peenemünde looked as if she was about to cry. Her eyes brimmed. The tears fell.

Braemar flew into the spasming vacuum, into abstraction piled upon abstraction. She flew through the vast pomegranate halls of the cosmos, skins of matter holding in a casual hive the rich juicy cells of void. She was cradling in her hands a drop of salt water, the most precious possession of her life.

She saw a pool, a wellspring bubbling up in starlight. The professor was sitting beside it. Clavel was there, that powerful young *feminine person* with the sad and fearless eyes. The two were talking together. Braemar felt a great ocean of outraged loss open inside her. You have no right to be here! she shouted. This is ours! We found it! The professor lifted a handful of liquid, and Clavel seemed to drink.

She arrived in Aleutia knowing something new, a secret irony that she would carry to her death.

It was shocking to discover how completely the gut-deep uncertainty returned: how his flesh was not real, how his hands were not his own, how his mind opened and spilled. There were so many fictional accounts of faster than light travel: only the few can bear it, drugs have to be taken; the undrugged captain screams and dissolves into dancing, tortured pixels as he passes through the cosmic wringer. It was all true.

The experience was the same, but far more manageable second time. On the brink of psychosis, terror receded as he thought: *people will take shots for this.* He was one of the first to endure what would be the commonplace motion sickness of interplanetary travel. His historic privilege dizzied him more than the effect itself.

They had attempted to script themselves this time. It had worked, pretty well exactly. Johnny came awake walking in what looked like the same narrow passageway as he'd landed in before. He pulled himself into the new *situation* like someone shrugging on a suit of clothes: and there was Braemar. They found a cupboard, dressed themselves.

'I'm scared to go out there,' whispered Braemar, the first time either of them had spoken. 'We don't know what happened last time, only our hallucination. We don't know how much time has passed – '

At the moment the previous trip seemed entirely real to Johnny, the ftl a concrete, technical marvel. He supposed there was a tiny Einstein effect involved in travelling to the moon in seconds, but nothing to worry about. He gripped Braemar's hands.

'Calm down. Last time, we had a real-life accident that happened to rouse some psychic demons in us. This time, we understand the effect and we can fight it. We were here three weeks ago, we're back. They may have some kind of red alert on, but did you never sneak into somewhere that was trying to keep out the media? Think positively. You're an innocent passer-by. Think of Clavel in Fo.'

She stared at him, horrors in her eyes. He didn't know what she was seeing. They were lucky that his own sickness was controllable this time: no grisly hyper-associative arousal, no violence. He was Johnny Guglioli, eejay, dodging the authorities in a foreign city. He was taking a trip to normality, out of the nightmare of the last few years.

They found a map and took a bus. It was a quiet time of day. The lights were low, the streets half-empty. Motes in the hazy air were maybe taking messages of intrusion: there was nothing to be done except to get on with the job.

The wide irregular plaza outside the communications centre was planted with trees, and the kind of municipal bludgeonry that gives sculpture a bad name. The sky was indigo-grey, with a sunset blur of dim ruby around the rooftop horizon. An old couple sat nodding companionably on a bench by the sculpture. Shop windows were shuttered. A small group of pre-teens raced about playing some kind of chasing game. The evening silence was so clear you could hear their breath across the square.

Clavel in Fo. The autopilot normaliser gets to work, busily feeding you analogue translation. Johnny shut his eyes to clear his vision, forgetting what a horrible effect that had. He yelped, a ludicrous infantile gasp of fear. Braemar took his arm. They passed, unremark-able, through the great arched doorway.

The main hall was huge, vaulted, lit and decorated only by the screens themselves and the glassy boxes of memorabilia. It was quite empty. Johnny and Braemar walked about like casual visitors, stopping occasionally to peer into the lives of the famous, depicted in 2D through the same faintly blurry material that Johnny had met before. It was odd to think that these were not the famous *dead*. These Aleutians would live again, maybe were living now. There were galleries around the walls, and stairs to other levels. But, as Johnny had seen, the working studios were at the far end of the main hall, opposite the great doors. They strolled up there.

'Hey – '

Johnny's whisper echoed like distant thunder. He broke away.

'*Look at this!*'

There was a new exhibit in the hall of remembrance. The form was the same as the others, a boxy single-screen tv on a pedestal, a display case beside it. But the video playing on this screen was absolutely riveting.

'*Shit*,' hissed Johnny, entranced. 'Now *that* is alien. I can't think of a city on earth where people wouldn't be standing in line around the block . . .'

The rape had begun. The adventurers had started to ship back their loot, the first tiny instalments. Braemar was filled with horror as if, like an Aleutian herself, she saw snippets of her own flesh on display. Johnny pored over the case, cheerfully criticising the aliens' taste in souvenirs. She didn't dare to go near.

'But how did they get it here, Brae? Have you heard of any rocket launches from Uji? Shit, maybe we're wrong and they have a matter transporter after all.'

For God's sake, come away. She swallowed in desperation, and the horribly familiar situation threatened to engulf her. Be a good boy-baby and do what smiling Mama wants you to do. She fought to keep her feet through a tumbling wave of meaning.

'We don't know how much time we've got.'

He came away.

The studios were closed, the front walls dark. They heard no sound, there were no warning lights. There was a distinct impression that the place was deserted. They found an open door. Johnny moved quickly to the desks. He looked, and looked: not touching anything yet. He stood back, frowning intently.

'Oooh-kay.' One hand reached to the shoulder of his dun overalls. He looked at it, and laughed softly: embarrassed. 'Thought I had my totebag.'

'Well? *Well?*'

'One can but try. I've seen kookier setups. Not much, not many, but . . . Let's see how we lock ourselves in.'

He studied the desk nearest the door, identified a row of iconed keys. There was a split circle, one half-light, one dark. He touched it, *rubbed* it. The outer wall, the clear one, darkened and lights came up inside the room. The icon next to it was a circle with a notched line down the middle. He rubbed that one. 'Try the doors.'

The glassy stuff had melded, seamlessly, in three bands around head and knee and waist height.

He cackled in delight.

'Open it again, Johnny. I'm going outside.'

This was no place for the battle of the sexes. It was time to be practical. Johnny was the engineer. He had been trained by the State for just such an occasion as this – the naked reporter, far from home, faced with almost unrecognisable equipment. Johnny frowned in puzzlement. This moment had not been covered in their script. He wanted her to stay, but she was right. Out there in the alien cathedral she might be able to hold off trouble for a few precious moments.

'Johnny, I may not get back to you. When you're done, or if an alarm sounds, *go home*. The way you came here, by an act of will.'

He'd have liked to stay and crow over the Aleutians, but it wouldn't be wise. In the heat of the moment, he might end up with his throat cut.

'Right,' he said. 'Good luck.'

'You too.'

She stood wrapped in impenetrable mystery, alone in her version of Buonarotti's travel mode. Johnny held out his arms. They embraced. He kissed her face, the unreal flesh, a Braemar-replica of interplanetary plasma. He tasted salt.

'Don't cry. We're going to be famous.'

A whole floor of the Multiphon complex was secretly given over to the handling of Aleutian mothership material. They were trying to contain it, protecting the incoming data from frame-grabbers. It was a hopeless task. The secret caucus included the President of the USSA and an undisclosed chain of informants behind her. It was impossible to discover how many nationals and corporations already had access to this dynamite information. It might be none. The world at large paid little attention to old space science. But they must be prepared. At any moment the deafening silence could be shattered. The conspirators struggled to formulate a rightly balanced response, and squabbled about the correct moment to take this amazing news to the Multiphon.

As soon as the government of the world was told, they'd insist on telling the Aleutians. That was inevitable. But then the whole world would know, and humanity might not take this demotion of their angels very well. The Aleutians would be in danger. It seemed wise to stretch this pause as long as possible: the more they could learn before the story broke the better.

Their security arrangements within the Multiphon building had not yet aroused suspicion. There were a lot of secrets at Dusit in those days: a lot of different groups of people behaving strangely while they deliberated on enclave evacuation and future projects for the superbeings. Some of the waste-disposal problems the Aleutians might be asked to resolve were highly sensitive.

They had made it their business, since the conspiracy began, to secure first sight of any forensic information. One long, anxious day among many, a report arrived from the Abdus Salam institute in Banjul. This was Asean, kissing cousin to the Pacific Rim, where everything really *is* joined up at the back. They were taking isolation seriously. Information moved about on pieces of quickly degradable paper, if not by word of mouth. The report had been hand-copied from the Multiphon document handler. They were sitting around a table, each reading a different section and passing it on.

The coarse texture of instant paper took Ellen back to the raw and desperate years of the '04 when the whole world pulled together, and courage and virtue were the currency of political life (this wonderful effect paid for by the death of millions). But that wasn't a true analogy. She felt like a government official in some seventeenth-century court crisis throwing aside the printed books of science, taking refuge in astrology on animal skin. She was aware that everything she read had been passed by the censors of a major corporation, as yet unidentified, which had taken control of the African material quite early on. Possibly every word was false.

'These "active alien cell complexes",' said Chas softly. 'Any connection with their body lice?'

No one could answer that. No one had paid much attention to the lice. It was rather embarrassing by earth standards that the superbeings should be verminous.

'And what happens when humans ingest this living dust?'

There was silence while sections shuffled around and other

people found the connection between his question and the report. The alien artefacts were packed with tiny organisms. The same kind of organisms had been found in samples of the research lab's air.

The down-to-earth hazards of contamination had been almost forgotten, since the visitors were accepted as superbeings on prime-time television. The assumption was that they would never do harm unintentionally: and what defence could there be against angelic punishment?

Ellen frowned over the close-written pages. 'It seems that these "organisms" have to do with the function and manufacture of their artefacts. I'd like to see a report on one of our machines that was affected in the "mad machine plague" – if any of them survived.'

This was unlikely. After the plague, no one had dared to examine the machines involved. Everything had been throughly incinerated.

'But if I read the figures right, the *dispersed* "active material" was in vanishingly low concentrations.'

'So perhaps it's okay to have just a few Aleutians. But the new settlers? What about them?'

We will have to abandon coralin, if we want to keep them out of our business. Douglas Milne decided this briskly: as if he really were a ruler of the world and could order it done, this afternoon. Then he remembered that Carlotta had already begun to do it. He suffered a moment of fugue, staring into time.

What is going to become of us . . .?

Poonsuk propped her head on both hands. *I was there, the night the world was made one.* It was impossible not to glory in that memory. But it was an article of faith with Poonsuk that she had been no more present, in the Multiphon, than any one of the billions who joined her through the lightlines. The lightlines, the networks, were the means to the Buddhahood of all mankind, female and male. What if the aliens, who did not believe in telecommunication, were to do away with that?

She was too tired to read. Deadly weakness overwhelmed her, it seemed as if the weight of the air would break her bones. She had schooled herself for so long to think no further than: this is a bad day, this is a good day. She had fought to disregard her illness in the same spirit as it coolly disregarded medical science. Now she was thinking: I am dying, they could cure me. It was a catastrophic breach of discipline.

Martha murmured to Robin, 'D'you think someone should warn Carlotta?' It wasn't quite a joke. Poonsuk hadn't given a sign of displeasure after Carlotta's rash words about the princesses. But you don't, you just *don't* show disrespect to the Thai royals.

Ellen overheard. 'I don't see why,' she said in the unsibilant undertone that gives the adept privacy even in livespace. 'The President was disgracefully rude. If she suffers for it, serve her right.'

Martha wasn't sure if Ellen knew how rough things could get behind the mask of KT politics. She slid a curious glance; but the English woman's face gave nothing away.

She doesn't want me. Robin shifted himself a psychic millimetre out of Martha's space. It's over. He smiled faintly, looking away from her: *I can speak Aleutian.* The euphoria of that night in the Multiphon was long gone. Here was the reality. They are refugees. More bloody refugees. Is that what it comes to? Just that? Something terrible and beautiful has passed us by, he thought. The rest is politics.

The handwriting of a Thai technician, only partially familiar with English script, melted into haphazard dots and curls. Words became heaps of electron-magnified genes, solid and mysterious. He stopped trying to decipher them. He would get interested in the implications of alien bio-chemistry another day.

He decided that the government of the world would want to send earthlings to Aleutia, to the mothership. He would volunteer.

Life is made of glorious moments. There is no meaning. I will build my career on the fact that I was one of the first at Uji. I will excel, because I play the game for sensation and not for any conventional kind of gain. He rubbed his face with his hands.

The KT air was hot and tainted in spite of the filtration. The room grew very quiet. This conspiracy had been begun as an attempt to normalise relations with Aleutia – to debunk the superbeings, to put it bluntly. As soon as the ship was discovered, and Carlotta's analysts began to lay bare its less-than-supernatural secrets, the impulse to protect their protégés had returned. But yet another mood was taking over. If the Aleutians were not superbeings, then their behaviour – their very presence – looked entirely different. The reflex of the human animal was growing stronger.

Go away, thought Ellen. *Come back in five hundred years. We can't attend to you people at the moment. We're too busy.*

But whenever the aliens came they would find the same world: a mass of petty wars, longstanding grievances working to the surface, fragile new beginnings. And as soon as they arrived they would become part of what was happening. The alien infestation would become, inextricably, a factor in the situation.

Rajath and his crew were the unchanging catalyst, speeding up a purely human process. Already the shape of affairs on earth had been shifting towards a new gestalt. The old power blocs were fragmenting, the fragments moving towards a different kind of union. But it had become too fast, too fragile. Without the Aleutians as angels, the hothouse plant in the Multiphon could not possibly survive.

The message was delivered by a slender young man with the token tonsure and yellow scarf of a temporary vocation. He weied as he handed it over to Ellen. The words were English but unintelligible. She looked at him in bewilderment.

'A human person has been seen in space,' explained the part-time monk.

The sequence was short, and perfectly clear. The face was well known to the conspirators. Johnny Guglioli, White Queen's tame ex-eejay. Robin Lloyd-Price began to laugh.

'My God, it was a hoax! It's not the mothership at all. It's an obscure new way to deliver a letterbomb!'

'Perhaps sir,' said the tech, watching code on his subscreen. He glanced up, smiling politely. 'Anything can be faked. But the weight of the evidence is heavy. We think he is out there.'

Suddenly Robin's grin vanished. He grabbed a desk and began to hit keys urgently.

Poonsuk, in her motored chair, looked from face to face. 'What does it mean?'

'Letterbombing is a very minor criminal offence,' said Robin. 'We know that White Queen has committed worse crimes, in the means they've used to get hold of information. But you don't take media-manipulators to court . . . Unfortunately, no one has access to Wilson's phone. We do get some information about the phone calls of another gamer, a rather unsavoury character quite apart from

the White Queen activities. A few days ago Braemar Wilson spent
some time on that tuning, talking to a third member of the group.
He's called the White Knight. He's a retired nuclear physicist. We
don't yet know what was said. We're still waiting for the police to
let us have sight of the transcript.'

'I didn't like that,' muttered Martha.

Johnny had vanished. The Peter Rabbit necklace saw only the big
hall, quiet and empty as it had been since the ceremony Carlotta
showed them.

'They may have known about the ship before us. They've always
insisted it was there. Damn, I can't find Carlotta's techies' report.'

The alien spaceship was being studied like a new asteroid.

Poonsuk stared. The faces around her were horror-struck.

'What are you saying?'

Ellen explained: 'Guglioli and Wilson left London a few days ago.
We think they crossed the Channel. We don't know where they
went. Guglioli has no passport, but clearly they've found some way
to get round that. As Robin said, we don't have the authority to do
more than observe. We've never wanted to demand it. It's been
important to keep the whole question of anti-Aleutian activism
low key.'

Suddenly, the White Queen conspiracy loomed enormous. To get
someone out into space, it must be backed by some of the richest
people in the world. But Johnny's means of transport was not their
present concern.

'Johnny's there,' said Martha. 'He's not alone, you bet. Where's
the lady?'

She looked around, taking in an atmosphere that laid bare the
secret they had kept from themselves for a long time: the covert
terror.

'I think we have to assume the aliens have a sabotage problem.
What the fuck do we do?'

It wasn't too far from the cathedral to her destination. She could
read a symbolic map as well as Johnny, and remember it. You have
to have a good memory in the communications business. The
evening street was quiet, but her body was shouting fear and guilt.
She saw an alley heading the right way and ducked into it. It was a
dusty tunnel, the kind of shortcut that children use, never adults.

The dust was a good sign: few live wanderers here. It became very narrow, but it was heading in the right direction so she persevered. For this sequence, some deep down dirty jingoism. Charles Villiers Stanford, *Songs of the Sea*. Can we get tape of that? We may have to go back to black vinyl: this is not exactly Youro-Age music.

> *Drake, he's in his hammock an' a thousand miles away,*
> *(Capten, art tha sleeping there below?)*
> *If the Dons sight Devon,*
> *I'll quit the port o' Heaven.*
> *And drum them up the channel, as I drummed 'em long ago* . . .

The imaginary letterbomb, cynically sentimental, drained emotion and made it possible to function.

Rataplan, rataplan rataplan, beat the little drum.

The dusty crevice delivered her into daylight. She had crossed a timezone boundary, or something. There were people. There were hundreds of people bustling about, twitching their animal faces; even speaking out loud. There was traffic: trambuses, things like mopeds . . . Braemar stared in horror. She put her hands over her face. She sobbed.

Courage.

If this was earth, the power station would have been sited far from human habitation. Maybe they were being pragmatic. There was nowhere very far to run, nor much point in trying to hide if this balloon went up. Maybe they simply were not scared. Braemar walked in off the street. The staff looked up as she passed them. She fed them disinformation: *I'm none of your concern. I'm supposed to be here.* They believed her. Politics must be quiet in Aleutia at present; and apparently no one feared for her safety.

No one was wearing anything special. Dun-coloured monotony, with the black seaweed hair slick to the shoulder: a few bangles, brooches and scarves. In Aleutia, basic clothing is not a product. You don't buy it, you use it like a paper towel in a public toilet. Few things have the status of consumer goods: extras, decoration. The domain of economic activity is much smaller than in our world . . . The rousing sea shanty rattled on behind the social analysis. As long as she went on making tape in her head, no matter if the tracks didn't match up, she would be all right.

Getting close, by the symbols, to the reactor chamber, and still nobody challenged her. When quiet footsteps approached (the silence of Aleutia!) she always had time to duck into a doorway or another passage. She found her way barred, an icon that wouldn't open the door no matter how she rubbed it. Then found the closet with (at last) helmets, gauntlets, suits. A gauntleted fingertip opened the door.

What can one take out of a virtuality? Information. What can one carry back? The White Knight had given her the tools she needed to plunge Aleutia into utter chaos. The looking-glass parallels continued. Everything that we are not they are, everything that we can't do they can. But the join is not completely sealed, a tiny trickle breathes through. Aleutia lives on the edge of our possibilities.

She heard the White Knight's slow words, sealing her fate.

What you saw sounds very like a fusion reactor. We can make something much like it: a thing called a 'spheromak'. But for us, the beast will not behave: we can't tame it.

They had an analogy for everything. Even gender identity, even metaphysics. Even death. The immortals had never known the crushing weight of mortality. But they, too, surrounded by their own life everywhere, recognised a realm that was unreachable, awesome: the domain of incalculable powers. When they entered this realm 'themselves', it was under the protection of what humans call religion. In other circumstances, those powers were the same in Aleutia as anywhere in the cosmos. Force, energy: the stuff that makes the wheels go round; fuels the processing.

She was alone in the antechamber, a corridor that circled the reactor's core. There was a great cylinder of the thick blurry glass. She saw what she had glimpsed the last time she dreamed this dream. Last time she had got as far as the corridor outside the door to this chamber: then it opened and she had to run away. She had run away half-blinded, believing herself asleep or dead – fled in horror from a nightmare impulse. But she had carried away her glimpse of the heart of Aleutia, knowing even before she spoke to the White Knight approximately what it was that she'd seen. And now she was back.

The sun in a cage: a fearsome captive, held in a state of anomalous stability. That meant something that ought not to be possible. On earth it was not possible for any sensible length of time. The White Knight thought the Aleutians must have discovered some way of doping super-hard metal to stop it from weakening under neutron bombardment. How the mini-sun had been manufactured or captured in the first place he couldn't fathom.

What Braemar had to do was to increase the pressure, to squeeze the bars of the cage. This must be possible, for the anomalous state of the blue sun must be constantly shifting, being corrected. She did not have to alter the super-metal. The important part of the cage was not material at all.

Through the glass, the blue sun. It was unbearably bright, even through the dark visor of her helmet. She couldn't imagine how her eyesight had survived the last time. The light roared like a million silent furnaces. The fuzzy blue sphere had the aspect of a ferocious animal struggling against the irregular coils of metal between which it hung, enchained.

The Aleutians on earth, the landing party, had made themselves look big because they were afraid. As far as they knew they were among equals, and they had nothing behind them but this vulnerable wandering home. It was natural for them to take short-term advantage of the hopelessly impressionable locals. If only the aliens had been what they honestly believed themselves to be – just folks, just people, completely unremarkable . . .

But they were not. The Aleutians were exactly what their emissaries had pretended to be: superbeings with magical powers. They would not mean any harm. At full expression they were still few, if Clem was right. But those 'three to five million' would soon rule, and change utterly, the miserable savage race that they'd stumbled upon. How could they help it?

It will be gone. Everything we ever did, everything we ever made: dead and worse than dead, *meaningless* . . .

Braemar found a panel of simple iconic controls. She stared at them. So far every button she or Johnny had tried had responded. They had wanted nothing that needed the live chemistry of a certain touch. It might be different here. But the gauntlets told her otherwise. She could see eyeless things like the alien camcorders at Uji clinging to the walls. They weren't turned towards the control panel. The Aleutians had no fear of each other. If one of their own turned mad enough to want to tamper here, it would be known long before they got anywhere near. But if conditions altered inside the actual chamber, presumably she'd have company pretty quickly.

Leave the door of the sun's cage ajar. Run back to Johnny. Fly back to Prussia. He'll never know what I did. A terrible coincidence. He'll guess, but he'll forgive me. Live happily ever after.

I am mad. I am mad and dead.

The drum went on beating. Tears filled her eyes and fell inside the mask. How horrible, to kill because of something generations in the future. How could anyone be so certain? But she was certain. The cold equations of history would not be denied.

In Krung Thep the government of the world, in session, had been plunged into secrecy. The press gallery was going crazy, demanding to know who'd pulled the plug on them. Inside the Multiphon the news had just been broken. There is a mothership, we have a surveillance device on board. We have discovered human saboteurs out there. What is to be done?

Poonsuk Masdit had abandoned her desk and taken a seat down in the Asean ranks. Not many people realised that this had happened, it was only clear that the speaker's screen was changing hands with indecent speed and informality: a matter of whose fingers were speediest and more adept. No one could remember that this was a secret session. These professional performers harangued a nonexistent global audience, struck attitudes and turned profiles. Who authorised surveillance of the Aleutians? Is this a faster-than-light starship? Who authorised the sabotage? Has Uji been informed? Is this story not obviously misinformation, fed to us by the ICI . . .?

Can we please take it as fact, demanded Martha Ledern, that the physical whereabouts of our surveillance device is not in question. The ship is really there. We know little about its technical specifications: we can infer, but we can discuss those inferences later. The question now is about terrorist sabotage. And it's urgent.

No, Uji doesn't know anything. So far as we're aware.

Martha's speech cleared up some of the confusion and revealed the existence of an inner circle, mysteriously well informed. But before outrage could break out (practised outrage: the Multiphon was riddled with inner circles) the delegates suddenly understood just what they were being asked to decide.

Whose side are we on?

The uproar diminished considerably. Martha asked for a vote. Taking into account that we will have to reveal that we have discovered their ship. Taking into account their maybe hostile reaction, and the fact that they may not believe that these saboteurs are acting on their own, and the fact that though they don't have an ftl ship, they may still have devastating weaponry . . . Taking everything into account: shall we inform the Aleutians?

Ellen could not watch the chamber. She and Poonsuk had insisted that the secret had to be blown. They'd won the vote in the inner circle, and then Ellen had been terrified that events would overtake them. To tell the Multiphon meant to invite babel, and meanwhile there was a terrorist on the loose in an innocent and vulnerable community. But it was only twenty minutes now since the messenger had called them: not much more than that since Johnny Guglioli had been spotted. No time, really. A long time in politics.

Normal service is restored. If not angels, then enemies . . . Ellen was agonised. She tried to tell herself that Wilson was planting a letterbomb. But her inner vision painted the horror that was commonplace in so much of the world: scattered limbs and shattered glass in some Aleutian indoor street. The families in tears. She must be mad, she must be having a breakdown, to feel this inexplicable longing that Wilson might succeed at whatever she planned, that the Multiphon might decide to keep silent. Though nothing would make her vote that way herself . . . Her eyes were screwed shut when a roar went up.

She stared at the voting board on her desk, and slowly her hands relaxed. She was saved.

The Aleutian effect had triumphed. Partly, perhaps, out of fear, partly from a genuine sense of honour: the government of the earth decided unanimously to protect the aliens and betray the terrorists. Poonsuk took the big screen, and made a short speech.

Uji was contacted immediately. Predictably, Rajath and his people made no fuss about their blown cover.

She was a little girl again in that great land of heat and birth, sweating in a scratchy uniform from far away. She stood and sang the war songs of a cold, small island, poured her heart out. Wrong skin, wrong sex, wrong culture: but the need to belong was stronger than self-respect. She had always wanted to have adventures, to be brave, to be the hero of her own life. She felt a weight on her shoulders, the armour and the crown. The champion entered the lists, a woman with the heart and stomach of a man.

And a white man, at that. What shameful nonsense.

She rubbed the icon that announced its perilous meaning in the Common Tongue. Ice blue filaments snaked from the fuzzy sphere. Its light became even more intense.

No one sane could do this. She felt meaning shift again, further still from reason, and did not try to pull it back. She was Mother, she was Queen. The living Person of earth's brood of consciousness had become a woman to do battle with the Person of the invader. Mother must do this, take the responsibility, be the one to blame . . . I don't believe my cause is just, no cause is just. But I must fight you. Please understand, it's an obligation.

She knew that she had no idea how to return to Prussia. She had never intended to return. No sane grown-up becomes a terrorist without accepting that their own life is forfeit. Johnny said that. But when things started to break up he would escape. She knew he would go.

She hoped he didn't know what she was doing.

Ah, to have a lover instead of a child. Too late.

The blue sun had become an ellipse. It burned deepest violet.

Obligation. For your sake, baby –

The door opened. The Aleutians stared at her. Livid light played over their helmeted heads, flickered on eyeless visors, blank and dark. Four of them flew at her, two more fell on the control panel, caressing it desperately. No one spoke.

Ideally, modern telecommunication worked with chemistry and modulated light, coralin and the lightlines. In practice, technically obsolete electronics continued to thrive: in tv networks, in state bureaucracies, in Braemar's abused housebox. The developed world had a cat's cradle of translation mechanisms, out of one spectrum, into the other and back again. In the wilderness, outside the White North, an eejay like Johnny Guglioli was the living link: the kid who could coax the most ancient electronic devices into talking to the new systems. That wouldn't be the problem here. By everything anyone had learned, Aleutian telecoms had to run on chemistry and light. But how to get in?

He stood in the middle of the studio. He didn't know what was recorded here, or what was transmitted; or for what purpose. He saw smooth bulky consoles, desks at his hand height. Above every double desk there was a roughly rectangular blank screen, in front of each a pair of seats. The screens were probably some kind of chemical processing film, modulated by light – or sound. Under them were bars of glowing coloured lozenges – maybe feedback indicators. In front of each right hand seat there was a handshaped dimple in the desk. He was reminded of a driving instruction simulator – one seat for you and one seat for the instructor: but there was no head-up. The desk by the door was the only one with rub-a-dub buttons. He hadn't the slightest idea what to do.

He was terrified that Aleutians, alerted by a chemical tinge of alien panic in their air, might come rushing in. He reasoned with himself, pointing out that this was unlikely. If you don't know how to decode it, a signal is mere noise. If the Aleutians could read each other's chemical messages, that didn't mean they could read the human version.

This plan had begun as a wild dream that some brilliant technical fix would be possible, permitting him to force the aliens' own outreach satellite to squirt earthling binary code at one of the Lagrange nodes – or even straight into the earth's comsat network. He must have been crazy to imagine he could achieve that. But he *must* be able to do something.

Boldly, he sat down and stuck his hand on a dimple.

'I want to – '

The dimple warmed faintly. A wash of coloured movement flooded the lozenges: a face swam up in the screen. Johnny leapt backwards.

He recovered quickly. Well, he said to himself. Apparently monkey has found the on-switch.

He didn't have to hack their 'moon'. He didn't have to understand their tech. There must be an extraordinarily powerful transmitter somewhere around here. He only had to find the right button, then talk to the screen like a dumb presenter. His video transmission, flooding the void, would force the Lagrange to bombard a comsat with high quality signals. Johnny Guglioli would burst in on global tv. The Lagrange sats were dual system, light and e/m, futuristic marvels in their day; they'd have no problem. They were constantly pumping stuff back to earth, and the newsagencies sampled it the way they sampled everything. If Johnny did end up on tv, he might even get paid for it.

He might be blocked by alien-loving censorship. It didn't matter. There were enough hams, hackers and marginal science researchers tuned to the lost frontier, to ensure that something got through. It would be passed around, and grabbed, and checked out: and then, too bad for those who wanted to keep the aliens' secret.

He went back to the icon buttons. There was one that looked like the Aleutian equivalent of an emergency siren: concentric broken circles, a stick figure in the middle. *Abandon ship?* It could be. Or it could be *All Aboard, About To Cast Off!* Whatever it was, his intuition swore it was worth trying. A reckless confidence in this stunt returned to him. He would rub the buttons that looked right, and then talk to the world. Maybe it would work, why not? He remembered the aliens, big-eyed with surprise on the tv: *but naturally we understand your 'computers'. What's to understand?* Time to turn that around.

Try and stop me, alien scum.

He still didn't feel solid. He was dreaming, his body lay in a coma in Germany. The uncertainty was a constant strain. It was like the QV: there and not there. A therapist at Amsterdam had told him the infection was real, but he'd infected himself. 'The QV is an analogue of your political activities: your need to break open the citadel.' It was crazy to talk like that about a designer virus – but Americans are all crazy.

When he got back to earth the first thing he'd do – after the victory parade – would be to demand that Carlotta investigate the whole QV story. He would be cleared. He could go back to work, with this stunt in his bag and the Aleutians no longer a problem. The prospect was bliss.

He'd better hurry, Braemar would be getting scared.

As soon as he thought that, he realised that he knew she was not waiting outside. Braemar had been alone in Aleutia for a long time, on their first trip. Also, she'd been behaving suspiciously the last few days in London. He had a psychic, *Aleutian* feeling that she was up to something that involved the White Knight, the old guy who used to be one of those free-lunch wizards, into high energy physics. He didn't want to think about exactly what she might be doing. If he knew, he might have to go after her and stop her.

Trouble was, as soon as he started blasting out on the lightlines he was bound to start up some kind of alarm, even in this easy-going set up.

He looked at the console that had recognized his touch . . . 'Hi, I'm Johnny Guglioli, late of New York City . . .'

He knew why he was recognised. Fury suddenly swept through him. He was contaminated. Clavel had known it from the start. The petrovirus was the link – the taint. He hated the idea of being close to her in any way. He remembered the hideous humiliation of the rape, the abject fear that he'd been made to live with since the first night in Africa. *They made me eat shit*, he thought. The image of Braemar, being slapped around *and learning to like it* pumped him full of disgust. No, I'm not going to live in their world. Not at any price.

If this was real life he'd have to control his anger. He'd have to set off the alarms here, and stop Brae. You can't let yourself be ruled by anger, you can't take stuff out on the innocent. Luckily, this was only a dream.

If Brae did something terrible, in the dream, it wasn't his fault. He didn't know, he wasn't to blame.

From behind him there was a sound like cloth ripping. The studio doors had been forced open. Johnny flung himself at a recording desk, slapped his hand down . . . But somebody had pulled a plug somewhere.

Ellen Kershaw found herself in dialogue with an alien prince over the fate of the saboteurs. The prince used Lugha as interpreter. 'He' watched the demon child closely, and after the second interview took over for himself in a stylish aphoristic English. It turned out that the attribute of namelessness was not linked with an inability to use articulate language. It was natural to Aleutia. Ellen *felt* the prince, marginally more masculine than feminine, taking shape as a presence. She would know him anywhere, but his 'name' was a circumstantial label. It changed incessantly in the course of a conversation.

The dialogue went on for weeks. Things were complicated by the fact that the prince considered himself to be taking part in a religious ritual; and he was not greatly interested in religion.

'You-we were not of one mind about the attack. You were a house divided.'

'We had found your mothership,' replied Ellen. 'We detected it in its hiding place behind our moon. We acknowledge that you on our planet had a right to keep the secret of its position: even to the extent of actively deceiving us. But you must see that its presence put your arrival on earth in a different light. Braemar Wilson is a brave person, Johnny Guglioli also. We have no reason to believe that she is capable of violence. No harm came of their gesture, which we do not entirely repudiate.'

It was a terrible strain: to speak the truth, the whole truth and nothing but the truth. The prince's face changed like quicksilver. He wore a robe of deep blue scattered with gold tassels: this finery, flung over the eternal dun overalls, made him look like a child who's been at the dressing-up box. He would rise from his couch and fidget about. The way he tossed the open, trailing sleeves behind him spoke volumes in a language in which Ellen could barely stumble through a sentence.

'Johnny Guglioli merely interfered with some church furniture.'

Ellen agreed, guardedly. No one on earth had been allowed access to Guglioli or Wilson. Apparently they had made statements, or at least what the Aleutians took for statements, but access to these wasn't possible either. It seemed likely that the Aleutians didn't understand the request. Everyone who'd had contact experience agreed that it would be unwise to push it. The only way to save the prisoners was to behave normally – in Aleutian terms.

Lugha sat passive: he was not obliged to pay any attention to this sort of thing. Ellen tried to peer into the room beyond. The future lay there, the future of two races. In some real sense it hung in the balance. There was a mandatory death sentence for major sabotage, that had been made clear and in principle accepted. But the government of the world needed to save the lives of the two humans. It was important to extract that concession. The Aleutians couldn't know how important. They didn't know what mercy meant in earth politics (or did they?). But as she struggled she was distracted by the years ahead.

She could see nothing behind the prince and the demon child, nothing but midnight shadows.

'Yet he is the younger, and the truechild is parent to the trueparent. That's the way it is in all the stories I know.'

She had no idea what he was getting at: she followed her instinct. 'The Beloved rules the Lover? Yes, we have stories like that too. There was once a person called Achilles . . .'

The person whose favourite colour is blue settled on the couch in his private chapel. He lifted a tassel on his sleeve and stroked the gold filament. The person who likes the brightness of gold was arriving at our judgement.

'What turns out to have been a harmless prank didn't start that way. Someone has to be taught a lesson. Let us return to the land of the living.' The person who believes in respect for forms made a gesture: rearranging his sleeves. He was replacing his hat on the church steps, brisk and slightly irritated at the end of a tiresomely long service. He keyed a backdrop of the great character shrine. It appeared briefly, chasing the shadows from Ellen's screen, and ended the transmission.

*

The person whose aspect is often an exasperating purity of motive had arrived home. The prince went to meet Clavel in the office of criminal justice in the city of the sun. There were several interested persons gathered there: some obligate scientists, some scholars; and notably an artisan, who kept his distance from the signifiers but seemed very much at home. The person whose purity is actually riddled with abysses of error stared at this artisan, and his nasal grew pinched and white-edged.

The doctor from the wilderness first-aid post, who had treated Johnny Guglioli, stood with arms folded, resentful.

<I blame you,> stared Clavel. <You could have stopped them before this happened. I blame you for ever.>

The doctor glared in return, and made a speech. 'I run a first-aid post,' he said. 'People fall in the rocks and hurt themselves. I fetch them in and fix them. It is categorically none of my business to get tied up in meaningless bureaucracy.'

<Excuse me.> One of the science people asked, mildly, for attention. <You pumped this stranger full of ordinary blood plasma?>

The doctor raised his eyebrows. <Certainly not. We made a synthesis from a sample. The companion refused to donate: for reasons I could well understand. My course was obvious.>

Some of those present became guiltily excited.

<Is it possible that some trace of the original survived?>

<You insult my obligation. I'm a doctor, not a weapons developer. We cleaned everything away.>

No one in Aleutia could take seriously what Braemar had been trying to do. The averted cataclysm had left no scar. There was no sense of outrage against the saboteurs – especially since they had both made statements which, though confused, were certainly penitent. But the event had come soon after Lugha's return, and it served to bring the whole question of that big planet out there into focus. It was a very long time since the wanderer had left a giant world of its own. Only the most stubbornly conservative minds had preserved any active notion of a goal, of final landfall. If it hadn't been for Johnny and Braemar, Rajath's invitation would have tempted a few and left most people unmoved. But now, suddenly, everybody was interested in the new world next door.

The person who is always aware of the attention of the

thousands, and the thousands upon thousands who are presently unborn, stroked his sleeve thoughtfully.

<If we pat those two on their heads and send them home, we go belly-up to these new neighbours. That is obvious. What is the precise relationship between them? I understand there was something to do with a war? A story of true love thwarted? My pure-hearted cousin cannot be mistaken, so who is it who has stolen his lover?>

Clavel endured this. The person who goads Clavel whenever he gets the chance of course knew all. And none of it. No one at home, nobody had the slightest notion of how things were on earth. He made a speech.

'You've seen there are two broods. Braemar is an obligate childbearer, Johnny the parasite kind. They were born in different camps, but became lovers.'

<Ah! Everything becomes clear. It was a love suicide, nothing to do with us.>

<No!> cried Clavel. <It was not like that. It was a gesture directed against us. A statement we can't ignore!>

<Really? Could you make a speech to that effect?>

Clavel could not. Not in here; not under oath. He was not sure.

The prince turned to the scientists. <They've both made statements, but there's a claim that one of them was unduly influenced, which seems to be substantiated. That suits us well. There will be a body. Your sneaky feelings may be justified. Maybe we'll try to secure it: but not if we can't think of a plausible excuse.>

Clavel stopped trying to keep calm. He flew across the room in a fanged leap that would have taken the prince's throat out. But those days were long gone. His people grabbed his sleeves. The prince sighed.

<Control the pure person. Take him away and make him lie down with some unfortunate. We understand he's discovered rough trade: that should take the froth off.>

Ah, Clavel. Always the same Clavel.

Clavel had come to Johnny, joined him in the small clean room.

'So it was your idea, Johnny?'

Johnny didn't know what was to become of him yet, and they wouldn't let him see Braemar. He had gathered that *her* stunt had failed completely, whereas he'd been caught in the act. He had resigned himself to spending a long time in this room. It was ridiculous, but he felt sad to find that in Aleutia there were police cells, and prison guards, and machineries of justice. When they let him at an interpreter he could present a case. But it was hard to accept Clavel as that interpreter. He shrugged.

She drew herself together, knee and hip joints turning backwards inside her clothes. 'You sent Braemar to disintegrate the magnetic sheath around the core of our main reactor?' Clavel hunched herself into a gaunt knot of limbs, like a sick cat.

Johnny took this news. It entered him and filled him until he choked. He blinked. 'Is that what she says?'

'Apparently.'

'Then that's fine by me.'

She said nothing for a while. She looked to him like someone lost in contemplation of a tragic drama. 'Your lover is a complicated person.'

'So am I,' said Johnny. 'But I'll get better press. And *la lutte continue.*'

The detention cell was perfectly comfortable. Braemar lived in it quietly: eating, sleeping, keeping herself clean. She knew she must try to survive. But she couldn't bring herself to plead innocence, so she kept silent and tried to silence her face and body. She was visited once by other residents of the detention block. They were concerned, rather priggish. She thought they were probably saying: *Buck up, you're not in here for a rest cure. Come and do some occupational therapy.* They didn't come again.

At last Clavel came and told her that her plea of undue influence had been accepted, and Johnny had taken full responsibility. She said not a word: and whatever she told Clavel in the Common Tongue, it seemed she didn't change her plea. When Clavel was gone she lay tearless, like an animal in a cage. She would not cry. The choice was made and she would take no painkillers, not even those distilled from her own blood. She waited and dreamed of Johnny; immersed herself in sweet memory. She had a persistent fantasy that some kind of rescue was due when things got really bad. But this was nonsense.

For much of the time Johnny was sure that when the climax came he would wake from his long and complicated dream. He fostered this illusion, because he didn't want to panic and make a fool of himself. He was more and more certain that *fear* was the root cause of their problems. He thought of the night in Africa: his craven terror, Braemar with her deadly weapon. The whole story was there.

He found himself thinking a great deal about Bella, not as a sore place in his memory but as a living person. He remembered dancing with her in his arms: cavorting round the floor of that cluttered little partition to some schmaltzy C&W waltz. He looked down at the two-year-old face, so lost in bliss. You won't remember a moment of these years, he thought. It will be gone, I'll be an aged geezer who never gives you anything but aggravation. But one day you will be dancing in someone's arms: and you won't know it but *this* is what you'll be looking for. It takes love to make love, sweet baby. He decided there was not much to choose between the Aleutian and the earthly view, after all.

He thought of Izzy too. Sorry, Izabel. You weren't the love of my life, nor I yours. But you were a good friend, and I pushed you too fucking hard.

Most of all, he remembered Braemar. Even now, the glow-worm dress: the amused and delicate arrogance of her step as she came down into the garden bar at L'Iceberg. She danced to *musique naturelle* with David Mungea: and smiled wickedly into his dog-hungry eyes. In the water-coloured drawing room she sat with a very straight back, eau-de-nil skirts, bare shoulders, whispering to Larrialde. She glanced at him where he stood attempting to dissemble his pathetic jealousy: caught his eye and drowned him.

The scent of her hair. Those fabulous transitions from wordplay into naked lust. *I am the place that you come into.* Even now he was drowning again, though he knew exactly what went on behind the magic. He knew how a lovely creature like his lover was made, he saw the inevitable chain of events that ran from the forces that made her to this desperate predicament. He could taste the poison, fear and the abuse of power: between human and alien, between men and women. But how could he want to change anything that had ever happened?

No one asked him how they'd reached Aleutia. He was hazy about the details himself. It didn't seem to matter much. He was glad the White Queen spacers seemed to have got clean away.

*

Johnny walked into the shrine, flanked by detention centre people. The executioner had been to the cell and introduced himself earlier. He came up and they walked together. Johnny seemed composed. As he stepped on to the open floor he stopped dead.

'Is this being recorded?'

There was quite a crowd gathered around the edge of the dancing floor and between the serried ranks of characters. The outburst of speech bewildered Johnny's guards, but almost immediately his request was understood. There was a flurry of embarrassment. By some extraordinary oversight, no arrangements had been made.

'I want to see the cam,' said Johnny stubbornly. He looked likely to avail himself of the sentenced criminal's immemorial right to fight or flight: to make things difficult. Shortly, the executioner was able to assure the prisoner that his death would be recorded. Across the floor the other prisoner smiled. Evidently Johnny felt that touch. His eyes were seen to scan the crowd, meet the eyes of his partner.

As soon as she saw him, she remembered everything.

'Johnny!' she shouted, leaping forwards, electrified. 'Johnny, it doesn't have to be this way. You don't have to die! Fly away! Vanish!'

The disturbance was contained. The person whose aspect is often comfort of the defeated hurried over there.

'I want to make a speech,' announced the prisoner.

The person who is always aware that spilled blood can spatter and leave a stain was not presiding. Several of his close friends were present, and they made it known that this was perfectly in order.

'I know that I don't have to be here.'

Johnny's speech was clear in the Common Tongue, but his physical attention was so focused that not many Aleutians could make out what he was saying. It didn't matter. He wasn't speaking to them.

'I'm here of my own choice. I know what we meant to do and I know my life is forfeit. This is my real situation. I don't want to change it. I would not change an instant,' he said. 'I would not change one measly, virtual particle in the sum of things that made you.'

Clavel was with Braemar. He had persuaded the guards to stand back and give the prisoner space. He stayed close, quelling the grief and pain that could only seem a meaningless intrusion.

<Would you like me to hold you?>

Braemar shook his head.

Now. The knife edge. The fountain of life.

To the Aleutian, Braemar seemed to take the stroke in his own body. He would have fallen, but Clavel held him up.

'Go to Johnny,' he whispered urgently. 'You must. The newly dead remember: so he will know you when you two wake again.'

She ran across the dancing floor, dropped on to her knees. She pulled him up and held him. She tried to wake, to be rescued, to plunge into the void. But they had stayed too long and the dream had come true. There was only Johnny, warm and lax in her arms; and heavier than usual, like a sleeping child. She laid her cheek against his hair, closed her eyes. No one disturbed them for what seemed a blessedly long while.

Braemar Wilson came back to earth in an Aleutian spaceplane, along with Johnny Guglioli's body and the record of his death. It had been proposed that she would serve the UN mandatory life sentence for peacetime terrorism in an English prison. Nothing came of that: no appeals, no public debate; she escaped from police custody on her way home from Thailand. The mystery of how Johnny and Braemar had reached Aleutia was investigated with zeal, for the record: and then, along with active pursuit of Braemar, quietly abandoned. This was not a time when the government of the world wished to find itself unveiling an anti-Aleutian conspiracy among space-capable governments and the super-rich.

The White Queen group continued its activities under the name 'Oroonoko', on a smaller scale. Braemar did not contact any of her associates and she never returned to London or to the house in New Cross. Eighteen months after Johnny's death she surfaced: a face in the front line at an Eve-riot in Leipzig. Once a terrorist, always a terrorist. Nobody who knew anything about Wilson believed she had turned feminist. It was feared that the White Queen was gathering new allies, adepts in guerrilla violence.

But there was no need to worry about Braemar Wilson any more. She surfaced again at the registration desk of a large public hospice in an English city. By swift and devious means, the news reached tv screens around the world before it reached the police or the Aleutian Office. To the global audience Braemar was a minor item. It was a long time since the sabotage drama, and anti-Aleutian feeling was not widespread. Enough interest was generated, however, to hold the forces of law and order at bay for a short while.

Braemar remained a symptomless carrier of the deadly virus to the end. Her problem was lung cancer, a hazard of nicotine addiction. She'd waited too long before surfacing and it was too late for any treatment. She was sixty-six years old.

She lay under the white sheet, a thinking egg balanced on top of the ruin inside her skin. She'd refused a flotation tank. The bed approximated a narrow hospital cot of another age, for her reassurance, but it kept her miraculously comfortable. So long as you have enough money, you're in good favour when you're dying. People feel grateful.

The Aleutians will stack us in arcologies, she thought. Because that's what they know. And we will thank them for it. How ridiculous. Considering the Japan Sea Factor, the cancer rate and the rest of it . . . By the end of this century, the last thing we'll be worrying about is over-population. She was making tape, still. Braemar Wilson, New Things: a topical opinion on any subject, any time. She lifted her hand, the one not braceleted with the pain-blocker. It still looked human. Could be quite well and whole, really. Could be waking with a bad hangover, or out of one of those thick cloying dreams that weighs on the heart like stone.

Sometimes she remembered lying down on the couch in Buonarotti's cell, she remembered that fall into the void as if she was still waiting to return. But the ftl trip was incredible. It couldn't have happened, her memory must be a delusion. Human beings cannot pass through the gates of death and live. Naked souls cannot commit terrorist acts . . . Sometimes she thought, and it seemed very sensible, that this was the reason why she and Johnny had failed.

She had been in such a strange state then, when she condemned herself to live and go on trying to kill Aleutians; and condemned Johnny to die. *There's no way back to civilisation from here.* She had always been so set on protecting his innocence. When your mind's unravelling, you cling to the few fixed ideas that remain with crazy devotion. She often thought of his last words. Did he understand what he was saying? She liked to think so. He had died on his own feet, for his own reasons. And she would never look into his sweet eyes now and see a racist killer. She would have laughed if she had the strength. How perversely it had turned out. But to love one's enemy: to heal the divided self, is not simple. Compound that struggle with the cosmic shock of first contact, and what can two poor humans do but cry: *This is is the world of our love, rotten to the core maybe, but I wouldn't change a word of it.*

I'm glad we tried. I'm desperately grateful that we failed, but fuck it, I'm glad we tried. You and me, together.

It was a pity to give up the work, still a lot that could be done in damage limitation. At least she was freed from the company of those dreadful women.

Johnny?

She laid her hand down, with the impression that she had been writing something on the air. An epitaph for the old world? *Exoriare aliquis nostris ex ossibus ultor?* No. She closed her eyes. In a moment she would wake. *Fail again. Fail better.*

'I like that,' she murmured. 'I'll have that.'

It was getting on for five in the afternoon. At this hour, in the warm broken light of a monsoon sky, the fort was at its best. Palms nodded their graceful heads in the shadow of its romantic walls. In the crumbling slit holes that had been made for cannon ferns and flowers were shining after the rain. The West African Office of Aleutian Affairs was next door. Its gardens joined the public grounds of the monument, the white-painted front verandah looked across a sweep of smooth green lawn to the old stronghold.

Ellen sat out on the verandah to watch the road. She was expecting a visitor, and she had nothing else to do. The Asabaland office was the quietest of their locations, scarcely more than a resthouse for Aleutian travellers. There were a few of those now: the curious, the thoughtful, the adventurous. She helped them with quarantine regulations and sorted out their collisions with local custom.

Not many people understood why Ellen had taken this post. She had access to the Multiphon, and was often consulted by the main office in Krung Thep. But effectively she had abandoned what could have been a prestigious third career. She said she was feeling old and it was time to slow down.

The last local bus of the day came struggling along the grande-route Macmillan. It was an open-backed truck, one of those near-immortal African machines: a makeshift conversion of an old gashog somewhere in the mess. It stopped. A passenger got down. The driver came round to collect his fare, and met a ferocious harangue. He backed away as if from a physical force. The battered *capot* went up, the passenger pointed into the dreadful depths within and made cutting, sarcastic suggestions.

All this could be read from gesture.

Ellen saw no reason to intervene. Soon enough the bus was on its way again, the driver uncowed. It would take more than the indignation of a few tourists to inculcate kindness to machinery in the stony hearts of humanity's poor.

Clavel was wearing a dark business suit, the lightweight and well-cut jacket open over a DONT BLOCK THE EXIT teeshirt. It was a shock. Ellen had not seen the person they used to call the poet-princess for over a year. She had heard that Clavel had 'joined the ICI', and wondered what that meant. She had never expected to see the alien actually wearing executive uniform.

'You have seen the news?' said Clavel. 'There wasn't much in the way of services. I was surprised.'

The story of Clavel and Johnny and Braemar was already legend back in the home world. That tragic collision of loyalties, and the 'self' who finds the 'other self' in the wrong camp: it was the very stuff of Aleutian romance. It would be difficult to convince Clavel that the death of Braemar Wilson didn't mean much to the global audience. He tried, but he was *obliged* to assume that the human race was a single entity. As far as he was concerned the whole of this creature (the brood-self) had participated almost as closely as he in that drama – the chamber tragedy which had been going on behind the tumultuous headlines of the past three years.

There was no use in fighting these assumptions. The Aleutians wouldn't change. Humans had to find ways around the obstacles. Wasn't it always so, in the dialogue between native culture and their far-come conquerers?

'Come inside,' she said, aware that she had been speaking in her pidgin Aleutian; and had probably given offence. She was not in control of that language, even now. Sometimes she tried hard. Sometimes she didn't care.

They went inside. Ellen made tea. They sat together in the cool of Ellen's living space, the Aleutian curled on the floor; the human woman preserving her dignity on a rattan sofa. They spoke of Robin, who was living in Aleutia. He was teaching English to adventurous young signifiers who planned to visit earth.

They spoke of Clavel's decision: but only briefly. The alien's determination to enter the service of humanity's God (as Clavel saw it) was intimately connected with his tragic love for Johnny. Ellen understood that, but she didn't want to discuss it.

Clavel was reading Marx as part of her studies: and was enthralled. She produced an antique paperback from her daypack.

Aleutians disliked to carry earthling communications gadgets around with them. They found it hard to come to terms with compact books, personal stereos, headboxes: things which both had no live Aleutian chemistry in them and carried messages from the dead world. There would be artisans who would convert these toys, but for the moment Aleutia rejected them.

'It is hard going. But oh, listen to this, Ellen. "*Along with the tool, the skill of the worker in handling it passes over to the machine. The capabilities of the tool are emancipated from the restraints inseparable from human labour power. This destroys the technical foundation on which division of labour.*" You see what that means? So do I! I learned it long ago. Self is both tool and hand. Division of one from the other is one of the *basic lies* which allow us to function.'

Clavel was not aware that he had broken off the quotation mid-sentence. Whatever the Aleutian did to serve as 'reading', it didn't work like the human version. Perhaps his eyes sent out little motes to reconstruct, chemically, the ur-hieroglyphs behind the letters: something mind-boggling like that. Their physiology, especially the neurological part, was a bizarre mystery.

'Ah,' said Ellen. 'That reminds me.' She got up, went into an inner room and returned with a curious padded tabard which she pulled over her head. It was dun-coloured and quilted, shaped into two exaggerated breasts before; two jutting buttocks behind.

'I had forgotten to put on my uniform.'

The Aleutians could not get the 'war between the two broods' out of their heads. They were certain that the Eve-riots, and the festering problem they represented, formed *the* most important factor in earthling politics. No amount of official denial could convince them otherwise.

Clavel was mortified. He sat back sharply, hips twisting into an animal crouch. If he'd been human he'd have been blushing scarlet.

'Now then.' Ellen saw no harm in letting Clavel know exactly how she felt. She advanced and the alien recoiled before a blast of fury. 'What's this about "cupmen" and "clawmen"?'

'It won't last.' Clavel bared his teeth and shrugged placatingly. 'There are some total idiots. They reckon that if we don't know the difference between one brood and the other, we'll always be getting into the firing line by accident. Don't worry, Ellen. *They are just trying it on.*'

The idiom made Ellen smile in spite of herself. 'I don't worry. I stopped worrying about you people one hot winter's day in Thailand two years ago. What will be, will be. But don't ask me to like it.'

'I'm sorry.'

There was silence. For both of them, the immortal alien and the old warhorse of human politics, that silly tabard opened vistas of the harm that might be done in generations ahead.

Clavel sighed. 'You people see our signifiers, users of formal language, as rulers.' His nasal puckered, thoughtful. 'We don't have rulers. We are, I think, an *anarchy* – from the Greek an, arche. Each of us works out things for himself.'

'Hmph.'

Clavel shrugged, accepting Ellen's scepticism. 'Oh, well, of course: there are people who are naturally inclined to look big, and have followers. But that's different. . . . To use language, though, means something else. I think you should call us the *consciousness* of Aleutia. Ask yourself, as a "single person". For better or for worse: does that mean we are in control?' He rearranged his limbs, recovering composure. 'But I came to cheer you up. You must believe me, Ellen. Johnny is not dead. He is not gone for ever, nor is our friend Braemar. Your friends are not lost, you should not grieve. What they did was beautiful and tragic, and *right*. They will be welcomed as heroes when they come again.'

No one at Uji would help when Ellen was begging them to intervene. Later Aleutians had learned of the horrific belief in permanent death, and humans had learned that Aleutians were immortal. The sentence had been a grim misunderstanding. Aleutia had had no notion of what it was doing to Johnny. The Aleutian reaction was typical. They simply refused to believe in permanent death. But Clavel had called Ellen up and told her everything: the first meeting here, the sweet courtship (as Clavel had imagined it), the rape, the raid on Braemar's house; Clavel's belated understanding.

Ellen had claimed the job of defence lawyer partly from a secret sense of guilty complicity. By the end of that ordeal she knew more than she ever wanted to know about the two terrorists, and her grudging sympathy had become real. She had never liked Braemar Wilson. She had considered the pair her enemies. But she knew that the fate of those lovers would haunt her for the rest of her life. Scenes from the execution video still recurred to her on the edge of sleep. Braemar and Johnny, separated by the alien crowd: their complicated human love and desperate gallantry. The witness of that record was so clear that it had never been allowed near the global audience.

Clavel gazed earnestly. 'You let her escape.'

Ellen frowned. 'Anyone with any sense knows that.'

'Of course. I meant: you did the sensible thing. But you could not stop them before. Don't blame yourself, they were doomed. Ellen, that business of the cupmen and the clawmen is so wrong. I started it, but I know better now. I don't pretend to be able to prove it with science, but you *are* one brood. Johnny and Braemar were true lovers, I'm convinced of that: and self can only love self. In reality, you know, that's why they were driven to suicide. They believed they were incestuous lovers, committing exogamy.'

'Exogamy', Ellen noticed, had been a sin that had not worried Clavel himself when he fell for Johnny. The alien was a proper little Jesuit with his own religion, twisting it any way he chose. But that was typical. Whenever you fell into thinking of them as magic savages they'd show you another face, no more 'bound by obligation' than any bourgeois-individualist earthling.

Clavel lowered his eyes, nasal flaring. 'I have joined the ICI to learn. I am an adventurer, trade is my obligation. But I had to come to earth to find a world where *trade* is a vision of the whole: of the WorldSelf. You have healed something like a division deep in me. But there's more. I have done you an injury. I was in love, and I was confused by new ideas: and that's my fate, to know what's right and go on doing wrong. But for Johnny's sake I will do everything I can, for all the lives to come, to make amends.'

Ellen took off the tabard and went to put it away. When she came back she found Clavel out on the verandah, ready to leave: in an unguarded pose of great loneliness. She sighed. In certain lights she could still see a young girl with a face like a flame, the ardent purity of a teenage idealist.

If the talkers are consciousness, she thought, then you are conscience itself. She wondered how many like Clavel there were, even at full expression: very few, she guessed sardonically. It was irony on irony that Clavel's status in Aleutia was exactly that of his 'voice' in humanity. Humans and aliens were so alike. They were two almost identical surfaces, at first glance seamlessly meeting: at a closer look hopelessly just out of sync, in every tiny cog of detail.

'I will go now. May I call on you sometimes?'

'I'd like that. Please do.'

Clavel walked away across the lawn. The cut of the dark jacket straightened the line of his shoulders and covered the lumpy oversized hip joints. His seaweed hair had been coaxed into a skinny pigtail that flopped on his shoulder. He had forgotten to put Das Capital back in his pack and the book bulged in his jacket pocket. Ellen frowned, and wanted to rub her eyes.

She had asked Rajath about the love story once. She understood by now something of the way Aleutians recognised identity. Those dun overalls signalled that physical feature wasn't important. The nameless, thousand-named presence resides elsewhere.

'And Clavel's fantastic mistake? Were they alike? You've seen records of Johnny Guglioli.'

'Actually, yes.' Rajath screwed his shoulders up to his ears, eyes sparkling. His bumptious personality overspilled the screen. He would always be her favourite. Talk loudly and carry a little stick, Rajath liked to say. He thought he'd stolen this fine aphorism, and admired it greatly. Ellen didn't correct him. She preferred the alien's version. 'Like as two pees in a pot, Ellen. Damndest thing I ever saw.'

Clavel stopped and stared at the Devereux fort. The swift tropic dusk was falling. He walked on down to the road, and joined a few Africans who were waiting by the unmarked bus and taxi stop for a ride back into Fo.

From indoors came the quiet chatter of the satellite news. There were the Eve-riots, there were big problems surfacing between the ex-Japanese and their various hosts. The Americas war was still trying to happen, the Indonesian Empire was in bloody eruption. The West Africa Federation Initiative was pulling itself into shape, looking set to become some kind of major power. For so much of the human earth the 'government of the world' in Thailand remained a sideshow, and the aliens an exciting curiosity.

Sometimes Ellen felt like a stranded time traveller, trapped in a world that didn't exist yet: a kind of relic of a future that she would not live to see.

In earth's terms, it could be that both Aleutian 'immortality' and their 'telepathy' were cultural artefacts shaped by their exotic physiology: obligate illusions. But that was logic-chopping. Aleutians remained, in their own reckoning, telepathic immortals. Where could they go from there? They couldn't be better protected from alien influence. But humanity would change. Ellen foresaw the working out of Clavel's amends: the third sex that would develop, schooled to alien ways. The devaluation of the masses who failed that standard.

Earth would give up the use of coralin for fear of alien contamination, would give up bio-chemical technology because the aliens could achieve the same effects so easily. In a couple of hundred years, if faint traces of another version of this meeting were discovered in old texts, neither the 'superior' nor the 'inferior' race would believe their eyes.

So it would go on. The unconsummated wedding, the irremediable almost-matching of two worlds. There was a powerful voice in Aleutia that said they should continue the journey: leave this soft and fascinating landfall, prefer the dark ocean and the stars. But they would stay. And it would be Clavel, more than anyone, who would keep them here. Clavel, with his intuitive grasp of the alien culture; and his poetry, and his earnest desire to do good.

No, she would not give way to self-pity. The human race had made a nest of horrors for itself, and the Aleutians were still saviours, no matter what. Strange things happen: and the strangest is that things happen (that was Buonarotti). The two races might be good for each other, in the long run. Some kind of fruitful union might be achieved.

Good luck to Clavel. No language matches another, no language models the world. But almost, almost . . . and between the dropped and the caught stitches of that immaterial, impossible weaving somehow: the meaning comes.

But I'm too old a dog to learn new tricks.

Clavel was still standing at the bus stop. The Africans were puzzled, bemused by the rich tourist's eccentric slumming.

I must tell him about that teeshirt, she thought.

Clavel rocked in the back of the truck, dreaming of Uji. The manor house. It was almost deserted now, the gardens overgrown. Everyone else had gone home or moved on. The sound of the rain, the sound of the river: pouring away, pouring away. He slept in the main hall. He woke in the night with tears on his face, and wondered how long grief could continue to be so poignant.

The river rushed on, eddies spilling around the sunken timbers, shining faintly out until they vanished into the stream. A door would open one day into another world: how far away or how near to this one he could not know. He would see Johnny again, and go to him and cry, *Daddy, baby, don't you know me?* This time it would come true. It would not come true. Johnny belonged to someone else, and Clavel had no right even to dream of him.

But he would cling to the lovely fiction, knowing it false. He was learning. He had found out at last why people flee from doubt, and what it means to call something a 'necessary lie'. So much that was painful! This is good, thought Clavel. I will learn this, I will make it mine. Time is cheap. And the lesson of humanity, the unappeasable sorrow, passed through him into Aleutia: sinking into the depths and spilling outward.

The river. Dark water in starlight. Sorrow is real.

Over Neubrandesburg, the summer night sky was a grey canvas roof of unbroken cloud. Peenemünde climbed heavily to her secret laboratory, a huge empty water tank on the roof of her building. She had moved everything up here. There was business to be done with the aliens these days. Professor Buonarotti was back at work, her cell no longer invisible.

She sat, puffed out, at the foot of the last iron ladder, and looked up at the murk that hid the beautiful land, the dark and bright plains of time.

No one would ever know what she had done. The Aleutians thought an illicit space shuttle could be crumpled and stuffed in the nearest waste chute. The facts of earthling limitation didn't yet penetrate far enough into the Aleutian mind for them to realise there *was* a mystery. The governments of earth didn't wonder because everybody suspected everybody else, and nobody wanted to know the secret truth.

'And so,' muttered Peene, 'the legend will lie fallow, one day to give rise to tales of mystical earthling magic. Pah.'

She clambered again. Human beings cannot use faster than light travel. Every time she lay down Peenemünde was aware of the risk. So easily one can mislay one's return ticket, even if one has a life as placid as porridge, as neat as silicon circuitry.

She descended into the chill, echoing interior of the tank, and began to ready herself. In her own bed, every time she looked up the eyes of her friends reproached her. Stupid Peenemünde! There must have been another way. If only she had been the kind of person who can speak out, a person with some moral fibre. The beautiful lady with the iron eyes and that romantic boy would have been convinced by gentle and invincible argument to give up their plan. She'd known they were going to be in no state to harm anyone. She had not foreseen the consequences for them. She was stupid about 'situations', always.

We carry nothing into the world, and it is certain that we can carry nothing out of it . . . Peenemünde had noticed that this mournful warning quite possibly did not apply to the aliens. Those spaceplanes of theirs, as it were budded from their own living selves. What of them? It could be that Buonarotti could give them what they'd pretended was theirs already: the freedom of the stars.

The couch wrapped itself around her. Temptation was sometimes painful, but she could do this much for Braemar and Johnny. She could keep silent. Someone else would stumble over the Buonarotti discovery soon: doesn't that always happen in science? Let someone else tell.

'Time's cheap. Don't they say that? Let them wait.'

She was gone.

Also available in Vista paperback

North Wind

GWYNETH JONES

Peenemunde Buonarotti was one of the last to know, when the Aleutians announced their presence on Earth. She was far too busy inventing faster-than-light travel to turn on the tv that night . . . and after two humans used her device to sabotage the Aleutian mothership, she hid it, to prevent it falling into alien hands. Now, almost a hundred years later, they are hot on its trail.

Caught up in the hunt are Bella, an invalid alien, and 'her' very human protector, known as Sidney Carton. Their complex affair changes as much as their role in the game, as secrets and identities unravel and fluctuate against a backdrop of hidden loyalties, sexual misunderstandings and terrifying urban chaos.

'Puts a genuinely poetic and hauntingly memorable spin on loving the alien' *Time Out*

'Blows away male–female concepts of sexuality with a sardonic power' *The Times*

ISBN 0 575 60248 1

VISTA

Phoenix Café

GWYNETH JONES

It is three hundred years since the Aleutians arrived on earth. In a city that was once Paris, Michael Connelly – son of the *quartier*'s game warden, keeper of the virtual wilderness – meets Catherine, human ward of the alien Lord Maitri.

Both damaged by the consequences of the Aleutian Invasion, Misha and Catherine recognize in each other a capacity for suffering and a need for pain that will draw them into a strange and shocking private world.

But there are worlds within worlds, in these last days of the alien empire on earth. The Buonarotti Device, disputed and perilous key to the kingdoms of heaven, has not given up all its secrets.

'Hyper-imagined, strenuously intelligent'

Observer

ISBN 0 575 60075 6

VISTA

Chaga

IAN McDONALD

On the trail of the mystery of Saturn's disappearing moons, network journalist Gaby McAslan finds herself in Africa researching the Kilimanjaro Event: a meteor which landed in Kenya causing the striking African landscape to give way to something equally beautiful – and indescribably alien. Dubbed the Chaga, the alien flora destroys all man-made materials, and moulds human flesh, bone and spirit to its own designs. And when Gaby McAslan finds the first man to survive the Chaga's changes, she realizes it has its own plans for humankind . . .

'First contact has been written about so many times, but rarely with such compassion' *New Scientist*

'As usual McDonald's prose scintillates as it weaves its captivating course. He has a wicked way with words. And the denouement is simply stunning. All this and football too' *SFX*

ISBN 0 575 60022 5

VISTA

Sacrifice of Fools

IAN McDONALD

They're ancient, they're enigmatic, they're alien and they're here. The Shian arrive on Earth, not as conquerors, but as settlers. Outwardly similar but inwardly deeply different, the Shian are a challenge to all mankind's established notions of society, family, gender, sex and law.

When a prominent Shian family is brutally murdered, human and alien cultures find themselves on a collision course, with only Andy Gillespie, ex-con and aspirant to the mysteries of the Shian law, standing between them.

His search for justice takes him through corrupt religious sects and sinister political organizations with the police and paramilitaries hot on his heels – for Shian justice always comes at a price . . .

'One of the finest writers of his generation' *New Statesman*

'Powerfully good storytelling . . . cleverly written, intelligent and unflinchingly truthful' *SFX*

ISBN 0 575 60059 4

VISTA

Fairyland

PAUL J. McAULEY

WINNER OF THE ARTHUR C. CLARKE AWARD

In twenty-first-century Europe, endlessly ravaged
by the changes of war and technology, gene hacker
and psychoactive virus designer Alex Sharkey is a
bare step ahead of the police and the Triads. But
when he helps a scarily super-smart little girl
called Milena to turn a genetically engineered doll
into the first of a new, autonomous species, the
Fairies, he doesn't realize he's giving history a
dangerous shove.

Milena has her own reasons. Some of the folk,
as fey and malign as any in legend, have other
ideas about their destiny . . .

A giddying baroque journey through the crumbling counter-cultures, obsolete magic kingdoms
and war-torn realities of post-nanotech Europe.

'McAuley is part of a spearhead of writers who for
pure imagination, hipness, vision and fun have
made Britain the Memphis Sun Records of SF'
Mail on Sunday

ISBN 0 575 60031 4

VISTA

THE FIRST BOOK OF CONFLUENCE

Child of the River

PAUL J. McAULEY

Confluence: an artificial world orbiting an obscure star beyond the edge of the galaxy, a flat strip twenty thousand kilometres long, bounded on one side by the Rim Mountains, on the other by the Great River.

Confluence: home to thousands of alien races raised to intelligence by god-like descendants of humanity who long ago retreated from the Universe into an artificial Black Hole.

As a baby, Yama was found on the breast of a dead woman in a white boat floating on the Great River. Raised by an obscure bureaucrat in an obscure town, he attracts the attention of schemers who discover that he has the ability to control the machines which maintain the fabric of the world. Yama must journey to the ancient capital of Confluence to reconcile his human nature with his dangerous powers. He must unravel the riddle of his birth before he can understand whether he is to be the saviour of Confluence – or its nemesis.

ISBN 0 575 60168 X

VISTA

Other Vista Science Fiction titles include

VISTA